A Secret Love

Stephanie Laurens

W F HOWES LTD

This large print edition published in 2010 by
W F Howes Ltd
Unit 4, Rearsby Business Park, Gaddesby Lane,
Rearsby, Leicester LE7 4YH

1 3 5 7 9 10 8 6 4 2

First published in the United Kingdom in 2007
by Piatkus Books

A CIP catalogue record for this book is available
from the British Library

ISBN 978-1-40745-948-6

Typeset by Palimpsest Book Production Limited,
Falkirk, Stirlingshire
Printed and bound in Great Britain
by MPG Books Ltd, Bodmin, Cornwall

PROLOGUE

April 17, 1820
Morwellan Park, Somerset

Disaster stared her in the face.

Again.

Seated at her desk in the library of Morwellan Park, Alathea Morwellan gazed at the letter she held, barely seeing the precise script of her family's agent. The substance of the missive was burned into her brain. Its last paragraph read:

I fear, my dear, that my sentiments concur with yours. I can see no evidence that we have made any mistake.

No mistake. She'd suspected, virtually expected that that would be the case, yet . . .

Exhaling, Alathea laid the letter down. Her hand shook. A youthful cheer reached her, borne on the breeze wafting through the long windows. She hesitated, then stood and glided to the French windows standing open to the south lawn.

On the rolling expanse separating the terrace from the ornamental lake, her stepbrothers and stepsisters played an exuberant game of catch. Sunlight flashed on one fair head – Alathea's eldest

1

stepbrother, Charlie, leaped high and snatched the ball from the air, denying Jeremy, only ten but always game. Despite his emerging elegance, Charlie, nineteen, was good-naturedly caught up in the game, indulging his juniors, Jeremy and Augusta, just six. Their older sisters, Mary, eighteen, and Alice, seventeen, had also joined in.

The entire household was currently in the throes of preparing to remove to London so Mary and Alice could be introduced to the ton. Nevertheless, both girls threw themselves into the game, ringlets framing innocently happy faces, the serious business of their come-outs in no way dampening their joy in simple pleasures.

A whoop from Charlie signaled a wild throw – the ball flew over all three girls and bounced toward the house. It struck the flags of the path and bounced even higher, clearing the shallow steps to land on the terrace. Two more diminishing bounces, and it tumbled over the library threshold and rolled along the polished boards. Raising her skirt, Alathea placed one foot on the ball, stilling it. She considered it, then looked out to see Mary and Alice racing, laughing and gasping, toward the terrace. Stooping, Alathea scooped up the ball; balancing it on one palm, she strolled out onto the terrace.

Mary and Alice skidded to a halt before the steps, laughing and grinning.

'Me, Allie, *me*!'

'No! Al-a-the-a! *Sweet* Allie – me!'

2

Alathea waited as if weighing her choice while little Augusta, left far in the rear, panted up. She stopped some yards behind the older girls and raised her angel's face to Alathea.

With a grin, Alathea lobbed the ball over the older girls' heads. Open-mouthed, they watched it soar past. With a gurgling laugh, Augusta pounced, grabbed the ball, and raced away down the slope.

Flashing Alathea conspiratorial grins, Mary called after Augusta, Alice cheered, and both set out in pursuit.

Alathea remained on the terrace, the warmth suffusing her owing nothing to the bright sunshine. A movement beneath a large oak caught her eye. Her stepmother, Serena, and her father, the earl, waved from the bench where they sat indulgently watching their children.

Smiling, Alathea returned the wave. Looking back at her stepsiblings, now headed in a wild melee toward the lake, she drew in a long breath, then, lips firming, turned back into the library.

Crossing to the desk, she let her gaze dwell on the tapestries gracing the walls, the paintings in their gilded frames, the leather-bound, gilt-encrusted spines lining the shelves. The long library was one of the features of Morwellan Park, principal seat of the earls of Meredith. Morwellans had occupied the Park for centuries, from long before the earldom's creation in the fourteenth. The present gracious house had been built by her great-grandfather, the grounds expertly land-scaped under her grandfather's exacting eye.

Regaining the large carved desk, hers for the last eleven years, Alathea looked at the letter lying on the blotter. Any chance that she would crumple in the face of such adversity as the letter portended was past. Nothing – *no one* – was going to steal the simple peace she'd sacrificed the last eleven years of her life to secure for her family.

Gazing at Wiggs's letter, she considered the enormity of what she faced, too practical not to recognize the difficulties and dangers. But it wasn't the first time she'd stood on the lip of the abyss and stared ruin – financial and social – in the face.

Picking up the letter, she sat and reread it. It had arrived in reply to an urgent missive from her dispatched post haste to London three days before. Three days before, when her world had, for the second time in her life, been rocked to its foundations.

While dusting her father's room, a maid had discovered a legal document stuffed inside a large vase. Luckily, the girl had had the wit to take the paper to the housekeeper and cook, Mrs Figgs, who had immediately bustled into the library to lay it before her.

Satisfied she'd missed nothing in Wiggs's reply, Alathea set his letter aside. Her glance strayed to the left desk drawer where the wretched document at the heart of the matter lay. A promissory note.

She didn't need to read it again – every last detail was etched in her brain. The note committed the earl of Meredith to pay upon call a sum that exceeded the present total worth of the earldom. In return, the earl would receive a handsome percentage of the profits realized by the Central East Africa Gold Company.

There was, of course, no guarantee such profits would ever materialize, and neither she, nor Wiggs, nor any of his peers, had so much as heard of the Central East Africa Gold Company.

If any good would have come of burning the note, she would happily have built a bonfire on the Aubusson rug, but it was only a copy. Her dear, vague, hopelessly impractical father had, entirely without understanding what he was about, signed away his family's future. Wiggs had confirmed that the note was legally sound and executable, so if the call was made for the amount stipulated, the family would be bankrupt. They would lose not only the minor properties and Morwellan House in London, all still mortgaged to the hilt, but also Morwellan Park, and everything that went with it.

If she wished to ensure that Morwellans remained at Morwellan Park, that Charlie and his sons had their ancestral home intact to inherit, that her stepsisters had their come-outs and the chance to make the marriages they deserved, she was going to have to find some way out of this.

Just as she had before.

Absentmindedly tapping a pencil on the blotter,

Alathea gazed unseeing at the portrait of her great-grandfather, facing her down the long length of the room.

This wasn't the first time her father had brought the earldom to the brink of ruin; she'd faced the prospect of abject poverty before. For a gentlewoman reared within the elite circle of the haut ton, the prospect had been – and still was – frightening, all the more so for being somewhat beyond her ken. Abject poverty she had no more than a hazy notion of – she had no wish for either herself or, more importantly, her innocent siblings, to gain any closer acquaintance with the state.

At least, this time, she was more mature, more knowledgeable – better able to deal with the threat. The first time . . .

Her thoughts flowed back to that afternoon eleven years before when, as she was poised to make her come-out, fate had forced her to stop, draw breath, and change direction. From that day, she'd carried the burden of managing the family's finances, working tirelessly to rebuild the family's fortunes, all the while maintaining an outward show of affluence. She'd insisted the boys go to Eton, and then to Oxford; Charlie would go up for the autumn term in September. She'd scrimped and saved to take Mary and Alice to town for their come-outs, and to have sufficient funds to puff them off in style.

The household was eagerly anticipating removing to London in just a few days. For herself, she'd anticipated savoring a subtle victory over fate when her stepsisters made their curtsies to the ton.

For long moments, Alathea stared down the room, considering, assessing – rejecting. This time, frugality would not serve her cause – no amount of scrimping could amass the amount needed to meet the obligation stipulated in the note. Turning, she pulled open the left drawer. Retrieving the note, she perused it again, carefully evaluating. Considering the very real possibility that the Central East Africa Gold Company was a fraud.

The company had that feel to it – no legitimate enterprise would have cozened her father, patently unversed in business dealings, into committing such a huge sum to a speculative venture, certainly not without some discreet assessment of whether he could meet the obligation. The more she considered, the more she was convinced that neither she nor Wiggs had made any mistake – the Central East Africa Gold Company was a swindle.

She was not at all inclined to surrender meekly all she'd fought for, all she'd spent the last eleven years securing – all her family's future – to feather the nest of a pack of dastardly rogues.

There had to be a way out – it was up to her to find it.

CHAPTER 1

May 6, 1820
London

Swirls of mist wreathed Gabriel Cynster's shoulders as he prowled the porch of St George's Church, just off Hanover Square. The air was chill, the gloom within the porch smudged here and there by weak shafts of light thrown by the street lamps.

It was three o'clock; fashionable London lay sleeping. The coaches ferrying late-night revelers home had ceased to rumble – an intense but watchful quiet had settled over the city.

Reaching the end of the porch, Gabriel swung around. Eyes narrowed, he scanned the stone tunnel formed by the front of the church and the tall columns supporting its facade. The mist eddied and swirled, obscuring his view. He'd stood in the same place a week before, watching Demon, one of his cousins, drive off with his new wife. He'd felt a sudden chill – a premonition, a presentiment; perhaps it had been of this.

Three o'clock in the porch of St George's – that

was what the note had said. He'd been half inclined to set it aside, a poor joke assuredly, but something in the words had tweaked an impulse more powerful than curiosity. The note had been penned in desperation, although, despite close analysis, he couldn't see why he was so sure of that. The mysterious countess, whoever she was, had written simply and directly requesting this meeting so she could explain her need for his aid.

So he was here – where was she?

On the thought, the city's bells tolled, the reverberations stirring the heavy blanket of the night. Not all the belltowers tolled the night watches; enough did to set up a strange cadence, a pattern of sound repeated in different registers. The muted notes faded, then died. Silence, again, descended.

Gabriel stirred. Impatient, he started back along the porch, his stride slow, easy.

And she appeared, stepping from the deep shadows about the church door. Mist clung to her skirts as she turned, slowly, regally, to face him. She was cloaked and veiled, as impenetrable, secret, and mysterious as the night.

Gabriel narrowed his eyes. Had she been there all along? Had he walked past her without seeing or sensing her presence? His stride unfaltering, he continued toward her. She lifted her head as he neared, but only slightly.

She was very tall. Halting with only a foot between them, Gabriel discovered he couldn't see over her head, which was amazing. He stood well over six feet tall; the countess had to be six feet tall herself. Despite the heavy cloak, one glance had been enough to assure him all her six feet were in perfect proportion.

'Good morning, Mr Cynster. Thank you for coming.'

He inclined his head, jettisoning any wild thought that this was some witless prank – a youth dressed as a woman. The few steps she'd taken, the way she'd turned – to his experienced senses, her movements defined her as female. And her tone was soft and low, the very essence of woman.

A mature woman – she was definitely not young.

'Your note said you needed my help.'

'I do.' After a moment, she added, 'My family does.'

'Your family?' In the gloom, her veil was impenetrable; he couldn't see even a hint of her chin or her lips.

'My stepfamily, I should say.'

Her perfume reached him, exotic, alluring. 'Perhaps we'd better define just what your problem is, and why you think I can help.'

'You can help. I would never have asked to meet you – would never reveal what I'm about to tell you – if I didn't know you could help.' She paused, then drew breath. 'My problem concerns a promissory note signed by my late husband.'

'*Late* husband?'

She inclined her head. 'I'm a widow.'

'How long ago did your husband die?'

11

'Over a year ago.'

'So his estate has been probated.'

'Yes. The title and entailed estate are now with my stepson, Charles.'

'Stepson?'

'I was my husband's second wife. We were married some years ago – for him, it was a very late second marriage. He was ill for some time before his death. All his children were by his first wife.'

He hesitated, then asked, 'Am I to understand that you've taken your late husband's children under your wing?'

'Yes. I consider their welfare my responsibility. It's because of that – them – that I'm seeking your aid.'

Gabriel studied her veiled countenance, knowing she was watching his. 'You mentioned a promissory note.'

'I should explain that my husband had a weakness for engaging in speculative ventures. Over his last years, the family's agent and I endeavored to keep his investments in such schemes to a minimum, in which endeavors we were largely successful. However, three weeks ago, a maid stumbled on a legal paper, tucked away and clearly forgotten. It was a promissory note.'

'To which company?'

'The Central East Africa Gold Company. Have you heard of it?'

He shook his head. 'Not a whisper.'

'Neither has our agent, nor any of his colleagues.'

'The company's address should be on the note.'

'It's not – just the name of the firm of solicitors who drew up the document.'

Gabriel juggled the pieces of the jigsaw she was handing him, aware each piece had been carefully vetted first. 'This note – do you have it?'

From beneath her cloak, she drew out a rolled parchment.

Taking it, Gabriel inwardly raised his brows – she'd certainly come prepared. Despite straining his eyes, he'd caught not a glimpse of the gown beneath her voluminous cloak. Her hands, too, were covered, encased in leather gloves long enough to reach the cuffs of her sleeves. Unrolling the parchment, he turned so the light from the street lamps fell on the single page.

The promissor's signature – the first thing he looked at – was covered by a piece of thick paper fixed in place with sealing wax. He looked at the countess.

Calmly, she stated, 'You don't need to know the family's name.'

'Why not?'

'That will become evident when you read the note.'

Squinting in the poor light, he did so. 'This appears to be legal.' He read it again, then looked up. 'The investment is certainly large and, given it is speculative, therefore constitutes a very great risk. If the company had not been fully investigated and appropriately vouched for, then the investment was certainly unwise. I do not, however, see your problem.'

'The problem lies in the fact that the amount promised is considerably more than the present total worth of the earldom.'

Gabriel looked again at the amount written on the note and swiftly recalculated, but he hadn't misread. 'If this sum will clean out the earldom's coffers, then . . .'

'Precisely,' the countess said with the decisiveness that seemed characteristic. 'I mentioned that my husband was fond of speculating. The family has for more than a decade existed on the very brink of financial ruin, from before I married into it. After our marriage, I discovered the truth. After that, I oversaw all financial matters. Between us, my husband's agent and I were able to hold things together and keep the family's head above water.'

Her voice hardened in a vain attempt to hide her vulnerability. 'That note, however, would be the end. Our problem in a nutshell is that the note does indeed appear legal, in which case, if it is executed and the money called in, the family will be bankrupt.'

'Which is why you don't wish me to know your name.'

'You know the haut ton – we move in the same circles. If any hint of our financial straits, even leaving aside the threat of the note, was to become common knowledge, the family would be socially ruined.

14

The children would never be able to take their rightful places in our world.'

The call to arms was a physical tug. Gabriel shifted. 'Children. You mentioned Charles, the youthful earl. What others?'

She hesitated, then said, 'There are two girls, Maria and Alicia – we're in town now because they're to be presented. I've saved for years so they could have their come-outs . . .' Her voice suspended. After a moment, she continued, 'And there are two others still in the schoolroom, and an older cousin, Seraphina; she's part of the family, too.'

Gabriel listened, more to her tone than her words. Her devotion sounded clearly – the caring, the commitment. The anxiety. Whatever else the countess was concealing, she couldn't hide that.

Raising the note, he studied the signature of the company's chairman. Composed of bold, harsh strokes, the signature was illegible, certainly not one he knew. 'You didn't say why you thought I could help.'

His tone was vague – he'd already guessed the answer.

She straightened her shoulders. 'We – our agent and I – believe the company is a fraud, a venture undertaken purely to milk funds from gullible investors. The note itself is suspicious in that neither the company's address nor its principals are noted, and there's also the fact that a legitimate specu-lative company accepting a promissory note for such an amount would have sought some verification that the amount could indeed be paid.'

'No check was made?'

'It would have been referred to our agent. As you might imagine, our bank has been in close touch with him for years. We've checked as far as we can without raising suspicions and found nothing to change our view. The Central East Africa Gold Company looks like a fraud.' She drew in a tight breath. 'And if that's so, then if we can gather enough evidence to prove it and present such evidence in the Chancery Court, the promissory note could be declared invalid. But we must succeed before the note is executed, and it's already over a year since it was signed.'

Rerolling the note, Gabriel considered her; despite the veil and cloak, he felt he knew a great deal of her. 'Why me?'

He handed her the note; she took it, slipping it once more under her cloak. 'You've built something of a reputation for exposing fraudulent schemes, and' – lifting her head, she studied him – 'you're a Cynster.'

He almost laughed. 'Why does that matter?'

'Because Cynsters like challenges.'

He looked at her veiled face. 'True,' he purred.

Her chin rose another notch. 'And because I know I can entrust the family's secret to a Cynster.'

He raised a brow, inviting explanation.

She hesitated, then stated, 'If you agree to help us, I must ask you to swear that you will not at any time seek to identify me or my family.' She halted, then went on, 'And if you don't agree to help, I know I can trust you not to mention this meeting, or anything you deduce from it, to anyone.'

Gabriel raised both brows; he regarded her with veiled amusement, and a certain respect. She had a boldness rarely found in women – only that could account for this charade, well thought out, well executed. The countess had all her wits about her; she'd studied her mark and had laid her plans – her enticements – well.

She was deliberately offering him a challenge.

Did she imagine, he wondered, that he would focus solely on the company? Was the other challenge she was flaunting before him intentional, or . . . ?

Did it matter?

'If I agree to help you, where do you imagine we would start?' The question was out before he'd considered – once he had, he inwardly raised his brows at the 'we.'

'The company's solicitors. Or at least the ones who drew up the note – Thurlow and Brown. Their name's on the note.'

'But not their address.'

'No, but if they're a legitimate firm – and they must be, don't you think? – then they should be easy to trace. I could have done that myself, but . . .'

'But you didn't think your agent would approve

17

of what you have in mind once you discover the address, so you didn't want to ask him?'

Despite her veil, he could imagine the look she cast him, the narrowing of her eyes, the firming of her lips. She nodded, again that definite affirmation. 'Precisely. I imagine some form of search will be required. I doubt a legitimate firm of solicitors will volunteer information on one of their clients.'

Gabriel wasn't so sure – he'd know once he located Thurlow and Brown.

'We'll need to learn who the principals of the company are, and then learn the details of the company's business.'

'Prospective business.' He shot her a look, wishing he could see through her veil. 'You do realize that any investigating risks alerting the company's principals? If the company is the sham you think it, then any hint of too close interest from anyone, particularly and especially me, will activate the call on promised funds. That's how swindlers will react – they'll grab what they've got and disappear before anyone can learn too much.'

They'd been standing for more than half an hour in the mausoleum-like porch. The temperature was dropping as dawn approached; the chill of the mists was deepening. Gabriel was aware of it, but in his cloak he wasn't cold. Beneath her heavy cloak the countess was tense, almost shivering.

Lips tightening, he suppressed the urge to draw

her closer and ruthlessly, relentlessly stated, 'By investigating the company, you risk the note being called in and your family being made bankrupt.' If she was determined to brave the fire, she needed to understand she could get burned.

Her head rose; her spine stiffened. 'If I don't investigate the company and prove it's a fraud, my family will *definitely* be bankrupt.'

He listened but could detect no hint of wavering, of anything less than informed but unshakable resolution. He nodded. 'Very well. If you've made the decision to investigate the company, then yes, I'll help you.'

If he'd expected gushing thanks, he'd have been disappointed – luckily, he'd had no such expectation. She stood still, studying him. 'And you'll swear . . . ?'

Stifling a sigh, he raised his right hand. 'Before God, I swear—'

'On your name as a Cynster.'

He blinked at her, then continued, 'On my name as a Cynster, that I will not seek to identify you or your family. All right?'

Her sigh fell like silk in the night. 'Yes.' She relaxed, losing much of her stiff tension.

His increased proportionately. 'When gentlemen reach an agreement, they usually shake hands.'

She hesitated, then extended one hand.

He grasped it, then changed his hold, fingers sliding about hers until his thumb rested in her palm. Then he drew her to him.

He heard her in-drawn breath, felt the sudden leaping of her pulse, sensed the shock that seared her. With his other hand, he tipped up her chin, angling her lips to his.

'I thought we were going to shake hands.' Her words were a breathless whisper.

'You're no gentleman.' He studied her face; the glint of her eyes was all he could see through the fine black veil, but with her head tipped up, he could discern the outline of her lips. 'When a gentleman and a lady seal a pact, they do it like this.' Lowering his head, he touched his lips to hers.

Beneath the silk, they were soft, resilient, lush – pure temptation. They barely moved under his, yet their inherent promise was easy to sense, very easy for him to read. That kiss should have registered as the most chaste of his career – instead, it was a spark set to tinder, prelude to a conflagration. The knowledge – absolute and definite – shook him. He lifted his head, looked down on her veiled face, and wondered if she knew.

Her fingers, still locked in his, trembled. Through his fingers under her chin, he felt the fragile tension that had gripped her. His gaze on her face, he raised her hand and brushed a kiss on her gloved fingers, then, reluctantly, he released her. 'I'll find out where Thurlow and Brown hang their plaque and see what I can learn. I assume you'll want to be kept informed. How will I contact you?'

She stepped back. 'I'll contact you.'

He felt her gaze scan his face, then, still brittlely tense, she gathered herself and inclined her head. 'Thank you. Good night.'

The mists parted then reformed behind her as she descended the porch steps. And then she was gone, leaving him alone in the shadows.

Gabriel drew in a deep breath. The fog carried the sounds of her departure to his ears. Her shoes tapped along the pavement, then harness clinked. Heavier feet thumped and a latch clicked, then, after a pause, clicked again. Seconds later came the slap of reins on a horse's rump, then carriage wheels rattled, fading into the night.

It was half past three in the morning, and he was wide awake.

Lips lifting self-deprecatingly, Gabriel stepped down from the porch. Drawing his cloak about him, he set out to walk the short distance to his house.

He felt energized, ready to take on the world. The previous morning, before the countess's note arrived, he'd been sitting morosely over his coffee wondering how to extract himself from the mire of disaffected boredom into which he'd sunk. He'd considered every enterprise, every possible endeavor, every entertainment – none had awakened the smallest spark of interest.

The countess's note had stirred not just interest but curiosity and speculation. His curiosity had largely been satisfied; his speculation, however . . .

Here was a courageous, defiant widow staunchly

21

determined to defend her family – stepfamily, no less – against the threat of dire poverty, against the certainty of becoming poor relations, if not outcasts. Her enemies were the nebulous backers of a company thought to be fraudulent. The situation called for decisive action tempered by caution, with all investigations and inquiries needing to remain covert and clandestine. That much, she'd told him.

So what did he know?

She was an Englishwoman, unquestionably gently bred – her accent, her bearing and her smooth declaration that they moved in similar circles had settled that. And she knew her Cynsters well. Not only had she stated it, her whole presentation had been artfully designed to appeal to his Cynster instincts.

Gabriel swung into Brook Street. One thing the countess didn't know was that he rarely reacted impulsively these days. He'd learned to keep his instincts in check – his business dealings demanded it. He also had a definite dislike of being manipulated – in any field. In this case, however, he'd decided to play along.

The countess was, after all; an intriguing challenge in her own right. All close to six feet of her. And a lot of that six feet was leg, a consideration guaranteed to fix his rakish interest. As for her lips and the delights they promised . . . he'd already decided they'd be his.

Occasionally, liaisons happened like that – one

look, one touch, and he'd know. He couldn't, however, recall being affected quite so forcefully before, nor committing so decisively and definitely to the chase. And its ultimate outcome.

Again, energy surged through him. This – the countess and her problem – was precisely what he needed to fill the present lack in his life: a challenge and a conquest combined.

Reaching his house, he climbed the steps and let himself in. He shut and bolted the door, then glanced toward the parlor. In the bookcase by the fireplace resided a copy of *Burke's Peerage*.

Lips quirking, he strode for the stairs. If he hadn't promised not to seek out her identity, he would have made straight for the bookcase and, despite the hour, ascertained just which earl had recently died to be succeeded by a son called Charles. There couldn't be that many. Instead, feeling decidedly virtuous, not something that often occurred, he headed for his bed, all manner of plans revolving in his head.

He'd promised he wouldn't seek out her identity – he hadn't promised he wouldn't persuade her to reveal all to him.

Her name. Her face. Those long legs. And more.

'*Well?* How did it go?'

Raising her veil, Alathea stared at the group of eager faces clustered about the bottom of the stairs. She had only that instant crossed the threshold of Morwellan House in Mount Street;

behind her, Crisp, the butler, slid the bolts home and turned, eager not to miss any of her tale.

The question had come from Nellie, Alathea's maid, presently wrapped in an old paisley bedrobe. Surrounding Nellie in various stages of deshabille stood other members of Alathea's most stalwart band of supporters – the household's senior servants.

'Come now, m'lady, don't keep us in suspense.'

That from Figgs, the cook-housekeeper. The others all nodded – Folwell, Alathea's groom, his forelock bobbing, Crisp, joining them, carrying the rolled promissory note she had handed him for safekeeping.

Alathea inwardly sighed. In what other tonnish establishment would a lady of the house, returning from an illicit rendezvous at four in the morning, meet with such a reception? Quelling her skittish nerves, telling herself that the fact he'd kissed her didn't show, she set her veil back. 'He agreed.'

'Well – there now!' Thin as a rake, Miss Helm, the governess, nervously clutched her pink wrapper. 'I'm sure Mr Cynster will take care of it all and expose these *dreadful* men.'

'Praise be,' intoned Connor, Serena's severe dresser.

'Indeed' – Alathea walked forward into the light thrown by the candles Nellie, Figgs and Miss Helm were holding – 'but you should all be in bed. He's agreed to help – there's nothing more to hear.' She caught Nellie's eye.

24

Nellie sniffed, but buttoned her lip.

Alathea shooed the others off, then headed up the stairs, Nellie on her heels, lighting her way.

'So what happened?' Nellie hissed as they reached the gallery.

'Shh!' Alathea gestured down the corridor. Nellie grumbled but held her tongue as they passed Alathea's parents' rooms, then Mary's and Alice's, eventually reaching her room at the corridor's end.

Nellie shut the door behind them. Alathea untied her cloak, then let it fall – Nellie caught it as she stepped away.

'So now, my fine miss – you're not going to tell me he didn't see through your disguise?'

'Of course he didn't – I told you he wouldn't.' He wouldn't have kissed her if he had. Sinking onto her dressing table stool, Alathea pulled pins from her hair, freeing the thick mass from the unaccustomed chignon. She normally wore her hair in a knot on the top of her head with the strands about her face puffed to form a living frame. It was an old-fashioned style but it suited her. The chignon had suited her, too, but the unusual style had pulled her hair in different directions – her scalp hurt.

Nellie came to help, frowning as she searched out pins in the silky soft mass. 'I can't believe after all the years you two spent rollin' about the fields that he wouldn't simply look at you, veil and cloak or no, and instantly know you.'

'You forget – despite the years we spent "rollin'

about the fields," Rupert has barely seen me for over a decade. Just the odd meeting here and there.'

'He didn't recognize your voice?'

'No. My tone was quite different.' She'd spoken as she would to Augusta, her tone warm and low, not tart and waspish as when she normally spoke with him. Except for those few breathless moments . . . but she didn't think he'd ever heard her breathless before. She couldn't recall ever feeling so nervous and skittish before. With a sigh, she let her head tip back as her hair finally fell loose. 'You're not giving me sufficient credit. I'm a very good actress, after all.'

Nellie humphed but didn't argue. She started to brush Alathea's long hair.

Closing her eyes, Alathea relaxed. She excelled at charades; she could think herself into a part very well, as long as she understood the character. In this case, that was easy. 'I kept to the truth as far as possible – he truly thinks I'm a countess.'

Nellie humphed. 'I still can't see why you couldn't simply write him a nice letter, asking him to look into this company for you.'

'Because I would have had to sign it "Alathea Morwellan".'

'He would have done it, I'm sure.'

'Oh, he wouldn't have *refused*, but what he would have done was refer it to his agent – that Mr Montague. Without telling Rupert *why* it's so desperately needful to prove this company a fraud, it wouldn't have seemed important – important enough to stir him personally to action.'

'I can't see why you don't just tell him—'

'No!' Eyes opening, Alathea straightened. For an instant, the lines between mistress and maid were clear – there in the matriarchal light in Alathea's eyes, in her stern expression, and in the suddenly wary look in Nellie's face.

Alathea let her expression ease; she hesitated, but Nellie was the only one with whom she dared discuss her plans, the only one who knew them all. The only one she trusted with them all. While she suspected that meant she was trusting the entire little band downstairs, as the others never presumed to mention it, she could live with that. She had to talk to someone. Drawing in a breath, she settled on the stool. 'Believe it or not, Nellie, I still have my pride.' She shut her eyes as Nellie resumed her brushing. 'Sometimes, I think it's all I truly have left. I won't risk it by telling even him all. No one knows just how close to ruin we came – what depth of ruin we now face.'

'He'd be sympathetic, I should think. He wouldn't noise it abroad.'

'That's not the point. Not with him. I don't think you can imagine, Nellie, just how rich the Cynsters are. Even I have trouble assimilating the sums I know he regularly deals with.'

'Can't see why it matters, meself.'

Alathea felt the familiar tugs as Nellie started braiding her hair. 'Let's just say that while I can cope with fraudulent companies and imminent disaster, the one thing I really don't think I could face is pity.'

His pity.

Nellie sighed. 'Ah, well, if that's the way it must be . . .' Alathea sensed her fatalistic shrug. After a moment, Nellie asked, 'But how'd you get him to agree to help if'n you didn't tell him about the family all but being rolled up if that wretched company asks for their money?'

'*That*' – Alathea opened her eyes – 'was the main point of my masquerade. I did tell him. All of it. I could hardly expect him to help without knowing the details, and he certainly wouldn't have helped if there hadn't been a real family and a real threat. He's never been easy to stir to action, but he is a Cynster and they always respond to certain prods. He had to be convinced of both the family and the threat, but the way I told it, it's the countess's family. I cast my father as my dead husband, with me as the countess, his second wife, and all the children as my stepchildren, instead of my stepbrothers and stepsisters. Serena I made into a cousin.'

She paused, remembering.

'What happened?'

Alathea looked up to see Nellie regarding her in concern.

'It's no use telling me something didn't go wrong – I can always tell when you look like that.'

'Nothing went *wrong*.' She wasn't about to tell

28

Nellie about that kiss. 'I just hadn't thought of names for all the children. I used Charles for Charlie – it's a common enough name after all – but I hadn't expected Rupert to ask me about the others. When he did . . . well, I was so deep in being the countess, I couldn't really think. I called them to mind and had to put names to them instantly or he would have grown suspicious.'

Dropping her completed braid, Nellie stared at her. 'You didn't go and call them by their real names?'

Rising, Alathea stepped away from the table. 'Not exactly.'

Nellie started unlacing her gown. 'So what did you call them?'

'Maria, Alicia, and Seraphina. I skipped the others.'

'So what happens the first time he finds himself in a room with one of those books that list the lot of you? All he'll have to do will be to look up the earls – you being a countess – and it'll jump off the page at him. And he'll know who you are then, too.' Straightening, Nellie helped her out of her gown. 'Wouldn't want to be in your shoes then, miss – not when he finds out. He won't be pleased.'

'I know.' Alathea shivered, and prayed Nellie thought it was because she was cold. She knew exactly what would happen if luck dealt against her and Rupert Melrose Cynster discovered *she* was his mysterious countess – that she was the woman he'd kissed in the porch of St George's.

All hell would break lose.

He didn't have a temper, any more than she did.

Which meant he didn't appear to have one, until he lost it.

'That's why,' she continued, head emerging from the nightgown Nellie had thrown over her, 'I made him swear not to try and identify me. The way I have it planned, he need never learn the truth.'

She knew he wouldn't appreciate having the wool pulled over his eyes. He had a deep, very real dislike of any form of deception. That, she suspected, was what lay behind his growing reputation for unmasking business frauds. 'For now, everything's perfect – he's met the countess, heard her story, and agreed to help. He actually wants to help – wants to expose these men and their company. That's important.' Whether she was reassuring Nellie or herself she wasn't sure; her stomach hadn't relaxed since he'd kissed her. 'Lady Celia's forever complaining about him being too indolent, too bored with life. The countess's problem will give him something to work on, something that interests him.'

Nellie snorted. 'Next you'll be saying being gulled will be good for him.'

Alathea had the grace to blush. 'It won't hurt him. And I'll be careful, so there's no reason to think he ever will know that he's been "gulled", as you put it. I'll make sure he never meets the countess in daylight, or in any decent illumination. I'll always wear a veil. With heels to make me even

30

taller' – she gestured to the high-heeled shoes she'd discarded by the dressing table – 'and that perfume' – another wave indicated the Venetian glass flacon standing before her mirror – 'which is nothing like anything Alathea Morwellan has ever worn, I really do not see that there's any danger of him knowing me.'

Alathea glided to the bed; Nellie bustled ahead, turning down the covers and removing the copper warming pan. Slipping between the sheets, Alathea sighed. 'So all is well. And when the company's exposed and her family saved, the countess will simply' – she waved gracefully – 'disappear in a drift of mist.'

Nellie humphed. She shuffled about, tidying things away, hanging up Alathea's clothes. From the wardrobe, she looked back at Alathea. 'I still don't see why you couldn't simply go and see him, and tell him to his face what this is all about. Pride's all very well, but this is serious.'

'It's not only pride.' Lying back, Alathea gazed at the canopy. 'I didn't ask him to his face because he very likely would not have helped me, not personally. He'd have directed me to Montague as fast as he politely could, and that simply won't do. I – we – need *his* help, not the assistance of his henchman. I need the knight on his charger, not his squire.'

'I don't see that – he'd have helped, why wouldn't he? It's not as if you two don't go back near to all your lives. He's known you since you

31

was in your cradle. You played as babies and all through the years, right up until you was fifteen and ready to be a lady.' Her tidying done, candle in hand, Nellie approached the big bed. 'If you was just to go to him and explain it all, I'm sure he'd help.'

'Believe me, Nellie, that wouldn't work. While he'll extend himself to help the mysterious countess, he would never do the same for me.' Turning onto her side, Alathea closed her eyes and ignored Nellie's disbelieving sniff. 'Good night.'

After a moment, a soft, grumbling 'Good night' reached her. The candlelight playing on her eyelids faded, then the door clicked as Nellie let herself out.

Alathea sighed, sinking deeper into the mattress, trying to relax the muscles that had tensed when he'd kisssed her. That was the one development she hadn't foreseen but it was hardly serious, presumably the sort of sophisticated dalliance he practiced on all likely ladies. If she could start her charade again, she'd think twice about making herself a widow, one already out of mourning, but it was done – the masquerade had begun. And while she might not be able to fully explain it to Nellie, her charade was absolutely essential.

Rupert Melrose Cynster, her childhood play-mate, was the one, perfectly armed knight she'd had to win to her side. She knew his true mettle – what he could accomplish, would accomplish, once he was fully committed to a cause. With him as her champion, they would have a real chance of triumphing over the Central East Africa Gold Company. Without his aid, that feat had appeared close to impossible.

Knowing him of old – so well, so thoroughly – she'd known that to secure his commitment, she would need to fully engage his oft-times fickle interest. She needed him to *focus* on her problem, willingly bringing his considerable abilities to bear. So she'd invented the countess and, cloaked in beguiling mystery, had set about recruiting him, body and soul, to her cause.

She'd won her first battle – he was ready to fight beside her. For the first time since Figgs had placed the wretched promissory note before her, she allowed herself to believe in ultimate victory.

As far as the ton would see, the Morwellans were in town as expected to allow the younger daughters to make their curtsies to society and for Charlie to make his bow. She, the eldest daughter, now an ape-leader, would hug the shadows, assisting with her stepsisters' come-outs, in her spare moments donning cloak and veil to masquerade as the countess and remove the sword presently poised over her family's future.

She smiled at such melodramatic thoughts. They came easily to mind – she knew precisely what she was doing. She also knew precisely why Rupert wouldn't have helped her as he would the countess, although it wasn't something she was eager to explain, even to Nellie.

They disliked being in the same room, certainly not within ten feet of each other. Any closer proximity was like wearing a hair shirt. The peculiarity had afflicted them from the age of eleven and twelve; since then, it had been a constant in their lives. What caused it remained a mystery. As their younger selves, they'd tried to ignore it, pretend it wasn't there, but the relief they'd both felt when her impending lady-hood had spelled an end to their all but daily association had been too real to ignore.

Of course they'd never discussed it, but his reaction was there in the sharpening of his hazel gaze, the sudden tensing of his muscles, in the difficulty he had remaining near her for more than a few minutes. Uncomfortable wasn't an adequate description – the affliction was far worse than that.

She'd never been able to decide if she reacted to him as he did to her, or if her aggravation arose in response to his. Whatever the truth, their mutual affliction was something they'd learned to live with, learned to hide, and ultimately, learned to avoid. Neither would unnecessarily precipitate a prolonged encounter.

That was why, despite growing up as they had, despite their families being such close neighbors, he and she had never waltzed. They had danced – one country dance. Even that had left her breathless, waspish and thoroughly out of temper. Like him, she wasn't given to displays of temper – the only one able to provoke her, all but instantly, was he.

And that – all of that – explained why the countess had walked the porch of St George's. While she could not, absolutely, know his mind and thus be certain he would not have personally helped her, she imagined his instincts would have prompted him to help, but his reaction to her would have mitigated against it. Dealing with the company for her would mean seeing her frequently, often alone, which usually made the affliction worse. They'd met briefly only a few months ago – their affliction was stronger than ever. They'd reduced each other to quivering rage in under three minutes. She couldn't believe, if she asked for his help, that he'd break the habit of years and readily spend hours in her company – or, if he did, that it wouldn't drive them both demented.

More to the point, she hadn't been able to risk finding out. If she'd presented her problem to him as herself, only to have him send her to Montague, she couldn't then have appeared as the countess.

No choice.

He would never forgive her if he ever found out – ever learned *she* was the countess. He would probably do worse than that. But she'd had no choice – her conscience wasn't troubling her, not really. If there'd been any other sure way of getting him to help her without deceiving him, she would have taken it, but . . .

She was halfway asleep, drifting in the mists, her mind revisiting bits and pieces of their rendezvous, revolving more and more about that unnerving kiss, when she started awake. Blinking, eyes wide, she stared up at the canopy – and considered the fact that their decades-old mutual affliction had not reared its head that night.

CHAPTER 2

'Ala-*the*-aaa. Whoo-hoo! Allie! Can you pass the butter, please?'

Alathea focused – Alice was pointing across the luncheon table. Bemusedly glancing in that direction, her brain belatedly caught up with reality; lifting the butter dish, she passed it across.

'You're in a brown study today.' Serena was sitting next to her, at the end of the table.

Alathea waved dismissively. 'I didn't sleep all that well last night.' She'd been so keyed up, primed to play the countess, desperate to secure Rupert's aid, that she'd rested not at all before her three o'clock appointment. And afterwards . . . after her success, after that kiss, after realizing . . . she shook aside the distraction. 'I'm still not used to all the street sounds.'

'Perhaps you should move to another room?'

Glancing at Serena's sweet face, brow furrowed with concern, Alathea clasped her stepmother's hand. 'Don't worry. I'm perfectly happy with my room. It faces the back gardens as it is.'

Serena's face eased. 'Well . . . if you're sure.

But now Alice has woken you up' – her eyes twinkled – 'I wanted to check how much we can afford to spend on the girls' walking dresses.'

Alathea gladly gave Serena her attention. Short, plump, and fashionably matronly, Serena was gentle and retiring, yet in the matter of her daughters' come-outs, she'd proved both shrewd and well up to snuff. With real relief, Alathea had consigned all the details of their social lives, including their wardrobes, to Serena, more than content to play a supporting role in that sphere. They'd been in town for just over a week and all was on track for a pleasant Season all around.

All she had to do was prove the Central East Africa Gold Company a fraud, and all would be well.

The thought returned her mind to its preoccupation – and to the man she'd recruited last night. She glanced around the table, viewing her family as if through his eyes. She and Serena discussed materials, trimmings and bonnets, with Mary and Alice hanging on every word. At the table's other end, her father, Charlie, and Jeremy discussed the more masculine entertainments on offer. Alathea heard her father muse on the attractions of Gentleman Jackson's Boxing Saloon, a prospect guaranteed to divert both Charlie as well as his precocious younger brother.

Leaving Serena, Mary, and Alice debating colors, Alathea turned to the youngest member of the family, sitting quietly beside her, a large doll on her lap. 'And how are you and Rose today, poppet?'

Lady Augusta Morwellan raised huge brown eyes to Alathea's face and smiled trustingly. 'I had a lovely time in the garden this morning, but Rose here' – she turned the doll so Alathea could inspect her – 'has been *fractious*. Miss Helm and I think we should take her for a walk this afternoon.'

'A walk? Oh, yes! That's a lovely idea – just what we need.' Having settled her sartorial requirements, Mary, all bouncing brown ringlets and glowing eyes, was ready for the next excitement.

'I'm starting to feel hemmed in with all these houses and streets.' With fair hair and doelike eyes, Alice was more serious and contained. She smiled at Augusta. 'And Augusta won't want us disturbing Rose with our chatter.'

Augusta returned the smile sweetly. 'No. Rose needs quiet.' Too young to share in the excitement that had infected the rest of the family, Augusta was content to stroll the nearby square, her hand in Miss Helm's, and stare, wide-eyed, at all the new and different sights.

'Is there somewhere else we can go – other than the park, I mean?' Alice looked from Alathea to Serena. 'We won't have our new dresses until next week, so it's probably better we don't go there too often.'

'I would prefer that you didn't haunt the park anyway,' Serena said. 'Better to appear only a few times a week, and we were there yesterday.'

'So where shall we go? It has to be somewhere with trees and lawns.' Mary fixed her glowing gaze on Alathea's face.

'Actually . . .' Alathea considered – just because she'd successfully recruited her knight didn't mean she had to sit on her hands and leave all the investigating to him. She refocused on her stepsisters' faces. 'There's a particular park I know of, quiet and pleasant, cut off from all the noise. It's very like the country – you can almost forget you're in London.'

'That sounds perfect,' Alice declared. 'Let's go there.'

'We're going to Bond Street!' Jeremy pushed back his chair.

Charlie and the earl did the same. The earl smiled at his womenfolk. 'I'll take these two off for the afternoon.'

'I'm going to learn to box!' Jeremy danced around the table, thrusting his fists through the air, dealing summarily with invisible opponents. Laughing, Charlie caught Jeremy's fists, then half-waltzed, half-wrestled him out of the room. Jeremy's piping protests and Charlie's deeper amused taunts faded as they progressed in the direction of the front door.

Mary and Alice rose to follow. 'We'll get our bonnets.' Mary looked at Alathea. 'Shall I fetch yours?'

'Please.' Alathea rose, too.

The earl stopped by her side, his fingers light on her arm. 'Is everything all right?' he asked quietly.

40

Alathea looked up. Despite his age and the troubles resting heavily on his shoulders, her father, two inches taller than she, remained a strikingly handsome man. Glimpsing shadows of pain and regret in his eyes, she smiled reassuringly; she caught his hand and squeezed. 'Everything's going well.'

He'd been devastated when he'd learned about the promissory note. He'd thought the sum pledged was much smaller – the wording of the note was such that arithmetic was required to determine the total sum. All he'd intended was to gain a few extra guineas to spend on the girls' weddings. She'd spent some time comforting him, assuring him that although the situation was bad, it was not the final end.

It had been hard for him to carry on as if nothing had happened so the children wouldn't suspect. Only the three of them – he, she and Serena – knew of the latest threat or, indeed, of the perilous state of the earldom's finances. From the first, they'd agreed that the children were never to know that their future hung by such a slender thread.

Despite the fact she had spent all her adult life putting right the problems her father had caused, Alathea had never been able to hold it against him. He was the most lovable, and loving, man – he was simply incapable when it came to money.

Now he smiled, a sad, forlorn smile. 'Is there anything I can do?'

She hugged his arm. 'Just keep doing what

you've been doing, Papa – keep Jeremy entertained and out of mischief.' She drew back. 'You're so good with them – they're both a real credit to you.'

'Indeed,' Serena agreed. 'And if Alathea says there's nothing to worry about, then there's no sense worrying. She'll keep us informed – you know she always does.'

The earl seemed about to speak, then muffled cries and thumps came from the front hall.

The earl's lips twitched. 'I'd better get out there before Crisp hands in his notice.' He touched his lips to Alathea's temple, stooped to kiss Serena's cheek, then he strode out to the hall, squaring his shoulders and lifting his head as he crossed the threshold.

With Serena, Alathea followed more slowly. From the dining room doorway, they watched the melee in the hall resolve itself under the earl's direction. 'He's really a wonderful father,' Serena said as the earl ushered his sons out of the front door.

'I know.' Alathea smiled at his departing back. 'I'm really very impressed with Charlie.' She glanced at Serena. 'The next earl of Morwellan will hold a candle to all comers. He's an amazing amalgam of you both.'

Pleased, Serena inclined her head. 'But he's also got a very large dose of *your* common sense. Thanks to you, my dear, the next earl of Morwellan will know how to manage his brass!'

They both laughed, yet it was true. Not only was Charlie handsome, unruffleably good-natured, never high in the instep, and always game for a lark, but he was, largely due to Serena, thoughtful, considerate and openly caring. Thanks to the earl's influence, he was a gentleman to his toes and, as he also spent at least one session a week with Alathea in the estate office, and had for some years, he was at nineteen in a fair way to understanding how to successfully manage the estate. While he still did not know the level to which the earldom's coffers had sunk, Charlie now knew at least the basics of how to keep them filling up.

'He'll make an excellent earl.' Alathea looked up as Mary and Alice came clattering down the stairs, bonnets on, ribbons streaming, her own bonnet dangling from Mary's hand. Augusta had slipped out earlier; Alathea glimpsed her littlest stepsister heading out to the garden, her hand in Miss Helm's.

Charlie, Jeremy, Mary, Alice, and Augusta – they were the ultimate reasons she'd invented the countess. Even if he discovered her deception, Alathea couldn't believe her knight would disapprove of her motives.

'Come on!' Alice waved her parasol at the door. 'The afternoon's winging – we've already ordered the carriage.'

Accepting her bonnet, Alathea turned to the mirror to settle it over her top knot.

Casting a critical eye over her daughters, Serena

43

straightened a ribbon here, tweaked a curl there. 'Where do you intend going?'

Alathea turned from the mirror as the clop of hooves heralded the carriage. 'I'd thought to go to Lincoln's Inn Fields. The trees are tall, the grass green and well tended, and it's never crowded.'

Serena nodded. 'Yes, you're right – but what an odd place to think of.'

Alathea merely smiled and followed Mary and Alice down the steps.

Gabriel discovered the bronze plaque identifying the offices of Thurlow and Brown along the south face of Lincoln's Inn. Surrounding a rectangular cobbled courtyard, the Inn housed nothing but legal chambers. Its inner walls were punctuated with regularly spaced open archways, each giving access to a shadowy stairwell. On the wall beside each archway, bronze plaques bore witness to the legal firms housed off the stairway within.

After consulting a book listing the solicitors of the Inns of Court, Montague had directed Gabriel to Lincoln's Inn, describing the firm as small, old, but undistinguished, with no known association with any matter remotely illegal. As he climbed the stairs, Gabriel reflected that, if he'd been behind the sort of swindle it seemed likely the Central East Africa Gold Company was, then the first step he'd take to lull gullible investors would be to retain such a firm as Thurlow and Brown. A firm stultifyingly correct and all but moribund, unlikely to boast the talents or connections that might give rise to unanswerable questions.

Thurlow and Brown's rooms were on the second level, to the rear of the building. Gabriel reached for the knob of the heavy oak door, noting the large lock beneath the knob. Sauntering in, he scanned the small reception area. Behind a low railing, an old clerk worked at a raised desk, guarding access to a short corridor leading to one room at the rear, and to a second room off the reception area.

'Yes? Can I help you?' The clerk clutched at the angled desktop. Frowning, he flipped through a diary. 'You don't have an appointment.' He made it sound like an offense.

His expression one of affable boredom, Gabriel shut the door, noting that there were no bolts or extra latches, only that large and cumbersome lock.

'Thurlow,' he murmured, turning back to the clerk. 'There was a Thurlow at Eton when I was there. I wonder if it's the same one?'

'Couldn't be. His nibs' – the clerk waved an ink-stained hand at the half-open door giving off the reception area – 'is old enough to be your dad.'

'That so?' Gabriel sounded disappointed. Clearly 'his nibs' was out. 'Ah, well. It was really Mr Browne I came to see.'

Again the clerk frowned; again he checked his book. 'You're not down for this afternoon . . .'

'I'm not? How odd. I was sure the pater said two.'

The clerk shook his head. 'Mr Brown's out. I'm not expecting him back until later.'

Letting annoyance flash across his features, Gabriel thumped the reception railing with his cane. 'If that isn't just like Theo Browne! Never could keep his engagements straight!'

'*Theo* Brown?'

Gabriel looked at the clerk. 'Yes – Mr Browne.'

'But that's not *our* Mr Brown.'

'It isn't?' Gabriel stared at the clerk. 'Is your Browne spelled with an "e"?'

The clerk shook his head.

'Damn!' Gabriel swung away. 'I was sure it was Thurlow and Browne.' He frowned. 'Maybe it's Thirston and Browne. Thrapston and Browne. Something like that.' He looked questioningly at the clerk.

Who shook his head. 'I'm sorry I can't help you, sir. Don't know of any firms with names like that. Mind you, there is Browne, Browne and Tillson in the other quad – might they be the ones you're after?'

'Browne, Browne and Tillson.' Gabriel repeated the name twice with different inflections, then shrugged. 'Who knows. Could be.' He swung to the door. 'The other quad, you say?'

'Aye, sir – across the carriage road through the Inn.'

Waving his cane in farewell, Gabriel went out, closing the door behind him. Then he grinned and strolled down the stairs.

Regaining the sunshine, he strode across the cobbles. He'd seen enough to confirm Thurlow and Brown's standing – precisely as Montague had said, Stuffily, dustily dull. He'd learned which room was whose, and through the open doors he'd seen the locked client boxes lining the walls of both partners' rooms. They didn't lock the boxes away somewhere else. They were there, within easy reach, and the only lock between the landing and the boxes was the old wrist-breaker on the main door.

There had also been no sign of any junior clerk. There'd been only one desk, and little space outside the partners' rooms – no area for a clerk or office boy to spend the night.

Entirely satisfied with his afternoon's work, Gabriel saluted the gatekeeper with his cane and strode through the secondary gateway into the adjoining Fields.

Before him, a small army of old trees, like ancient sentinels, spread their branches protectively over gravel walks and swaths of lawn. Sunlight streamed down. The breeze ruffled leaves, shedding shifting shadows over the green carpets on which gentlemen and ladies strolled while waiting for others consulting in the surrounding chambers.

Gabriel paused in the cobbled forecourt beyond the gate, gazing unseeing at the trees.

Would the countess be impatient enough to contact him that evening? The possibility tantalized, even more so as the realization sank in that

47

her impatience could not possibly match his. While with her, he'd felt he knew her, knew the sort of woman she was; away from her, he'd realized how little he knew of the real woman behind the veil. Learning more, quickly, seemed imperative – he especially needed to learn how to put his hand on a woman who thus far had been a phantom in the night.

Unfortunately, he couldn't learn more until she contacted him – at least now, when she did, he'd have something to report.

Shrugging off his distraction, he settled on Aldwych as his best bet for a hackney and set out along the south side of the Fields. Halfway along, he heard himself hailed.

'Gabriel!'

'Over here!'

The voices coming from the Fields were assuredly feminine, equally assuredly young. Halting, Gabriel scanned the shaded lawns; two sweet young things, their parasols tilted at crazy angles, were bobbing up and down and waving madly. Squinting against the sunlight, he recognized Mary and Alice Morwellan. Raising his cane in reply, he waited until a dowager's black carriage rolled soberly past, then started across the narrow street.

Alathea saw him coming, and had to fight down an urge to screech at her sisters – what had they *done*? She'd seen him walk through the gates of the Inn and pause. Her attention locked on him, she'd assured herself that he wouldn't notice her in the shadows, that there was no reason for her heart to gallop, for her nerves to twitch.

He'd remained safely ignorant of her presence – she'd been surprised he'd acted so swiftly on the countess's behalf. That was, she presumed, why he was here – if she'd known, she would never have risked coming. Having him find her anywhere near any location he would associate with the countess had formed no part of her careful plans. She needed to keep her two personas completely distinct, especially near him.

As he'd walked along the street, cane swinging, broad shoulders square, sunlight had gleamed on his chestnut hair, gilding the lightly curling locks. Her thoughts had slowed, halted – she'd completely forgotten Mary and Alice were with her.

They'd seen him and called – now there was no escape. As he crossed the grass toward them, she drew in a breath, lifted her chin, tightened her fists about her parasol's handle – and tried to quell her panic.

He couldn't recognize lips he'd kissed but not seen, could he?

Smiling easily, Gabriel strode into the trees' shadows. As he neared, Mary and Alice stopped jigging and contented themselves with beaming; only then, with his eyes adjusting and with their dancing parasols no longer distracting him, did he see the lady standing behind them.

Alathea.

His stride almost faltered.

She stood straight and tall, silently contained, her parasol held at precisely the correct angle to protect her fine skin from the sun. Not, of course, waving at him.

Masking his reaction – the powerful jolt that shook him whenever he saw her unexpectedly and the prickling sensation that followed – he continued his advance. She watched him with her usual cool regard, her customary challenge – a haughty watchfulness that never failed to get his goat.

Forcing his gaze from her, he smiled and greeted Mary and Alice, veritable pictures in mull muslin. He made them laugh by bowing extravagantly over their hands.

'We were utterly amazed to see you!' Mary said.

'We've been to the park twice,' Alice confided, 'but that was earlier than this. You probably weren't about.'

Refraining from replying that he rarely inhabited the park, at least not during the fashionable hours, he fought to keep his gaze on them. 'I knew you were coming to town, but I hadn't realized you were here.' He'd last met them in January, at a party given by his mother at his family home, Quiverstone Manor in Somerset. Morwellan Park and the Manor shared a long boundary; the combined lands and the nearby Quantock Hills had been his childhood stamping ground – his, his brother Lucifer's, and Alathea's.

With easy familiarity, he complimented both girls,

fielding their questions, displaying his suave London persona to their evident delight. Yet while he distracted them with trivialities, his attention remained riveted on the cool presence a few feet away. Why that should be so was an abiding mystery – Mary and Alice were effervescent delights. Alathea in contrast was cool, composed, still – in some peculiar way, a lodestone for his senses. The girls were as bubbling, tumbling streams, while Alathea was a deep pool of peace, calm, and something else he'd never succeeded in defining. He was intensely aware of her, as she was of him; he was acutely conscious they had not exchanged greetings.

They never did. Not really.

Steeling himself, he lifted his gaze from Mary's and Alice's faces and looked at Alathea. At her hair. But she was wearing a bonnet – he couldn't tell whether she was also wearing one of her ridiculous caps, or one of those foolish scraps of lace she'd started placing about her top knot. She probably was concealing some such frippery nonsense, but he couldn't comment unless he saw it. Lips thinning, he lowered his gaze until his eyes met hers. 'I hadn't realized you were in London.'

He was speaking directly to her, specifically of her, his tone quite different from when he'd spoken to the girls.

Her lashes flickered; her grip on her parasol tightened. 'Good afternoon, Rupert. It is a lovely day. We came up to town a week ago.'

51

He stiffened.

Alathea sensed it. Her stomach knotted with panic, she looked at Mary and Alice and forced herself to smile serenely. 'The girls will be making their come-outs shortly.'

After a fractional hesitation, he followed her lead. 'Indeed?' Turning back to Mary and Alice, he quizzed them on their plans.

Alathea tried to breathe evenly, tried to hold her sudden lightheadedness at bay. She refused to let her gaze slide his way. She knew his face as well as her own – the large, heavily hooded eyes, the mobile lips given to wry quirks, the classic planes of nose and forehead, the uncompromisingly square chin. He was tall enough to see over her head – one of the few who could do so. He was strong enough to subdue her if he wished, and ruthless enough to do it. There was nothing about him physically that she didn't already know, nothing to set such a sharp edge to her usual tension.

Nothing beyond the fact that she'd seen him last night in the porch of St George's, while he hadn't seen her.

The memory of his lips covering hers, of the beguiling touch of his fingers beneath her chin, locked her lungs, tightened her nerves, set her senses leaping. Her lips tingled.

'Our ball will be in three weeks,' Mary was telling him. 'You'll be invited, of course.'

'Will you come?' Alice asked.

'I wouldn't miss it for the world.' His gaze flicked to Alathea's face, then he looked back at the girls.

Gabriel knew exactly how a cat with its fur rubbed the wrong way felt – precisely how he always felt near Alathea. How she did it he did not know; he didn't even know if she had to do anything – it simply seemed his inevitable reaction to her. He'd react, and she'd snap back. The air between them would crackle. It had started when they were children and had grown more intense with the years.

He kept his gaze on the girls, ruthlessly stifling the urge to turn to Alathea. 'But what are you doing here?'

'It was Allie's idea.'

Blithely, they turned to her; gritting his teeth, he had to do the same.

Coolly, she shrugged. 'I'd heard of it as a quiet place to stroll – one where ladies would be unlikely to encounter any of the more rakish elements.'

Like him.

She'd chosen to live her life buried in the country – why she thought that gave her the right to disapprove of his lifestyle he did not know; he only knew she did. 'Indeed?'

He debated pressing her – both for her real reason for being in the Fields and also over her impertinence in disapproving of him. Even with the girls all ears and bright eyes before them, he could easily lift the conversation to a level where they wouldn't understand. This, however, was Alathea. She was intractably stubborn – he would learn nothing she didn't wish him to know. She was also possessed of a wit quite the equal of his; the last time they'd crossed verbal swords – in January, over the stupid Alexandrine cap she'd worn to his mother's party – they'd both bled. If, eyes flashing, cheeks flushed with temper, she hadn't stuck her nose in the air and walked – stalked – away from him, he would quite possibly have strangled her.

Lips compressed, he shot her a glance – she met it fearlessly. She was watching, waiting, as aware of the direction of his thoughts as he. She was ready and willing to engage in one of their customary duels.

No true gentleman ever disappointed a lady.

'I take it you'll be accompanying Mary and Alice about town?'

She went to nod, stopped, and haughtily lifted her head. 'Of course.'

'In that case' – he smiled disarmingly at Mary and Alice – 'I'll have to see what amusements I can steer your way.'

'There's no need to put yourself out – unlike some I could mention, I don't require to be constantly amused.'

'I think you'll discover that unless one is constantly amused, life in the ton can be hellishly boring. What, other than boredom, could possibly have brought you here?'

'A wish to avoid impertinent gentlemen.'

'How fortunate, then, that I chanced upon you.

If avoiding impertinent gentlemen is your aim, a lady within the ton can never be too careful. There's no telling precisely where or when she'll encounter the most shocking impertinence.'

Mary and Alice smiled trustingly up at him; all they heard was his fashionable drawl. Alathea, he knew, detected the steel beneath it; he could sense her increasing tension.

'You forget – I'm perfectly capable of dealing with outrageous impertinence, however unamusing I might find such encounters.'

'Strange to say, most ladies don't find such encounters unamusing at all.'

'I am not "*most ladies*." I do not find the particular distractions to which you are devoted at all amusing.'

'That's because you've yet to experience them. Besides,' he glibly added, 'you're used to riding every day. You'll need some activity to . . . keep you exercised.'

He raised eyes filled with limpid innocence to hers, expecting to meet a narrow-eyed glance brimming with aggravation. Instead, her eyes were wide, not shocked but . . . it took him a moment to place their expression.

Defensive. He'd made her defensive.

Guilt rose within him.

Hell! Even when he won a round with her, he still lost.

Stifling a sigh – over what he did not know – he looked away, trying to dampen what he thought of as his bristling fur – that odd aggression she always evoked – and act normally. Reasonably.

He shrugged lightly. 'I must be on my way.'

'I dare say.'

To his relief, she contented herself with that small barb. She watched as he bowed to the girls, setting them laughing again. Then he straightened and deliberately caught her gaze.

It was like looking into a mirror – they both had hazel eyes. When he looked into hers, he usually saw his own thoughts and feelings, reflected over and again, into infinity.

Not today. Today all he saw was a definite defensiveness – a shield shutting her off from him. Protecting her from him.

He blinked, breaking the contact. With a curt nod, which she returned, he swung on his heel and strode off.

Slowing as he neared the edge of the lawn, he wondered what he would have done if she'd offered her hand. That unanswerable question led to the thought of when last he'd touched her in any way. He couldn't remember, but it was certainly not in the last decade.

He crossed the street, wriggling his shoulders as his peculiar tension drained; he called it relief at being out of her presence, but it wasn't that. It was the reaction – the one he'd never understood but which she evoked so strongly – subsiding again.

Until next they met.

★   ★   ★

Alathea watched him go; only when his boots struck the cobbles did she breathe freely again. Her nerves easing, she looked around. Beside her, Mary and Alice blithely chatted, serenely unaware. It always amazed her that their nearest and dearest never saw anything odd in their fraught encounters – other than themselves, only Lucifer saw, presumably because he'd grown up side by side with them and knew them both so well.

As her pulse slowed, elation bloomed within her.

He hadn't recognized her.

Indeed, after the total absence of his typical reaction to her when he'd met the countess last night, combined with the strong resurgence of it in the last hour, she doubted he'd ever make the connection.

This morning, she'd woken to the certain knowledge that it wasn't her physical self that he found so provoking. If he didn't know she was Alathea Morwellan, nothing happened. No suppressed irritation, no sparks, no clashes. Blissful nothing. Cloaked and veiled, she was just another woman.

She didn't want to dwell on why that made her feel so happy, as if a weight had suddenly lifted from her heart. It was clearly her identity that caused his problem – and it was, she now knew, his problem, something that arose first in him, to which she then reacted.

Knowing didn't make the outcome any easier to endure, but . . .

She focused on the wrought-iron gates through which he had emerged. They were open to admit coaches to the courtyard of the Inn. She could see the Inn's archways and the glint of bronze plaques – it wasn't hard to guess the purpose of the plaques.

He'd seemed satisfied and confident when he'd strolled away from the gates.

Drawing in a determined, fully recovered breath, Alathea smiled at Mary and Alice. 'Come, girls. Let's stroll about the Inn.'

Evening came, and with it a strange restlessness.

Gabriel prowled the parlor of his house in Brook Street. He'd dined and was dressed to go out, to grace the ballroom of whichever tonnish hostess he chose to favor with his presence. There were four invitations from which to choose; none, however, enticed.

He wondered where the countess would spend her evening. He wondered where Alathea would spend hers.

The door opened; he paused in his pacing. His gentleman's gentleman, Chance, pale hair gleaming, immaculately turned out in regulation black, entered with the replenished brandy decanter and fresh glasses on a tray.

'Pour me one, will you?' Gabriel swung away as Chance, short and slight, headed for the sideboard. He felt peculiarly distracted; he hoped a stiff brandy would clear his mind.

He'd left Lincoln's Inn buoyed by his small success, focused on the countess and the sensual game unfolding between them. Then he'd met Alathea. Ten minutes in her company had left him feeling like the earth had shifted beneath his feet.

She'd been part of his life for as long as he could remember; never before had she shut him out of her thoughts. Never before had she been anything but utterly free with her opinions, even when he'd wished otherwise. When they'd met in January, she'd been her usual open, sharp-tongued self. This afternoon, she'd shut him out, kept him at a distance.

Something had changed. He couldn't believe his comments had made her defensive; it had to be something else. Had something happened to her that he hadn't heard about?

The prospect unsettled him. He wanted to focus on the countess, but his thoughts kept drifting to Alathea.

Reaching the room's end, he swung around – and nearly mowed Chance down.

Chance staggered back – Gabriel caught his arm, simultaneously rescuing the brimming tumbler from the wildly tipping salver.

'Hoo!' Chance waved the salver before his unprepossessing visage. 'That was a close one.'

Gabriel caught his eye, paused, then said, 'That will be all.'

'Aye, aye, sir!' With cheery insouciance, Chance headed for the door.

Gabriel sighed. 'Not "Aye, aye" – a simple "Yes, sir" will do.'

'Oh.' Chance paused at the door. 'Right-oh, then. "Yessir," it is!'

He opened the door, and saw Lucifer about to enter – Chance stepped back, bowing and waving. 'Come you right in, sir. I was just a-leaving.'

'Thank you, Chance.' Grinning, Lucifer strolled in. With unimpaired serenity, Chance bounced out – then remembered and returned to shut the door.

Closing his eyes, Gabriel took a large swallow of brandy.

Lucifer chuckled. 'I told you it wouldn't simply be a matter of a suit of clothes.'

'I don't care.' Opening his eyes, Gabriel regarded the exceedingly large quantity of brandy in the tumbler, then sighed, turned, and sank into a well-stuffed armchair to one side of the hearth. 'He'll become something employable if it kills him.'

'Judging by his progress to date, it might kill you first.'

'Quite possibly.' Gabriel took another fortifying swallow. 'I'll risk it.'

Standing before the mantelpiece checking his own stack of invitations, Lucifer shot him a look. 'I thought you were going to say you'd "chance" it.'

'That would be redundant – I *am* "chancing" it. Precisely why I named him that.'

Chance was not Chance's real name – no one, including Chance, knew what that was. As for his age, they'd settled on twenty-five. Chance was a product of the London slums; his elevation to the house in Brook Street had come about through his own merit. Caught up in the stews while helping a friend, Gabriel might not have made it out again but for Chance's aid, given not for any promise of reward, but simply in the way of helping another man with the scales weighted heavily and unfairly against him. Chance had, in a way, rescued Gabriel – Gabriel, in turn, had rescued Chance.

'Which have you chosen?' Lucifer looked from his invitations to the four lined up on Gabriel's side of the mantelpiece.

'I haven't. They all seem similarly boring.'

'*Boring?*' Lucifer glanced at him. 'You want to be careful of using that word, and even more of giving way to the feeling. Just look where it got Richard. And Devil. And Vane, too, come to think of it.'

'But not Demon – he wasn't bored.'

'He was running, and that didn't work, either.' After a moment, Lucifer added, 'And anyway, I'm sure he *is* bored now. He's not even sure they'll come up for any of the Season.' His tone labeled such behavior incomprehensible.

'Give him time – they've only been married a week.'

A week ago, Demon Harry Cynster, their cousin and a member of the group of six popularly known as the Bar Cynster, had said the fateful words and

61

taken a bride, one who shared his interest in horse-racing. Demon and Felicity were presently making a prolonged tour of the major racecourses.

Nursing his brandy, Gabriel mused, 'After a few weeks, or months, I dare say the novelty will wear off.'

Lucifer threw him a cynical look. They were both well aware that when Cynsters married, the novelty did not, strange as it seemed, wear off at all. Quite the opposite. To them both, it was an inexplicable conundrum, however, as the last unmarried members of the group, they were exceedingly wary of having it explained to them.

How on earth men like them – like Devil, Vane, Richard, and Demon – could suddenly turn their backs on all the feminine delights so freely on offer within the ton, and happily – and to all appearances contentedly – settle to wedded bliss and the charms of just one woman, was a mystery that confounded their male minds and defied their imaginations.

Both sincerely hoped it never happened to them.

Resettling his cloak, Lucifer selected one gilt-edged card from his stack. 'I'm going to Molly Hardwick's.' He glanced at Gabriel. 'Coming?'

Gabriel studied his brother's face; anticipation glinted in the dark-blue eyes. 'Who'll be at Molly Hardwick's?'

Lucifer's quick smile flashed. 'A certain young matron whose husband finds the bills before Parliament more enticing than she.'

That was Lucifer's speciality – convincing ladies

of insufficiently serviced passions that permitting him to service them was in their best interests. Considering his brother's long, lean frame and rakishly disheveled black locks, Gabriel raised a brow. 'What's the odds?'

'None at all.' Lucifer strolled to the door. 'She'll surrender – not tonight, but soon.' Pausing at the door, he nodded at the glass of brandy. 'I take it you're going to see that to the end, in which case, I'll leave you to it.' With a wave, he opened the door; an instant later it clicked shut behind him.

Gabriel studied the dark panels, then raised his glass and took another sip. Transferring his gaze to the fire burning in the grate, he stretched out his legs, crossed his ankles, and settled down for the evening.

It was, he felt, a telling fact that he would rather wait out the hours until midnight here, safe and comfortable before his own hearth, than risk his freedom in a tonnish ballroom, no matter how tempting the ladies filling it. Ever since Demon's engagement had been announced nearly a month ago, every matron with a daughter suitable in any degree had set her sights on him, as if marriage was some poisoned chalice the Bar Cynster was handing around, member to member, and he was the next in line.

They could live in hope, but he wasn't about to drink.

Turning his head, he studied the pile of journals stacked on a side table. The latest issue of the

Gentlemen's Magazine was there, yet . . . he'd rather consider the countess – all six feet of her. It was rare to meet a lady so tall . . .

Alathea was nearly as tall.

Three minutes later, he shook aside the thoughts that, unbidden, had crowded into his mind. Confusing thoughts, unsettling thoughts, thoughts that left him more distracted than he could ever remember feeling. Clearing his mind, he focused on the countess.

He enjoyed helping people – not in the general sense but specifically. Individual people. Like Chance. Like the countess.

The countess needed his help – even more, she had asked for it. Alathea didn't, and hadn't. Given how he felt, that was probably just as well. His gaze fixed on the flames, he kept his mind on the countess – on plotting the next phase in their investigation, and planning the next stage in her seduction.

CHAPTER 3

At twenty minutes past midnight, Gabriel stood outside the oak door guarding the offices of Thurlow and Brown and studied the old lock. He'd seen no one while crossing the quiet courtyard. Light had shone from a few windows, where clerks were presumably laboring through the night; the rooms directly below were occupied, but no one had heard him slip past on the stair.

He felt in his pocket for the lockpick he'd brought, one capable of dealing with such a large lock. Simultaneously, without thought, he tested the door, turning the knob—

The door eased open.

Gabriel stared at the door, at the lock that had been unlocked, and tried to imagine the old clerk shutting up and going home without locking up.

That scenario wasn't convincing.

He could see no light through the crack between door and jamb. He eased the door further open. As earlier in the day, it opened noiselessly. The reception area and the room off it were in darkness.

In the room at the end of the corridor, however, faint light gleamed.

Shutting the door, Gabriel eased the bolt home. Leaning his cane beside the door, he paused, letting his eyes adjust to the denser gloom, noting again the position of the wooden gate in the railing of the reception area through which clients were admitted to the chambers beyond.

That, too, opened noiselessly.

His footfalls muffled by the runner, he made his way silently along the corridor and wondered if it was remotely possible that Mr Brown without an 'e' was working late. The occasionally pulsing light presumably came from a lamp turned very low; the lamp was also partially screened, the light thrown back into the room, away from the windows, presumably toward Brown's desk. Pausing at the threshold, Gabriel listened – and heard the steady flick of pages being turned. Then came the soft thump of a book being closed, then papers were shuffled. That was followed by a different sound – he eventually placed it as papers and books being placed into a tin box, and the box shut.

Another box was opened. A second later came more flicking – steady, even, purposeful.

It didn't sound like Mr Brown.

Beyond curious, Gabriel stepped over the threshold into the shadowed gap created by the half-open door and looked around its edge.

A tall cloaked and hooded figure stood before

the large desk, rifling the papers she'd lifted from one of the boxes stacked on the desktop. Her gloved hands gave her away, as did the curve of her jaw, fleetingly revealed when she tilted her head, angling a document so that the light fell more definitely on it. The lamp stood on the desk to her left, a tall ledger propped around it to act as a screen.

Conscious of the tension leaving muscles he hadn't been aware he'd tensed, Gabriel leaned against the bookshelves and considered.

He waited until she'd methodically searched the contents of the now open box and restacked the papers. Then he reached out and pushed the door.

It squeaked.

She gasped. Papers scattered. In a furious flurry she flicked down her veil and whirled, so quickly that, despite watching closely, he failed to catch even a glimpse of her face. One hand at her breast, the other clutching the edge of the desk against which she'd backed, the countess stared at him, as deeply incognito as she'd been in Hanover Square.

'*Oh!*' Her voice wavered as if uncertain of its register, then, with an obvious effort, she caught her breath and said in the same low tone he recalled, 'It's you.'

He bowed. 'As you see.'

She continued to stare at him. 'You . . . gave me quite a start.'

'I would apologize, but' – he pushed away from

the bookshelves and advanced upon her – 'I hadn't expected to find you here.' Halting before her, he studied the glint of eyes behind her veil, and wished the veil were thinner. 'I thought *I* was supposed to locate Messrs Thurlow and Brown. How did you know they were here?'

She was breathing rapidly, her gaze locked on his face, then she looked away. With a sliding step, she slipped out of the trap between him and the desk, smoothly turning so she faced the desk again. 'I chanced upon them.' Her voice was very low; it strengthened as, collecting the scattered papers, she went on, 'I had to visit our family solicitor in Chancery Lane and on impulse I strolled into the Inn. I saw the plaques, so I wandered about – and found them.'

'You *should* have left it to me. Sent a note and stayed safely at home while I did this.' Why he was so annoyed, he couldn't have said. She was, after all, a free agent – except that she'd asked for his help.

She shrugged. 'I thought, as I'd found them, I'd see what I could discover. The sooner we locate the company, the better. All we need is their address.'

Gabriel inwardly frowned. Had his kissing her made her regret approaching him? If so, too late – she had. Her breathless skittishness reached him clearly, but he knew women too well to confuse resistance with rejection. If she wasn't seriously tempted, she wouldn't be skittish. 'How did you get in? The door was unlocked . . .' Only then did he notice that the boxes she'd been searching were padlocked. Only one was presently open, but . . . 'You can pick locks.'

She shifted. 'Well – yes.' She gestured briefly. 'It's a small talent I have.'

He wondered what other talents she was concealing. 'As it happens, it's a talent I share.' He reached for one of the boxes she'd yet to search. Each was labeled but only with a surname. The one he held was labeled 'Mitcham.' He looked at the small lock.

'Here.'

He glanced up. One delicate hand, gloved in the finest Cordovan leather, offered a hairpin.

'It's just the right size.'

His hand surrounded hers as he plucked it from her fingers. He had the box open in a trice; setting back the lid, he picked up the mass of papers within. 'Have you stumbled on any details yet – names or other references to the company?'

'No. Nothing. There's no box here or in the other room with the company's name on it, but there must be a box for them, surely? If they're a client, they would have a box, don't you think?'

'So one would imagine.' Gabriel glanced around the room. It confirmed his impression of the firm's incumbents. 'Messrs Thurlow and Brown appear staunchly conservative – if the company's a client, they'll have a box.'

Side by side, they searched swiftly but thoroughly.

An hour ticked by. Eventually, the countess sighed. Setting the papers back in the last box, she closed it, and pushed the box to Gabriel to relock. 'Nothing.'

'We've still got Thurlow's room. This will only have been half the practice.' Replacing the locked box on the top of the last shelf, Gabriel returned, picked up the lamp, and waved her on.

She'd already closed and replaced the ledger she'd used as a screen; now she gave the desk one last, comprehensive glance, checking all was as it had been, then she preceded him out of the door.

'Was this ajar?'

'Yes.' She glanced back and nodded at how he'd left the door. 'Like that.'

In Thurlow's room, they arranged their work-place – the desk cleared, the lamp set and screened as before – then set to. It was slow, demanding work, scanning document after document, looking for any mention of the Central East Africa Gold Company. If anything, Thurlow's room held more boxes than Brown's; the bookshelves were taller.

Gabriel was halfway through yet another box, when he heard a strangled '*Oh!*' He looked up – just in time to drop the papers he held, cross the room in two strides, and catch the stack of boxes teetering over the countess's head.

She was tall enough to reach the top shelf but, in this room, she hadn't been able to grip the boxes, only touch them. At full stretch, she'd coaxed a

70

stack of boxes to the edge of the shelf; they'd tipped, then started to slide . . .

He reached over her head and grabbed them, his arms outside hers, his shoulders enclosing hers. They both froze, gripping the tin boxes, desperate not to let them clatter to the floor.

There was less than an inch between them.

Her perfume rose, wreathing his senses; her womanly warmth, clothed in soft, sensual flesh, teased them. The urge to close that small gap, to feel her lean against him, waxed strong.

He sensed the leap of her pulse, the sudden fluster that gripped her. He heard her indrawn breath, sensed her uncertainty—

Tilting his head, he touched his lips to her veiled temple. She stilled – the tension that gripped her changed in a flash from physical to sensual; from clinging to a physical pose, she was now teetering on a sensual precipice. He shifted, closing the gap between them until she stood stretched upward against him, touching but not pressing. Sliding his lips from her temple, caressing the line exposed by her backswept hair, he dipped his head and traced the whorl of her ear, then slid his lips lower to tease and tantalize the sensitive spot below her lobe.

Skillfully he tempted her to ease her locked muscles and lean against him. The silk veil shifted beneath his lips, a secondary caress. She caught her breath on a shaky sob and held it; he bent his head and traced the long line of her throat until, at last, she exhaled. Tentatively, ready to take flight at the slightest sign, she let her shoulders ease against his upper chest.

Inwardly smiling in triumph, he angled his head upward, pressing gentle kisses into the hollow of her throat, encouraging her to raise her chin until finally her head tipped back against his shoulder. The warm curves of her back sank more definitely against him.

He wanted much more, but their hands were locked on the boxes still held high and he didn't dare break the spell. She was sweetly responsive but oh-so-skittish, like a mare never gentled to a man's hand. So he kept each caress simple, direct, unthreatening, and as each moment passed, she sank more definitely against him. The subtle warmth of her flowed over his hardness; he was aroused but held the pain at bay. It flashed into his mind that she was a castle he intended storming; his present victory was much like watching her drawbridge come down.

Eventually, she was leaning fully back against him. A fine tension still gripped her, but that derived more from fascinated anticipation than resistance. He pressed a firmer kiss in the hollow beneath her ear, and heard her shivery breath. A tremor shook her, followed by a shaky gasp.

'I'm going to drop these boxes.'

He raised his head and looked, and stifled a sigh. Her arms were quivering. He straightened – instantly, she did, too. She drew in a breath and held it. He eased back. Very carefully, she shifted her hands and gripped the lower two boxes, allowing him to lift the upper three away.

Lowering her arms, she stepped sideways, then turned and, spine poker straight, unmistakable resolution in every line, carried the two boxes back to the desk.

Leaving him with three tin boxes and a definite ache.

Jaw setting, Gabriel carried the boxes to the desk, stacking them atop hers. She'd already opened one box. Without glancing at him, she lifted the papers from it and started flicking through them. Eyes narrowing, he considered simply hauling her into his arms; the stiff, abrupt way in which she was turning pages argued against it.

Gritting his teeth, he picked up the pile of papers he'd been searching. He sent her a hard-edged glance. If she saw it, she gave no sign.

They continued to search in silence.

Just as he was wondering if, perhaps, he'd been wrong, and the Central East Africa Gold Company for some unknown reason had not merited a box, the countess straightened.

'This is it.'

Gabriel glanced at the box; it was labeled 'Swales.'

Holding a stack of papers to the lamplight, the countess swiftly studied each in turn. He shifted to stand behind her so he could read over her shoulder.

'Those are documents the company would need for registration to conduct business in the City of London.' He scanned the sheet she held. 'And the company is a formal client of Thurlow and Brown.'

'Because all these list Thurlow and Brown as the contact?'

'Yes. The firm must have been hired when the company first entered the City. That means there'll be very few pieces of legal paper listing the company's address.'

'There must be one, surely?' She looked up at him over her shoulder; her lips were outlined by her veil. His gaze locked on them and she froze, then a fragile shiver shook her. She looked away and breathlessly asked, 'Or will we need to search some government office to find it?'

She didn't see the subtle smile that curved his lips. 'There should be at least two documents listing the company's address. One is the main registration of the company, but that will in all likelihood be with the company. The other, however, is a document all solicitors prepare, but which many clients don't know about.'

Reaching out, he tugged at the last sheet in the stack; she let him draw it free. He held it up, and smiled. 'Here we are – the internal instructions for the firm on how to make contact with the client.'

'Mr Joshua Swales,' she read. 'Agent of the Central East Africa Gold Company, in the care of Mr Henry Feaggins, 142 Fulham Road.'

74

They reread the names and address, then Gabriel returned the sheet to the box. Taking the sheaf from the countess's hands, he rifled through it.

'What are you looking for?'

'I wondered if we'd be lucky enough to find a list of investors . . . or a list of promissory notes the firm's prepared . . . but no.' Frowning, he restacked the papers. 'Whoever they are, the company are certainly careful.'

She held the box as he set the papers back in, then he closed and relocked it. Carrying the other boxes, she followed him back to the shelf. He restacked the boxes in the right order, then turned to discover her already back at the desk, setting it to rights, straightening the blotter, realigning the inkstand.

Completing a last visual scan of the room, he lifted the lamp. 'Where did this come from?'

'The little table out here.'

She led the way. Gabriel set the lamp down on the side table she indicated, then waited until she passed through the gate in the railings before turning the wick down. The light died. 'Let's hope,' he murmured, moving around the clerk's desk to the gate, 'that the clerk is not the sort to keep a careful eye on the level of his lamp oil.'

She returned no comment, but waited by the door.

Retrieving his cane, he opened it. She stepped through. He followed, shutting the door, then crouching down to turn the heavy tumblers of the lock. Not a simple task. They finally fell into place. 'How on earth did you manage it?' he asked as he straightened.

'With difficulty.'

Certainly not with a hairpin. Stifling his curiosity, he followed her down the stairs. Her heels clicked on the stone. Crossing the cobbles silently would be impossible. At the bottom of the stairs, he took her hand and placed it on his sleeve. She looked up at him – he assumed in surprise. 'I presume your carriage is waiting?'

'At the far corner of the Fields.'

'I'll escort you to it.' In the circumstances, she could hardly argue, yet he knew she considered it. If she'd tried, he would have informed her that, courtesy of five tin boxes, she now had more chance of flying to her carriage than of dismissing him with nothing more than words.

There were rules to all engagements, in seduction as in war; he knew them all and was a past master at exploiting them for his own good. After the first clashes, every lady he'd ever engaged with had decided his exploitation had been for her good, too. Ultimately, the countess would not complain.

They set off, openly crossing the courtyard. He felt her fingers on his sleeve flutter nervously, then settle. He glanced at her veiled face, then let his gaze skate down her cloaked form. 'You appear to be a recently bereaved widow who could thus have good reason for visiting the Inn late.'

She glanced at him, then gave a slight nod and lifted her head.

Approving the imperious tilt to her chin, Gabriel looked ahead. She was no mean actress – there was now not a hint of trepidation to be seen. If he had to have a female partner, he was glad it was she. She could think, pick locks, and carry off a charade – all definite positives. Despite his irritation on first finding her here, he now felt in considerable charity with her role.

He would, of course, put his foot down and ensure she engaged in no more midnight searches, but that would have to wait until after they got past the porter nodding in his box by the gate. Head up, spine straight, the countess walked past as if the porter didn't exist. The man touched his fingers respectfully to his cap, then yawned and slouched back on his stool.

They walked on. In the shadows cast by the huge trees of the Fields, a small black carriage waited, the horses' heads hanging. As they neared, the coachman glanced around, then hunched over his reins.

Halting by the carriage, Gabriel opened the door.

The countess put out her hand. 'Thank you—'

'In a moment.' Taking her hand, he urged her into the carriage. He felt her puzzled glance as she complied. As she settled on the seat, he glanced at her coachman. 'Brook Street – just past South Molton.' With that, he followed the countess into the carriage and shut the door.

She stared at him, then scooted further over as he turned and sat beside her. The carriage rocked into motion.

After an instant's fraught silence, she said, 'I wasn't aware I had offered you a ride.'

Gabriel considered her veiled face. 'No doubt you would have – I thought I'd save you the trouble.'

He heard a small spurt of laughter, instantly suppressed. Lips curving, he faced forward. 'After all, we need to consider our next move.' He'd already mapped out several; all could be attempted in a closed carriage rolling through the night.

'Indeed.' Her tone was equable.

'But first, a point I should have made plain at the outset. You asked for my help and I agreed to give it. You also asked for my promise not to seek out your identity.'

She stiffened. 'Have you?'

His lightheartedness evaporated. 'I promised. So no. I haven't.' Each word was clipped, each sentence definite. 'But if you want me to play your game any further – if we're to continue our alliance and save your stepfamily from ruin – *you'll* have to promise to abide by my rules.'

Her silence lasted for a good fifty yards. Then, 'Your rules?'

He could feel her gaze on the side of his face; he continued to look forward.

'And what are they? These rules of yours.'

'Rule number one – you must promise never again to act without my knowledge.'

She stirred slightly. 'Your *knowledge*?'

Gabriel hid a cynical smile; he'd dealt with women long enough not to label it 'permission.' 'If you and I act independently, especially in such a delicate affair as this, there's a good chance we'll cross tracks to disastrous effect. If that happens, and we reveal our interest to the company too early, then all you've worked for will go for nought. And you are not sufficiently *au fait* with how matters are dealt with in the City to appreciate all the ramifications of what we might learn, which is, after all, why you sought my help in the first place.'

She had none of her sex's usual wariness of silence; again, she claimed it to calculate, to consider. As they swayed around a corner, she asked, 'These rules – what are the others?'

'There are only two – I've told you one.'

'And the second?'

He turned his head and looked at her. 'For each piece of information we gather, I get to claim a reward.'

'A reward?' Wariness had crept into her tone.

He suppressed a wolfish smile. 'Reward – a customary token of gratitude given in return for services rendered.'

She knew precisely what he meant, her knowledge clear in the fine tension that gripped her. After a moment, she cleared her throat. 'What reward do you want?'

'For locating Thurlow and Brown – a kiss.'

She went still – so still he wondered if he'd shocked her. But she could hardly be surprised – she knew very well who and what he was. From behind her veil, she stared at him, but if she was flustered, there was no sign of it – her hands, folded in her lap, remained still. 'A kiss?'

'Hmm.' This time, he couldn't stop his lips curving, couldn't suppress the seductive purr that entered his voice. 'Without the veil. Take it off.'

'No.' Calm – absolute.

Arrogantly, he raised his brows.

She shifted on the seat. 'No. The veil . . . I . . .'

He sighed resignedly. 'Very well.' Before she could think of some pretext on which to refuse the kiss altogether, he framed her face with one hand, his thumb under the edge of her veil, lifting it from her lips as he covered them with his.

Her lips had parted on a startled exclamation – as he caught them, she stilled. She didn't freeze, didn't panic – she simply sat, warm and alive, and let him fashion his lips to hers. He tilted her chin slightly; her face moved easily – she wasn't stiff. But there was no response as he pressed the caress upon her.

He wasn't having that, but he knew when to be patient. He kissed her lightly, gently shifting his lips on hers, artfully dallying, waiting . . .

Her first surrender was a shiver – piercingly sweet, a ripple of pure sensation. He sensed the hitch in her breathing, the increasing tension in her spine.

Then her lips moved, firming under his, still not giving, but alive. It was as if she was a statue coming to life, cool marble slowly heating, stone carapace melting, giving way to flesh, blood, and life.

He held her face steady and increased the pressure of the kiss. Acutely focused on her, he knew when she lifted one gloved hand from her lap, raising it to where his hand cupped her face. Her fingers hovered, an inch from his hand, then, very gently, almost as if she wasn't sure he – his hand – was real, she touched her fingertips to the backs of his.

The hesitant touch rocked him – it held a wondering innocence that captivated and held him.

Her leather-encased fingertips trailed, tracing the back of his hand; they hesitated for one quivering instant, then settled.

Like a butterfly on the back of his hand.

Her fingers didn't grip, didn't tug – they simply touched. He drew breath – drew her perfume deep – and deepened the caress. Asking – for once in his life, not demanding.

And she gave. Of her own accord, she tipped her face further, swaying toward him as she offered her lips.

He swooped like a conqueror and took, claimed – but immediately reined back when he sensed her sudden skitter. She was unused to being kissed. Strange as that seemed, he knew it for fact – he didn't ponder the cause but set himself to ease her, tease her, encourage her.

She was a quick study – soon she was kissing him back, gently but without reserve. He longed to draw her into his arms, but experience warned against it. Her nervousness was now explained – for whatever reason, she wasn't used to this. His lips on hers, his hand about her face, seemed, at this moment, all she could assimilate, so he set himself to work with that.

Set himself to cajole and tease, to lead her to yield more, to seek more. When she hesitantly parted her lips, he felt he'd won a siege, but he was careful, this time, of taking advantage too quickly – which meant he savored every sweet moment of her surrender, the whole extended like a necklace of precious, individual gems of sensation.

When she tentatively touched his tongue with hers, then slowly, sinuously, caressed him in return, his head very nearly spun.

She was like fine wine – best savored slowly.

He finally drew back as the carriage rumbled around a corner. Chest swelling, he studied her lips, briefly illuminated by a street flare. They were full, deeply rosy, slightly swollen. 'Now, for learning Swales's address . . .'

Her lips parted – whether in protest or invitation he didn't wait to learn. He covered them again; they molded easily, this time, to his, and parted fully the instant he touched them with his tongue.

Brook Street couldn't be much farther. The thought spurred him to drink more deeply, to take all she offered – then seek, search, and tempt her further.

She gave – not so much easily as willingly, taking hesitant steps along a path he instinctively knew she'd never trod. She'd never before been passionately kissed, never been awakened in this way. He had to wonder about her late husband, and whether she'd been awakened at all.

He held her steady, urging her on, his lips ruthless, just this side of hard. He would have taken her further, much further, but tonight they'd run out of time.

The carriage slowed, then rocked to a halt.

Reluctantly, he released her lips. For one instant, as their breaths mingled, he was tempted . . . then he drew away his hand and let her veil fall. She would reveal herself to him of her own accord. That was one moment he intended to fully savor.

He straightened. She sank against the seat. She tried to speak and almost choked; clearing her throat, she tried again. 'Mr Cynster . . .'

'My name is Gabriel.'

Despite her veil, their gazes locked. She stared at him, her breasts rising and falling beneath her cloak. 'I thought you had to consider our next move.'

His gaze didn't waver. 'Believe me, I am.'

He waited; when she made no reply but continued to stare at him, he inclined his head. 'Until our next meeting.' He reached for the door. 'Incidentally, when will that be?'

After a moment, she managed, 'I'll contact you in a day or two.'

She was still breathless; he hid a triumphant smile. 'Very well.' Deliberately, he let his gaze harden, pinning her where she sat. 'But you will remember what I said. Leave Swales to me.'

Although it was no question, he waited. Eventually, she nodded – one of her usual crisp nods. 'Yes. All right.'

Satisfied, he opened the door and stepped down to the pavement. Shutting the door, he signaled to the coachman. The reins flicked; the coach rumbled on.

He watched it roll away, then turned and climbed his steps, a great deal more than merely satisfied with the achievements of the night.

CHAPTER 4

She'd never felt so *breathless* in her life.

One elbow propped on the dining table, Alathea toyed with her toast and struggled to bring some order to the chaos of her mind. Not a simple task with her senses still reeling.

How naive she'd been to ignore the portent of that first, oh-so-innocent kiss. Sealing a pact, indeed! It hadn't occurred to her that, with no prickly reaction to stop him, he would most assuredly kiss her again. So now here she was, in a totally unexpected, never-before-experienced fluster. Just the thought of last night's kiss – *series* of kisses – was enough to addle her brain. One conclusion, however, was horrifyingly clear. Her errant knight believed she was a married woman – an *experienced* married woman – one with whom he could freely dally. But she wasn't. Thus far, he hadn't suspected that fact, but how far could she travel his road of rewards without giving herself away?

Without *having* to give herself away?

All that was bad enough, but to top it all, he'd filched the reins from her grasp. God alone knew where her carefully laid plans were now headed.

She should have foreseen his move to take control; he'd always been the leader in their childhood games. But they were no longer children, and for the last ten years she'd been accustomed to command; being summarily relegated to the rank of follower was a little hard to take.

About her, the rest of her family talked, ate, laughed; sunk in her thoughts, she barely heard them. Picking up her toast, she crunched, and decided she'd have to allow at least the appearance of him being in charge. His Cynster self would settle for nothing less; it was pointless beating her head against that wall. That didn't mean she had to meekly let him make all the decisions, only let him think he was. Which led to the question of how she could ensure that he didn't forge on and simply leave her in ignorance.

She would have to meet with him regularly, a prospect that made her edgy. Organizing their next meeting was logically her next step, but she'd yet to recover from their last. She'd counted on his deep vein of chivalry in enticing him to her aid – not in her wildest dreams had she imagined he'd extrapolate so fiendishly as to claim a reward.

Even that word was now forever altered in her mind. Now it instantly evoked something illicit. Something exciting, thrilling, tempting—

Seductive.

Her thoughts whirled; her lungs seized. Simply recalling that moment in the carriage when, with typical high-handedness, he'd set his lips to hers still made her dizzy. Remembering what had followed sent color rushing to her cheeks.

Instantly, she banished the mental visions, and the remembered sensations as well. If anything, the latter were worse. Lifting her teacup, she sipped and prayed no one had noticed her blush. She hadn't blushed in the last five years, possibly not in the last ten. If she suddenly started coloring up over nothing, questions would be asked – speculation would be born. Quite the last thing she needed.

Ruthlessly burying all memories of the drive to his house, she told herself she had no reason to berate herself; she couldn't have avoided it – any of it – without raising his suspicions. There was no point considering it further, beyond sending heartfelt thanks to her guardian angel – she'd very nearly blurted out his name when he'd released her. 'Rupert' had hovered on the tip of her tongue; she'd only just managed to swallow the word. Uttering it would have spelled an immediate end to her charade; she was the only female younger than his mother who persisted in calling him by his given name. He'd told her so himself.

Why she was so stubborn about it she didn't know – it was like clinging to a simpler time long gone. She'd always thought of him as Rupert.

My name is Gabriel.

His words rang in her mind. Gazing at the windows, she pondered; he was right – he was Gabriel now, not Rupert. Gabriel contained the boy, the youth, the man she'd known as Rupert, but also encompassed more. A greater depth, a greater spectrum of experience – a deeper reserve.

After a moment, she mentally shook herself and finished her tea. As the countess, she would have to remember to call him Gabriel, while Alathea still dubbed him Rupert.

And she would have to find a way to limit the rewards Gabriel would, without doubt, attempt to claim.

'I think we should call on Lady Hertford this morning.' Checking the day's invitations, Serena looked consideringly at Mary and Alice. 'She's giving an at-home, and I *think*, if you wear those gowns that were delivered yesterday, it would be a useful venue at which to be seen.'

'Oh, yes!' Mary exclaimed. 'Do let's start going about.'

'Will there be other young ladies there?' Alice asked.

'Naturally.' Serena turned to Alathea. 'And you must come, too, my dear, or else I'll have to spend all my time explaining your absence.'

That was said with a sweet but determined smile; Alathea smiled back. 'Of course, I'll come, if nothing else to lend support.'

Mary and Alice brightened even more. Amid serious discussion of ribbons, bonnets and reticules, they all retired upstairs to prepare for the projected excursion.

It was, indeed, very like a military sortie. An hour

later, standing at the side of Lady Hertford's drawing room, Alathea hid a grin. Serena had led the metaphorical charge into her ladyship's arena, positioning her troops with keen eye and shrewd judgment. Mary and Alice were engaged with a group of similarly young and inexperienced damsels, chattering animatedly, all initial shyness forgotten. Serena was sitting with Lady Chelmsford and the Duchess of Lewes, both of whom also had under their wings young ladies making their come-outs. Alathea would have wagered a tidy sum that the talk had already veered to which gentlemen might be expected to unearth handkerchiefs to drop this Season.

For herself, she stood quietly at the side of the room, although she knew she'd been noted by all. As Serena had remarked, if she hadn't appeared, her whereabouts would have been questioned, but now that the matrons present had confirmed that the earl's eldest daughter – unmarried, which was a mystery, but quite an ape-leader now – was in no way out of the ordinary and was quite comfortable with her stepsisters and stepmother – well, with no grist for the gossip mill to be found, she'd been dismissed from their collective consciousness.

That suited her very well.

Finishing her tea, she glanced around for a table on which to set her cup. Spying one beyond the *chaise* on which her hostess sat chatting to one of her bosom-bows, Alathea glided along the wall, passing behind the *chaise* to set her cup down. She was about to retreat when the words 'Central East Africa Gold Company' froze her where she stood.

She stared at the back of Lady Hertford's frizzy red head.

'An absolutely *certain* return, my cousin said, so naturally I told Geoffrey. I gave him the name of the man in charge, but Geoffrey's been hemming and hawing, dragging his feet.' Leaning closer to her friend, Lady Hertford lowered her voice. 'You may be sure I pointed out that what with the *unexpected costs* his heir has incurred at Oxford, he should be eager to better his current standing – I told him plainly that this year, Jane would need not just better gowns but more in her portion as well. But would he be moved?'

Lady Hertford sat poker straight, disapproval for her errant spouse in every line. 'I'm convinced,' she hissed, 'that it's only because my dearest cousin Ernest suggested it, and Geoffrey's never liked Ernest.'

Her friend murmured sympathetically, then turned the conversation to their offspring. Alathea moved away. Clearly, Lord Hertford shared her reaction to the Central East Africa Gold Company – in his case, if her ladyship was to be believed, because of who was 'in charge.'

From across the room, a turbaned dowager beckoned; Alathea obeyed the summons. With a serene smile firmly in place, she withstood an intensive inquisition on her obsession for the country and her spinster state. Not, of course, that the words 'unfashionable recluse' or 'husband' ever featured in the conversation.

Invincible serenity and an adamant refusal to be drawn finally won her her release from Lady Merricks, who snorted and waved her away. 'Unconscionable – that's what it is, miss! Your grandmama would have been the first to say so.'

With that observation ringing in her ears, Alathea gravitated back to the side of the room, and wondered if she dared broach the subject of the Central East Africa Gold Company with her hostess. One glanced at Lady Hertford's round and ruddy countenance put paid to that idea. Her ladyship was unlikely to have any information beyond what she'd already divulged. More to the point, she would be amazed by Alathea's inquiry. Ladies of her ilk, young or otherwise, should have no interest in such matters – ladies of her ilk were not supposed to know such matters existed.

Which was a definite hurdle, for she could not, on the same count, beard his lordship, either.

Alathea glanced at the door. Did she dare slip out and search Lord Hertford's study? She debated the likelihood of finding anything helpful; if learning the name of the man behind the company had been enough to cool his lordship's interest, it seemed unlikely he would have needed to write it down.

The probable return did not seem worth the risk

of getting caught searching Lord Hertford's study. She could just imagine the scandal *that* would provoke, especially if her reasons for searching ever came out.

And what if Gabriel learned of it?

No. She'd have to be patient. The very word chafed – she trenchantly repeated it. In the matter of the Central East Africa Gold Company, she was the countess and the countess had put her trust in Gabriel.

Patience and trust were all very well, but such virtues did nothing to ease her curiosity or allay the conviction that, if she left him too much to his own devices, Gabriel would either solve the entire matter and then present himself before her expecting to claim some impossible reward, or he'd become mired in some distracting detail and lose the thread entirely. Either was possible. If *he* had always been the leader, she had always been his *eminence grise*. It was time to reclaim that position.

They were attending an evening party at Osbaldestone House. Standing by the *chaise* on which Serena sat conversing with Lady Chadwick, Alathea scanned the crowd gathered to celebrate Lady Osbaldestone's sixtieth birthday. For her purpose, the setting was perfect.

Two days had passed since their unplanned meeting at Lincoln's Inn, two days in which Gabriel should have investigated the company's agent and his place of business. It was time for the countess to ask for a report.

Before her, the flower of the ton mingled and met. There was no dancing, just a string quartet installed in an alcove, vainly striving to be heard over the din. Talk – gossip and repartee – were the primary occupations of the evening, activities at which the guest of honor excelled.

Lady Osbaldestone was sitting on a *chaise* facing the room's center. Alathea glanced her way. The old lady thumped her cane on the floor, then pointed it at Vane Cynster, currently standing before her. Vane stepped back as if taking refuge behind the willowy figure of his wife. Alathea had met Patience Cynster in the park a few days before. Patience curtsied with unruffleable calm before her ladyship.

Alathea wished *she* had a little more patience – her eyes strayed to the clock for the third time in ten minutes. It was not yet ten o'clock; the party had barely begun. Guests were still arriving. Gabriel was already here, but it was too early for the countess to materialize.

The Cynsters were here *en masse*, Lady Osbaldestone being a connection. Alathea was watching two beauties presently holding court under Gabriel's oddly unimpressed eye when long fingers wrapped about her elbow.

'Welcome to town, my dear.'

The fingers slid down to tangle with hers and briefly squeeze. Alathea turned, a smile lighting her face. 'I wondered where you were.' She ran an appreciative glance over the tall, dark-haired, dark-garbed figure beside her. 'Now what am I supposed to call you – Alasdair? Or Lucifer?'

His smile flashed, the pirate beneath the fashionable facade showing briefly. 'Either will do.'

Alathea raised a brow. 'Both accurate?'

'I do my poor best.'

'I'm sure you do.' She looked across the room. 'But what's he doing?'

Lucifer followed her gaze to his brother. 'Guard duty. We take turns.'

Alathea studied the girls and caught the resemblance. 'They're your cousins?'

'Hmm. They don't have an older brother to watch over them, so we do. Devil's in charge, of course, but he's not often in town these days. Very busy taking care of the ducal acres, the ducal purse, and the ducal succession.'

Alathea's gaze shifted to the tall, striking figure of the Duke of St Ives. 'I see.' Devil was paying amazingly close attention to a haughtily commanding lady standing by his side. 'The lady with him . . . ?'

'Honoria, his duchess.'

'Ah!' Alathea nodded; Devil's intent gaze was now explained. She'd met all Gabriel's and Lucifer's male cousins occasionally over the years; she had no difficulty picking them out from the crowd. The family resemblance was definite, their general handsomeness a byword, although they were all identifiably distinct, from Devil's striking, piratical looks, to Vane's cool grace, to Gabriel's classical features and Lucifer's dark beauty. 'I can't see the other two.' She scanned the crowd again.

'They're not here. Richard and his witch are resident in Scotland.'

'His witch?'

'Well, his wife, but she truly is a witch of sorts. She's known as the Lady of the Vale in those parts.'

'Indeed?'

'Mmm. And Demon's busy escorting his new wife on a prolonged tour of the racetracks.'

'Racetracks?'

'They have a shared interest in racing thoroughbreds.'

'Oh.' Alathea checked her mental list. 'That leaves only you two still unwed.'

Lucifer narrowed his eyes at her. '*Et tu, Brute?*'

Alathea smiled. 'Merely an observation.'

'Just as well, or I might be tempted to point out that those who live in glass houses shouldn't throw stones.'

Alathea's smile didn't waver. 'You know I've decided marriage isn't for me.'

'I know you've told me so – what I've never understood is why.'

Shaking her head, she looked away. 'Never mind.' Her gaze returned to the two blond beauties chatting gaily, studiously ignoring Gabriel's lounging, deliberately intimidating presence mere yards away. 'Your young cousins – are they twins?'

'Yes. This is their second Season, but they are only eighteen.'

'Eighteen?' Alathea glanced at Lucifer, then back at the girls, confirming the modish gowns a touch more elegant than permissable for a girl in her first Season, the more sophisticated hairstyles, the assurance in the girls' gestures. Considering Gabriel watching over them like a potentially lethal avenging angel, Alathea shook her head. 'What on earth does he – you – think you're doing? If they're eighteen . . . why' – she swung to look at Mary and Alice talking in a group nearby – 'Alice is only seventeen.'

'She is?' Lucifer turned to stare at Mary and Alice. 'Good Lord – I didn't notice they were here.' He frowned, then glanced across the room at his cousins. 'If you'll excuse me?'

Without waiting for an answer, he swooped on Mary and Alice. With effortless charm, he detached them from their circle. One on each arm, he bore them across the room. Alathea watched, the question of what he was doing fading from her mind as the answer presented itself. He introduced her sisters to his cousins – a moment later, he slipped away from the enlarged circle now containing all four young ladies surrounded by a bevy of exceedingly safe, exceedingly careful young gentlemen.

The pleased-with-himself look on Lucifer's face as he slid into the crowd had Alathea shaking her head, not in wonder so much as resignation.

96

She'd been the recipient of the protectiveness of Cynster males often enough to recognize the impulse. Knowing she was supposed to approve, although she wasn't at all sure she did, she smiled in reply to Lucifer's questioning glance.

Lucifer headed for Gabriel. Smoothly, Alathea joined the circle about Serena's *chaise*. From the corner of her eye, she watched Lucifer explain his new arrangement; Gabriel nodded and passed the watch to Lucifer. Lucifer pulled a face but acquiesced, taking Gabriel's place by the wall.

Alathea darted a glance at the clock. Perfect. Lucifer's maneuvers were going to prove unexpectedly helpful; for the next hour she felt sure she could rely on him and his fair cousins to keep Mary and Alice happily occupied. And any minute now . . .

Majestic, yet blending into the glittering scene, Lady Osbaldestone's butler cleaved through the crowd. He stopped before Gabriel and presented a silver salver. Gabriel lifted a note from the salver, dismissing the butler with a nod. Opening the folded sheet, he scanned it, then refolded it and slipped it into his pocket.

The entire proceedings had taken no more than a minute – unless one had been watching Gabriel specifically, in the crush, nothing would have been seen. Not a flicker of expression betrayed his thoughts – on anything.

Trusting he'd respond to the instructions in the note, Alathea looked away, giving her attention to

Serena and her neighbors until it was time for her next move.

She reached the gazebo five minutes early, already slightly breathless. She told herself it was because she'd hurried, because she'd kept trying to watch in every direction at once to make sure no one saw her slip away. The vise locked about her lungs owed nothing to the fact that she was soon to meet Gabriel – not Rupert, but his far more dangerous alter ego – once more in the dark of night.

Folwell had been waiting as instructed in the thick bushes lining the carriage drive. He'd brought her cloak, veil and high-heeled shoes, and her special perfume. Drawing in a deep breath – steeling herself – Alathea let the exotic scent wreathe through her brain. She *was* the countess.

In her disguise, she actually felt like someone else – not Lady Alathea Morwellan, spinster, ape-leader. It was as if her anonimity and the seductive perfume brought out another side of her – she had little difficulty sliding into her role.

The gazebo stood tucked away at the end of the shrubbery – she'd remembered it from years ago. It was far enough from the house to be safe from the risk of others chancing by, and so overhung by trees and rampant shrubs that she need not fear any stray beam of light, a pertinent consideration as she'd been unable to change her gown.

Outside, gravel crunched. A sudden thrill shot through her; tingles of excitement raced over her skin. Facing the archway, she drew herself up, head erect, hands clasped before her. Anticipation slid, insidiously compelling, through her veins. Ruthlessly quelling a reactive shiver, she drew in a tight breath. Tonight, she was determined to hold her own.

He appeared, a black silhouette filling the doorway, her sworn knight come to report. He was a dark presence, intensely masculine, achingly familiar yet so unnervingly unknown. Pausing on the threshold, he located her in the dark; he hesitated – she felt his gaze rake her, felt an inexplicable urge to turn and flee. Instead, she stood still, silent and challenging.

He strolled forward.

'Good evening, my dear.'

She was a creature of night and shadow, discernible only as a darker shape in the dense gloom within the gazebo. Her height, her veil and cloak – Gabriel could see nothing beyond that, but his senses had abruptly focused; he was sure it was she. Halting directly before her, he studied her, very conscious of the alluring perfume that rose from her flesh. 'You didn't sign your note.'

Despite not being able to see it, he knew she raised a haughty brow. 'How many ladies send you messages to meet them in dark gazebos?'

'More than you'd care to count.'

She stilled. 'Were you expecting someone else?'

'No.' He paused, then added, 'I was expecting you.' Not here at Osbaldestone House, under his very nose, but he hadn't imagined she'd calmly sit in her drawing room and wait for a week before contacting him again. 'I expect you'd like to know what I've learned?'

He heard the purr in his voice, and sensed her wariness.

'Indeed.' She lifted her chin; he could feel the challenge in her gaze.

'Swales doesn't live at that address on the Fulham Road – it's a public house called the Onslow Arms. Henry Feaggins is the proprietor. He holds the mail for Swales.'

'Does Feaggins know where Swales lives?'

'No – Swales simply stops by every few days. There was no mail to be collected, so I sent a letter – a blank sheet. Swales came in this morning and picked it up. My man followed him – Swales went to a mansion in Egerton Gardens. It seems he lives there.'

'Who owns the mansion?'

'Lord Archibald Douglas.'

'Lord Douglas?'

He looked sharply at her. 'Do you know him?'

She shook her head. 'Could Lord Douglas be the chairman of the company?'

Her question effectively answered his. 'Unlikely – Archie Douglas cares for nothing beyond wine, women, and cards. Spending money is his forte, not making it. However . . .' He paused, considering how much to reveal. Looking at her veiled face, upturned to his, he inwardly admitted that it was her investigation as much, if not more, than his. 'If Swales is the company agent and he's using Archie's home as his base, then there's a very good chance – better than even money – that a good friend of Archie's, who also happens to be in residence at this time, is the real power behind the Central East Africa Gold Company.'

'And who is this friend?'

'Mr Ranald Crowley.' The name hung heavy on the air, laden with dislike.

'You know him.' It wasn't a question.

'We've never met. We have, however, crossed swords, financially speaking, and I know a great deal of his reputation.'

'Which is?'

'Not good. He's a black-hearted scoundrel. He's been thought to have been involved in a number of less-than-straightforward dealings, but whenever the authorities show any interest, the venture simply evaporates. There's never been any proof against him, but in the . . . shall we say, underworld of business, he's well known.' He hesitated, then added, 'And well feared. He's said to be cunning and dangerous – few doubt he would balk at murder if the gain was sufficient.'

She shivered and wrapped her arms about her. 'So he's a *clever*, black-hearted scoundrel.' A moment later, she said, 'I overheard that Lord Hertford declined to invest in the company purely because of "the man in charge".'

Focused on her, Gabriel waved dismissively. 'Don't worry about Crowley – I'll look into the situation.'

He reached for her – she was in his arms before she knew it. Amazed to find her hands resting on his chest, she looked up. 'What—?'

He heard the fluster in her voice, sensed the anticipation that flashed through her. Inwardly, he grinned. 'My reward for locating Swales.'

She hauled in a rushed breath. 'I never said anything about rewards.'

'I know.' Tightening his arm about her, he brushed her veil aside and lowered his lips to hers, touching them lingeringly once, twice . . . she quivered, then surrendered. He caught his breath as her supple, womanly warmth sank against his much harder frame – a tentative, evocative caress. His lips a mere whisker from hers, he murmured, 'You'll need to pay nevertheless.'

She made no effort to deny him – he claimed his due, his lips firming, then hardening on hers. She met him, not proactive but ready to follow his lead, her reactions a mirror reflecting his desire, her giving a reflection of his need. Inch by unconscious inch, her hands stole upward, eventually sliding over his shoulders. She angled her head, inviting him to deepen the kiss.

He did. She sank into his embrace and he tightened his arms, and his hold, on her. Her perfume sank into his brain.

All he asked for, she gave, not just willingly but

with an open-hearted generosity that was an invitation to plunder. So he plundered, but with no sense of seizing anything that wasn't freely given. If he wanted, she gave – readily, easily, as if she delighted in the giving. Which only made him want more.

He pushed her veil back; with her head tipped up, there was no need to hold it. Sliding his hand down, he found the opening of her cloak. With her arms over his shoulders, he couldn't flick the cloak up and over hers. Instead, he parted it, sliding his palm over the silk of her gown, around to the back of her waist. Supporting her there, he transferred his other hand beneath the heavy cloak; closing both hands about her hips, he drew her nearer.

She obliged without a murmur of dissent – she was so tall, they were nearly hip to hip, her thighs against his, the hollow at their apex a cradle for his erection. If she was aware of it, she gave no sign, not that he gave her time to think. His lips remained on hers, commanding her senses while his sought wilder pleasures.

When he closed his hand about her breast, he wondered if he'd gone too far – the shock that lanced through her was very real. He instinctively soothed, distracting her with his lips, his tongue, with increasingly explicit kisses, but he didn't remove his hand. Moments later, she drew in a shaky breath. Beneath his hand, her breast swelled; against his palm, he felt the furling of her nipple.

Only then did he caress the soft flesh, feeling it heat and firm. She was wearing nothing more than two layers of fine silk; the temptation to do away with them, to lower his head and set his mouth to her sweet flesh, grew with every second, with every shared breath.

He let the compulsion grow, caressing, teasing, taunting, kneading, stroking until he knew her breasts were aching, longing for more. Only then did he slip the tiny buttons closing her bodice free. Sliding his fingers across her silken shoulder, he searched, and found the ribbons of her chemise.

She knew what he was doing. Her awareness, focused, heightened, followed his fingers; the fine tension investing the supple muscles along her spine tightened – then locked as he tugged. The tiny bow unraveled; the ribbons slid free. He paused, deliberately easing back from their kiss, giving her a chance to stop him if she would. He knew very well she wouldn't. He searched, found, and tugged again. Her breath shivered against his lips. Smoothly, he drew her chemise down, Deliberately dragging the silk over her sensitized flesh.

Then, deliberately, he pressed aside the heavier silk of her bodice and closed his hand, skin to petal-soft skin, about her breast.

Her breathing fractured. His fingers firmed and she gasped.

He took her lips again, too hungry, too needy,

even while his senses feasted. She'd never been touched, not as he was touching her, caressing her until she whimpered and clung. Her flesh was warm, her nipples tight buds as she gave herself up to his touch. She was a sensual innocent, as generous with her body as she had been with her lips, every bit as instinctively giving. The hot mounds of her breasts were a sensual delight far too tempting to ignore.

She murmured incoherently when he drew his lips from hers, nudging her head back so he could trace the line of her throat, remembering just in time not to mark her. The sweet flesh filling his hand beckoned; he lowered his head and heard her stifled cry.

It was a warning, one he was too experienced not to heed. He was driving too fast, pushing her relentlessly along a path she'd never trod. So he slowed, introducing her to each sensation, letting her assimilate the glory of each before moving on to the next. Only when she was fully prepared did he draw one aching peak into his mouth. Her fingers sank into his shoulders; she arched in his arms, but not to pull away. She was hot and malleable under his hands, the very essence of sensual woman in the night.

She was fascinating, a houri, a woman of endless temptation – he basked in her warmth, feasted on her bounty, secure in the knowledge that she would eventually be his. Not tonight, but soon. Very soon.

When, at last, he lifted his head, she pressed herself to him, her body afire, helpless in her need. He took the lips she offered, glorying in her eagerness. He sent his hands roaming over her hips, over the smooth swells of her derriere, tracing the hemispheres, then artfully caressing until she shifted her hips sensuously against his, searching instinctively for ease.

He gave her none – not tonight. She might be wondrously responsive, gloriously giving, but tonight would be too far, too fast. She was sensually naive, definitely untutored, even if she could not be precisely innocent. Having known only a much older husband who had clearly failed to appreciate her, that was obviously the case. She was following his lead blind; he knew it. He, however, knew precisely what they were about, knew very well how the timing went, how the play should pan out. And even though he'd restructured the script and advanced her lessons to the point where her ultimate surrender was imminent, that time was not yet.

Thus spake the coldly calculating mind of a highly experienced rake. His body, unfortunately, was far from cold and didn't want to listen; most of his mind was similarly enthralled with the wonder in his arms.

It took iron will and every ounce of his determination even to think of letting her go, to accept that this interlude filled with burgeoning sensuality and such gloriously heady promise had to come to a close. An unfulfilled close. Even when his mind was finally won over, convincing his lips, tongue, arms and hands to comply was a battle.

He finally succeeded in lifting his head. Drawing in a huge breath, feeling her breasts hot and firm against his expanding chest, he stole just one more minute to revel in the feel of her against him, in the trusting way she leaned into him, the soft huff of her breath against his jaw, the heady temptation of her perfume. And her.

She sighed – a shivery exhalation laden with arousal, her breath caressed his check.

His arms, about to relax, tightened instead; he turned his head, his lips seeking hers, his script forgotten—

She stopped him with a hand on his cheek. 'Enough.'

For an instant, he teetered on the brink, her injunction at odds with the way she lay, supple and enticing in his arms.

As if she sensed the clash of will and desire, she repeated, 'You've had reward enough.'

He caught her hand, held it – unsure even in his own mind what he would do next. Then he drew breath, turned her hand, and placed a kiss in her palm. 'For now.'

He straightened, setting her on her feet, supporting her until she was steady.

Her first movement was to raise her hand and – weakly – flip down her veil. He could now see her outline clearly; transparently dazed, she looked down at her gaping bodice. He reached for her. 'Here – let me.'

She did. He drew her chemise up, tied the ribbons loosely, then closed her bodice. Her nervousness grew. The instant the last button was secured, she resettled her cloak, then glanced around. 'Ah . . .' She was clearly having trouble reassembling her wits. Drawing in another breath, she waved – weakly still – to the house. 'You go back first.'

Despite having found her here, he wasn't about to leave her here, alone in the dark. 'I'll walk you to the edge of the shrubbery, then I'll go on ahead.'

For one instant, he thought she'd argue, but then she nodded. 'Very well.'

He offered his arm and she took it; pacing slowly, he led her out of the gazebo.

She said nothing as they strolled the winding walks, leaving him to reflect on how at ease in her company he felt, and how, despite the sensual flickering of her nerves, she was confident enough, reassured enough, not to invoke conversation's protective screen. Now he thought of it, she'd yet to make an aimless remark. Meaningless patter was not the countess's style.

They reached the last hedge and she stopped. He scanned her veiled face, then inclined his head. 'Until next time.'

Turning, he strode across the lawn.

Her pulse still galloping, her head still whirling, Alathea watched her broad-shouldered knight cross to the house, saw him silhouetted by its blazing windows. He went up the terrace steps and in through the open doors without once looking back.

Shrinking back into the darkness, she waited for long minutes while her fevered skin cooled, while her heartbeat steadied, while the exhilaration that had gripped her – the daring, the compulsion, and that frighteningly wild and wanton desire – waned. She tried to think but couldn't. Finally, hugging the shadows, she made her way around to the carriage drive.

Folwell was waiting; she handed him her cloak and veil, and changed her shoes. He slipped away, taking her disguise back to the carriage. Once more herself – at least in appearance – she re-entered the house by a side door, then made her way to the withdrawing room.

Luckily, the event wasn't a major ball; the withdrawing room was quiet. Sitting before a table provided with a mirror, she ordered warm water and towel and set about bathing her wrists, temples, and throat, removing all trace of the countess's exotic scent. Then she asked for cold water, dipped in a corner of the towel, and when no other lady was looking, held the cold compress to her swollen lips.

She didn't dare peek, but she was sure he must have marked her. Scalded her, or so it had felt. Thank God nothing showed above her neckline. Just the thought of his mouth on her breasts sent heat rushing to them. She could feel his hands caressing her – she wished they still were.

In the mirror, she met her own eyes. She looked deep for long minutes, then grimaced. Looking down, she dipped the towel into the cold water; after a surreptitious glance around, she reapplied it to her still rosy lips.

She wasn't in the habit of deceiving herself – there was no point pretending that she hadn't known he would claim a reward if he'd uncovered any new facts, and that the likelihood of his having done so had been high. She'd gone to the gazebo knowing her protests would very likely prove too weak to stop him claiming all he wished.

She'd been right about that, but it was too late for regrets. In truth, she wasn't sure she harbored any.

That, however, did not alter the fact that she was now in deep trouble.

He thought they were playing a game – one at which he was an acknowledged expert but which she had never played before. She knew some of the rules, but not all of them; she knew some of the moves, but not enough of them. She'd initiated the charade, but now he'd taken control and was rescripting her role to suit his own needs.

To suit his own desires.

She tried to summon a suitable degree of annoyance; the thought that he desired her wouldn't let annoyance form. The very concept intrigued her, lured her. No serpent had ever been so persuasive; no apple so tempting.

No knight so invincibly demanding.

That last made her sigh – changing direction was impossible. She'd started the charade; she'd have to play her part. Her options were severely limited.

She studied her reflection, then, with her usual deliberation, decided: While alone with him, she wasn't Lady Alathea Morwellan but his mysterious countess. It was the countess he'd kissed and the countess who'd responded.

Not her.

There'd been no harm done; none would be done.

She lowered the towel. He'd seemed to find her kisses – and the rest of her – quite satisfactory as a reward. She'd sensed his hunger – his appetite; she was certain that was not something he would fabricate. Their interaction was in no way harming him, and while it might be unsettling – even eye-opening – it wasn't hurting her.

And the fact that her kisses were enough to satisfy one of the ton's most exacting lovers was an invisible feather she'd proudly wear in her spinster cap – the cap she'd wear for the rest of her life.

Refocusing on the mirror, she critically surveyed her face and lips. Almost normal.

Her lips twisted wryly. Impossible to play the hypocrite and pretend that she hadn't enjoyed it – that she hadn't felt a thrill, an excitement beyond anything she'd previously known. In those long minutes when he'd held her in his arms, claiming her, she'd felt a woman whole for the first time in her life.

Indeed, he made her feel like a woman other than herself – or did he simply make her feel things she shouldn't, compulsions she'd had no idea she could experience. She was twenty-nine, on the shelf, very definitely an old maid. In his arms, she hadn't felt old at all – she'd felt alive.

Driven by necessity, she'd set aside all hope of ever knowing what it was to be a woman with a man. She'd had her longings, but she'd locked them away, telling herself they could never be fulfilled. And they never could be – not all of them, not now. But if, in protecting her family again as she was, the chance was offered to experience just a little of what she'd had to forgo, wasn't that merely justice?

And if she knew she was playing with fire? Tempting fate beyond the bounds of all sanity?

Setting down the towel, she stared into her eyes, then she stood and turned toward the door.

She couldn't turn her back on her family, which meant she couldn't walk away from Gabriel.

Whether she wished it or not, she was trapped in her charade.

CHAPTER 5

Heathcote Montague's office looked down on a small courtyard tucked away behind buildings a stone's throw from the Bank of England. Standing before the window, Gabriel stared down at the cobbles, his mind fixed on the countess.

Who *was* she? Had she been a guest at Osbaldestone House, lips curving with secret laughter as she waltzed past him? Or, knowing he, together with all the Cynsters, would be there, had she slipped in uninvited, waited in the garden until their meeting, then slipped away through the shadows again? If so, she'd taken a considerable risk – who knows whom she might inadvertently have met. He didn't like her taking risks – that was one point he fully intended to make clear.

But only after he'd made love to her – after he'd had his fill of her feminine delights and pleasured her into oblivion.

He had a strong suspicion she didn't even know what sexual oblivion was. But she would – just as soon as he had her alone again. After last night, that much was certain – he'd already had his fill of restless nights.

'Hmm. Nothing here.'

It took him a moment to return to the present, then he turned.

Heathcote Montague, perennially neat, precise but self-effacing, set the three notes he'd just received to one side of his desk and looked up. 'I've heard back from nearly everyone. None of us, nor any of our clients, have been approached. Precisely what one would expect if the Central East Africa Gold Company is another of Crowley's crooked schemes.'

'Us' referred to the select band of 'men of business' who handled the financial affairs and investments of the wealthiest families in England.

'I think' – deserting the window, Gabriel started to pace – 'given it is Crowley behind it and he's avoiding all knowledgeable investors, then we can reasonably conclude the scheme's a fraud. Furthermore, if the amounts involved are comparable to that on the promissory note I saw, this scheme's going to cause considerable financial distress if it runs its course.'

'Indeed.' Montague leaned back. 'But you know the law's view as well as I. The authorities won't step in until fraud is apparent—'

'By which time it's always too late.' Gabriel faced Montague. 'I want to shut this scheme down, quickly and cleanly.'

'That's going to be difficult with promissory notes.'

114

Montague held his gaze. 'I assume you don't want this note you saw executed.'

'No.'

Montague grimaced. 'After last time, Crowley's not going to explain his plans to you.'

'Not that he explained them to me last time.' Gabriel returned to the window. He and Ranald Crowley had a short but not sweet past history. One of Crowley's first ventures, floated in the City, had sounded very neat, looked very tempting. It had been poised to draw in a large number of the ton, until he had been asked for his opinion. He'd considered the proposal, asked a few pertinent but not obvious questions, to which there were no good answers, and the pigeons had taken flight. The incident had closed many doors for Crowley.

'You're probably,' Montague observed, 'one of Crowley's least favorite people.'

'Which means I can't appear or show my hand in any way in this case. And nor can you.'

'The mere mention of the name Cynster will be enough to raise his hackles.'

'And his suspicions. If he's as cunning as his reputation paints him, he'll know all about me by now.'

'True, but we're going to need details of the specific proposal made to investors to secure their promissory notes in order to prove fraud.'

'So we need a trustworthy sheep.'

Montague blinked. 'A sheep?'

Gabriel met his gaze. 'Someone who can believably line up to be fleeced.'

'Serena!'

Together with Serena, seated beside her, Alathea turned to see Lady Celia Cynster waving from her barouche drawn up beside the carriageway.

Waving in reply, Serena spoke to their coachman. 'Here, Jacobs – as close as you can.'

Spine poker straight, Jacobs angled their carriage onto the verge three carriages from Celia's. By the time Alathea, Mary, and Alice had stepped down to the grass, Celia and her girls were upon them.

'Wonderful!' Celia watched her daughters, Heather, sixteen, and Eliza, fifteen, greet Mary and Alice. The air was instantly abuzz with chatter and innocent queries. The four girls had the years of their shared childhoods to bind them in much the same way as Alathea, Lucifer, and Gabriel. Celia gestured at her offspring. 'They insist on coming for a drive, only to become bored after the first five minutes.'

'They have yet to learn that social chatter is the . . . *comme ca va?* – oil that makes the ton's wheels go around?'

'Oil that greases the ton's wheels.' Celia turned to the speaker, a strikingly beautiful older lady who had strolled up in her wake.

Alathea curtsied deeply. 'Your Grace.'

Serena, still seated in the carriage, bowed and echoed the words.

Smiling, Helena, Dowager Duchess of St Ives, put out a gloved hand to tip up Alathea's face. 'You grow more attractive with the years, *ma petite.*'

Through her frequent visits to Quiverstone Manor, the Dowager was well known to the Morwellans. Alathea smiled and rose; the Dowager's brows rose, too. 'Not so petite.' Catching Alathea's eye, she lifted one brow even higher. 'Which makes it even more of a mystery why you are not wed, *hein?*'

The words were uttered softly; Alathea smiled and refused to be drawn. While she was used to such queries, the intelligence behind the Dowager's pale-green eyes always left her with the uncomfortable feeling that here was one who suspected the truth.

The carriage rocked as Serena rose, clearly intending to join them. Helena waved her back. 'No, no. I will ascend and we can chat in comfort.' She gestured at Celia and Alathea. 'These two must stretch their legs in the service of propriety.'

Alathea and Celia looked in the direction of Helena's nod; the four girls, heads together, arms linked, were already strolling the lawn.

Celia sighed resignedly. 'At least we can stroll together and chat.'

Leaving Helena settling in beside Serena, Alathea and Celia followed the four girls, but with no intention of joining them. They only needed to keep the girls in sight, leaving them free to talk without reserve.

117

Celia immediately availed herself of that freedom. 'Have you spoken to Rupert since coming up to town?'

'Yes.' Alathea mentally scrambled to recall the meeting – the one with Rupert, not Gabriel. 'We met briefly while the girls and I were out walking.'

'Well, then. You'll have seen. What *am* I to do with him?'

Alathea swallowed the observation that no one had ever been able to 'do' anything with Rupert Melrose Cynster. He was as malleable as granite and always on guard against manipulation. As for Gabriel . . . 'I saw nothing unusual. What worries you so?'

'Him! *He*!' Celia's fists clenched on the handle of her parasol. 'He's even more infuriating than his father. At least, by his age, Martin had had the good sense to marry me. But will Rupert turn his mind to the same task?'

'He's only thirty.'

'Which is more than old enough. Demon has married, and Richard, too – Richard's only a bare year older than Rupert.' A minute later, Celia sighed. 'It's not so much the marrying as his frame of mind. He doesn't even *look* at ladies properly, at least not with a view to any legitimate connection. And even the other sort of connection – well, the reports are hardly encouraging.'

Alathea tried to keep her lips shut, but . . . 'Encouraging?'

Ahead, the four girls burst out laughing; glancing

their way, Celia explained, 'It is apparently common knowledge that Rupert is cold – even with his mistresses he remains distant and aloof.'

'He always was . . .' About to say 'reserved,' Alathea reconsidered. 'Guarded.' That was much closer to the mark. 'He always keeps his feelings under very close control.'

'Control is one thing – true disinterest is another.' Celia's concern shadowed her eyes. 'If he can't catch fire even in that arena, what chance is there for any acceptable lady to set tinder to his wick?'

Alathea fought to keep her lips straight. By any standard, their conversation was exceedingly improper, but she and Celia had a decade-long habit of discussing her sons – Alathea's childhood companions – with a frankness that would have made their subjects' ears burn. But Rupert cold? It wasn't an adjective she'd ever associated with him, not as Alathea Morwellan and even less as the countess. 'Are you sure you're getting the true picture? Mightn't you be hearing solely from those ladies he hasn't been . . .' – she gestured – '"interested in"?'

'Would that that were so. But my information *has* frequently come from disgruntled ladies he *has* been 'interested in.' One and all, they've despaired of making any serious impression on him. If half the tales told are true, he barely remembers their names!'

Alathea's brows rose. Rupert being vague over

a name was a sure sign he was not paying attention, which meant he was not truly 'interested' at all. 'Perhaps,' she said, steering the conversation away from her nemesis, 'Alasdair will marry first.'

'Hah! Don't be fooled by all that easy-going charm. He's even worse than Rupert. Oh, not that he's cold – quite the opposite. But he's feckless, footloose, and over-indulged. He's busy enjoying himself without any long-term ties – he's developed a deep-seated conviction he doesn't need any shackles on his freedom.' Celia's humph was the definition of disapproving. 'All I can do is pray some lady has what it takes to bring him to his knees.' She looked up, checking the girls still strolling ahead. After a moment, she murmured, 'But it's really Rupert who worries me. He's so detached. Uninvolved.'

Alathea frowned. Gabriel hadn't treated the countess as if he were detached or uninvolved. Far from it, but she could hardly reassure Celia with that news. It seemed odd that the portrait Celia was painting was so different from the man she knew, let alone the man she was discovering, the man who had held her in his arms last night.

Celia sighed. 'Put it down to a mother's concern for her first-born if you will, but I can't see how any lady is going to break through Rupert's defenses.'

It was possible if one had known him for years and knew where the chinks were. Nevertheless, Alathea inwardly admitted that she could easily see him steadfastly refusing to let any lady close, not in the emotional sense. He didn't like close – he didn't like emotional. He and she had been emotionally close all their lives, and look how he reacted to that. If Celia was correct, she was the only female he had ever allowed within his guard . . .

Everything within her stilled. Had his experience with her, of her, hardened him against all women?

Then she remembered the countess. With the countess, he was intent, attentive, certainly not distant and cold. Perhaps distant and cold came later? After . . . ?

Inwardly frowning, she shook aside her thoughts. Looking ahead, she saw the four girls nearing a group of budding dandies. 'Perhaps we'd better catch up.'

Celia looked; her gaze sharpened. 'Indeed.'

Where in London was he to find a suitable sheep?

Leaving Lucifer and the friends with whom they'd lunched in the smoking room of White's, Gabriel scanned the occupants of the rooms through which he passed. None fitted his bill. It had to be someone with no obvious connection to the Cynsters, yet someone he could trust. Someone sharp enough to play a part but appear vacuous. Someone willing to take orders from him. Someone reliable.

Someone with money to invest and some hope of appearing gullible.

While he had contacts aplenty who would qualify on most counts, that last criterion excused them all. Where was he supposed to find such a someone?

Pausing on the steps of White's, he considered, then strolled down and headed for Bond Street.

It was the height of the Season and the sun was shining – as he'd expected, all the ton and their relatives were strolling the fashionable street. The crowd was considerable, the traffic snarled. He ambled, scanning the faces, noting those he knew, assessing, rejecting, considering alternatives – trying to ignore the female half of the population. He needed a sheep, not a tall lady.

Even if he saw the countess, he doubted he'd know her. Other than her height and her perfume, he knew so little of her. If he kissed her, he'd know, but he could hardly kiss every possible lady on the off-chance she was his houri. Besides, he'd already determined that the fastest way to get the countess precisely where he wanted her was to learn more about the company – and that necessitated finding a sheep.

He was halfway along the street when, immediately ahead, four ladies stepped out of a milliner's shop and congregated on the pavement. In the instant he recognized the Morwellans, Alathea raised her head and looked directly at him. Serena, Mary, and Alice followed her gaze – their faces promptly lit with smiles.

There was nothing for it but to do the pretty.

Sliding into his fashionable persona, he shook Serena's hand, exchanged nods with Mary and Alice, and lastly, more stiffly, with Alathea. As all four ladies stepped free of the throng by the shop windows, closer to the curb so they could converse more easily, Alathea hung back, then took up a position a good yard away from him, so that they both had their backs to the congested carriageway with Serena, Mary, and Alice strung between, facing them.

'We met your mother and your sisters only this morning,' Serena informed him.

'In the park,' Mary added. 'We strolled – it was such fun.'

'There were some silly gentlemen about,' Alice said. 'They had *monstrous* cravats – nothing like yours or Lucifer's.'

He responded easily, in truth without thought. Even though Serena, Mary, and Alice ranked high on his list of people to be kind to, with Alathea three feet away, his senses, as always, slewed to her.

And prickled, and itched.

Even though he'd barely glanced at her, he knew she was wearing a lavender walking dress and a chip bonnet that covered her haloed hair. Under the bonnet, he was certain, would lurk one of those scraps of lace he found so offensive. He couldn't comment, not even elliptically, not with Serena before him . . . on the other hand, if he caught Alathea's eye, she would know what he was thinking.

With that in mind, he glanced her way.

The carriage horse behind her reared, kicking over the traces—

He grabbed Alathea and hauled her to him, swinging around, instinctively shielding her. A hoof whizzed past their heads. The horse screamed, dragged the carriage, then tried to kick again – the rising knee caught him in the back.

He jerked, but stayed upright.

Pandemonium ensued. Everybody yelled. Men ran from all over to help. Others called instructions. One lady had hysterics – another swooned. In seconds, they were surrounded by a noisy crowd; the driver of the green horse was the center of attention.

Gabriel stood motionless on the curb, Alathea locked in his arms. His senses were reeling, his wits no less so. At the edge of his awareness, he heard Serena, Mary, and Alice shrilly scolding the driver – they were incensed but not hysterical. Everyone around them was watching the melee in the road, temporarily ignoring him and Alathea.

He tried to catch his breath, and couldn't. A host of emotions poured through him, relief that she was unhurt not the least. He hadn't been gentle – he'd slammed her against him, then held tight; she was plastered to him from shoulder to knee. She'd gasped, then gasped again as his body had jolted with the horse's kick.

Her gaze was fixed over his shoulder, but from her fractured breathing, he suspected she saw nothing.

A light, flowery fragrance rose from her breasts, crushed to his chest; soft whorls of hair peeked from under her bonnet, mere inches from his face.

He felt her catch her breath; a slight shiver went through her. She gathered herself – he could feel steel infuse the fine muscles in her back – then she turned her head and looked into his face.

Their gazes met and held – hazel drowning in hazel. Hers were clouded, so many emotions chasing each other across her eyes that he couldn't identify any of them. Then, abruptly, the clouds cleared and one emotion shone through.

He recognized it instantly, even though it had been years since last he'd seen it. Concern poured from her eyes and warmed him – he'd forgotten how it always had.

'Are you all right?' Her hands, trapped between them, fisted in his coat. 'The horse kicked you.'

When he didn't immediately reply she tried to shake him. Her body shifted against his. He caught his breath. 'Yes, I'm all right.' But he wasn't. 'Only the knee connected – not the hoof.'

She stilled in his arms, open concern for him filling her face. 'It must hurt.'

All of him hurt – he was so aroused he was in agony.

He knew the instant she realized. Flush against him, she couldn't help but know. Her gaze flickered, then her lashes lowered – her gaze fell to his lips, then to his cravat. An instant later, she sucked in a small breath and wriggled – just a little. It was a long ago sign between them; she wasn't attempting to break free – she knew she couldn't – she was asking to be let go.

Forcing his arms to unlock, then setting her back from him was the hardest physical labor he'd ever performed. She immediately fussed with her skirts and didn't look at him.

He felt flustered, awkward, embarrassed . . . he swung on his heel to view the disaster in the road, praying she hadn't noticed the color in his cheeks.

Alathea knew the instant his gaze left her. She couldn't breathe; her wits were reeling so crazily she felt disorientated as well as dizzy. Straightening, she pretended to watch as the fracas was resolved, grateful when it required Gabriel's intervention. Rigid, she waited on the pavement, stiffly inclining her head when the gentleman who'd been in charge of the young horse approached with profuse apologies.

In her mind, she repeated a single refrain: Gabriel hadn't realized.

Not yet.

The question of whether he would suddenly see the light kept her stiff as a poker.

Then Serena bustled up, all matronly concern, both for her and her protector.

'Are you *sure* you're all right?' Uninhibited by age or elegance, Serena grabbed Gabriel's arm and made him swing around.

Alathea allowed herself a fleeting glance at his face as Serena brushed off his coat.

He frowned and all but squirmed. 'No harm done.' Freeing himself from Serena's grasp, he gathered Mary and Alice with a glance. 'It would be wise to retreat.' He hesitated, then asked Serena, 'Is your carriage close?'

'Jacobs is waiting just around the corner.' Serena waved back along the street.

For the first time since he'd let her go, Gabriel looked directly at her; Alathea immediately waved Mary and Alice before her, then turned in the direction of the carriage. The last thing she needed was to stroll on his arm.

He offered his arm to Serena; she was very ready to lean on his strength. She filled the distance back to the carriage with sincere and copious thanks for his prompt and efficient action. Safely separated from him by Mary and Alice, Alathea murmured her agreement, allowing her stepmother's praise to stand in place of her own.

She was grateful – she knew she should thank him. But she wasn't game to get too close to him, not when she'd so recently been in his arms. She had no idea what might trigger a fateful convergence of memories; holding her head high, she walked to the carriage, apprehension crawling along her spine.

By lengthening her stride, she reached the carriage first and climbed in without waiting for his assistance. He shot her a hard glance, then handed the others up. He stepped back and saluted; Jacobs flicked his reins.

At the very last, Alathea turned her head – their gazes met, held . . . she inclined her head and looked forward.

Gabriel watched the carriage rattle away down the side street, his gaze locked on Alathea's chip bonnet, on her shoulders encased in lavender twill. He watched until the carriage disappeared around a corner, then, his expression turning grim, he headed back to Bond Street.

Rejoining the bustling throng, he walked along, his gaze fixed ahead, unseeing. He still felt stunned – pole-axed to be precise. To be so aroused by Alathea. He couldn't understand why it had happened, but he could hardly pretend it hadn't – he was still feeling the definite effects.

He was also feeling rocked, off balance, and hideously uncomfortable. He'd never felt that way about her – they'd always been such close friends, *that* had never raised its head.

He walked on; gradually, his mind cleared.

And the obvious answer presented itself, much to his intense relief.

Not Alathea – the countess. He'd spent all last night plotting the how and where of her ultimate seduction, teasing himself with all the details; this morning, he'd set out to implement his plan. Then fate in the guise of a horse had flung Alathea into his arms. Obvious.

It was hardly surprising that his body had confused the two women – both were tall, although the countess was definitely taller. They were both slender, willowy – very similar in build. They both had the same fine, supple muscles in their backs, but that, he assumed, was to be expected of any very tall, slender woman – an architectural necessity.

The physically obvious, however, was the limit of their similarity. If he dared kiss her, Alathea would tear a verbal strip off him – she certainly wouldn't melt into his arms with that gloriously seductive sensual generosity the countess displayed.

The thought made him smile. His next thought – of what Alathea would make of his reaction once she'd had time to consider it – eradicated all inclination to levity. Then he recalled her long-standing opinion of him and his rakish lifestyle; once again, he smiled. She would doubtless put his reaction down to unbridled lust – and she wouldn't be wrong. But it was the countess he lusted after, his houri of the night.

He wanted her intensely. Somewhat to his surprise, that want went further than the physical. He actually wanted to know her – who she was, what she enjoyed, what she thought, what made her laugh. She was mysterious and intriguing, yet, oddly, he felt very close to her.

She was a puzzle he intended solving – taking apart at every level.

To do that, he needed to press on with his plan . . . Lifting his head, he refocused on his surroundings. He'd nearly reached the end of Bond Street. Crossing the road, he started back, once again scanning the crowds. He still needed a sheep. There had to be *someone*—

'Gracious! And what's got into you?'

The query and the cane levelled at his navel jerked him to attention.

'Going about with your nose in the air in Bond Street! Why, you don't even know who you're cutting.'

Looking into a pair of bird-bright eyes in an old, soft face, Gabriel smiled. 'Minnie.' Brushing aside her cane, he dropped a quick kiss on her cheek.

'Humph.' Minnie's tone was unmollified but her eyes twinkled. 'Remind me to tell Celia about this, Timms.'

'Indeed.' The tall lady beside Minnie lost her fight to keep her lips straight. 'Quite unconscionable, going about Bond Street without due regard.'

Gabriel bowed extravagantly. 'Am I forgiven?' he asked as he straightened.

'We'll consider it.' Minnie looked around. 'Ah! Here's Gerrard.'

Gabriel watched as Minnie's nephew, Gerrard Debbington, brother to Patience, Vane's wife, crossed the street, the bag of nuts he'd clearly been dispatched to fetch in one hand.

'Here you are.' Handing the bag to Minnie, Gerrard smiled easily.

Gabriel returned the smile. 'Still keeping watch on Minnie's pearls?'

'No more threat, thank goodness. I'm staying with Vane and Patience, but I stop by to take a stroll with Minnie now and then.'

Although just eighteen, Gerrard appeared older, his assurance in part due to his brother-in-law's influence; it was Vane's elegant hand Gabriel detected behind Gerrard's fashionable town rig. At close to six feet, Gerrard had the height and breadth of shoulder to carry the austere lines. The rest of his appearance, his easygoing demeanor, his directness and self-confidence, could largely be laid at his sister's door; Patience Cynster was the very epitome of directness.

Gabriel opened his mouth, then quickly shut it. He needed to think. Gerrard was, after all, only eighteen, and there were risks involved. And he was Patience's brother.

'We're going to look in at Asprey's.' Minnie fixed him with an innocent look. 'Perhaps there's some little thing you need from there?'

Gabriel returned the look with one equally innocent. 'Not at present.' The image of the countess drifted through his mind. Perhaps, after she'd rewarded him, he would reward her. Diamonds would look well on such a tall woman. Filing the thought away, he bowed. 'I won't keep you.'

With a humph softened by a smile, Minnie nodded. Timms took her arm and they moved on. With a grin and a nod, Gerrard turned to follow.

Gabriel hesitated, then called, 'Gerrard?'

Gerrard turned back. 'Yes?'

'Do you know where Vane is at present?'

'If you want him, try Manton's. I know he was going to meet Devil there sometime this afternoon.'

With a brisk salute, Gabriel headed for Manton's.

'It'll have to be August.' Devil extended his arm and pulled the trigger. His shot was an inch off the center of the target.

Vane squinted down the alley. 'That seems awfully close. Is Richard sure?'

'As I understood it, it's Catriona who's sure. Richard, at this stage, isn't sure of anything.'

Moving past Devil to take his shot, Vane grimaced. 'I know the feeling.'

'What's this?' Lounging against the partition wall, Gabriel fixed them with a look of mock dismay. 'A lesson for expectant fathers?'

Devil grinned. 'Come to learn?'

'Thank you, no.'

Grimly, Vane sighted down the long barrel of his pistol. 'You'll come to this, too.'

Gabriel grimaced. 'Someday perhaps, but spare me my innocence. No details, please.'

Both Honoria, Devil's duchess, and Patience were pregnant. While Devil was displaying the detachment of one who'd been through the wringer before, Vane was already edgy. He pulled the trigger. As the smoke cleared, they saw his bullet had barely nicked the target.

Devil sent the attendant to get another pistol, then

turned to Gabriel. 'I assume you've heard that our mothers have determined on a special family gathering to welcome Catriona into the family?'

'She's definitely coming down, then?'

Devil nodded. 'Mama had a letter from her yesterday. Catriona's decreed she can travel until the end of August. What with Honoria due early July and Patience later that month, it'll have to be August for this celebration of theirs.'

Gabriel blinked, replaying Devil's words. 'Don't tell me Richard's joined your club.'

'He has indeed.' Vane grinned evilly. 'Now all it needs is for Demon and Flick to get back from their wanderings with Flick blooming, so to speak, and just think where that'll leave you come August.'

Gabriel swore. 'I'd better warn Lucifer. Mama is going to be impossible.'

'You could, of course, cheer her up.'

The look Gabriel leveled at Devil was that of a man betrayed. 'That is a truly horrible thought.'

Devil laughed. 'Strange to say one gets used to the state.' One black brow arched suggestively. 'There are compensations.'

'There'd have to be,' Gabriel muttered.

'But if you didn't come to discuss our impending paternity, what brings you here?' Vane, too, settled his shoulders against the wall.

'A swindle.' Briefly, Gabriel outlined Crowley's scheme, avoiding all mention of the countess.

'Crowley.' Devil cocked a brow at Gabriel. 'Wasn't he the one with the investment in some diamond mine?'

Gabriel nodded.

'You exposed that one, too, didn't you?' Vane asked.

Again Gabriel nodded. 'Which is why I need help this time, and not from you or the others.' He looked at Vane. 'I need someone not obviously connected.'

Vane looked puzzled; Gabriel quickly explained the necessity of learning the precise details of the offer made to investors.

'And . . . ?' Vane prompted.

'What do you think about using Gerrard Debbington?'

Vane blinked. 'As your sheep?'

'I haven't been seen about with him, and if he gives Minnie's address rather than yours, then there's no reason anyone will immediately connect him with any Cynsters. I know Crowley's not *au fait* with the ton – he uses Archie Douglas as his source in that arena, and Archie wouldn't know Gerrard from Adam.'

'True.'

'And even if Archie did ask around, checking Gerrard's background, all he'd hear is that Gerrard is reasonably wealthy and owns a nice manor in Derbyshire. He wouldn't think to ask after Gerrard's connections, or Gerrard's sister.'

'Or Gerrard's guardians.'

'Precisely. Gerrard appears distinctly older than he is.'

Vane considered. 'I can't see any reason why Gerrard couldn't develop an interest in gold mining.' He looked at Gabriel. 'Provided, of course, that we don't tell Patience.'

'I hadn't imagined doing so.'

'Well, then.' Vane straightened away from the wall as the attendant slipped back into the alley. 'I'll explain the matter to Gerrard, if you like, and see what he thinks. If he's agreeable, I'll send him to see you.'

Gabriel nodded. 'Do.' Picking up the extra pistol the attendant had brought, he hefted it. 'So what's the score?'

They fired ten rounds. Gabriel beat the others easily, a fact that made him frown. 'Marriage,' he observed, 'has dulled your edges.'

Vane shrugged. 'It's just a game – hardly important. Marriage has a way of re-scripting your priorities.'

Gabriel stared at him, then looked at Devil, who merely looked back, making no attempt to correct Vane's strange thinking.

Reading his thoughts in his eyes, Devil grinned. 'Start thinking about it, for as sure as August follows July, your time will come.'

The words froze Gabriel, just as they had at Demon's wedding; again, a tingle of presentiment glissaded down his spine. He managed to suppress his reactive shiver. Adopting an easy expression and his usual debonair manner, he accompanied the other two outside.

At five o'clock, Gabriel was idly scanning the *Gentleman's Magazine* when someone knocked on his door. Listening, he heard Chance's footsteps all but dance up the hall; smiling, he returned to the magazine.

A minute later, the parlor door opened. Chance stood in the doorway. 'A Mr Debbington to see you, m'lord.'

Gabriel inwardly sighed. 'Thank you, Chance, but I'm not a lord.'

Chance's brow furrowed. 'I thought as how all the Quality was lords.'

'No.'

'Oh.' Catching a glimpse of Gerrard, waiting at his elbow to get past, Chance stepped aside, and all but shooed Gerrard over the threshold. 'Well, here you are. Do you want me to pour you some brandy?'

'No. That will be all.'

'Very good, sir.' With commendable aplomb, Chance bowed himself out, and remembered to shut the door.

Gerrard stared at the closed door, then looked questioningly at Gabriel.

'He's in training.' Gabriel waved Gerrard to a chair. 'Would you like some brandy?'

Gerrard grinned. 'No. Patience would be sure

to notice.' Once at ease in the chair, he met Gabriel's gaze. 'Vane told me about this swindle you're trying to expose. I'd be happy to help. What do you need me to do?'

Omitting all mention of the countess, Gabriel outlined his plan.

CHAPTER 6

At noon the next day, Gabriel descended the steps of the Burlington Hotel, well satisfied with the arrangements he'd made. His plan was in motion and developing nicely. Soon the countess would be his.

Turning into Bond Street, he looked ahead. His steps slowed.

Alathea stood on the corner of Bruton Street, hanging back by the shop facade, her gaze on the crowd surrounding a nut vendor.

She'd always been particularly partial to nuts – and she was clearly debating pushing into the crowd to secure a bag. At this hour, the rowdy crew about the vendor's stall was composed of young sprigs and boisterous bucks.

Lips setting, Gabriel had crossed the street before he'd even thought of what he was doing – or going to do. The memory of his last encounter with Alathea flashed – too hotly – into his mind. His jaw set more firmly. Perhaps a bag of nuts would go some small way toward mending his fences with her.

He could hardly excuse his reaction to her by explaining he'd confused her with another lady.

Alathea eyed the circle of male backs between her and the source of the wonderful smell of roasting nuts. That succulent smell had lured her from the doorway of the modiste's where Serena, Mary, and Alice were engaged in making last-minute adjustments to their ball gowns. The salon had been airless and cramped, so she'd come down to the street, intending to simply wait.

That smell had made her stomach growl. Pushing into the crowd, however, would very likely expose her to a score of impertinent remarks. Still . . . her mouth was watering. Deciding she could not exist a minute longer without a bag of nuts, she stepped forward—

'Here.'

A strong hand closed about her elbow and drew her back – her heart nearly leaped free of her chest!

Without meeting her eyes, Gabriel moved past her. 'Let me.'

She did, for the simple reason that she dared not move – her legs had turned to jelly. Her latest plan for survival dictated she avoid him at all costs – she'd intended to do just that. She'd been *doing* just that – she was in *Bruton* Street at *noon*, for heaven's sake! What was *he* doing here? She'd never have left the safety of the salon if she'd known he was about.

She clung to her irritation – undoubtedly wiser than surrendering to her panic.

Gabriel turned back to her, a brown paper bag in his hand. 'Here.'

She took the bag and busied herself opening it. 'Thank you.' She popped a nut into her mouth, then offered the nuts to him.

He took a handful, his gaze on her face. 'What are you doing here?'

She met his eyes fleetingly. 'I'm waiting for Serena and the girls.' She gestured down Bruton Street. 'They're at a fitting.'

Looking down, she took her time selecting another nut. If she gave him absolutely no encouragement, perhaps he would go away. She was acutely aware that the longer she was alone with him as herself, the greater the danger of his recognizing his countess.

Then her conscience prodded – hard. *Damn*! She didn't want to, but . . . Lifting her head, she fixed her gaze on his right ear. 'I have to thank you for yesterday. I would have been kicked if you hadn't . . .'

Grabbed her, held her – been aroused by her.

She quickly ended her sentence with a gesture, but her consciousness must have shown in her eyes. To her amazement, from under her lashes, she saw color trace his cheekbones. He was embarrassed? Good lord!

'It was nothing.' His accents were clipped. After a moment, he added in a low voice, 'I'd rather you forgot the incident entirely.'

She shrugged and turned to stroll back to the modiste's. 'If you wish.' Dare she suggest he do the same?

He fell into step beside her – there seemed little point suggesting he leave her to walk the street alone. Luckily, the bag of nuts gave her a perfect reason for not taking his arm; touching him again would be inviting disaster. As it was, she could stroll with a good two feet separating them – reasonably safe. She flourished the bag of nuts between them, inviting him to help himself as they strolled. It felt like feeding tidbits to a potentially lethal leopard to keep him distracted while she strolled to the cage door.

Thankfully, the door of the modiste's wasn't far. She stopped beside it, contemplating handing him the almost empty bag in lieu of her hand. 'Thank you for the nuts.' She met his gaze and realized he was frowning.

She froze – apprehension locked her lungs. Had she said something? Done something?

'You don't happen to know . . .' His tone was diffident. He glanced away. 'Have you met a countess, one recently widowed—?'

Gabriel broke off. What was he *doing*? One glance at Alathea's face confirmed he'd said enough. Her expression was deadpan, her eyes blank.

'No.'

He mentally kicked himself. She knew him well enough to guess why he'd asked. A spurt of resentment surfaced; she'd always turned aside any reference to Lucifer's conquests with an amused glance, but she'd never extended the same leniency to him.

He frowned. 'Forget I asked.'

She looked at him, blank still. 'I will.'

Her voice sounded odd.

He was about to step back, make his excuses, and leave, when the rowdy crew from the nut vendor's stall came barrelling past. One jostled his shoulder. He turned, stepping closer to the shop front, closer to Alathea, instinctively shielding her once more. The group streamed past, then were gone. Turning back to Alathea, his farewells froze on his tongue. 'What's the matter?'

She'd paled – she was breathing quickly and leaning against the doorframe. Her eyes had been shut – now they flew open.

'Nothing. Here!' Alathea thrust the nut bag at him, then whirled and opened the modiste's door. 'Serena will be wondering where I've got to.'

With that, she fled – there was no other word for it. She dashed into the small foyer, grabbed up her skirts and flew up the stairs to the salon. She didn't care what he thought of her departure – she simply couldn't bear to be so near him – not anymore. Not as Alathea Morwellan.

Two days later, Alathea stood at the window of her office, sunk in thought. Wiggs had just left. In light of his worry over the promissory note, she'd felt compelled to reveal that she'd engaged the services of Gabriel Cynster. Wiggs had been impressed – and hugely relieved. He'd recalled that the Cynsters were their neighbors in Somerset.

Luckily, she'd remembered to suggest that, given the necessary secrecy surrounding their investigations, Wiggs should not communicate with Mr Cynster other than through her.

The rotund man of business had gone off much happier than when he'd arrived. She'd asked him to clarify the procedure for approaching the Chancery Court to have the promissory note declared invalid once they'd secured proof of fraud. She hoped the matter could be dealt with via a petition direct to the bench, avoiding any mention of the family name in open court and the added expense of a barrister.

In the matter of their investigations, all was proceeding smoothly; she wished she could feel as comfortable over the way matters were proceeding between her and Gabriel.

For the past two days, she'd done all she could to avoid meeting him. Not seeing him, however, didn't ease the guilt she felt over his embarrassment. It was doubtless irrational but the feeling was there.

Lurking in her mind was the recognition that he always stepped forward whenever she needed him; incidents like the horse in Bond Street, the crowd about the street vendor – those were not unusual, not for him and her. Despite their difficulty – indeed, in the teeth of it – he'd always helped her whenever he'd known she needed help. He was helping her now, even if, this time, he didn't know it was her he was helping.

He deserved better from her than deceit, but what could she do?

She sighed and concentrated, forcing herself to deal with the latest twist in her charade. For a start, she would make an effort to re-institute their old relationship and behave normally toward him so he'd forget his embarrassment. As herself, beyond that moment in Bond Street, she'd barely touched his sleeve over the past decade – surely she could get through the next weeks without touching him more than that?

And secondly, regardless of all else, no matter the struggle, she would not allow – *could not* allow – the susceptibility that had overcome her in Bruton Street to surface again. If he came close, she would suffer in stoic silence. That much, she owed him.

She frowned, realizing she now thought of him by his preferred name. Then she shrugged. Better to think of him as Gabriel – Gabriel was the man she had to deal with now. Perhaps, if she bore that in mind, the hurdles she kept encountering might not be quite so surprising.

Gazing at the shifting greens beyond the window, she set aside her resolutions and turned to her next problem: how to learn of his plans. That he had plans, she didn't doubt. He'd told her to leave Crowley to him; it was tempting to simply do so. Unfortunately, as he didn't know her family's identity, that course was too risky. And she needed some control over his capacity to claim rewards.

That was another hurdle. While she desperately wanted to arrange another meeting to ask what he'd learned, what he was doing, what he had planned, justifying the likely indiscretion was not easy. It was perfectly possible he'd discovered something new, some significant fact – what reward would he claim if he had?

Her experience was insufficient to provide an answer. And she wasn't sure she trusted herself – not while in his arms.

That was the part she understood least. While with him as the countess, she seemed to occupy a position in relation to him that had never been available to Alathea Morwellan, despite the fact she knew him so well. It wasn't only the illicit nature of their interaction, but some different, deeper linkage, a sharing more profound. A sharing she coveted but knew she couldn't have.

She'd never been the sort to throw her cap over the windmill; she'd never been the least bit wild. Yet while she was the countess and he treated her as someone different, she'd started thinking and feeling differently, too.

Her charade had taken on new and dangerous dimensions.

A knock fell on the door. She turned. Folwell, her groom, looked in. He saluted respectfully; she smiled and waved him forward, returning to the desk. 'Anything to report?'

'Nothing today, m'lady' – Folwell halted before the desk – 'but that Chance . . . he's a right talker, he is. With due respect, m'lady, I had to put him right – tip him the wink. He talks far too free about Mr Rupert. That's not how it's done, m'lady, as you know.'

'Indeed, but in this case, Chance's talkativeness has been useful.'

'Oh, he still chatters to me and Dodswell, of course. But we don't want him chattering to no one else.'

'Quite so.' Alathea restrained a smile at Folwell's instructing Gabriel's odd new gentlemen's gentleman. She'd already received a highly colored account of how Chance had come into his position; all she'd subsequently heard had made her quite keen to meet him. The eccentricity Gabriel had displayed over Chance was both familiar and endearing. As she'd told Celia, Gabriel wasn't cold, but rather, controlled. She was prepared to wager Celia didn't know about Chance.

'Mr Rupert's not met with Mr Debbington again?'

'No, m'lady. Just that one meeting like I mentioned. Mr Debbington hasn't been back.'

'No notes or letters?'

'There was one note last night, m'lady, but Chance doesn't know who it was from. Mr Rupert read it and seemed pleased, but he didn't say anything to Chance, of course.'

'Hmm.' Celia's complaints wafted through Alathea's brain; she considered Folwell. 'What about ladies? Have there been any women visiting?

Or has he gone out . . . ?' With her back to the window, Folwell couldn't see her blush.

'No, m'lady. No one. Dodswell says there's been no females in the house for an age – weeks, at least. He says Mr Alasdair's hunting a new one' – it was Folwell's turn to blush – 'but Mr Rupert's been staying quiet at home, except for going to family gatherings and to meet some mysterious person. That'd be you, m'lady.'

'Yes – thank you Folwell.' Alathea nodded. 'Keep stopping by every day, but try to avoid Mr Rupert's notice.'

'I'll do that, m'lady.' Folwell ducked his head. 'You can count on me.'

After he'd gone, Alathea considered the picture that was emerging of Gabriel's life. Celia had always given the definite impression that there was a constant stream of ladies going through the Brook Street house. Admittedly, there were two of them, Lucifer as well as Gabriel, but it certainly seemed that at present, Gabriel was not pulling his weight. Not, at least, in that arena.

Pencil tapping absentmindedly, she pondered that fact.

Augusta, Marchioness of Huntly, held a *grande balle* two nights later. What distinguished it from other balls, Alathea could not have said; it was just as crowded, just as boring. She'd never had much time for balls; the Hunt Ball and one or two others through the year were quite enough for her. To be forced to endure a major ball every night was fast becoming her personal definition of torture. However, the Marchioness was the Dowager's sister-in-law, a Cynster by birth; there'd been no question of declining her invitation.

At least the ball gave her an opportunity to keep an eye on her nemesis; it was possible his plans included meetings at balls. From the side of the ballroom, to which she doggedly clung, she watched him prowl. She was tall enough to see him easily, but she was careful not to fix her gaze. In her mind, she repeated her latest resolution: She would avoid him if possible, but if they were to meet, she would behave as she always had, as if she'd never stood locked in his arms in Bond Street – or anywhere else.

Thankfully, he was heading away from her, broad shoulders shifting under a coat of walnut-black. The brown tint in the material turned his hair to burnished brown; the stark simplicity of the cut only emphasized his stature and intensified the predatory aura he exuded.

After a moment, she unfocused her gaze and shifted it to the crowd between them. Then she glanced at the walls. Their crepe decorations caught her eye. She fell to considering how to reduce the cost of decorating the huge ballroom at Morwellan House while still achieving a satisfactory result. The ball at which Mary and Alice would make their formal curtsies to the ton was all too rapidly nearing.

'Why the *devil* can't you leave those wretched things at home? Or better yet, fling them in the fire.'

Alathea whirled; her heart leaped to her throat. She'd been so absorbed, he'd been able to walk right up to her. Her eyes searched his – he was watching her, waiting . . . her resolution rang in her ears. 'I'm twenty-nine, for heaven's sake!'

'I know precisely how old you are.'

She lifted her chin. 'People expect me to wear a cap.'

'There's no more than ten people in this room who can even *see* the horrendous thing.'

'It is *not* horrendous – it's the very latest style!'

'There's a style in horror? Amazing. Nevertheless, it doesn't suit you.'

'Indeed? And why is that?' Heat flooded her cheeks. 'Its color, perhaps?'

The cap was the exact same shade as her gown of pomona green silk, an exceedingly fashionable hue that suited her to perfection. Eyes narrowed, she dared him to suggest otherwise; they were right back to normal, no doubt about that.

His gaze swept her face, then returned to his aversion. 'It could be solid gold, and it would still be tawdry.'

'*Tawdry?*'

Up to then, their conversation had been conducted in muted tones; Alathea nearly choked trying to preserve her outward calm. Her gaze on his face, she drew in another breath and in tones of unswerving defiance stated, 'As I so choose, I will wear a cap for the rest of my life, and there's not one thing you can do about it. I therefore suggest you either grow accustomed to the fact or, if that's too much to ask, keep your opinions to yourself.'

His jaw clenched; his gaze swung down to lock with hers. Eyes hard, lips compressed – all but toe to toe – they stood by the side of the Huntlys' ballroom, each waiting for the other to back down first.

'Oh, *Allie!*'

The anguished tone had them both turning. Alice materialized from the crowd. '*Look.*' Woebegone, she lifted her skirt to show the trailing flounce. 'That stupid Lord Melton trod on it during the last dance, and now my lovely new gown is ruined!'

'No, no.' Alathea put her arm around Alice and hugged her. 'It's no great problem. I've pins in my reticule. We'll just go to the withdrawing room and I'll pin it up so you won't miss the rest of the dances, and then Nellie can mend it as good as new when we get home.'

'Oh.' Alice looked at Gabriel, blinked and gave him a watery smile. Then she looked at Alathea. 'Can we go now?'

'Yes.' Alathea threw a haughtily dismissive glance at Gabriel. 'We've concluded our conversation.'

There was heat in his eyes when they met hers, but by the time his gaze reached Alice, his expression was mild. 'Flounces rip all the time – just ask the twins. They rip one every second ball.'

Alice smiled sweetly and glanced expectantly at Alathea.

'Come along. The withdrawing room will be just along the corridor.' As she led the way, Alathea could feel Gabriel's gaze on her back. He'd been carping about her caps for the last three years, ever since she'd first started wearing them. The cause of his vehement dislike was a mystery, to him, she suspected, as much as to her – and nothing had changed, thank God.

They were back to what passed for normal for them.

As Alathea walked out of the ballroom, Gabriel heaved an inward sigh of relief and turned away. Good! Everything was back as it used to be – the concern that had nagged at him for the past few days literally evaporated. After his blunder in Bruton Street, the need to set matters straight with Alathea and re-establish their habitual interaction had distracted him, even impinging on his concentration on his plans for the countess.

But all was now settled. Alathea had clearly harbored a similar wish – she'd been ready to revert to their customary behavior as soon as he'd offered the opportunity; he'd seen that consideration flash through her eyes before she'd first snapped at him.

The sense of release he felt was very real – now he could turn his attention fully to the matter that, increasingly, called to his warrior's soul. The countess and her seduction – now all his energies could be focused on that.

The torn flounce took five minutes to fix. In no rush to return, Alathea called for a glass of water and sipped; the exchange with Gabriel had shaken her more than she cared to admit. She was finding it increasingly hard to rip up at him, to keep her voice sharp and shrewish, and not let it soften to the countess's tone – the tone she used privately to those she loved.

Yet another difficulty when she had difficulties enough.

Ten minutes later, she re-entered the ballroom in Alice's wake. Gabriel was nowhere in sight.

Alice returned to her circle of very young ladies and equally youthful gentlemen. Alathea strolled; scanning the crowd, she located Gabriel. Unobtrusively, she took up a position beside the wall opposite him, this time near a protective pillar. Not, it seemed, that anything could protect her from the attentions of Cynsters – Lucifer strolled up almost immediately.

'Torn flounce?'

Alathea blinked. 'Yes. How did you know?'

'The twins try that all the time.'

'*Try* it?'

'Try to use the excuse to slip away. Mind you, the flounce or ruffle or whatever usually *is* torn, but if one was to accept that the plethora of injuries their wardrobes sustain was due to the clumsiness of their partners, you'd expect the entire male half of the ton to be clod-footed.'

Alathea didn't smile. 'But why do the twins try to slip away?'

'Because they have fantasies of meeting with

152

unsuitable gentlemen if only they could escape from our sight.'

Alathea checked; Lucifer's expression was perfectly serious. He scanned the crowd, then glanced her way. 'But you know what it's like – I saw you keeping watch over young Alice.'

'I wasn't keeping watch over her – she'd never ripped a flounce before and didn't have pins, or know how to pin it up. I was simply helping her.'

'Maybe so, but you know the ropes – you were watching over her as well.'

Alathea had had a surfeit of male Cynsters that evening. Drawing in a breath, she held it for a moment, then turned to her companion. 'Alasdair.'

That got his attention. He glanced her way, one brow rising.

'You and your equally misguided brother have got to put an end to this ridiculous obsession. The twins are eighteen. I've met them; I've conversed with them. They are sensible and level-headed young ladies, perfectly capable of managing their own lives, at least to the extent of interacting with suitable gentlemen and selecting their own consorts.'

Lucifer frowned. He opened his mouth—

'No! Be quiet and hear me out. I've had quite enough of arguing with Cynsters this evening, and you may tell your brother that, too!' She flashed him a darkling glance. 'You must both understand that your constant surveillance is driving the twins demented. If you don't give them the space to find their stride, they'll kick over the traces, and then you'll be left trying to make a poor fist out of some unholy mess. How would you feel if you were cabin'd, cribb'd and confin'd every time you set foot in a ballroom?'

'That's different. We can take care of ourselves.' Lucifer searched her face, then he sighed. 'I'd forgotten you haven't spent much time in London.' His smile flashed, the essence of brotherly condescension. 'There are all sorts of bounders drifting through the ton – we couldn't possibly leave the twins unwatched. It would be like staking out two lambs and then walking away and letting the wolves have at them. That's why we watch. And you needn't worry about Mary and Alice – it's as easy to watch four as it is to watch two.'

He was in earnest. Alathea considered a heartfelt groan. 'Has it ever occurred to you that the twins just possibly might be able to take care of themselves?'

'In this arena?' Glancing at the subjects of their discussion, Lucifer shook his head. 'How could they possibly? And you must admit, when it comes to sweeping ladies off their feet, we are the reigning experts.'

Alathea resisted rolling her eyes to the skies. She was determined to puncture, or at least dent, their Cynster egos. Scanning the ballroom, she searched for inspiration.

And saw Gerrard Debbington stroll up to Gabriel, who was chatting with an acquaintance. Gerrard nodded easily. Gabriel nodded back. Even from across the room, Alathea could sense the sudden focusing of his awareness.

'You see,' Lucifer said, shifting closer, 'take the case of Lord Chantry, currently sniffing around Amelia's skirts.'

'Chantry?' Alathea's gaze was fixed across the room. The gentleman who'd been conversing with Gabriel departed, leaving him alone with Gerrard. Instantly, the tenor of the conversation changed. Gerrard shifted; she could no longer see his face.

'Hmm. He's supposed to have a nice little estate in Dorset and is a thoroughly charming fellow, as far as the ladies can see.'

'Really?' Alathea could tell from the intensity of Gabriel's expression that whatever Gerrard was saying was extremely important.

'However, there's another side to Chantry.'

She had to get closer so she could overhear; they were obviously discussing something vital.

'He's in dun territory. All but rolled up.'

About to move, Alathea focused nearer to hand – and found herself face to face with Lucifer. 'What?'

'He's under the hatches and looking for a quick wedding with a nice bit of brass tied to the bouquet.'

'Who?'

'Lord Chantry.' Lucifer frowned at her. 'I've been

telling you about him so you'll understand why we watch over the twins. Haven't you been listening?'

Alathea blinked. Pushing past Lucifer, hurrying across the crowded ballroom, and somehow getting close enough to Gabriel to overhear what was being said was impossible. Aside from anything else, Lucifer would be at her heels. 'Umm . . . yes. Tell me more.'

She shifted so she could keep Gabriel in view.

Lucifer eased back. 'So that's Chantry. And of course Amelia's been smiling sweetly at him for the last week. Silly puss. I tried to tell her but would she listen? Oh, no. Stuck her nose in the air and insisted Chantry was amusing.'

Alathea considered telling him Amelia was probably encouraging Chantry simply to tease him and Gabriel.

Gabriel looked up. As if summoned, Devil, the object of Gabriel's glance, detached himself from Honoria's circle and made his way to join the conference.

Something major was being planned.

'Another perfect example of a bounder is Hendricks – there – to Amanda's right. He's even worse than Chantry.'

Letting Lucifer's monologue roll past her, Alathea watched the meeting taking place across the room. Vane strolled up as if just passing by; he, too, joined the discussion. Ideas – arrangements? – were batted back and forth; that much was clear from the shifting glances, the occasional gestures. At last, a decision was made. Whatever it was, it involved Gerrard Debbington. Gerrard and Gabriel. Devil and Vane appeared to be advisers, less involved in the details of whatever was planned.

She had to learn the plan.

'So, you see, that's why we watch over them. Do you understand now?'

She refocused on Lucifer. What was the right answer? Yes? No? She sighed. 'Never mind.' The twins would have to fight their own battles. Putting a hand on his arm, she eased him back. 'There's a waltz starting – come and dance. I need distraction.'

'I can't – I'm on watch.'

'Gabriel's free – signal to him. He can take over.'

Lucifer did, and Gabriel did, and she got her distraction.

Much good did it do her.

By the time she was in the carriage rolling home through the deserted streets, she'd accepted the fact that she would have to meet with her knight again. Cudgeling her brains, she tried to devise some way for the countess to meet him in safety. Somewhere that would inhibit him from claiming any further reward.

He'd had reward enough.

She couldn't, in all conscience, allow him to claim anything more, not even if he'd learned further facts. He'd taken liberties enough as it was.

But how to prevent his taking more?

CHAPTER 7

'**G**ood morning, Mr Cynster.'
Gabriel halted and turned; the countess was walking toward him.

Along the pavement of Brook Street in broad daylight.

She was, as usual, fully cloaked and veiled. Gabriel arched a brow. The hunter in him recognized her strategy, but if she thought to deny him all reward, she'd yield something else, instead.

No veil was impenetrable in daylight.

Then she stopped before him, her face high, and he saw the black mask she wore under the veil.

He wondered if she played chess.

'Good morning . . .' He let his greeting die away for want of a name or specific title; as he straightened from his bow, he amended, 'Madam.'

He sensed her smile, concealed beneath the mask, then she gestured in the direction he'd been heading. 'May I walk with you?'

'By all means.' He offered his arm and she laid her gloved hand on his sleeve. As they strolled in the direction of Bond Street, he was intensely aware of her height. He could see over the heads of most ladies; it was consequently easy to largely ignore them even when they were on his arm. Ignoring the countess was impossible; she impinged on his awareness in so many ways.

It was just past midday and the ton was slowly stirring, gentlemen emerging from their doors as he had to seek refuge or congenial company in the clubs around St James's.

'I assume,' his companion said, her voice, as ever, soft and low, 'that you're proceeding with the matter of the Central East Africa Gold Company?'

'Indeed.' Swiftly considering, he continued, 'In order to prove fraud, it's imperative we have witnesses to and evidence of the precise details of the proposal the company representatives present to prospective investors. My man of business has made discreet inquiries, but none of the more wealthy, experienced investors, nor their men of business, have been approached by the company. That being so, we'll need to send the company a potential investor.'

She looked down. They crossed South Molton Street before she asked, 'Who do you have in mind for the role?'

'A young friend by the name of Gerrard Debbington. He has the presence to pass as over twenty-one, although in fact he's a minor. That, of course, gives him a perfect and valid reason to not, after the company's presentation, sign any promissory note himself.'

'His guardians would have to sign.'

'Quite. But he's not going to mention them until the end of the interview.'

She looked up. 'What interview?'

His expression impassive, Gabriel considered the bright glint that was all he could see of her eyes. He didn't know their color, yet he suspected they wouldn't be blue. Brown? Green? 'Gerrard has spent the last few days ambling about in all the right places, making vague noises about finding something better to do with his brass than buy up more fields.'

'And?'

'Yesterday, Archie Douglas just happened to bump into him.'

'And?'

The repeated word held a note of impatience; Gabriel kept his lips straight. 'Archie chatted about the Central East Africa Gold Company. When Gerrard showed the right sort of interest, a meeting with the company's representatives was mooted.'

'When?'

'Archie had to confirm the details with his friends, but Gerrard, as per instructions, suggested tomorrow evening at the Burlington Hotel.'

'Do you think the company representatives, by which I assume you mean Crowley, will agree?'

'I'm quite sure they'll agree. Archie wouldn't have approached Gerrard if Crowley hadn't already singled out his mark.'

'But . . .' Anxiety colored the word. 'I believe Gerrard Debbington is a connection of yours. Of the Cynsters. Is that wise?'

Gabriel inwardly frowned. Who was she? 'He is, but the connection isn't obvious, at least not in this sense. Archie Douglas is not highly regarded by the ton's hostesses; he won't know of the connection. Crowley's scrutiny will focus on Gerrard's background, which shows he's a wealthy young gentleman from the shires. If the company was in the habit of more prudently checking their marks, they wouldn't have bothered with your late husband.'

'Hmm.'

His fair companion sounded less than convinced. 'Put it this way, if Crowley had any inkling that Gerrard Debbington was in any way associated with me, Gerrard would never have been approached.'

Her head lifted. She gave one of her distinctive nods. 'Yes, that's true. So . . . you think Gerrard Debbington can effectively pass himself off as a gullible investor?'

'I'm sure of it. I'll drill him in what we need to know, and give him pointers – a primer, if you will – so he'll know the most useful questions to ask, all couched in language appropriate for a young gentleman fancying himself the next Golden Ball.'

'Yes, but do you think he'll be able to carry off the' – she waved – 'characterization, as it were? If he's only eighteen . . .'

'He does a very good job of appearing less

161

intelligent than he is. He simply stares vaguely – vacuously – at whoever's talking. He has an innocent-looking face with large eyes and one of those charmingly youthful smiles. He appears as open as a book at all times – that doesn't necessarily mean he is.' Gabriel glanced at the countess. 'I don't know if you're aware, but he's a budding painter, so even in the most social of settings he's usually considering the line of people's faces, their clothing, coloring, and so on, even while he's supposedly engaged in conversation.'

The countess looked him in the eye. 'I see.'

So she did play chess, but he was a master. 'So Gerrard will meet with the company's representatives tomorrow evening. I've chosen the Burlington as it's the sort of place at which someone like Gerrard's supposed self would stay. He'll have a suite, and while he speaks with whoever arrives to make the presentation in the sitting room, I'll be listening from the adjoining bedchamber.'

'Do you expect Crowley to appear?'

'Impossible to be sure. There's no reason he needs to show himself but, based on how he's behaved in the past, I suspect he'll be there. He seems to take delight in personally gloating over those he swindles.'

'I want to attend – to listen in on this meeting.'

Gabriel frowned. 'There's no need for you to be there.'

'Nevertheless. I'd like to hear for myself what the Company offers and, ultimately, it means we'll

162

have an extra witness to the presentation if need arises.'

Gabriel frowned harder. 'What about Gerrard? If you want to preserve your anonymity, surely you won't want him to know of your existence. While I might respect your request not to discover your identity, Gerrard is, after all, only eighteen and possesses an artist's eye.'

She stopped. 'He doesn't know that you're investigating the company at my behest?'

'As I've investigated other companies purely through my own inclination, there was no need to advance any reason for my interest in the Central East Africa Gold Company. Particularly not with Crowley at its helm.'

She fell silent; he could almost hear her mind working. Then she looked up. 'Will Mr Debbington actually be staying at the Burlington?'

'No. He'll arrive about half an hour before the meeting's due to start.'

'Very well – I'll arrive before him. I assume you'll be there?'

Gabriel set his lips. 'Yes, but—'

'There'll be no danger to me personally, or to my anonymity, if I secret myself in the bedchamber before Mr Debbington arrives, hear the presentation, and then wait until after he's left to do the same.'

Gabriel held her veiled gaze. 'I cannot fathom why you should be so set on senselessly exposing yourself—'

'I insist.'

Chin angled imperiously, she held his gaze. Lips thinning, he let the moment stretch, and stretch, then grudgingly gave way. 'Very well. You'll need to arrive at the Burlington no later than nine.'

He sensed the triumph that flooded her – she thought she'd won a round. Under her mask, she was no doubt beaming. He kept his lips compressed, his frowning gaze on her veiled face.

'I'll leave you now.' Withdrawing her hand, she looked back up the street.

He glanced around and saw a small black carriage, presumably the one that had driven him home from Lincoln's Inn, drawn up by the curb behind them. 'I'll walk you to your carriage.' Before she could blink, he recaptured her hand and trapped it on his sleeve. She hesitated, then acquiesced, somewhat stiffly.

Gabriel raked the carriage as they neared, but it was an anonymous affair – small, black and unadorned – identical to the second carriage most large households maintained in the capital. Used to ferry their owners about discreetly, such carriages carried no insignia blazoned on the door, or identifying detail worked into the body. No hint of the countess's identity there.

The horses were nondescript. He glanced at the coachman; he was hunched over the reins, his head sunk between his shoulders. The man wore a heavy coat and plain breeches – no livery.

164

The countess had thought of everything.

He opened the carriage door and handed her in. Pausing on the step, she looked back at him. 'Until tomorrow evening at nine.'

'Indeed.' He held her gaze for an instant, then let her go. 'I'll leave a message with the porter to conduct you to the suite.' Stepping back, he shut the door, then stood and watched the carriage drive away.

Only when it had rumbled around the corner did he allow his victorious smile to show.

He was waiting in the best suite at the Burlington when, at five minutes to nine o'clock the next evening, she knocked on the door. He opened it and stood back, careful not to smile too intently as, inevitably veiled and cloaked, she swept past him.

Shutting the door, he watched as she scanned the room, taking in the two lamps on side tables flanking the hearth, spilling their light over the scene. Two armchairs and a sofa were drawn up in a comfortable arrangement around a low table before the hearth. Heavy curtains screened the windows; the fire dancing in the grate turned the scene cozy. A well-stocked tantalus stood within reach of one of the armchairs.

When she turned to face him, he got the distinct impression she approved of his stagecraft. 'When will Mr Debbington arrive?'

Gabriel glanced at the clock on the mantelpiece.

'Soon.' He nodded at the door opposite the hearth. 'Perhaps you'd care to inspect our vantage point?'

Her skirts swirled as she turned; he followed as she crossed the room.

Pausing beyond the threshold, she looked around. 'Oh, yes. This is perfect.'

Gabriel thought so, too. In the cave-like gloom created by the heavy curtains, a huge four-poster bed sat in stately splendor. It possessed a goodly number of plump pillows and the mattress was thick. He'd already confirmed it met his standards; the countess would have no reason to cavil.

She, of course, paid no attention to the bed; her comment was occasioned by the convenient gap between the half-closed door and its jamb, a gap that gave anyone standing behind the door a perfect view of the seats before the sitting-room fireplace.

She was squinting at them when another knock fell on the door.

Gabriel met her questioning glance. 'Gerrard. I'll need to rehearse his lines – he won't know you're here.'

He spoke in a whisper. She nodded. Leaving her, he crossed to the door.

Gerrard stood in the corridor looking sleekly debonair, his youth revealed only by the expectant light in his eyes. 'All ready?'

'I was about to ask you the same question.'

Waving him to the seats by the fire, Gabriel shut the door. 'We should go over your lessons.'

'Oh, yes.' Gerrard made himself comfortable in what was clearly the host's chair. 'I hadn't realized how much there was to learn about giving people money.'

'Many don't, which is precisely what men like Crowley count on.' Gabriel walked to the other armchair, then hesitated. Then he walked to the wall, picked up a straight-backed chair, and carried it over to face Gerrard. 'Better to play safe . . .' Sitting, he fixed Gerrard with a keen glance. 'Now . . .'

He led Gerrard through a catechism of terms and conditions, couched in popular investing cant. At the end of twenty minutes, he nodded. 'You'll do.' He glanced at the clock. 'We'd better speak in whispers from now on.'

Gerrard nodded. His gaze drifted to the tantalus; he rose and poured himself a small amount of brandy, swirling it around the glass to make it appear there'd been more originally. He met Gabriel's gaze as he resat, cradling the balloon in his fingers. 'I'll offer them a drink, don't you think?'

'Good idea.' Gabriel nodded at the glass in Gerrard's hand.

Gerrard grinned.

An aggressive knock fell on the door.

Rising, Gabriel held up a hand to stay Gerrard, then picked up his chair and silently returned it to its place against the wall. After one last glance about the scene, he crossed to the darkened bedchamber and stepped behind the door.

Gerrard set down his glass, then stood, straightened his sleeves, and strolled to the door. Opening it, he looked out. 'Yes?'

'I believe you're expecting us.' The deep booming voice carried clearly to the two behind the bedchamber door. 'We represent the Central East Africa Gold Company.'

Gabriel took up his position behind the countess. In the darkened bedchamber, she was no more than a dense shadow, her veiled face lit by the weak light shafting between door and jamb. Slightly to one side of her, Gabriel watched Gerrard greet his visitors with earnest affability.

After shaking hands, Gerrard waved the two men to the sofa. 'Please be seated, gentlemen.'

Gabriel struggled to block out the countess's perfume and concentrate; this was his first view of Crowley. Although he'd only been able to hear the names exchanged, he had no doubt which of the two was he. He was a bull of a man; comparing his height with Gerrard's, Gabriel pegged him at just on six feet. Six feet of muscled bulk; Crowley would easily have made two of Gerrard. Heavy black brows, thick and strong, slashed across his face, overhanging deep-set eyes. His face was fleshy, his features as coarse as the black hair that curled thickly over his large head.

That head appeared sunk directly into hulking shoulders; his arms were heavily thewed, as were his legs. He was wide and barrel-chested; he looked as strong as an ox and probably was. The only weakness Gabriel could discern was that he moved heavily, with no suppleness to his frame; when Gerrard offered a drink just as Crowley was about to sit, he had to turn his entire body toward Gerrard to answer, not just his head.

He was a distinctly unlovely specimen, but not specifically ugly. His thick lips were presently curved in an easy smile, softening the pugnacious line of his jaw and lending his otherwise unprepossessing countenance a certain charm. Indeed, there was raw energy – an animal magnetism – conveyed in the brilliance of his gaze and in the sheer strength of his movements.

Some women would find that attractive.

Gabriel glanced at the countess. Her attention was riveted on the scene in the sitting room. He looked back to see Crowley lean back on the sofa, completely at ease now he'd seen Gerrard. The expression on his face reminded Gabriel of a cat about to start playing with a mouse – anticipation of the kill oozed from Crowley's pores.

A soft sound reached Gabriel. He glanced at the countess, and realized he'd heard her swiftly indrawn breath. She'd tensed; as he watched, she almost imperceptibly shuddered.

Looking back at the scene playing out before them, Gabriel could understand. At his vacuous

169

best, Gerrard was chatting amiably with the other man; he wasn't looking at Crowley's face. Yet Gerrard, sensitive and observant, wouldn't be – couldn't be – unaware of Crowely's potent menace. Gabriel's respect for the younger man grew as, with every evidence of artless innocence, Gerrard turned to Crowley.

While Gerrard engaged Crowley in banal preliminaries, asking about the basic nature of the company's business, Gabriel studied the other man, Swales, the company's agent.

He was average in almost every way – average height, average build, common in his coloring. His features were indistinguishable from those of countless others, his clothing likewise anonymous. The only thing that set Swales apart was that while his face with its bland expression seemed like a mask, his eyes were never still. Even now, although there was no one in the room bar Gerrard and Crowley, Swales's gaze darted constantly, now here, now there.

Crowley was the predator, Swales the scavenger.

'I see.' Gerrard nodded. 'And these gold deposits are in the south of Africa, you say?'

'Not the south.' Crowley smiled patronizingly. 'They're in the central part of the continent. That's where the "Central East" in the company's name comes from.'

'Oh!' Gerrard's face lit. 'I see now, yes. What's the country's name?'

'There's more than one country involved.'

170

Gabriel listened, occasionally tensing as Gerrard artfully probed, but Patience's brother possessed a real knack for pressing just so far, then sliding away into patent and unthreatening ignorance one word before Crowley tensed. Gerrard played his part to perfection, and played Crowley just as well.

The countess was equally on edge, equally concerned; she tensed at precisely the same moments he did, then relaxed as Gerrard once again played out Crowley's line. Crowley was the one hooked on the lure, being artfully reeled in, not the other way about.

By the end of an hour, when Gerrard finally allowed Swales to show him the promissory note, they had heard all they could hope to hear, and that from Crowley's lips. He'd named the locations of three of the company's mining claims, and also cited towns where he said the company had a workforce and buildings established. He'd dropped a host of names supposedly of African officials backing the company, and of African authorities from whom permissions had been received. Under subtle prompting, he'd revealed figures aplenty, enough to keep Montague busy for a week. He'd also twice mentioned that the company was close to commencing the next phase of development.

They'd learned what they needed to know, and Gabriel was exhausted by the constant ebb and flow of helpless tension. The countess was sagging, too. Gerrard, on the other hand, was positively glowing. Crowley and Swales saw it as enthusiasm;

Gabriel knew it was suppressed excitement at his triumph.

'So you see' – Swales leaned closer to Gerrard, pointing to the lower portion of the promissory note, now unrolled on Gerrard's knees – 'if you just sign here, we'll be all right and tight.'

'Oh, yes. Right-ho!' Gerrard started rerolling the note. 'I'll get it signed right and tight, and then we'll all be happy, what?' He grinned at Crowley and Swales.

There was an instant of silence, then Crowley said, '*Get* it signed? Why can't you sign it now?'

Gerrard looked at him as if he'd admitted to lunacy. 'But . . . my dear man, *I* can't sign. I'm a minor.' Having dropped his bombshell, Gerrard looked from Crowley to Swales and back again. 'Didn't you know?'

Crowley's face darkened. 'No. We didn't know.' Shifting forward, he held out a hand for the note.

Gerrard grinned and held onto it. 'Well, there's no need to worry, y'know. M'sister's my main guardian and she'll sign whatever I tell her to. Well, why wouldn't she? She's got no head for business – she leaves that to me.'

Crowley hesitated, his gaze fixed unwaveringly on Gerrard's innocent countenance. Then he asked, 'Who's your other guardian? Do they have to sign, too?'

'Well, yes – that's how things usually are if there's a female involved, don't y'know. But my other

172

guardian's an old stick – bumbling old fool – my late pater's old solicitor. He lives buried in the country. Once m'sister signs, then he will, too, and all will be right as a trivet.'

Crowley glanced at Swales, who shrugged. Crowley looked back at Gerrard, then nodded. 'Very well.' He stood, slowly bringing his bulk up off the sofa.

Gerrard unfolded his long limbs with the effortless grace of the young and held out his hand. 'Right then. I'll get the deed done, the note signed, and get it back to you forthwith.'

He shook hands with Crowley, and then with Swales, then accompanied them to the door. As they reached it, Crowley paused. Gabriel and the countess shifted, craning to keep them in sight.

'So when can we expect to get the note back?'

Gerrard grinned, the epitome of foolish vacuity. 'Oh, a few weeks should do it.'

'Weeks!' Crowley's face darkened again.

Gerrard blinked at him. 'Why, yes – didn't I say? The pater's old solicitor lives in Derbyshire.' When Crowley continued to glower, Gerrard's brows rose, his expression degenerating to that of a child fearing denial of a promised treat. 'Why? There's no tearing rush, is there?'

Crowley studied Gerrard's face, then, very gradually, drew back. 'As I said, the company's close to commencing the next phase of operations. Once we reach that point, we won't be accepting any more promissory notes. If you want a share in our profits, you'll need to get the note signed and returned to us – you can send it to Thurlow and Brown, of Lincoln's Inn.'

'But if you don't get it to us soon,' Swales put in, 'you'll miss out.'

'Oh, no chance of that! I'll get m'sister to sign and get it off tomorrow. If I send it by rider, it'll be back before we know it, what?'

'Just make sure it is.' With one last intimidating glance, Crowley hauled open the door.

Swales followed him into the corridor. Gerrard stopped on the threshold. 'Well, thank you, and good-bye.'

Crowley's growled farewell rumbled back to them, drowning out Swales's reply.

Gerrard stood at the door, watching them depart, his silly smile still in place, then he stepped back, closed the door, and let his mask fall.

Gabriel closed his hands about the countess's shoulders. She sagged back against him – for one blissful moment, from shoulder to hip, she caressed him – then she remembered herself and stiffly straightened. Smiling in the dark, Gabriel squeezed her shoulders, then released her. Leaving her behind the door, he went out to Gerrard.

He put a finger to his lips as Gerrard faced him. Gerrard dutifully held silent. They both waited, listening, then Gabriel signaled Gerrard to open the door and look out.

Gerrard did, then stepped back and closed the door. 'They're gone.'

Gabriel nodded, scanning Gerrard's face. 'Well done.'

Gerrard smiled. 'It was the longest performance I've ever given, but he didn't seem to suspect.'

'I'm sure he didn't. If he had, he wouldn't have been anywhere near as accommodating.' Crossing to the escritoire by the windows, Gabriel drew out paper and pen. 'Now to the last act. We need to write down everything we heard, and sign and date it.'

Gerrard drew up a chair. Together, they recounted the conversation, noting down names, locations and amounts. With his sharp visual memory, Gerrard was able to review the conversation, verifying Gabriel's recollections and adding further snippets. An hour had passed before they were satisfied.

Gabriel pushed back from the escritoire. 'That gives us a lot to check, a lot to verify – more than enough chance to prove fraud.' He glanced at Gerrard, just as Gerrard yawned. 'Now it's time you were off home.'

Gerrard grinned and rose. 'Tiring work, acting, and I'm driving to Brighton with friends tomorrow, so I'd best turn in.'

Gabriel followed Gerrard to the door. Gerrard stopped by the sofa. 'Here – you'd better take this, too.'

'Indeed.' Gabriel accepted the rolled promissory note. 'It's absolute evidence that this meeting took place.'

Reaching the door, Gerrard looked back. 'Are you coming?'

Stowing the note and their account of the meeting in the inside pocket of his coat, Gabriel shook his head. 'Not just yet. We shouldn't be seen together. You go ahead – I'll follow later. Duggan is waiting for you, isn't he?' Duggan was Vane's groom.

Gerrard nodded. 'He'll drive me back to Curzon Street. Let me know how it goes.' With a salute, he went out of the door, shutting it softly behind him.

Gabriel considered the closed door, then walked across and snibbed the lock. He surveyed the room, then strolled to the lamp beside the fireplace, turning it, then its mate, very low, shrouding the room in shadows. Satisfied, he headed for the bedchamber, for the epilogue to the evening's performance.

CHAPTER 8

The countess was waiting, no longer behind the door but seated on the end of the bed. A dark shadow, she rose as he neared.

'Do you really think there are mining claims in those places – Kafia, Fangak, and Lodwar?'

'I'd be greatly surprised if there's anything there at all. Towns or villages, maybe, but no mining. We'll check.' He couldn't see her other than as a denser figure in the gloom; the already dark room had darkened even further with the dimming of the light from the sitting room. So he had to rely on his other senses – they told him she was still absorbed with Crowley's revelations. 'He gave us more than enough facts, not only names and places but also figures and projections. I've got it all down. To get the company's notes declared invalid all we need do is prove *some* of those claims false, not all of them.'

'Still' – he heard the frown in her voice – 'it won't be easy to prove what really is happening in deepest Africa. Did you recognize any of the places he mentioned?'

'No, but there must be someone in London who will.'

'He also stated that they were close to commencing the next stage of development – surely that's his way of saying that they plan to call in the promissory notes soon.'

'He's not at that stage yet. Unless something triggers the call, he'll wait to see how many more gullible gentlemen up from the shires for the Season he can lure into his net.'

Silence ensued. Her gnawing anxiety reached him clearly. He stepped closer. 'It's a significant victory to have got that much detail from him.'

'Oh, indeed!' She looked up. 'Mr Debbington was quite splendid.'

'And what about the *eminence grise* behind the scenes?'

He knew precisely when she realized – realized she was alone with him in a very dark bedchamber with a very large bed a mere foot away. Her spine straightened, her chin tilted higher; a fine tension gripped her.

'You've been very . . . inventive.'

He slid one arm about her waist. 'I intend being a great deal more inventive yet.'

He drew her against him. After only the slightest resistance, she permitted it, settling breast to chest, hip to hip, thigh to thigh, as if she belonged there.

'You've been very successful.' Her tone was slightly breathless.

His lips curved. 'I've been brilliant.' He found the edge of her veil. Slowly, he lifted it. All the

178

way up. She caught her breath, one hand rising, hovering . . . but she allowed it. The room was so dark he couldn't possibly distinguish her features. Then he bent his head and set his lips – to the lips that were waiting for him.

Waiting, yearning, ready to pay his price – he knew she had no idea how precious, how heady, he found her lack of guile, her open generosity, the way she yielded her mouth at his demand, the way she sank against him, into him. The way she gave without restraint.

There was power in her giving. As before, it caught him, captured him, and held him in thrall. He had to have more – know more – of her. His fingers found the ties of her cloak; a minute later, it slid from her shoulders to pool on the floor at their feet. A curved clip across the crown of her head anchored her veil; he slid one hand under the veil, past her throat, and encountered the heavy weight of her hair, coiled at her nape. Soft as silk, it caressed the backs of his fingers; without conscious direction, they searched. Her pins pattered on the floor; her hair spilled over his hands, both the one at her throat and the one at her waist. Her hair was long and so soft; he caught strands between his fingers and played, enthralled by the texture.

He sensed the hitch in her breathing. Closing his fist in her hair, he drew her head back, exposing the column of her throat. Blind in the dense darkness, he slid his lips from hers to trace the supple line and find the spot where her pulse beat hotly. He laved it, then sucked – her breath hitched again. Her fingers had speared through his hair; they spread over his skull as he shifted his hold and closed his hands over her breasts.

Already firm, they swelled and filled his palms, heated flesh begging for his attention. Straightening, dragging in a swift breath, he caught her lips again. She kissed him back – avidly, greedily, as ravenous as he. When he rotated his thumbs about her already ruched nipples, she gasped. Without thought, he backed her until she came up against the wall. Inwardly, he tried to shake his head to clear it of the miasma of lust fogging it. He'd just moved her away from the bed, a patently silly move. Now he'd have to move her back again.

Later.

Trapping her lips with his, he pinned her to the wall and set his fingers to her laces.

He couldn't think – he hadn't planned, although he'd tried to. He rarely embarked on a seduction these days, especially not one he was particularly intent on, without some idea of what would work best, what possibilities were most likely, what avenues held most promise of fulfillment. In thinking of how he would have the countess, he hadn't been able to get past the need to touch her, to know her.

A surprisingly simple need for such an experienced lover as he, and one surprisingly compelling.

He had her laces free, her gown loose, in the

space of a heated minute. Using his weight to immobilize her, he reached up and dislodged her hands from his hair. Drawing her hands and arms down, he leaned into their kiss – she drew him deep, then played havoc with his senses. For one definable instant, he lost his will entirely and simply existed, utterly in thrall, then the hot pressure of her breasts against his chest recalled him to his urgent need.

He had to touch her, caress her – feel her. If she wouldn't allow him to see her, he would have to learn her by touch, by having her against him, skin to bare skin, heat to heat.

Without any veils, any cloaks, any barriers between them.

He needed to know her.

Releasing her hands, he reached for her shoulders and swiftly drew her gown down, pushing the sleeves down her arms, deftly freeing her breasts. He sensed her hesitation, the tremor of uncertainty that shook her; capturing her lips, her attention, in a searing kiss, he left her gown in folds about her hips and cupped her breasts, now covered only by the thin silk of her chemise.

Her hesitation evaporated. She gripped his face with both hands and kissed him back, every bit as urgent as he. Through the silk, her skin burned; the ripe swells tipped by nipples hard as pebbles beckoned. Her chemise was fastened by a row of tiny buttons. He ravaged her mouth as he swiftly undid them. He was already aching, rigid with need, but more than anything he wanted to savor each moment, each revelation. Each bit of her as he uncovered it.

Her breasts were a delight. Firm and full, they filled his hands, generous, hot and heavy. Pushing the open halves of her chemise wide, he kneaded and heard her moan. The evocative sound sent another, unnecessary rush of blood to his loins. Dragging his lips from hers, he ducked his head, trailing open-mouthed kisses over her throat, her collarbone, to where her flesh mounded in his hands.

Then he feasted.

She moaned, and panted, and even sighed his name as he tasted, licked, and suckled. He had to be marking her; although he couldn't see, the thought sent a surge of sheer possessiveness through him. He drew one peak deep into his mouth; she cried out. Her knees buckled. He leaned into her, holding her up, his erection hard against her lower belly, his balls cradled between her thighs.

Her softness flowed around him as she slid her arms about his shoulders and clung; her perfume, evocative as sin, wrapped about them.

He lifted his head and found her lips again, swollen and hot and needy. She drew him in, tongue tangling with his, boldly inciting. He slid his hands down to her hips, then further, tracing the smooth lines of her flanks. Her nipples, hard and tight, were twin points of flame surrounded by the fire of her breasts, crushed against his chest as he pressed her to the wall. Her hips tilted into his.

He wasn't even thinking when he grasped the folds of her gown in both hands and pushed them from her hips. His senses didn't register the sibilant 'swoosh' as he shifted and the silk slithered to the floor. His senses had seized.

She was like hot, supple silk, alive, enchanted, all his. Her limbs, all but naked, shifted sensuously against him, not to push him away but to enclose him more sweetly. If he'd ever dreamed of a houri, then she was here, in his arms, nubile, nearly naked, ready to fulfill his every want, ready to kill him with pleasure. He couldn't catch his breath, mentally or physically; lust closed like a fist about his gut and shut off his brain. His hands dove beneath the hem of her chemise to close possessively about the globes of her bottom.

Her kiss only grew hotter, sweeter, headier. She tasted like the elixir of the gods.

She levered herself up, tightening her arms about his shoulders. His legs had been outside hers, trapping hers; now he supported her and shifted, pressing one long thigh between hers. She murmured, an incoherent sound lost between their lips. He set her down; she balanced on her toes, held high by her hold on him and pinned by his chest. Shifting, he released her luscious derriere and slid both hands forward, caressing the sweet indentation where hip met thigh before moving on to the front of her naked thighs. With his thumbs, he found the crease at the top of each thigh; pressing lightly, he slid both thumbs slowly inward.

Her breathing fragmented; their kiss turned desperate as his thumbs tangled in her silky curls. He played, teasing, being tantalized, then, skillfully plundering her mouth, he sent one hand upward, fingers splaying over the delicate skin of her stomach, caressing, then kneading evocatively. In almost the same breath, he let the fingers of his other hand drift down, gently pressing in, searching through her heated softness to find her.

If he hadn't been kissing her, he sensed she would have gasped. She was slick, swollen, and so hot. Her breasts strained against his chest; he held her steady and gently probed, then stroked, soothed, only to take further liberties.

The intimacy was new to her – he knew that in his bones. Her late husband must have been a clod. Yet she was flowering sweetly for him; her nectar burned his fingers as he circled her entrance, then drew back to caress the nubbin of flesh now tight and throbbing with need.

She quivered, her fingers digging into his upper arms as she arched her head away. He allowed her to break the kiss and catch a shattered breath, then he deliberately reached deeper and circled her entrance again . . .

She shivered. He was asking and she understood – after a fractional hesitation, she bent one knee, sliding her slender calf around his leg. Opening herself for him.

The only thing he managed to remember after that was that she hadn't been pleasured like this before. So he penetrated her slowly, letting her feel every tiny increment as he slid one finger into her sheath. She was scalding hot; he wasn't surprised to discover she was tight as well. Her experience of intimacy appeared miniscule. She clamped firmly about his finger, her breath shivering in his ear. He turned his head, found her lips, and soothed her with a long, slow kiss. As he withdrew his finger, her hips instinctively tilted, her body begging for more. He gave it to her, clinging to the reins of his impulses, howling to have her, urgent and ravenous. He was too experienced a lover not to know what would be best for her; with his lips on hers, re-assuring, distracting, and inciting in turn, he set himself to show her what could be.

And when her fingers bit deep and she pulled back from their kiss as her body shattered in glory, he felt like a conqueror, victorious, triumphant, with the spoils of his conquest in his arms. Her released passion washed over him in waves, surge after surge of heat and fierce delight. The soft moan that escaped her, one of fulfillment laced with residual need, the waft of her ragged breaths against his cheek, the thundering of her heart pressed close to his, the evocative muskiness that rose from where his fingers filled her to combine with her perfume and drive him mad – all urged him on.

She was ready, so gloriously tall, and he was desperate.

It was the work of seconds to release his straining staff, to lift the leg she'd crooked about his knee to his hip. To draw his fingers from her hot wetness and set the head of his erection to her entrance. Gripping her hips, he caught her lips and plunged into her mouth, and into her heat.

She screamed.

The sound, trapped between their lips, reverberated through his head. Then she tensed, like a vise, about him.

He gasped, breaking their kiss, grimly fighting for control. It couldn't be – yet it was. Had been. The shock shook at least a few of his wits into place. After a fraught second in which he teetered on the brink of madness, he managed to block out the physical long enough to ask, 'How?'

He had barely enough air in his lungs to form the word, but with her face close by his, she heard.

'I . . .'

Her voice quavered; she was, it seemed, as shocked as he, if not for the same reason. That, he could understand. If this was her first time . . . he was buried to the hilt inside her.

She gulped in air. Her words came in a shaky whisper by his ear. 'I was a child bride. My husband . . . he was much older. And ill. He wasn't able to . . .' She released her grip on his arm to gesture. The movement caused her to shift upon him – she caught her breath on a fractured gasp.

186

'Shh. Gently.' He found her lips and soothed her with a kiss while he struggled to take it in. A child bride left virginal by her aging husband? No doubt it did happen, although it had never before happened to him. Her unexpected innocence, however, raised a most pertinent question. Had she known he would . . . ?

It took all his effort, and the last shreds of his will, to force himself to ask, 'Do you want me to stop?'

Hardly elegant phrasing, but it was all he could manage with her clamped, the tightest, hottest, wettest dream he'd ever had, about him.

Her answer was a long time coming. His teeth were gritted, every muscle straining against the driving need to have her. With what little wit he still possessed he fought to ignore the warmth of the lush body in his arms, the constantly fluctuating pressure against his chest as she breathed rapidly, raggedly. He was so aware of her breathing, he knew when she reached her decision and drew in a deeper breath to deliver it.

He steeled himself to accept it – and prayed.

She shook her head. 'No.'

He exhaled. 'Thank God.'

'What—?'

He kissed her deeply, reassuringly, then lifted his head. 'Don't think, just do as I say.' He hesitated, wishing for the hundredth time that he could see, then added, 'It'll feel a lot better very soon.' He could only guess what she was feeling – he couldn't remember the last virgin he'd had. But she was still very tense; every muscle below her waist was locked tight. She was certainly not comfortable; she might even be in pain.

Withdrawing from her and repairing to the bed would have been the simple option. Unfortunately, with her tensed as she was, withdrawing from her would probably cause her more pain. But the bed was a must. 'Raise your other leg – wrap it about my waist. I'll hold you.' When she hesitated, he brushed her lips with his. 'Trust me. I'll carry you to the bed.'

She drew in a breath, and lifted her other leg, moving more confidently when she felt his hands shift and he took her weight. Locking her legs about him, sliding her arms about his shoulders for balance, she levered herself up a little, easing herself from him.

He gripped her hips. 'That's enough.' Grimly denying the impulse to surge back into her, he turned and carried her the few feet to the bed. Carefully, he laid her down with her hips close to the edge. As he'd expected, she relaxed just a little on finding the bed beneath her. Just enough for him to ease out of her a fraction more as he straightened, not fully but so he leaned over her, his weight on his locked arms.

Keeping his hips still, he found her face and brushed back the strands of gossamer soft hair that had fallen across her cheek. Her veil was still in place, still brushed back – he left it as it was.

That, one day, she would remove for him, when she was ready to trust him with her name. Tonight, she was trusting him with her body – for tonight, that was enough.

Framing her jaw, he leaned forward and kissed her. For a moment, she lay passive, then responded. Once she was kissing him back freely, he flexed his hips and pressed into her again, filling her, stretching her even more than before. She sucked in a breath and tensed, but then eased. He drew back and pressed in again, then repeated the movement, his action steady and even. He kept the tempo slow until her muscles relaxed, until her legs were loose about his hips, her hands lax, fingers trailing on his sleeves, her body open and accepting and starting to stir, starting to lift and surge with his rhythm.

Mildly triumphant, he drew back. 'Don't move. Just wait.' Then he straightened completely. Reaching around, he felt for her shoes, and removed them. Tracing her long legs upward until he encountered her garters, he stripped them and her stockings off. Her chemise was the merest wisp of fine silk – he decided to ignore it for the moment. Shrugging out of his coat, he heard the crackle of the promissory note and their lists; he tossed the coat toward where he'd seen a chair. His waistcoat and shirt followed in short order, then he toed off his shoes and stripped off his trousers.

The lamps in the sitting room had gone out; the darkness was intense. He couldn't see her – only feel her, hear her, sense her. And she couldn't see him.

'What . . . ?'

He reached for her, sliding his hands along her flanks, up over her sides. 'Just trust me.' He joined her on the bed, rolling and lifting her as he did, moving them back so their long legs weren't hanging over the edge.

She gasped as he rose over her again, her hands clutching wildly as, palms flat on either side of her, he braced his arms and held himself above her. Wedging his hips between her widespread thighs, he surged and filled her until she was full. Then he lowered his head, searching for her lips. Her fluttering hands found his face, then her lips joined with his. She offered them, and her mouth, willingly, lovingly. He took both as he rocked her, rocked into her, until she was once again easy, accepting the smooth slide of his staff into her sheath with gratifying eagerness.

Pulling back from the kiss, he held himself above her and changed the tenor of their joining. He kept the rhythm slow, but rolled his hips as he entered her, encouraging her to spread her thighs wider, raise her knees higher.

Then her fingertips hesitantly touched his chest, another of her butterfly caresses. He bit his lip and concentrated on keeping to his slow beat. His muscles flickered and twitched as her fingers delicately traced over his chest, his waist, his flanks. Stifling a gasp, he thrust deeper. 'Wrap your legs around me like before.'

She obeyed instantly, locking her legs about his hips. 'Now what?'

She couldn't see his smile. 'Now we ride.'

They did. Together.

He'd purposely darkened the room to ease her fear of revealing herself, her identity, to him. In doing so, he'd unwittingly created a sensual situation beyond even his ken. Making love in total darkness emphasized the tactile sensations and amplified the soft, intensely sensual sounds. It was a new and very different experience, loving a woman blind.

He was aware of every square inch where they touched, aware of the screening quality of her silk chemise, nowhere near as fine as the skin beneath it. He heard every little hitch in her breathing, every soft sound she made; he was attuned to every moan, every gasped, incoherent entreaty. He knew her perfume, but it was another scent that wreathed his brain, that of her and her alone. In his arms, in the dark, she became the epitome of woman, in truth the houri he'd labelled her. She was the essence of joy and the essence of madness; she was the ultimate challenge.

His senses were full of her, focused most completely on where they joined. The heightened sensations left him reeling.

He'd never before had a woman to equal her.

That was borne in on him as they rode on, through their sensual landscape, scaling higher and ever higher peaks. She matched him – not just physically, although that was wonder enough; she clung, gasped, shattered, then rose again to ride on. But she was there, with him, urging him on, daring and challenging, joyously inviting him to dive into the sensual whirlpool her body had become. A whirlpool of giving.

He demanded and she gave – not just generously but with a wild abandon that shattered his control. He couldn't get enough of her; he drank greedily, yet her well was never dry.

She gave him joy and delight and pleasure unimaginable, and in the giving received the same. When the end finally came and their ride ended in soul-shattering glory, he was, for the first time in his life, utterly beyond this world.

One thought drifted past: He'd been the first to have her.

A second later, that deeply buried part of him he rarely let loose growled a correction: The *only* one to have her.

Holding her close, feeling her soften beneath him, he shut his eyes and drifted into pleasured bliss.

She woke slowly, her senses gradually returning, her scattered wits reassembling in fits and starts. The first thing she was aware of was that there were tears in her eyes. They weren't tears of regret but of joy – a joy too deep, too intense to find expression in word or thought.

So *that* was what lay between a woman and a man. The thought brought a surge of giddy delight, followed immediately by a rush of gratitude – to him who had demonstrated so well.

Her lips kicked up at the ends. She'd heard for years that he was an expert in that sphere – she could now attest to the fact. He'd been gentle and tender, at least once he'd realized she was a novice, but later . . . she didn't think he'd held back.

She was glad – glad of the experience, glad it had happened. Especially glad it had happened with him. That last made her frown.

Even though it was dark and had been throughout, so that he'd been no more than a phantom, kissing her, caressing her, she'd always known it was he.

Him. Her senses focused on the heavy body lying upon her, the heaviness within her, filling her, stretching her . . .

The realization jolted her fully awake.

Her immediate thought was that this wasn't she – or not the same she. She had a naked man in her arms and they were joined; she was changed forever physically. And emotionally; she couldn't forget how she'd writhed beneath him, wanton and wanting. She was incontrovertibly altered – she could never go back to who she'd been.

She waited for the recriminations to start, the dire prophecies, the hysterical outpourings. Nothing came. Instead, she remained at peace, filled with a warm glow she'd never known, never even imagined existed. And she couldn't regret it.

It had been no one's fault; she hadn't imagined it could happen against a wall, not with them both upright. Her feet had been firmly on the floor. Her head, of course, had been wholly in the clouds, her wits swept away on a tide of pure desire.

The thought brought the experience back to her – the burgeoning excitement, the scintillating thrill, the pure, unadulterated joy. This, here, with him, would be the only chance she'd ever have of experiencing it – the true magnificence of being a woman, a woman joined with a man. There was no one she was hurting; no one in her life to care. No one who would ever know. She'd been condemned by circumstance to die an old maid; what harm could there be in this, her one taste of glory? It would have to last her the rest of her life.

Although he'd been inside her before she'd realized his intention, she'd known precisely what she was doing when she'd told him not to stop. She'd had plenty of experience in making decisions; she knew how it felt when she'd decided right. It felt like this.

In the same way she'd never looked back, never regretted turning her back on London and her Season all those years ago, she would not regret this. No matter what complications arose, she'd experienced and enjoyed – and lusted.

A gurgle of inner laughter welled up inside her. Sternly quelling it, she tried to shift, only to find it impossible. The movement once more focused her senses on the hard male body pressing hers into the bed. He was heavy, yet oddly, she rather liked the feeling of his weighted limbs pressing her into the mattress. She wasn't uncomfortable, indeed, quite the opposite, strange though that seemed. Her legs had relaxed from about his waist but were still tangled with his. One of her arms was draped over his shoulder; her other hand lay against his side.

Him. She couldn't take it in; her mind kept shying from the thought, from allowing his image to form. In the dark, he'd simply been a magnificent male, one she trusted so deeply the thought that he might physically hurt her had simply not occurred. She'd given herself to him and he'd taken her, swept her up in his arms and introduced her to delights she could still only barely comprehend.

Yet she knew who he was.

Didn't she?

Frowning, she slipped her hand from his side and, very gently, touched his shoulder. When his breathing continued deep and even, she let her fingers wander, tracing the wide bone, the sleek muscle bands. Spreading her fingers, she explored the side of his chest, then his back, sensing the power in the steely muscles beneath the smooth skin.

She'd seen his naked chest years before; even then, it had fascinated her, although she'd told herself she was merely curious. Now she could indulge; letting her hands wander, she filled her senses with him.

Her skin came alive, all over. The sudden rush of sensation made her breath hitch; he was so warm, so male, so vibrantly real. A tide of heady feeling welled and surged through her. The wave reared and crashed – and rocked her, tore her from her moorings and tossed her into a turbulent swell. She caught her breath, quivering, helplessly adrift on an emotional sea whipped by sudden turmoil.

Rupert?

No – Gabriel.

The reality struck to her bones. He was deeply familiar in so many ways, yet in truth he was a man she'd only recently met. She could feel his hands on her, still holding her even in sleep. Those strong, clever hands had loved her, caressed her, brought her untold joy and delight. Their touch was burned into her memory, as was the empty ache that had swept her, the ache only he evoked and only he could ease.

Shifting her head, she peered at his face, but the darkness defeated her. All she knew was his warm weight, the touch of his hands, and the stream of feeling that welled and poured through her, from her, leaving her shaking inside.

It took a minute to catch her breath, to steady herself, to reground herself in reality and let the fantasy – and that exultation that left her so vulnerable – fade away.

He'd be horrified if he knew, if he realized it

was she. So why was every instinct she possessed screaming that this was right, so right, when she knew, logically, it was all wrong?

As she stared into darkness, confusion reigning in her mind, he stirred.

Then he shifted; she realized he was turning toward her, then the pressure on her chest eased. His warmth was still close, her lower body still pressed heavily into the bed. It took her a moment to realize that he was resting his weight on his elbows.

She remembered her veil. Propelled by sudden panic, she started to reach . . . then realized he was as blind as she. The darkness was so intense, even though she knew his face was mere inches from hers, she couldn't see it.

'That was quite a ride, countess.'

The lazy, gravelly words drifted down; his breath wafted across her cheek. His lips followed, searching and finding hers, then settling for a long, slow, exceedingly thorough kiss. When he finally brought it to an end and released her lips, she could tell his were curved.

'How do you feel?'

Stretched. Still full of him. 'Alive.' How true. Her skin was heating again. How could that be?

As if he could read her thoughts, his lips returned to hers, and he was smiling even more definitely. Another lengthy kiss left her close to conflagration; ending it, he murmured, 'Are you game for another gallop?'

He pressed inward, and she realized that he definitely was. Her hips tilted, inviting him deeper; she concluded she must be, too. She tightened her arms about him, wordlessly urging him closer. He settled upon her, settled his lips on hers, and sank deeply into her – into her mouth, into her body.

This time, he was in no hurry. Before, he'd been reined, restrained; this time, he savored her, rocking her deeply, pleasuring her well. The heat inside her grew until her bones melted. She drew back from their kiss to drag in a breath. His lips slid down her throat, then, to her surprise, she felt him shift, pull back. He withdrew from her, leaving her suddenly, achingly empty. Sliding lower, he fastened his mouth leisurely over one nipple.

The scalding heat was a shock; she gasped, then relaxed, then tensed again as he artfully played. The sound she made when he rasped her nipple with his tongue reminded her of a cat; when he grazed the tortured bud with his teeth, she nearly died.

'Gently.'

The word was a soothing sigh feathering over her heated flesh as he turned his attention to her other breast, to the neglected peak that was already aching for his touch. When it came, she arched like a puppet whose strings were in his hands. His warm chuckle rewarded her.

'How old are you?'

His lips drifted lower, skating over her midriff.

'Umm . . . late twenties.'

'Hmm.' He slid lower, his lips trailing a hot path to her navel. 'You've got a lot of catching up to do.'

'I have?'

He reached one hand up to fondle her breasts; the other slid down and around, stroking over her bottom and along the backs of her thighs. 'Oh, yes.'

He sounded very sure.

'You may as well start now.'

She didn't argue. She was sensing him, seeing him anew – and it was a fascinating insight. This tenderly passionate seducer set a completely new dimension to this male she'd never, it now seemed, completely known. She'd never met him as the sensual adult male – in that guise, he was an enticing creature, cloaked in darkness, maybe, but oh so tempting.

The world slid away; reality faded as his hands wove their magic.

'What should I do?'

He lifted his head from where he was nibbling his way across her stomach, the skin taut and flickering. Her nerves were similarly afflicted.

'Just lie back.' She could hear a certain male smugness in his voice. 'Lie back, relax, and let the pleasure take you.'

She had no strength, no motivation to do otherwise, so she did. If she'd had any inkling of what he had in mind, she would have summoned strength from somewhere. But she didn't. So she indulged her senses, and indulged herself with the indescribable pleasure of indulging him.

The warm, vibrant body arching beneath him held Gabriel's attention more completely, more effectively, than any woman before. Than anything in his life before.

Nothing had ever been this compelling. Never before had he experienced such total and abject surrender to the moment, to the worship of shared pleasure. There was something more here, something deeper, more powerful, more fascinating. The connoisseur was enthralled; the man was captivated.

Whatever new caress, whatever outrageous delight he pressed on her, she accepted – eagerly, gratefully – and, in return, she ravished him with her body, lavished upon him an unrestricted, unrestrained invitation to take, to plunder, to enjoy.

To search, to plumb, to discover – to know. Completely, absolutely, without barriers or guile. There was no part of her she hid from him, no part of her she denied him. He only had to reach, to wordlessly ask, to be inivited to take, to touch, to sate his hunger in her.

Her generosity was not limited to the physical. He sensed no reticence, no emotional distance, no private core of feeling she kept screened. Even as he steered her toward the culminating climax, he could sense the vulnerability she didn't try to hide.

It was that that ensnared him, focused his attention so completely. He'd opened sensual doors for her; in return, she'd opened a door he'd never imagined existed, a door into a realm of deeper intimacy, far more explicit, more dangerous, more exciting. An abject innocent, she'd shown him how much more there could be in this sphere – a sphere in which he'd thought he'd known it all.

He'd never known this – this all-consuming passion. She was open, honest, and soul-shatteringly courageous in her giving. Without conditions, she offered the ultimate satiation – something deep inside him shook as, driven, he reached to claim it.

And then it was his, and they were caught in the tide, buffeted by the glory. The intense release swelled, rose, then washed through them, and he was drowning in the bottomless well of her giving, in the ultimate ecstasy.

His last thought as he slid beneath the wave was that she was his. Tonight – and forever.

He woke in the depths of the night. For one instant, he savored the fluid stillness that held them, then reluctantly he disengaged, lifting from her and untangling their limbs, then sinking down beside her and gathering her to him. He would have liked to simply lie there, sharing the contentment, the aftermath of pleasure still warm in their veins, but she woke, too, and turned skittish. Not with any false modesty but with anxiety.

'I must go.' A reluctance to match his resonated

in her words, colored her determination. That last, however, was strong.

She pushed away and he let her go, shaken by the spike of need that drove him to pull her back. He'd never been possessive; it was, he told himself, simply that he'd enjoyed her so well, that the experience of her was so new to him.

He listened as she slipped from the bed, tracking her by sound as she rounded the bed to grope by the wall for her gown.

Rising, he found his trousers, pulled them on, then padded into the sitting room. He returned a moment later, having relighted both lamps. She was in her gown, her veil already down; she was struggling to redo her laces.

'Here.' Strolling up, he caught her about the waist and turned her. 'Let me.'

Expertly, he did them up, noting the fine tension that had gripped her the instant he'd touched her. He left her drawing on her stockings in the semi-darkness, and quickly finished dressing. By the time he shrugged into his coat, she was fully cloaked and veiled. He wasn't surprised by her sudden bolt back into secrecy, but he was very tired of that veil.

She glanced at him. 'I'll see myself out.' The words were slightly breathless.

'No.' Strolling forward, he stopped by her side. 'I'll see you to your carriage.'

She considered arguing; he could sense it in

her stance. But then she acquiesced with an inclination of her head. Not haughty, but careful.

Without another word, he escorted her from the room, down the stairs, and through the foyer. The sleepy doorman let them out with barely a glance, too busy stifling a yawn.

Her black carriage was waiting just along the street. He handed her in, then she turned back to him. He felt her gaze search his face, lit by a nearby street flare, then she inclined her head again.

'Thank you.'

The soft words feathered his senses, leaving him very sure that it was not his efforts regarding the company for which she was thanking him.

She settled into the dark of the carriage; he shut the door and nodded at her coachman. 'Drive on.'

The coach rattled away. Filling his chest with a slow, deep breath, he watched it turn the corner, then he exhaled and headed home. The sense of achievement that suffused him was profound and intensely satisfying. Intensely gratifying.

Everything – *everything* – was going very well.

CHAPTER 9

'Well, miss, and what's got into you?'
Alathea snapped to attention. Reflected in the dressing table mirror before her, she saw Nellie shaking out her pillows and airing her bed.

Nellie caught her eye. 'You've been staring at that mirror for the past five minutes, and seeing nothing is my guess.'

Alathea gestured, brushing the query aside, praying she wouldn't blush, that her face showed no evidence of her thoughts. Heaven forbid.

'That meeting of yours last night must have been a long one – four o'clock again before you got in. Jacobs said you was in there for all those hours.'

Alathea picked up her brush. 'We had to discuss what we'd learned.'

'So you've found something out about this wretched company – you and Mr Rupert?'

'Indeed.' Setting the brush to her hair, Alathea forced her mind to that aspect of the night. 'We've learned enough to frame our case. All we need do now is assemble the right proofs, and we'll be free.'

Easier said than done, no doubt, but she was

convinced last night had set their feet on the road to success. Despite her careful words to Gabriel, she'd felt buoyed by their first real gain, the first scent of ultimate victory.

She'd been careful to hide her elation, aware he'd sense it and take advantage.

He'd taken advantage anyway.

So had she.

'Here, let me.' Nellie lifted the brush from her slack grasp. 'Good for nothing, this morning, you are.'

Alathea blinked. 'I was just . . . thinking.'

Nellie shot her a shrewd look. 'Well, I dare say there are lots of facts from this meeting you need chew on.'

'Hmm.' Facts. Sensations, emotions – revelations. She had a lot to think about.

Throughout the day, her mind wandered, considering, pondering, reliving the golden moments, carefully fixing each in her memory, storing them away against the cold years ahead. Again and again, she was jerked back to the present – by Charlie asking after one of their tenants, by Alice wanting her opinion on a particular shade of ribbon, by Jeremy frowning over a piece of arithmetic.

Finally, in the quiet of the afternoon when, after luncheon, all the females of the family repaired to the back parlor for a quiet hour before driving in the park or attending an afternoon tea, Augusta climbed into Alathea's lap, sitting astride her knees. Placing her soft hands on Alathea's cheeks, Augusta stared into her eyes. 'You keep going away – far away.'

Alathea looked into Augusta's large brown eyes.

Augusta searched hers. 'Where is it you go?'

To another world, one of darkness, sensation, and indescribable wonder.

Alathea smiled. 'Sorry, poppet, I've got lots on my mind just now.' Rose had been dumped in her lap between them; Alathea lifted the doll and studied her. 'How is Rose finding London?'

The distraction worked, not for her but for Augusta. Fifteen minutes later, when Augusta slipped from her lap and went to play with Rose in a splash of sunlight, Alathea exchanged a fond and, she hoped, undisturbingly mild glance with Serena, then quietly left the room.

She sought refuge in her office.

Standing arms crossed before the window, she forced herself to concentrate on the company's plans, all that Crowley had disclosed the previous evening. Despite her senses' preoccupation, there was nothing requiring thought in all the rest. It had happened – she'd seized and enjoyed the experience, but that was all there was to it. She wouldn't rescue her family from destitution by dwelling on such matters – on the substance of dreams. Her only major worry arising from her interlude with Gabriel was the difficulty she would experience in facing him as Alathea Morwellan. Knowing him in the biblical sense, and knowing he knew her in the same way but

206

didn't know it was she, wasn't going to make her life any easier.

Despite her charade, she was not a naturally deceitful person; she'd never imagined having to deceive him in this way.

If he ever found out . . .

Dragging in a breath, she turned from the window. Sensibility was not her strong suit – whatever leanings she'd had in that direction had been eradicated eleven years ago. Determinedly, she focused on the company and Crowley. It took mere minutes to concede that she could not, no matter how much she wished it, proceed without Gabriel. Quite aside from the fact that dismissing him would probably be more difficult than summoning him in the first place, she could see no way forward without him.

She couldn't break in, or even organize to have someone else break in, to Douglas's mansion. She'd had Jacobs drive her around Egerton Gardens; Folwell had chatted to a street sweeper and discovered which of the large, new houses belonged to Douglas, but breaking in was too risky. Although they might find some of the proofs they needed, the chances of Crowley or Swales realizing their records had been searched and, as Charlie would phrase it, getting the wind up, was high. Then they'd call in the promissory notes and she'd be too busy beating off creditors to press any claim in court.

And she didn't like Crowley. The thought of meeting him at night alone and cut off from help was the substance of nightmares. He was evil. She'd sensed it very clearly, watching him as he'd watched Gerrard Debbington, seeing the cruel gleam in his eyes. Gabriel had said Crowley liked to gloat over his potential victims, but it was more than that. He viewed people as prey. There was viciousness and real cruelty beneath his semi-civilized veneer.

She wanted him as far away from her family as possible.

All things considered – and she did mean all – the only sensible way forward was to find the needed proofs without delay. Then Crowley would no longer be a threat, and the countess could fade into the mists.

'Fangak. Lodwar. What was the other one?' Sitting at her desk, she drew a sheet of paper onto the blotter and reached for a pen. 'Kafia – that was it.'

She wrote the names down, then settled to list all the names and locations she could recall Crowley mentioning.

'Mary? Alice?' Alathea peeked into Mary's bed-chamber, where her elder stepsisters often repaired when they were supposed to be resting. Sure enough, both were lolling on the bed wearing identical expressions of disgusted boredom. They both lifted their heads to look at her.

Alathea grinned. 'I'm going to Hatchard's. Serena said you could come if you wished.'

Mary sat bolt upright. 'They have a lending library, don't they?'

Alice was already rolling from the bed. 'I'll come.'

Alathea watched them scramble into shoes, struggle into spencers, grab bonnets, casting only the most perfunctory of glances at their reflections. 'There is a lending library, but before you go looking for Mrs Radcliffe's latest, I want you to help me find some books.'

'On what?' Alice asked as she joined her at the door.

'On Africa.'

'That was *boring*.' On a long-drawn yawn, Jeremy sank deeper into the seat of the hackney and leaned against Alathea's shoulder. 'I thought they would have known about digging up gold. All they wanted to talk about was melting it.'

'Hmm.' Alathea grimaced. She'd thought the gentlemen at the Metallurgical Institute would have known about mining, too. Unfortunately, the academy, whose sign she'd glimpsed when walking with Mary and Alice, had proved to focus solely on refining metals and the subsequent workings. The good gentlemen had known less than she about gold mining in Central East Africa. Despite reading late into the night, she knew virtually nothing about the subject.

Alathea glanced at Augusta, snuggled on her other side with Rose propped on her lap. At least Augusta was happy, unconcerned with mining gold. 'How's Rose?'

'Rose is good.' Augusta looked at Rose's face,

then turned her once more to the window. 'She's seeing more of the city – it's crowded and noisy, but she feels safe in here with me and you.'

Alathea smiled, closing her hand around the small fingers snuggled trustingly into hers. 'That's good. Rose is growing up – she'll be a big girl soon.'

'But not yet.' Augusta looked into her face. 'Do you think Miss Helm will be all better when we get back?'

Miss Helm had developed the sniffles, which was why Alathea had Augusta with her. 'I'm sure Miss Helm will be recovered by tomorrow, but you and Rose must be very good with her this evening.'

'Oh, we will.' Augusta turned Rose's face to hers. 'We'll be specially good. We won't even say she has to read to us before bed.'

'I'll come and read to you, poppet.'

'But you have to go to the ball.'

Alathea stroked Augusta's hair. 'I'll come and read to you first – I can go on later in the other carriage.'

'I say!' Jeremy jerked upright, staring out of the window. 'Look at *that*!'

Alathea did – it took a moment before she realized what she was looking at. 'It's a pedestrian curricle – at least, I suppose that's what it is.'

She'd heard of the contraptions. Both she and Jeremy leaned close to the window, with Augusta pressing between; they all watched the gentleman in a natty checkered coat balanced precariously above the large wheel weave in and out of the traffic until he disappeared from view.

'Well!' Eyes alight, Jeremy sank back.

Alathea looked at his face. 'No.'

Her tone was absolute; Jeremy's face fell. 'But, Allie – just think—'

'I am – I'm thinking of your mother.'

'I wouldn't fall off – I'd be extra specially careful.'

Alathea met his eye. 'Just like you were extra specially careful when I allowed you to drive the gig?'

'I only got tipped in the river – and anyway, that was old Dobbins's fault.'

Alathea held her tongue. The hackney rolled on, taking them back into the fashionable district. As they turned into Mount Street, she glanced again at Jeremy's face. He was still dreaming of the dangerous contraption; she knew he wouldn't let go of his dream until he'd experienced it, or something worse. He was adventurous, the sort who simply had to try things out. It was a compulsion she understood.

'Pedestrian curricles have been around for some years.' Her musing comment had Jeremy turning, his eyes lighting. She met his bright gaze. 'I'll ask your mama. Perhaps Folwell can find one—'

'Whoopee!'

'On one condition.'

Jeremy stopped bouncing on the seat, but his eyes still glowed. 'What condition?'

'That you promise not to use it in town at all,

211

but only once we're back at Morwellan Park.'
Where the lawns were thick and cushioning.

Jeremy considered for only a moment. 'All right.
I promise.'

Alathea nodded as the carriage rocked to a stop
before Morwellan House. 'Very well. I'll speak with
your mama.'

Propping up the wall at yet another ball, Alathea
stifled a yawn. She blinked her eyes wide, struggling to keep them open; she'd spent the past two
nights reading into the small hours after the rest
of the household was abed. It was the only time
she had to herself to wade through the tomes she'd
found on Africa.

Central East Africa, however, continued to elude
her. What little she could find on the region was
largely speculative, and exceedingly scant on detail.

A familiar head of burnished chestnut hove into
sight above the masses. The most peculiar thrill
shot through her; she immediately looked for cover.
There was not a palm or shadowy alcove anywhere
near. Besides, that might not be wise. Getting
trapped with him in the shadows was likely to
scramble her wits.

Beneath her skirts, she bent her knees and sank
just enough so that she was no longer so readily
detected by her height. Through gaps in the
horrendous crush, she caught glimpses of Gabriel
as he prowled the room.

For some peculiar reason, at least viewing him

from a distance, he seemed like a different man. She could see, appreciate, aspects of him she hadn't truly noticed before, like the perfection of his restrained elegance, and the subtle aura of leashed power that cloaked his tall frame. And his reserve, that distance, apparently unbreachable, that he maintained between himself and the world.

He was bored – truly bored. She could see why Celia and the ladies of the ton despaired. They were right in thinking he didn't see them at all; from the way his face was set, the steadiness of his gaze, she would have wagered Morwellan Park that he was thinking more of Central East Africa than of a glittering ballroom in Mayfair.

One lady braved his detachment and put her hand on his sleeve. He smiled, urbanely charming; gracefully, he lifted her hand and bowed over it. Straightening, he exchanged a light word, some quip to set the lady laughing, hoping . . . only to be disappointed as with no more than that superficiality, he smoothly moved on.

He was a master at sliding through a crowd, refusing to be anchored, ineffably polite, arrogantly assured, and utterly impossible.

'Alathea! Good gracious, my dear – what peculiar fetish do you have with walls?'

Abruptly straightening, Alathea looked around – into Celia Cynster's startled eyes. 'I was . . . just easing my legs.'

Celia gave her a hard, inherently maternal stare, but was distracted by a glimpse of her firstborn through the crowd. '*There* he is! I made him promise to attend – he's been to hardly any balls this entire Season – well, only family affairs. How on earth does he expect to find a wife?'

'I don't think securing a wife is uppermost in his mind.'

Celia nearly pouted. 'Well, he had better get started on the matter – he's not getting any younger.'

Alathea kept her lips sealed.

'Lady Hendricks has been dropping hints that her daughter Emily might suit.'

An image of the lovely Miss Hendricks popped into Alathea's mind. The young lady was sweet, modest, and excessively quiet. 'Don't you think she's a little too timid?'

'Of course she's too timid! Rupert wouldn't know what to do with her – and she certainly wouldn't know what to do with *him*.'

Alathea hid a smile. 'Are you really entertaining any hope that some lady will be able to influence Rupert? He's the least easy to influence person I know.'

Celia sighed. 'Believe me, my dear, the *right* lady could do a great deal with Rupert, because, you see, he'd let her.'

'Lady Alathea!'

Blinking, Alathea refocused on Mary and Alice, strolling with Heather and Eliza ahead of her on the lawns. It was clearly not they who had called.

Looking around, she discovered two blond beauties rushing to catch her up. Both held on to elegant bonnets, ribbons streaming in the breeze; profusions of golden ringlets danced on their shoulders.

Recognizing the twins, Alathea halted. She'd been introduced to them at a ball, but they hadn't had a chance for any lengthy chat.

Gaining her side, the twins waved at their cousins, then turned beaming smiles upon her as they flanked her. Alathea got the distinct impression she'd been captured.

'We wondered if we might speak with you,' one began.

Alathea smiled, a shrewd suspicion of what was to come dawning in her mind. 'You'll have to take pity on me – I can't remember which of you is which.'

'I'm Amelia,' the one who'd spoken testified.

'And I'm Amanda,' the other said, making it sound like a confession. 'We wondered if you'd mind giving us your opinion.'

'On what subject?'

'Well, you've known Gabriel and Lucifer since they were young. We've decided that the only way we'll be able to escape them and find our own husbands is for them to get married, so we wanted to ask if you could give us any pointers.'

'Any hints as to who might be suitable—'

'Or characteristics to avoid, like being hen-brained.'

'Although that does narrow the candidates.'

215

Alathea looked from one bright face to the other – they were earnest, eager, and totally serious. She stifled a gurgle of laughter. 'You want to marry them off so they'll no longer be in your way?'

'So they'll no longer guard us like the crown jewels!'

'We've heard,' Amelia said darkly, 'that some gentlemen won't even come near us, simply because of the ructions that might ensue.'

'They actually cross us off their lists, right from the first, all because of those two!' Amanda all but shook her fist at her absent cousins. 'How on earth can we reasonably assess all the possibilities—'

'And make sure they've assessed us properly, too—'

'If our watchdogs are forever snarling—'

'And they always snarl loudest at the most *interesting* gentlemen!'

'Well,' Amanda went on, 'you know what gentlemen are like. If there's the least hurdle, then they simply won't bother exerting themselves.'

'Well, they don't need to, do they? There's always so many other ladies about for whom they need exert themselves not at all.'

'So you see, when it comes to eligibility, we're laboring under an unfair disadvantage.'

'Oh, dear.' Alathea fought to straighten her lips. 'You know, I really don't think Gabriel and Lucifer would like you to think of them as an "unfair disadvantage".' She suspected they'd be hurt, their male egos bruised.

216

Amanda kicked at the grass. 'Well, we don't plan on telling them, but that doesn't excuse the fact. They *are* a disadvantage.'

'And they are unfair, too.'

Alathea didn't argue – she thought the same. They *were* being pigheadedly unfair, refusing to see that Amanda and Amelia had any modicum of sense and, regardless of all else, had every right to choose their own husbands. The way Gabriel and Lucifer had always treated her – as an equal companion – stood in stark contrast to how they treated the twins. Although they'd always inter-posed themselves between her and any threat, they hadn't tried to stop her from encountering those threats.

Looking up, she checked her charges ambling ahead; all four girls were engrossed in some avid discussion. Alathea glanced at the twins – at Amanda, scowling at the grass as she walked, then at Amelia, softer of face but with the same deter-mined set to her chin. 'Why do you think their marrying will help?'

Amanda looked up. 'Well, it has with all the others. They're no longer a problem.'

'All you have to do is look, and you'll see it. Why, Devil was the worst, but he's so much easier now.'

'Once they marry, it's as if all their attention is focused on the lady they wed.'

'And their families.'

Alathea pondered that.

'We think we should concentrate on Gabriel first.'

'Simply because he's the elder.' Amelia glanced at Alathea. 'Do you think that's the right tack?'

Alathea considered the picture of Gabriel trying to maintain his repressive watch over the twins while simultaneously fending off ladies the twins themselves introduced. He wouldn't have time to cause her any problems. 'I think . . . that your Aunt Celia could give you some names.'

Amanda brightened. 'That's a thought.'

'There would be no need,' Alathea mused, elaborating on the picture in her mind, 'to be overly subtle. The ladies won't care as long as they gain some time by his side, and he'll know what you're up to from the first, so there's no need to be careful on that count.'

Amelia stopped dead. 'He'll be trapped.' She swung to face Alathea and Amanda, her eyes alight. 'He won't be able to escape—'

'Except' – Amanda concluded with great relish – 'by leaving us alone.'

Hookhams Lending Library in Bond Street was Alathea's port of call the next morning. Unfortunately, their section on Africa was almost non-existent. Nevertheless, she borrowed all four books; old and rather tattered, they held out little promise. Juggling them under her arm, she stepped down to the pavement. The biggest book slipped – her shoe skidded off the last step—

'Careful!'

Hard hands gripped her arms and righted her.

218

Jerking her head up, Alathea stared – into Lucifer's face. She swallowed her sigh of relief, and struggled to calm her thudding heart. For one moment, with the sun behind him, she'd thought him his brother. 'Ah . . .'

'Here – give me those.'

He didn't, of course, give her any choice. 'Oh – yes!' Alathea drew in a quick breath. 'Have you been riding this morning?'

He looked at her. 'In the park? No. Why?'

She shrugged. 'I just wondered . . . I'd love to go for a ride, but it's so impossible here – only being allowed to amble in the park.'

'If you want to ride' – he tucked her books under one arm and fell in beside her – 'you'll need to organize an excursion to the country.'

Alathea grimaced. 'I may as well wait until we return home.' Her only hope was to keep him talking, to hold his attention so he didn't glance at the books. Africa was an unusual topic, certainly an odd one for her to be studying in depth. Given that Lucifer shared Gabriel's house, and she knew how they tossed tidbits and observations back and forth . . . she drew in a breath. 'But the Season's still got weeks and weeks to go.'

'Indeed, and those weeks are crammed with more balls than ever.' Lucifer frowned at the pavement. 'And now here's Gabriel threatening to eschew all but compulsory family events.'

'Oh? Why?'

'The damned twins have gone on the offensive.'

'Offensive? What do you mean?'

'Last night, they swanned up to Gabriel on three separate occasions with a different lady each time, and cornered him.'

Alathea wished she'd seen it. 'Couldn't he get away?'

'Not easy with one of the twins hanging on his arm and refusing to let go.'

'Oh, dear.'

'Oh, dear, indeed. You know what will happen, don't you?'

She looked at him questioningly.

'He'll wash his hands of the hussies.'

'Leaving you in the firing line.'

Lucifer stopped dead. 'Good God.'

She managed to keep him grumbling about the twins all the way to where her carriage waited. Deftly dropping a kiss on his cheek, she snagged her books from under his arm.

He frowned at her. 'What was that for?'

'Just for being you.' Safe in the carriage, the books on the seat beside her, she smiled gloriously.

He humphed, shut the carriage door, and waved her away.

She was still smiling when she crossed the threshold of Morwellan House; she nodded brightly to Crisp as he held the door. Stacking her books on the table beneath the mirror, she reached up to remove her bonnet.

'There you are, dear.'

Serena stood in the drawing-room doorway. Placing her hat on top of the books, Alathea crossed the hall. 'Do we have guests?' she whispered.

'No, no. I just wanted to speak with you.' Serena stepped back into the drawing room. 'It's about your father.'

'Oh.' Following her and shutting the door, Alathea raised her brows.

'He's in one of his states.' Serena raised her hands helplessly. 'You know – under the weather but not ill.'

'Has anything happened?'

'Not today. He was a little quiet when he came in yesterday, but he didn't say anything. You know he would normally be at White's by now, but instead he's sitting in the library.'

They looked at each other, concern mirrored in their faces. Then Alathea nodded. 'I'll go and speak with him.'

Serena smiled. 'Thank you – he always listens to you.'

Alathea hugged her stepmother. 'He always listens to you, too, but we talk about different things.'

Her smile strengthening, Serena returned the hug. 'Have you learned anything more about this promissory note?'

Alathea nodded. 'I think we've found a way – a legal way – to have the note declared invalid, but I don't want to get anyone's hopes up yet.'

221

'That's probably wise. Just tell us when we're free.'

They exchanged quick smiles, then Alathea headed for the library.

The door opened noiselessly; she slipped in, noting that the curtains were open, the room bright, not shrouded in gloom. A good sign. While her father did not make a habit of succumbing to the blue devils, he had, she knew, been inwardly berating himself over the wretched promissory note. He'd put on a brave face for her sake and Serena's, but he would feel the sense of failure, of self-reproach, deeply.

Sitting in his favorite armchair, the earl was looking out over the back lawn. Mary and Alice were cutting roses, each girl as delicately beautiful as the blooms they laid in their baskets. Beyond them, Charlie was teaching Jeremy the rudiments of cricket while Augusta and Miss Helm were seated on a rug in the sunshine, reading a book. The garden was enclosed by stone walls, visible here and there between trees and thick bushes. The scene could have been a painting depicting fashionable family life, but it wasn't a figment of anyone's imagination – it was real, and it was theirs.

Empowering certainty filling her, Alathea touched her father's shoulder. 'Papa?'

So engrossed had he been, he hadn't known she was there. He looked up, then his lips curved ruefully. 'Good morning, my dear.'

Catching her hand, he squeezed it; he continued

to hold it as she sat on the arm of his chair. Alathea leaned her shoulder against his, comforted by the solidity beneath his coat. 'What is it?'

He sighed, the sound deep and defeated. 'I really hoped you'd be wrong about that company – that the Central East Africa Gold Company would ultimately turn out to be legitimate. That I hadn't made yet another mistake.'

He paused; Alathea held his hand firmly and waited.

'But you and Wiggs were right. It was all a hum. Chappie I met at White's yesterday told me so. He was from those parts – Central East Africa. He knew the company. Condemned it as a racket set up to gull simpletons into parting with their brass.' He grimaced. 'I could hardly disagree.'

'You couldn't have known . . .' Alathea blinked. 'This man, who was he?'

'Sailor fellow – a Captain something. Didn't catch his last name.'

'What did he look like?'

At the sudden tension in her voice, the earl turned to meet her gaze. 'He was of middle height, rather portly. Had great grizzled whiskers down both cheeks. His clothes marked him as a seaman, senior rank – there's always a nautical air to such men.' He searched Alathea's face. 'Why? Is he important?'

Alathea reined in her excitement. 'He could be. Wiggs and I think there's a legal way of overturning the promissory note, but we need to learn more about the company's business. A man like this captain could be very helpful.' She gripped her father's hand. 'Was he with anyone you knew?'

Her father shook his head. 'No. But if it's important, I can ask around.'

'Do, Papa – it could be *very* important. And if you should stumble across him again, promise me you'll bring him home.'

Her father's brows quirked, but he nodded. 'Right, then. I suppose I'd better get on to White's and see if I can track him down.'

'Oh, yes!' Alathea bounced to her feet as he rose. 'This could help us *enormously*, Papa. Thank you!' She swooped at him and kissed him on the cheek.

Catching her within one arm, he hugged her. 'Thank *you*, my dear.' He looked into her face, then placed a gentle kiss on her forehead. 'Don't ever think I don't appreciate all you've done – I don't know what I did right to deserve you. I can only be glad you're mine.'

Alathea blinked rapidly. 'Oh, Papa!' She hugged him quickly, then broke away, glancing through the window. 'I must get Jeremy off to his lessons or he'll play cricket all day.'

Still blinking, she hurried out.

CHAPTER 10

That evening at Lady Castlereagh's ball, Alathea found herself plagued by gentlemen. With but little help from her, the number of mature bachelors who considered her an agreeable dance partner had been steadily growing as the Season progressed. Despite Celia's conviction that she hugged the walls, she was too astute to do so constantly. True anonymity meant doing nothing to make herself remarkable; she therefore duly danced and waltzed, not every dance but enough to ensure no one saw need to comment on her abstention.

Indeed, she enjoyed waltzing, although there were few men tall enough to meet her requirements. Yet despite the hurdle of her unusual height, the ranks of her admirers, as Serena insisted on terming them, had somehow swollen to the legion.

Which made life exceedingly awkward when, after two dances, she wanted to slink into the shadows, the better to consider her current difficulties. The principal one was present, garbed in severe walnut-black, his locks burnished, his manner ineffably urbane. He'd extended himself to dance the same two dances she had, but was now ambling, deliberately aimlessly, through the crowd. If he could dispense with the need to do the pretty and converse, she felt it only fair that she could, too.

'I'm afraid, dear sirs' – she beamed a smile at the gentlemen surrounding her – 'that I must leave you for the present. One of my stepsisters . . .' With an airy wave, she led them to believe she'd been summoned across the room. As joining Mary and Alice meant braving a gaggle of youthful damsels, none of the gentlemen offered to accompany her. They bowed and begged for promises of her return; she smiled and glided away from them.

The crush was unbelievable. Lady Castlereagh was one of the senior hostesses – her invitations could not be declined. That, Alathea suspected, accounted for the presence of most of the Cynsters, Gabriel included. Using the crowd to her advantage, she made her way to a narrow embrasure occupied by a pedestal topped by a bust of Wellington. She took refuge in the lee of the pedestal, screened from at least half the room.

Thankfully also screened from some of the noise – it was hard to hear her own thoughts. Across the room, she saw Gabriel, with obvious reluctance, relieve Lucifer of his watch on the twins. Taking up a position almost directly opposite her, Gabriel looked wary.

Alathea grinned. She searched the throng for the twins. Even using Gabriel's gaze for direction, she still couldn't see them. With an expectant sigh, she settled back, almost against the wall but not quite. Anyone seeing her would assume she was waiting for some gentleman or a youthful charge to return to her side.

Thus concealed, she settled to ponder how to tell her knight on a white charger where he should look for their relief. She'd issued the summons; he'd come galloping to her aid – now she was stuck with him and his notion of rewards. Dealing with him further was going to prove difficult, but she couldn't proceed without him.

Coming up with the captain, stumbling upon him in the crowd on a dance floor, was beyond unlikely – his sort stuck to the clubs, not the park or the ton's entertainments. The captain was effectively out of her reach. She didn't dare pin all her hopes on her father appearing one day for luncheon with the captain in tow.

She had to tell Gabriel about the captain, and as soon as possible. Who knew how long a seagoing captain would remain ashore? He might already have sailed, but she refused to consider the possibility. Fate couldn't be that cruel. But how to tell Gabriel in safety?

A letter had seemed possible until she'd drafted one. Even though she'd included her father's description of the captain verbatim, the letter lacked life, and reeked of cowardice. She couldn't even sign it other than as 'The Countess.' Instead of sending it off, she'd torn it up and resumed her pondering.

If she didn't see Gabriel face to face, she would have no way of knowing how he reacted to her news, nor could she question him over what he'd learned – she was quite sure he wouldn't have been idle in the five days since they'd last met.

At the Burlington Hotel.

The mere name sent a wave of uncertainty through her; she immediately blocked it off. She couldn't afford to let her emotions rule her, or dictate her moves. What had Gabriel learned? Had Crowley done anything more? These were questions to which she needed answers; she would get answers only if she met Gabriel face to face, of that she was absolutely sure.

But the thought of being private, alone with him in the dark, made her shiver – and not with dread. The fact only increased her wariness and made her question her arguments. Were they merely rationalizations?

Standing in the pedestal's shadow, she examined, dissected, and reassembled her thoughts – and got nowhere. The situation irked; her inability to make up her mind rasped her temper.

Then he moved. She'd been watching him from the corner of her eye. As he forcefully handed the twins' watch back to Lucifer, then stepped into the crowd, she straightened. A clamp slowly closed about her lungs. There was, she told herself, no reason he should stroll her way, no reason he even knew she was there.

She'd underestimated the power of her cap.

It drew him like a lodestone. He cleaved through the crowd so efficiently that, once she realized she was indeed his target, she didn't have time to beat a retreat. He halted beside her.

Trapped, she raised her chin and fixed him with a glare. 'Don't say a word.'

His eyes held hers for a pregnant moment; she inwardly quivered, and told herself he couldn't see through her disguise. That he'd never see the woman who'd lain naked in his arms in the lady who now stood before him.

Lips thinning, Gabriel nodded curtly. 'There's obviously no need, although I can't see why you bother – your hair will go gray soon enough.'

Alathea's eyes flashed, but instead of ripping up at him, she smiled. Acidly. 'I'm quite sure you'll have gray hairs aplenty if you persist in acting like a dog with a bone over your young cousins.'

'You know nothing about the matter, so don't start.'

'I know the twins are perfectly capable of taking care of themselves.'

He snorted derisively. 'Which shows how much you know.'

'I would have thought' – her tone had him tensing – 'that any females capable of routing one of the Cynsters, capable of detecting the chink in his armor and plotting and acting to press their advantage, and succeeding, would be thought capable of managing even the ton's most notorious rakes.' Her gaze slid around to his face. 'Don't you?'

Gabriel felt his eyes narrow; his temper surged. He would infinitely have preferred impassivity, but with her, that always seemed beyond him. He transfixed her with a glittering glance. '*You* told them.'

He didn't need the artful lift of her brows to tell him that was the truth.

'They approached me with their problem – I merely made an observation.'

'*You* are the cause of their current obsession with finding me a suitable bride.'

'Now, now' – she wagged a finger at him – 'you know perfectly well I couldn't be responsible for that. You're the one who's yet to marry. You're the one in need of a wife. The twins are merely trying to be helpful.'

What he muttered in response was far from polite; Alathea merely smiled. 'They're trying to be helpful in exactly the same way you're trying to help them.'

'And what way is that?'

She looked him in the eye. 'Misguidedly.'

He blinked.

When he didn't immediately respond, she looked away. 'I rather wondered how you'd react if the shoe was on the other foot.'

'You knew damned well how I'd react.' He gritted

his teeth. 'You only suggested it to plague me.' Her lips quirked, very briefly but enough to set his temper soaring. 'I know Lucifer attempted to explain the need for our watch on the twins – he clearly didn't succeed. So perhaps a demonstration's in order' – he lifted his gaze to the cap covering her soft hair – 'to drive the point through your demonstrably thick skull.'

Her head whipped around. She was frowning. He shifted closer, crowding her into the nook between the pedestal and the alcove wall. Clamping one hand on the pedestal's top, he caged her into the small space.

Meeting her gaze, fell intent in his, he was surprised to see her eyes flare – surprised to see how far into the gap between the pedestal and the wall she'd backed herself.

Her gaze falling to his chest, mere inches from hers, Alathea swallowed and wrenched her gaze back up to his face. She fought against the urge to press one hand to her breast in a vain effort to calm her leaping heart. *Oh, God!* In situations like this, she would customarily slap a hand to his chest and shove – she wouldn't hesitate, wouldn't stop to consider any possible impropriety. And although her strength couldn't possibly shift him, if she shoved, he'd move.

But she didn't dare touch him.

Couldn't guarantee what her hands would do if she did.

Gracious heavens! What on earth was she to do?

She could already see puzzlement dawning in his eyes.

Senses reeling – he was far too close! – she stiffened her spine, drew herself up to her full height, and made a passable attempt at looking down her nose at him. 'I do wish you'd *think*!' Her gaze locked with his, she did – frantically. 'Protecting them from real threats – threats that actually materialize – is all very well, but in this case, your' – she gestured, using her wave to make him lean back – 'constant *hovering* is actually limiting their opportunities. It's not fair.'

'Fair?' He snorted. To her immense relief, he eased back, letting go of the pedestal and turning to glance to where she imagined the twins must be. 'I can't see where fairness comes into it.'

'Can't you?' Able to breathe again, she dragged in a breath. 'Just think. You never used to stop me from . . . oh, riding neck or nothing with you and Alasdair – you wouldn't stop me doing it now.'

'You ride like the devil. There's no need to stop you – you'd be in no danger.'

'Ah, but if there was something dangerous in my path – if, for instance, I'd jumped a fence into a field with an enraged bull. Wouldn't you come racing to save me?'

The look he shot her was disgusted – disgusted she'd even asked. 'Of course I would.' After a moment, he added more softly, 'You know I would.'

She inclined her head, a very odd knot of emotion in her stomach; as children, he'd always been the first to interpose himself between her and any danger. 'Yes – and that's precisely what I mean about the way you're suffocating the twins.'

Deliberately, she fell silent. She sensed his reluctance; it poured from him in waves. He didn't want to hear her theory, didn't want to canvass the possibility that he, his brother, and his cousins might be wrong, might be over-reacting. Because if he did, he'd have to rein in his Cynster protectiveness, and that, she well knew, was very hard to do.

Eventually, he shot her a far from encouraging glance. 'Why suffocating?'

She looked away, across the sea of heads. 'Because you won't let them spread their wings. Rather than letting them ride wild, stepping in only if they're threatened, you're making sure they're not threatened in the first place by ensuring they never ride at all.' He opened his mouth; she held up a placating hand. 'A perfectly valid approach in other contexts, but in this arena, it means you're blocking off all chance of their learning to ride – all chance of their succeeding. Well' – she gestured across the room – 'just look at them.' She couldn't see them, but he could. 'They may be surrounded by ten gentlemen—'

'Twenty.'

'How ever many!' Her terse tone had him meeting her gaze. 'Can't you see they're the *wrong* men?'

Gabriel looked at the teeming masses around

the twins, and tried to tell himself he couldn't see it at all.

'Can you seriously imagine any of those innocuous gentlemen married to the twins? Or is it more accurate to say you – all of you – have been carefully avoiding imagining the twins married at all?'

She was like his conscience, whispering in his ear. Like his conscience, he couldn't ignore her. 'I'll think about it,' he growled, unwilling to even meet her eyes. All he would see was the truth, his own truth reflected back at him.

He dragged in a breath, chest swelling against the usual constriction, the constriction he always felt when around her. Lord, she made him uncomfortable. Even now, when they weren't tearing strips off each other but having what was, for them, a rational discussion, his insides felt scored, like claws had dragged down from his throat over his chest, then locked about his heart, his gut.

She'd shaken him, too. Again. Why the devil had she looked at him like that – eyes wide with *what?* – when he'd backed her against the wall? The sight had rocked him; even now, his skin was prickling just because she was close.

His impulse, as always, was to verbally lash at her, to drive her away even though, if she was in the same room, he would compulsively head for her side. Stupid. He wished he could tell himself that he disliked her, but he didn't. He never had. Keeping his gaze from her ridiculous cap – the sight would assuredly set him off – he drew in another breath, scanning the nearer guests, about to bow and excuse himself—

He narrowed his eyes. 'What the devil . . . ?'

The muttered question went unanswered as Lord Coleburn, Mr Henry Simpkins and Lord Falworth, all smiling easily, strolled up.

'There you are, my dear lady.' Falworth swept Alathea an elegant bow.

'We thought you might need rescuing,' Henry Simpkins stated, his gaze sweeping over Gabriel before coming to rest on Alathea's face. 'From the crush, don't you know?'

'It is indeed horrendous,' Alathea smoothly returned. She waited for Gabriel to excuse himself and move on; instead, he remained planted like an oak at her side. With Wellington immediately to her left, she couldn't escape; her would-be cavaliers were forced to deploy themselves in a semicircle before her and Gabriel. As if they were on trial. Heaving an inward sigh, she introduced him, quite sure the others would know him at least by reputation.

That last became rapidly apparent. By dint of various subtle quips, Coleburn, Simpkins and Falworth all made it plain they thought Gabriel would find better entertainment elsewhere. Alathea was not at all surprised when he shrugged their suggestions aside, looking for all the world as if he was fighting a yawn. He probably was. She certainly was. If she'd wanted to stand by the wall and converse with a gaggle of gentlemen,

Coleburn, Simpkins and Falworth would not have been her choice. She would rather converse with the Devil himself, presently on her right; at least, with him, she was never in danger of mentally drifting away and losing track of the conversation.

Despite the lack of stimulation, she was distinctly relieved that Gabriel did not decide to enliven proceedings by surgically dissecting Simpkins, who seemed intent on putting himself first in line with his studied and not-quite-nonchalant quips. Lady Castlereagh would not appreciate blood on her ballroom floor.

'And so Mrs Dalrymple insisted we ride on, but the oxer at the end of the fourth field forced her to retire. Well' – Falworth spread his hands – 'what could I do? We had to do a Brummel and take refuge in a nearby farmhouse.'

The other gentlemen seemed mildly intrigued by Falworth's description of his aborted outing with the Cottesmore. All except Gabriel, who was doing a remarkable imitation of a marble statue. An utterly meaningless smile on her lips, Alathea inwardly sighed and let Falworth's words flow past her.

Beyond their little circle, a tall gentleman, as tall as Gabriel, strolled nonchalantly by. His idle gaze passed over them, then halted. He stopped, noting Gabriel, then his gaze slid back to her.

The gentleman smiled; Alathea nearly blinked. Charming did as charming was, but this was something rather more. Her lips had curved in reply before she'd even thought. The gentleman's smile deepened; he inclined his head. His gaze on her face, he approached with the same easy, loose-limbed prowl that characterized the Cynsters and, Alathea surmised, certain of their peers.

Gabriel's reaction was immediate and intense. Alathea barely had time to consider the why before the wherefore was bowing before her.

'Chillingworth, my dear. I don't believe we've met.' Gracefully straightening, he flicked a glance at Gabriel. 'But I'm sure I can prevail upon Cynster here to do the honors.'

Gabriel let his silence stretch until it was just this side of insulting before grudgingly saying, 'Lady Alathea Morwellan – Chillingworth, earl of.'

Arching a warning brow at him, Alathea gave Chillingworth her hand. 'A pleasure, my lord. Are you enjoying her ladyship's offerings?' There was a string quartet laboring somewhere, and a busy cardroom.

'To be honest, I've found the evening a mite dull.' Releasing her hand, Chillingworth smiled. 'A little too tame for my liking.'

Alathea raised a brow. 'Indeed?'

'Hmm. I count myself lucky to have spotted you in this crowd.' His gaze was filled with appreciation, especially of her height. His lips curved. 'Fortunate, indeed.'

Alathea stifled a gurgle of laughter; beside her, Gabriel stiffened. Eyes dancing, she essayed, 'I'm engaged in planning a ball for my stepmother.

Tell me, what entertainments would best entice gentlemen such as yourself?'

The look Gabriel shot her was unmitigatingly censorious; Alathea ignored it.

So did Chillingworth. 'Your fair presence would greatly entice me.'

She met his gaze with a blank look. 'Yes, but beyond that?'

He nearly choked trying to swallow his laugh. 'Ah . . . *beyond* that?'

'Come now, Chillingworth. I'm sure, if you concentrate, you'll remember what it is that brings you to these affairs.' Gabriel's languid drawl deflected the earl's attention.

Chillingworth's brows rose. Leaning one arm on the pedestal's top, he frowned. 'Let me think.'

Gabriel snorted softly.

'Not hordes.' Catching Alathea's eye, Chillingworth continued, 'I can't think why the cachet of exclusivity isn't more widely appreciated.'

His gaze on the guests shifting and shuffling before them, causing the three other gentlemen, now relegated to the outer ranks, to have to give way constantly, then struggle back, Gabriel humphed in agreement. 'God knows why they imagine literally rubbing shoulders all evening to be fun.'

'Because no hostess is game to call the ton's bluff, so we're all left to suffer.' Alathea swept the gathering with a resigned eye.

'At least,' Gabriel muttered, 'we can see reasonably well. It must be worse for those who can't.'

'I'm sure it is,' Alathea returned. 'Mary, Alice and Serena seem to spend half their time trying to find their way about.'

Chillingworth had been watching them, taking in this exchange. 'Hmm. As to other requirements, while gentlemen such as I – and Cynster here – might be partial to sonatas and airs in their place, having a set of screeching violins set up in a corner merely constitutes unwarranted distraction.'

'Distraction?' Alathea glanced at him. 'Distraction from what?'

The direct question made Chillingworth blink. He slid a glance at Gabriel.

Alathea's lips quirked. 'From your customary pursuits?'

Chillingworth straightened; Gabriel merely threw her a resigned glance. 'Don't mind her,' he advised Chillingworth. 'Although perhaps I should warn you it only gets worse.'

Alathea favored him with a haughty look. 'You can't talk.'

Glancing from one to the other, Chillingworth stated, 'You know each other.'

Alathea waved dismissively. 'From birth – our association was decided for us, not by us.'

Gabriel's brows rose. 'Nicely put.'

The puzzled look in Chillingworth's eyes didn't entirely evaporate, but he settled beside Alathea again. 'Where were we?'

'The amenities you prefer for your customary pursuits.'

Alathea was enjoying herself; both Chillingworth and Gabriel sent repressive glances her way.

'Very well.' Chillingworth accepted the challenge. 'Not a dance schedule that includes only two waltzes. Apropos of that, my dear, I believe the orchestra is about to make itself useful and indulge us with a waltz.' Straightening, he smiled, both charming and challenging. 'Can I tempt you to brave the floor with me?'

Alathea returned the smile, perfectly ready to take up his challenge, equally ready to give Gabriel a chance to slope off. They'd been in each other's company without descending into cutting sarcasm for nearly half an hour; there was no sense in stretching their luck.

She held out her hand. 'Indeed, my lord – I'd be delighted.'

Gabriel gritted his teeth, held his breath, and willed himself to stillness. God knew, he didn't want to waltz with Alathea – the mere thought sent itching heat washing over his skin like a rash. But . . . he didn't want her waltzing with Chillingworth. Or anyone else, but Chillingworth was, typically, the worst choice she could have made of all the gentlemen in the room. Not that she hadn't chosen quite deliberately; she might be twenty-nine but she still possessed a healthy vein of minx-like tendencies, victim to a strain of considered recklessness.

He watched as Chillingworth led her to the floor, then took her lightly in his arms. She laughed at some quip and they began to revolve; as they

240

whirled down the room, Gabriel inwardly snorted. There she went, tempting fate with her eyes wide open.

Shifting his gaze, he saw Lucifer, still on guard but chatting with two friends while the twins danced. Gabriel located them, each in the arms of a suitably innocuous gentleman.

Alathea's words rang in his head; he inwardly humphed. He'd think about it. His gaze drifted over the dancers, and settled again.

The waltz was nearly over before Alathea identified the peculiar sensation afflicting her. It had started not when Chillingworth first took her into his arms but later, as they'd commenced their second revolution around the room.

She'd enjoyed the waltz. Despite his predilections, Chillingworth was charming, witty, and a gentleman to his toes. He was very like Lucifer and his Cynster cousins; she'd treated him as she would them – he'd responded in like vein, with a bantering air. She'd relaxed.

That was when the other sensation had made itself felt, like an intent gaze fixed directly between her shoulder blades. Its very intensity was what finally identified its source.

When Chillingworth gallantly returned her to the spot beside Wellington's bust, she was smiling and quietly simmering.

One look at Gabriel's face, into his hard hazel eyes, and her temper surged. She'd successfully reached through his armor to prick him about the twins; he was paying her back by watching her instead, simply to discompose her. Sliding into the space beside him, she muttered, 'Don't you have anything better to do?'

He looked at her blankly. 'No.'

It was impossible to shift him, so there he stayed; by the end of the evening, she was ready to commit murder. But in the carriage home, she had to bottle up her spleen and listen encouragingly to Mary and Alice prattle happily of their doings. To her considerable satisfaction, both had found their feet and were attracting the right sort of attention. As they left the carriage and climbed the steps to the front door, Alathea exchanged a speculative glance with Serena. Their campaign was progressing well.

She was doing less well. By the time she gained her room and Nellie had shut the door behind her, she felt like a human volcano.

'One of these days,' she informed Nellie through clenched teeth, 'he's going to come up to me when I have a dangerous weapon in my hands, and then I'll end in the Tower, and it'll all be his fault!'

'The Tower?' Nellie was totally confused.

'Imprisoned for *murdering* him!' Alathea let the reins of her temper fly free. 'You should have seen him! You can't imagine!' She fell to pacing before the hearth. 'He was more impossible than even I would have believed, even for him. Just because I told him – and convinced him, too – that he was wrong to so suffocate the twins, he left off suffocating them, and suffocated me, instead!'

'Suffocated . . . ?'

'Watched over me as if I was his sister! Tried to menace and chase away any entertaining gentleman.' She swung about, her skirts shushing furiously. 'At least he didn't succeed with Chillingworth, thank God! But all through supper – !' Words failed her; she threw a rapier-edged glance at the door. 'I have never felt so much like a bone with a large dog, teeth-bared, standing over me. And you should have seen his performance over the second waltz! I'd already danced the first with Chillingworth, and saw no reason why I shouldn't indulge him with the second as well – he is nicely tall, which is such a blessing in a waltz – but Gabriel behaved like a . . . a bloody archbishop! You'd have thought he'd never waltzed with a lady himself in his life!'

Arms folded, she paced on. 'It wasn't as if he wanted to waltz with me himself – oh, no! He's never waltzed with me in his life! He just wanted to be difficult! And he's so hard to counter! I sincerely commisserate with the twins, and can only be glad if I've shaken him to his senses over them.'

She scowled. 'Except that he now seems focused on me.' She pondered that, then shrugged. 'Presumably he was only doing it for tonight, just to pay me back. Whatever, I've had quite enough of the arrogant ways of Mr Gabriel Cynster.'

'Who?'

Alathea plonked herself down on the stool before her dressing table. 'Rupert. Gabriel's his nickname.'

Nellie let down her hair and started brushing it. Alathea let the familiar, rhythmic tug-and-release soothe her. Her mind reverted to the problem that had earlier consumed her, the problem she'd largely forgotten in the heat engendered by Gabriel's behavior in the ballroom.

When she'd been Alathea Morwellan.

That had been bad enough. His behavior when she was the countess seemed even further beyond her control.

'This has gone on long enough – I need to take charge.'

'You do?'

'Hmm. All very well for him to take the reins, but that's clearly too dangerous. It's *my* problem – he's *my* knight – I summoned him. He's going to have to learn to do my bidding, not the other way about. I'm going to have to make that point plain.'

She – the countess – was going to have to see him again.

Alathea frowned. 'I need to tell him about the captain.'

What happened at the Burlington would *not* happen again. That had simply been an opportunistic event, a combination of location, opportunity and elation – and her weakness – that he'd sensed, seen and seized.

She'd let him seize. She wouldn't, she swore, be so weak this time. Be so easily swept off her feet and onto a bed.

No. But it was senseless to take any chances.

'I can't risk another meeting in daylight.'

'Why not? He can't see your face even then, not if you wear that mask under your veil.'

'True. But he'll look more closely, and there'll be enough of my face showing . . .'

He might guess. He'd seen her at close quarters frequently enough in the past weeks. His powers of observation were acute when he concentrated, and after their last meeting at the Burlington, she was quite sure he'd be concentrating on the countess. Especially if she proved intent on keeping him at a polite distance.

Yet distance, polite or otherwise, was imperative.

'I've got to meet with him again.' Frowning, she drummed her fingers on the dressing table. If she could devise a meeting where opportunity was lacking, so he got no chance to seize anything at all, she'd be safe.

'A letter for you, m'lord – er, sir.' With a flourish, Chance placed the silver salver he'd taken to wielding at every opportunity on the breakfast table at Gabriel's right.

'Thank you, Chance.' Setting aside his coffee mug, Gabriel picked up the folded sheet of heavy white parchment and looked for the letter knife.

'Oh – ah!' Chance jigged and searched his

pockets. 'Here.' He brandished a small rusty knife. 'I'll do it.'

'No, Chance, that's quite all right.' Gabriel held on to the note. 'I can manage.'

'Right-ho.' Swiping up the salver, Chance departed.

Gabriel broke the seal with his thumbnail. Lips thinning, he opened the note.

He'd been expecting it for the last four days. He was more than a trifle aggrieved that the countess had taken so long to summon him to another meeting. The delay lay like a blot on his record, an adverse reflection on his skill. At least the note had finally come.

He scanned the few lines within, then rolled his eyes to the ceiling. A *carriage*?

He sighed. Well, she had been a virgin, so what could he expect? She was plainly a novice at arranging lovers' trysts.

CHAPTER 11

It was a moonless night. The wind soughed and sighed in the trees lining the carriage drive close by the Stanhope Gate. Waiting impatiently in the shadows, Gabriel resisted the urge to shake his head.

Midnight at the Stanhope Gate was only a marginal improvement on three o'clock in the porch of St George's. The countess had been reading too many gothic novels. In this case, she'd either forgotten that the park gates were locked at sunset, or was counting on him exercising his peculiar talents on the padlock that had secured the wrought-iron gates. He'd done so and left the gates wide. It wasn't unheard of for an open gate to be forgotten.

At least there wasn't any mist, only layers of shadows spreading over the parkland, shifting and drifting with the wind. There was just enough light to see by, to make out shapes but not their detail.

In the distance, a bell tolled, the first note in the midnight chorus. He listened as the other belltowers joined in, then the count was done, and the last note died into the brooding night. Silence returned, and settled.

The rattle of a carriage wheel was his first intimation that his wait was at an end. There were carriages aplenty rolling around Mayfair, but they were far enough away to ignore. The steady rattle continued, punctuated by the clop of hooves, then the small black carriage, lamps unlit, rolled between the gate posts into the gloom of the park.

Gabriel stepped onto the verge. The coachman redirected his horses; the carriage slowed and halted. Gabriel opened the door and climbed into a darkness even denser than had prevailed in the bedchamber at the Burlington.

He sat and felt leather beneath him, and sensed a warm presence beside him.

'Mr Cynster.'

Gabriel grinned into the dark. 'Countess.'

She gasped as she landed in his lap. It took only an instant for his fingers to find her veil, and then his lips were on hers.

It was a searing kiss – he made sure of that. A kiss to steal her wits, to make her senses reel. A kiss to light her fires, and his.

Her lips softened the instant his firmed; they parted the second he traced their contours. She melted in his arms as he grew more rigid; he didn't lift his head until she was dazed and dizzy, too breathless to utter the words her whirling mind couldn't begin to form.

He hesitated only a moment, their heated breaths mingling in the dark, the rhythm of their breathing already fragmented. He sensed her yearning, sensed the swollen, parted, hungry lips less than an inch from his.

Closing the distance, he sealed her fate. And his.

This time, however, he was determined to remain in control, to orchestrate their play until the very end. He'd plotted and planned and fantasized. After he'd had his wicked way with her and treated her to the full spectrum of sensations an experienced lover could evoke, he would wager his hardwon reputation that she wouldn't wait days to return to him.

His lips on hers, he quickly dispensed with her cloak and set her veil fully back. Drawing back from their kiss, he let his fingertips linger over the delicate skin of her forehead, the arch of her brows, the sweep of her cheeks. Her jaw was firm and finely wrought, her throat long, slender . . . elegant.

At the base of her throat, her pulse beat hotly. The scooped neckline of her gown revealed the upper swells of her full breasts. His fingers traced; his memories strengthened. Need burgeoned.

Her breath shivered on his lips; she quivered in his arms.

'Your coachman. What instructions did you give?'

She drew in a shaky breath; he sensed her struggle to think. 'I told him to drive slowly around the avenue . . . until we'd finished our meeting.'

'Perfect.' Reaching up, he rapped on the carriage roof. A second later, the carriage lurched, then ponderously rolled forward.

She straightened. 'I—'

Her breath caught on a hitch as, lowering his arm, he closed his hand possessively about one breast. He kneaded and she shuddered. Nudging her head up, he took her lips again, and set himself to cast her wits to the wind.

It wasn't difficult; she put up no resistance to speak of. She seemed a natural in this sphere, a deeply sensual woman, her consciousness surrendering willingly to the moment, to the physical thrill, the sexual excitement, the indescribable delight of give and take.

At first, it was he who took and she who gave, then he mentally drew back, inwardly reasserted control, then deliberately embarked on his script, his carefully plotted plan to bind her to him with sensual chains.

His lips on hers, he reached for her laces.

Divesting her of her gown was no great feat, not to one of his extensive experience. But he accomplished the deed slowly, savoring every inch of her curves as he exposed them, much to her shivering delight.

Not that she was cold. Thick curtains sealed the carriage windows. With their heated bodies enclosed within the small space, she would be in no danger of taking a chill despite the totality of his plans. That was just as well as, with her warm weight across his thighs, her luscious curves filling his arms and her hungry lips under his, he was in no state to rework them. Tonight, fate was on his side.

Lifting her, he eased the soft gown past her hips, then set her down, the bare backs of her thighs, exposed beneath her short chemise, in direct contact with his trousers. Through their kiss, he sensed the heightening of her tension. He set out to heighten it some more.

Deepening the kiss, he held her steady, one arm about her. Closing his hand on her bare thigh, he brushed her gown down by caressing her long limbs, first down one leg, then the other. Swiping up the gown, he tossed it on the seat beside him, and caught her foot. He slipped her shoe off, surprised to note its weight. As he dispensed with the other, he realized the heels were high. Skimming his hand up one leg, he located her garter, a few inches above her knee.

He toyed with the band. On? Or off? He reviewed his plan. Her lips shifted under his; she struggled to draw breath, to surface from the fog of desire in which he was deliberately shrouding her. He stilled her with a searching, ravishing kiss, and quickly rolled her stockings down and off, sending them to join her gown.

Leaving her clad only in her silk chemise.

He drew her to him, deeper into his embrace; tipping her head back, he plundered her mouth. She responded ardently, caught up in the hot tangle of their tongues, the melding of their lips.

His quick fingers slipped the tiny buttons closing her chemise free, all the way to her navel. The instant

251

the last slipped its mooring, he closed his fist in the fine garment; pulling back from the kiss, he drew the chemise up and over her head in one movement.

'Oh!' She grasped, not the chemise, but her veil.

His steadying hand now on bare skin, he grinned into the dark. Discarding the chemise, he reached for her face, touching gently, then framing her jaw. 'Your veil's still there.' That was part of his plan, having her totally naked except for that damned veil.

Her hands fluttered; the fingers of one touched the back of his hand as he drew her face nearer. He touched her lips with his tongue and they parted; he surged in, then retreated, settling to nibble, tantalize, tease . . . until she shifted on his thighs, trying to press her own demands, unsure what those demands should be.

He knew. Urging her hands, her arms, over his shoulders, he drew her around. Clasping one bare calf, savoring the smooth skin, he drew the limb up, lifting that leg over his thighs as he turned her, then released her, leaving her, blissfully naked but for her veil, sitting astride his long thighs.

Oh, yes. Before she had time to even try to think, he reached for her face with both hands, holding her steady for an incendiary kiss, one that left them both gasping, chests heaving, bodies heated and urgent. Hers had softened; his had hardened. Their panting breaths mingled. He slid his fingers under the back of her veil, finding the pins that anchored her hair. As they rained on the floor, their lips met again. Heat welled, swelled, grew.

Her hair cascaded down her back, long strands curling on her shoulders. He kissed her long and hard, then drew back.

She tried to lean closer, to follow his lips with hers, but he closed his hands about her shoulders. 'No.' Even though he couldn't see, could only feel with his senses at full stretch, he knew she was dazed, wanting but not yet frantic, her wits disengaged but her senses still aware. 'Not yet.'

They'd only just begun.

'Sit still, and concentrate on what you feel.'

She shuddered lightly, but did as he asked. He hadn't expected an argument – she was far beyond that – yet he went slowly; he had no intention of overwhelming her – not yet.

Curving his hands about her shoulders, he trailed his fingers lightly down, over the long sweeps of her arms, over her elbows and forearms, down to her wrists, then slid his fingertips along her palms, drawing them out across her fingers. Fingertip to fingertip, he held her arms out from her sides, then let them fall.

She was mesmerized; he knew that as he reached out again, and touched her breasts. They were already swollen, the peaks hard, begging for his attention. For long, heated moments he touched only with the pads of his fingers, listening as her breathing grew increasingly ragged. Then, leaning forward, he cupped one warm mound in his hand and took the peak into his mouth.

A cry died in her throat; her body arched convulsively. He suckled, one hand closing on her knee, the other lifting her flesh to his lips. When that nipple was aching and throbbing, he changed hands and tortured the other.

Her head fell back, her hair a gossamer curtain, its end brushing her hips, her bare bottom and his knees. Her spine bowed, every nerve drew taut; like the master he was, he let them tighten, and tighten, until she couldn't breathe, until she quivered, as fragile as spun glass, then he released her breast and leaned back.

He sensed the huge, shaky breath she drew in. Leaving his hand on her knee, more to reassure than to hold her, he gave her only a moment of surcease, then lifted his hand again.

To her ribs, tracing the fine skin over the smooth bones, then trailing his fingertips down to her waist. Releasing her knee, he closed both hands about her waist, circling her almost completely. Splaying his fingers over the supple muscles in her back, he touched, stroked, caressed.

She eased a little; his lips curving in a smile she couldn't see, he let his hands slide to caress her derriere, then sent them smoothly gliding over her flanks. And away.

For one instant, he left her there, posed on his knees in her naked glory. Then he reached out and touched her again.

He splayed his hand over her taut stomach. She shuddered, but her spine was so rigid she only swayed slightly, then tensed even more as he gently kneaded. She caught her breath on a sob. 'I—'

'Don't talk.' He waited a heartbeat, then added, 'Just feel.'

He waited until her senses refocused, then removed his hand. Clasping her knees, he slid his hands up, fingers gliding over the long, taut muscles of her outer thighs, his thumbs grazing the quivering inner faces. At the tops of her thighs, he ran his thumbs over and up, following the creases between thigh and torso outward. Then he removed his hands again.

Again he waited, leaving her quivering expectantly in the dark. Then, with one hand, he reached out again.

And touched her between her widespread thighs.

Her breath shook; she quaked.

'Shh.'

He traced the swollen folds, exposed and open to him. He suspected she hadn't realized, modestly shrouded by the dark.

She realized now; she reached out – he felt her fingers brush his sleeve.

'No. Leave your hands at your sides.'

She didn't immediately obey, but as he continued to caress her, the slow, steady stroking reassured her, and she let her arms fall.

Her breathing was shallow, racing with her heart.

He didn't want to speak again, to risk breaking the spell. She was hot and wet, his fingers slick with her dew. He found the tight nubbin concealed between her folds and circled it, but that wasn't his target. He waited until she'd steadied, until she'd stabilized on a narrow ledge one step away from the peak, then zeroed in.

The long slide of his finger entering her, spearing in, inexorably penetrating and filling her softness, sent her into spasm. Every muscle locked, so tight she was shivering, every fragment of awareness focused, waiting for the final touch that would shatter her.

He didn't administer it; the time was not yet. His finger buried in her sheath he held still, blocking all awareness of the heated softness that gripped him, the supple strength of her inner muscles, the hot honey that dampened his hand, the evocative scent that wreathed his brain.

Then she stabilized again, and the peak had moved away, one step further on. He knew, but doubted she did. He started to caress her again.

How long he prolonged the delicious torture, how many times he brought her almost to the peak, then let it shift away, he didn't know, but she was wild, sobbing in her need, her fingers clenched on his arms, her lips burning his, when he finally thrust deep and let her fly.

She came apart in his arms.

Cursing the darkness that stopped him from seeing it, from reaping the reward of his expertise, he gathered her to him, letting her cling, then cradling her as she collapsed completely.

He drew her closer, sensing her heartbeat, feeling it thunder, then slow. Then she stirred.

'I want you.'

His lips curved against her hair. 'I know.'

Her breath was a soft huff against his neck as she shifted, and reached, and found him. 'How?'

Her fist closed, and he shook. 'Ah . . .'

Fingers as quick as his slipped the buttons on his waistband, brushed aside his shirt. Slim digits dipped, then stroked, caressed . . .

Words were superfluous. He drew her hips nearer, sliding his own to the edge of the seat. They met – it was she who sank down, a long-drawn sigh shattering in her throat. It was all he could do to stifle his groan as she closed hotly about him. After that, he lost touch with the world as she became his reality, the hot, wet, generous woman who loved him in the dark.

She was everything he craved, mysterious, giving, intensely feminine; in some sensual way, she held a mirror to his soul. She filled his senses until he recalled no other, until he knew nothing beyond her luscious heat and the primal need that gripped him.

He sank into her and she wrapped herself about him; at his urging, she shifted her legs, awkward for a moment as she repositioned them, locking them around his hips. When she sank fully onto him again, she gasped. Gripping her hips, he lifted her, thrusting upward as he lowered her.

She sobbed, then found his lips. They clung, and loved, gave and took and gave again. The horses plodded slowly on.

The gloom inside the carriage became a heated cave, filled with lust, desire, and so much more. Hunger, greed, joy, and delirium all spun, a kaleidoscope in the dark. Then she flew high and he followed, soaring beyond the stars. The end left them shattered, broken and destroyed, reborn in each other's arms.

The gentle swaying of the carriage slowly drew them back to earth, yet they lay still, letting the long, achingly sweet moments wash over them, neither ready to lose the soul-deep communion.

His lips at her temple, her hair silk against his cheek, Gabriel dragged in a breath. His chest swelled, shifting her warm weight. He locked his arms around her; he didn't want to let go. Didn't want to lose the peace she'd brought him – she and she alone.

Never had he reached this state, this depth of feeling. Beyond sensation, beyond the world, a sea of unnameable emotion still lapped him. He wanted to deny it, shrug it aside. It frightened him. But it was a drug – he feared he was already addicted.

She stirred, first again. Sitting up, she sighed and shook back her hair. 'I meant to tell you . . .'

He got the distinct impression she'd intended to say, 'before you started this,' and, what's more, in a censorious tone. He was too sated to do more

258

than smirk in the dark. He was still buried to the hilt inside her. 'What?' Reaching for her, he drew her back into his arms.

She acquiesced, then relaxed; despite her resolution, she was still dazed. 'My stepson . . . he overheard a conversation at White's – between a Captain Something and another man. The captain was dismissing the Central East Africa Gold Company.'

He frowned. 'I thought your stepson was too young for White's.'

'Oh, he is. This was on the steps – he was walking in St James's Street.'

'Who was the captain talking to?'

'Charles didn't know.'

'Hmm.' It was difficult to think with her warm weight snuggled against him, with her body intimately clasping his. That last, and his resurging vigor, prompted him to say, 'A captain recently returned from Africa shouldn't be impossible to trace. The shipping lists, the Port Authority, the major merchant lines. He'll be known somewhere.'

'If we have a witness like that, we'd be able to petition the court immediately.'

But then there'd be no reason for them to meet, and he'd yet to learn her name. He frowned, grateful for the dark. 'Perhaps. It depends on how much he knows.' Turning his head, he squinted down at her, but still could see nothing. 'I'll look into it.'

'Have you heard anything else?'

'I have contacts in Whitehall sounding out the African authorities over the company's mining claims, and there are others I'm hunting up who might know of the company's presence in those particular towns.' Shuffling higher on the seat, he glanced upward. 'Now – tell your coachman to roll back, slowly, to Brook Street.'

She sat up, still clutching his coat, and cleared her throat. 'Jacobs?'

The carriage slowed, then halted. 'Ma'am?'

'Brook Street, please – you know where.'

'Aye, ma'am.'

Taking advantage of her uptilted head, Gabriel pressed his lips to her throat. She fought to stifle a giggle, then sighed.

Then her breath caught. A moment later, she asked, slightly dazed, 'Again?'

'I'm hungry.'

So was she. They devoured each other at speed, reckless and driven, reaching the bright pinnacle before the carriage even left the park.

It wasn't, unfortunately, all that far to Brook Street. Wrapping her in her cloak, Gabriel shifted her to the seat beside him. He righted his clothes, then leaned over her to press a long kiss to her swollen lips.

The carriage halted; he drew back. From over his shoulder a street flare shone in, laying a narrow swath of light across her face. She was exhausted, her eyes shut – he could just see the edge of a crescent of dark lashes lying on one pale cheek.

The strip of light illuminated only that cheek, her earlobe framed by a strand of soft brown hair, the edge of her jaw and the corner of her lips.

Not enough to identify her.

Gabriel hesitated, then he shifted and his shoulder cut off the light. 'Sweet dreams, my dear.'

Her murmured 'Good-bye' was soft and low, a lover's farewell.

Descending to the street, Gabriel watched her carriage roll away; it was all he could do not to call it back. Turning, he climbed his steps, frowning as he reached for his latchkey.

He'd seen her face before. The line of her jaw was familiar.

She was one of his circle.

Who?

Letting himself in, he went up to bed.

Sniff.

Alathea battled to lift her heavy lids, and lost.

Sniff.

Stifling a sigh, she tried again and managed to see through a slit. 'Nellie?'

Sniff. 'Yes, m'lady,' came in dolorous tones. *Sniff.*

Alathea struggled onto her back and raised her head. And saw Nellie, red-nosed with watering red eyes, shaking out her cloak. Alathea dragged in a breath. 'Nellie Macarthur! You go straight back to bed. I do not want to see you, or hear of you being about on your feet, not until you're better.' Fixing her old maid with a pointed glare, Alathea summoned strength enough to deliver the words 'Do you hear?' in appropriately intimidating tones.

Nellie sniffed again. 'But who'll see to you? You've got to go to all these balls and parties, and your stepmama rightly says—'

'The tweeny will do for me for the nonce – I'm not entirely helpless.'

'But—'

'Doing my hair in a simpler style for a few nights will be a relief. No one will think anything of it.' Alathea glared again. 'Now go! And don't you dare sneak about downstairs – I'll be speaking with Figgs immediately I get up.'

'All right,' Nellie grumbled, but Alathea could see from her lethargic movements that she was seriously under the weather.

'I'll tell Figgs to make you some of her broth.' Alathea watched Nellie open the door. 'Oh – and don't bother to send up the tweeny. I'll ring for her when I'm ready.'

With barely a nod, Nellie shuffled out.

The instant the door closed, Alathea dropped back on her pillows, closed her eyes, and *groaned*. Feelingly.

Her thighs would never be the same again.

CHAPTER 12

'Allie?'

Blinking, Alathea refocused. Concern in her eyes, Alice peered at her across the breakfast table.

'Are you coming out into the garden with us?' Mary, beside Alice, looked equally worried.

Alathea summoned a quick smile. 'Just wool-gathering. I'll get my hat – you go on ahead.'

She rose with them and parted from them in the hall to go up to her room to fetch her gardening hat. Nevertheless, it was half an hour later before she reached the garden.

Mary and Alice hadn't waited for her but had started weeding the long border. Although they looked up when she neared and smiled welcomingly, it was plain they'd been exchanging confidences, whispered comments on their hopes, their dreams. Returning their smiles, Alathea surveyed their endeavors, then looked around. 'I'll start on the central bed.'

Leaving them to their dreams, she went off to contend with hers.

The central bed circled a small fountain, a water

sprite caught in the act of springing free-showering droplets back into a wide bowl. Spreading her raffia mat by the bed, presently filled with pansies, Alathea knelt, tugged on her cotton gloves, and set to.

About her, her family went happily about their morning routines. Jeremy and Charlie appeared from around the house, dragging dead limbs cut from overgrown bushes. In half an hour, Jeremy's tutor would arrive, and Charlie would change into his town rig and go out to spend the day with his Eton chums. Miss Helm and Augusta, clutching the ever-present Rose, came out and sat on a wrought-iron seat; from what Alathea could hear, they were engaged in a simple botany lesson. After an hour or so, she, Mary and Alice would retire to wash, change, and prepare for their morning's excursion – whatever Serena had organized. Inside, Serena would be sifting through the invitations, sending notes, plotting their best course through the shoals of the Season. Alathea was content to leave the strategies to her; it was bad enough that she had to weed.

The fiction they'd concocted to hide the fact that they could not afford a second gardener, one to take care of the beds and borders at the Park and the garden of the London house, was that Alathea enjoyed planting and weeding and Serena felt it right that her daughters, too, became knowledgeable in the art of creating a stunning border. And, of course, all gentlemen should have some understanding of landscaping. Luckily, landscaping, borders, and beds were all the rage, although ladies and gentlemen generally only oversaw such projects, a fine distinction the earl, Serena and Alathea had omitted to mention.

As she reached for a blade of grass cheekily poking up between clumps of pansies, Alathea inwardly sighed. She would much rather never see a weed again, but . . . With a yank, she uprooted the interloper and dropped it on the grass beside her. Parting the pansy leaves, she searched for more.

Of course, as soon as her hands were mindlessly busy, her thoughts drifted . . .

She could never meet with him privately again. Not ever. The countess was going to have to retreat; she couldn't yet disappear. Despite the fact she'd enjoyed last night hugely, she couldn't possibly risk such a *meeting* again.

In a carriage. She still couldn't quite believe it. If she hadn't been there . . . Was there *anywhere* he couldn't . . . wouldn't . . .

Minutes later, she shook her head. Struggling to hide a smile, she looked down.

Thankfully, no one knew. She'd gathered enough strength to instruct Jacobs to drive around Grosvenor Square while she'd scrambled into her chemise, stockings, shoes, and gown. Her hair she'd had to leave down. Goodness knows what Jacobs had made of the pins he would by now have discovered on the carriage floor. Concealed beneath her veil and cloak, she'd been safe from Crisp's eyes. Other than Jacobs, who'd been busy with his team, only Crisp had been awake when she'd returned. She'd given strict instructions that not even Nellie was to wait up for her on pain of her considerable displeasure. She'd done the same the night she'd gone to the Burlington; she could only thank her stars she had.

So no one knew of her fall from grace. Her lips kicked upward. It had, to her, felt more like an elevation. A revelation certainly, an induction into a realm of earthly bliss. She was not of a mind to wallow in senseless regrets – she'd lived, all but died, and exulted last night, and for that she could only be glad.

Even now, she wasn't free of the lingering spell. She hadn't imagined that the activities theoretically restricted to the marriage bed could result in such an interaction – a voyage into another dimension of feeling where the world fell away and emotion reigned. She'd had her first inkling of that joyous state during their night at the Burlington. Last night, they'd journeyed much further, through landscapes of unutterable delight.

And it had been they, not just she. He'd been there, with her – had it been her inexperience, or had he been as stunned by the glory as she? Whatever, they'd shared it all – the journey, the discovery, the over-whelming satiation, followed by their plunge into that well of deep peace.

It had been the most glorious night of her life.

Her lips quirked. She had to wonder what he'd thought he'd been about, holding her naked on his knees. She assumed it had been part of some plan – he was always planning. She strongly suspected he'd intended her to feel in his power. She had to smile. He couldn't know that she'd sat there, naked before him, and gloried in the power she'd wielded over him.

For power there'd been – those dark, illicit moments had been charged with it – but for every tithe of power he'd held over her, she'd held the same measure over him.

She'd startled him with her statement that she wanted him. Other ladies would not have been so bold. But he hadn't been at all reluctant – oh, no. If she hadn't taken him, he'd have taken her.

Warm memories washed over her, through her – kneeling in the sunlight, she drifted away.

A conspiratorial giggle from Alice drew her back; she blinked – and saw the pansy plant she was holding, roots dangling, in one hand.

With a muttered curse, Alathea plunged it back into the hole from which she'd pulled it and quickly tamped it down. Then she checked her pile of 'weeds.' Two more pansies were rapidly returned to the soil. She could only hope that if they died, they wouldn't leave a hole in her border.

Inwardly sighing, she sat back on her heels, ignoring the twinges in her thighs. She had to stop thinking of last night. She had to determine how on earth she was going to proceed *after* last night. It seemed she would be safe only on a crowded street in broad daylight, and she'd have to wear a mask under her veil as well.

It would be easy for her to communicate with him by letter, but she couldn't see any way he could reply. And she knew him too well to beard the tiger; if she cut off all contact entirely, he'd come after her. Not trying to discover her identity, but trying to discover her. He'd be very intent, very focused; in such a state, he'd be unstoppable.

And where would that leave her?

She didn't like to think.

No. Folwell would keep her informed of Gabriel's movements. She would send him notes if necessary until they discovered something more, then she'd meet him in Grosvenor Square.

That brought her to the question of what more she could do to further their investigations. A vague recollection of Lady Hester Stanhope's diaries had her turning to scan the long border.

Rising, she dusted her gloves, then stripped them from her hands. Strolling to the long border, she made a show of evaluating the progress made, then nodded. 'We've done enough for today.' She met Mary's and Alice's bright eyes. 'I want to visit Hookhams again. Would you like to come?'

'Oh, yes!'

'Now?'

Alathea turned to the house. 'Just a quick visit – I'm sure your mama won't mind.'

She found what she was after in the biography of an explorer – a bona fide map of Central East Africa showing more than the major towns. The map told her Fangak, Lodwar and Kingi – Kafia Kingi, to be precise – were indeed towns, albeit small ones.

Leaning back in the chair behind the desk in her office, Alathea pondered her discovery. Was it good? Or discouraging?

About her, the house was peaceful and still. The lamp on her desk shed light onto the open book. In the grate, embers gleamed, warming the night. She'd stolen every moment she could throughout the day to wade through the stack of biographies and diaries she'd borrowed from Hookhams. At last, she'd uncovered something – something real.

The information was good, she decided – at least it gave them something to check. Surely they'd be able to find someone other than the mysterious captain who knew the area, now she knew where the area was.

On the stairs, the long-case clock chimed the hour. Three o'clock, the beginning of a new day. Stifling a yawn, Alathea closed the book and rose. It was definitely time for bed.

The next day, she spent the afternoon within the hallowed halls of the Royal Society.

'Unfortunately,' the secretary informed her, peering at her through a thick pair of *pince-nez*, 'there are no lectures presently scheduled on Central East Africa.'

'Oh. Can the society recommend any expert on the area with whom I could consult?'

The man pursed his lips, stared at her, then nodded. 'If you'll take a seat, I'll check the records.'

Retreating to a wooden bench along the wall, Alathea waited for fifteen minutes, only to have the man return, shaking his head and looking rather peeved.

'We do not,' he informed her, 'have any expert on East Africa listed. Three who could speak with authority on West Africa, but not the East.'

Alathea thanked him and left. Pausing on the steps, she considered, then headed for her carriage. 'Where can we find the city's map makers, Jacobs?'

Along the Strand, was the answer. She inquired at three separate establishments, and got the same answer at all three. For their maps on Central East Africa, they relied on explorers' notes. Yes, their present maps of the area were extremely short on detail, but they were awaiting confirmation.

'It wouldn't do, miss,' one rigidly correct gentleman lectured her, 'for us to publish a map on which we showed towns we weren't absolutely positive were there.'

'Yes, I see.' Alathea turned to leave, then turned back. 'The explorers whose notes you're waiting to confirm – are they in London?'

'Regretfully no, miss. They are all, at present, in Africa. Exploring.'

There was nothing to be done but smile, and leave. Defeated.

Alathea returned to Mount Street feeling un-accustomedly weary.

'Thank you, Crisp.' She handed the butler her bonnet. 'I think I'll just sit in the library for a while.'

'Indeed, miss. Do you wish for tea?'

'Please.'

The tea arrived but did little to alleviate the feeling of helplessness that dragged at her. Every time she thought she was on the brink of substantiating some solid fact, the proof evaporated. Her hopes would soar, only to be dashed. Meanwhile, the days were passing. The day Crowley would call in his promissory notes was inexorably approaching.

Doom leered at her through Crowley's eyes.

Alathea sighed. Setting aside her empty cup, she flopped back in the armchair and closed her eyes. Perhaps, if she rested just for a few minutes . . .

'Are you asleep?'

Realizing she had been, Alathea blinked her eyes wide, then smiled – a spontaneous smile of real joy – at Augusta's little face. 'Hello, sweetling. Where have you been today?'

Taking the question for the invitation it was, Augusta climbed into Alathea's lap and settled herself so she could see Alathea's face. Wedging Rose between them, she proceeded to distract Alathea with a detailed account of her day. Alathea listened, putting a question here and there, making understanding or sympathetic comments as required.

'So, you see,' Augusta concluded, hugging Rose to her chest and snuggling closer, pressing her head to Alathea's breast, 'it's been a *frightfully* busy day.'

Alathea chuckled; raising a hand, she smoothed Augusta's hair. Small arms, small body tucked close to her side, she felt a warm, emotional tug; Augusta was the daughter she wished she could have had. She banished the thought immediately; she was obviously overtired. Too much investigating.

Too many meetings.

Then Augusta wriggled and sat up. 'Hmm-mmm.' She sniffed at Alathea's throat. 'You smell extra nice today.'

Alathea's answering smile froze on her face as she realized the significance of Augusta's remark.

She was wearing the countess's scent.

Good God! She closed her eyes. What would have happened if she'd run into Gabriel? She'd been in the city and, earlier, not far from St James's, his habitual haunts.

Drawing in a breath, she opened her eyes. 'Come along, poppet. I need to go upstairs and wash before dinner.' Before anyone else noticed she was not quite the same woman she had been.

Two evenings later, Alathea was sitting with Jeremy in the schoolroom, Augusta in her lap, a detailed atlas from Hookhams open on the table, when the little tweeny appeared, breathless, at the door.

'If you please, Lady Alathea,' she piped, 'but it's time for you to get dressed, m'lady.'

Noting the way the little maid was wringing her hands and at a loss to account for it, Alathea looked at the mantel clock.

Then she understood the agitation.

'Indeed.' Lifting Augusta and settling her on the seat with a fond kiss, Alathea met Jeremy's eyes. 'We'll continue this tomorrow.'

Only too glad to escape the shackles of African geography, Jeremy grinned and turned to Augusta. 'Come on, Gussie. We can play catch before dinner.'

'I'm not *Gussie*.' The tone of Augusta's objection boded ill for the peace of the evening.

'Jeremy . . .' From the door, Alathea fixed him with a matriarchal eye.

'Oh, very well. *Augusta* then. Anyway, do you want to play or not?'

Leaving them in reasonable harmony, Alathea hurried to her room. By the time she reached it, she was even more agitated than the tweeny. They were to dine with the Arbuthnots, then attend the ball their old friends were giving to formally introduce their granddaughter to the ton. It was a major function; all the senior hostesses would be there. Being late for such a dinner without some cataclysmic excuse would sink one beyond reproach.

But the tweeny, who had thus far only helped her get ready for balls without dinners preceeding them, had not realized the earlier hour involved. Not until she'd noticed Serena, Mary and Alice were all busy dressing.

Oh, God Alathea stilled the panic that gripped her as her gaze swept her room and found no evidence of any chemise or stockings, let alone her gown, gloves, reticule . . . Nellie always had

273

everything ready, but with the tweeny she had to specify every item.

For one instant, Alathea considered developing a horrendous headache, but that would leave old Lady Arbuthnot with an odd number about her table. Stifling a sigh, she waved the maid forward. 'Quickly. Help me with these laces.' At least her hot water was ready and waiting.

As she stripped off her gown and quickly washed, she issued a steady stream of orders for all the items she required to appear presentable. From the corner of her eye, she kept watch on the little maid, making sure each item was correct before asking for the next.

Getting dressed in a scramble was one of her worst nightmares – she hated being rushed, especially for such a major event where she could count on her appearance being scrutinized by the sharpest eyes in the ton.

Blotting her face with the towel, Alathea shook her head. 'No – not those. My dance slippers. The ones with no heel.'

Hurrying to the bed, she stripped off her linen chemise, then slipped into the welcoming coolness of silk. At least with the present fashions, she didn't have to bother with petticoats. Throwing her gown of amber silk crepe over her head, she tugged it down, settled it, then whirled and let the tweeny tie the laces. The instant the last was secured, she rushed to her dressing table, plunked herself on the stool, and plunged her hands into her hair.

Pins flew. 'Quickly – we'll have to braid it.' There was no time for a more sophisticated style.

It was only as the maid reached the end of the long braid that Alathea realized she needed two plaits to make a coronet. 'Oh.' For one moment, she simply stared, then she waved the tweeny aside and grabbed the braid. 'Here – if we do it like this, it should pass muster.'

Under-rolling half the thick braid, she bunched it at her nape, then used the long end to circle and bind it. Pushing pins in right and left, up and down, she frantically secured what would pass for a braided chignon.

'There!' Moving her head, she confirmed the mass was anchored, then quickly eased the strands pulled back from her face so they formed a softer frame. One more quick check, then she nodded. 'Now . . .'

Opening a drawer in the table, she rummaged through her caps. Freeing a fine net heavily encrusted with gold beads, she grimaced. 'This will have to do.' Setting it over her hair so the lower edge curved about the braided bun, she pinned it in place.

Beyond her door, Mary's and Alice's voices rang, then their quick footsteps hurried for the stairs. Alathea quelled an impulse to look at the clock – she didn't have time. 'Jewelry.' Flinging open her jewelry box, she blinked. 'Oh.' Her hand hovered over the contents, all neatly arranged.

'I took the liberty of tidying, miss. Nellie said as how I had to dust and tidy every day.'

After one stunned glance at the tweeny's hopeful face, Alathea looked back at the box. 'Yes – well. That's all right.'

Except that now she hadn't a clue where her pearl earrings were, let alone the matching pendant. Spearing her fingers into the piles, scattering and disarranging as she went, Alathea unearthed the earrings. Standing, she leaned closer to the mirror and quickly fitted them.

'Allie? Are you ready?'

'Open the door,' Alathea instructed the maid. As soon as the door swung wide, she called, 'I'm coming!' And fell to ransacking her jewelry box again.

In one corner, she noted the Venetian glass flacon that contained the countess's perfume. After her recent mistake, she'd decided to take no further chances – the flacon was one of an identical pair. The other bottle contained her customary perfume; she'd left that out on the table. Her searching fingers finally touched the gold chain she sought; drawing the gold and pearl pendant free, she held the chain around her neck. 'Hurry.'

The tweeny's fingers were sure; the clasp closed as Mary came rushing to the door.

'The carriage is pulling up! Mama says we have to go *now*!'

'I'm coming.' Grabbing the flacon on her table, Alathea liberally sprinkled, then whirled – 'Oh, no! Not that reticule – the small gold one!'

The tweeny dived for her armoire; shawls and reticules went flying. 'This one?'

Grabbing her shawl from the bed, Alathea headed for the door. 'Yes!'

Waving the reticule, the tweeny chased her down the corridor. Settling her shawl over her elbows, Alathea grabbed the reticule, checked it contained a handkerchief and pins, then lengthened her stride, took the stairs two at a time, raced through the tiled foyer, out the door Crisp held wide, pattered down the steps and dove into the carriage.

Folwell shut the door behind her, and the carriage lurched into motion.

The crowd in Lady Arbuthnot's ballroom was unbearably dense. Having arrived as late as he dared, Gabriel inwardly girded his loins, then stepped off the stairs and plunged in. Prevented from propping his shoulders against the wall – there was no spare wall left – he circulated through the crowd, keeping an eagle eye out for those who most wished to see him, intent on seeing them first, and avoiding them.

High on his list of people to be missed were ladies such as Agatha Herries. He didn't see her early enough; she placed herself directly in his path. With no alternative offering, he halted before her. She smiled archly up at him and laid a hand on his sleeve.

'Gabriel, darling.'

He nodded. 'Agatha.'

His tone was the very essence of unencouraging.

Despite that, Lady Herries's smile deepened. Calculation gleamed in her eyes. 'I wonder if, perhaps, we might find a quiet spot.'

'For what?'

She studied him, then let her lids veil her eyes and slowly stroked her hand down his arm. 'Just a little proposition I'd like to put to you. A personal matter.'

'You can tell me here. In this din, it's unlikely anyone will overhear.'

The idea didn't suit, but she knew him too well to push.

'Very well.' She glanced around, then looked up at him. 'It seems you're destined to choose a wife soon. I wanted to make sure you were fully acquainted with all your options.'

'Indeed?'

'My daughter, Clara – I dare say you might remember her. She's been well trained to be an *accommodating* wife, and while our estate and lineage might not measure up to that of the Cynsters, there would, of course, be compensations.'

The purr in her voice, the lascivious gleam in her eyes, left no doubt as to what those 'compensations' might be.

Gabriel looked at her coldly, then he let his mask slip, let his contempt and revulsion show. Lady Herries paled and stepped back – then had to apologize to the lady she'd backed into.

When she looked back at Gabriel, his expression was impassive once more. 'You were misinformed.

I am not presently searching for a wife.' He inclined his head. 'If you'll excuse me.'

Stepping around Lady Herries, Gabriel continued on his way, searching, not for a wife, but for a widow. When he found her, after he'd wrung her neck and administered a few other physical torments, he'd turn his mind to marrying her.

First, he had to find her.

She ought to be here. Almost everyone of note was. She was of his circle – that he did not doubt – so where was she?

Behind his elegantly aloof facade, he felt decidedly grim. He'd been sure he'd get one of her countessly summonses the evening following their midnight drive. But he hadn't. He'd spent the whole evening with Chance popping in and out of the parlor like a Jack-in-the-box, wondering why he'd stayed in. Reining in his impatience – not easy after that midnight interlude and the tempest of emotions she'd unleashed – he'd waited at home the following night, with no greater success.

Now he was hungry – ravenous – not just for her, but even more to know she was his, to know where she was, to know he could put his hand on her whenever he wished. He was tense, wound tight with a need to possess far greater than any he'd previously experienced in all the years of his rakish career. He had to find out who she was, where she lived, where she was.

His copy of *Burke's Peerage* had started to exert

a hypnotic tug. He'd caught himself considering the leather-bound tome on a number of occasions. But he'd promised . . . given his word . . . the word of a Cynster.

He'd spent all last night, alone again, trying to devise some way around that promise. His Aunt Helena would know who the countess was – she always knew who was whose son, who had recently died, who married a young bride. Unfortunately, Helena would immediately inform his mother of his inquiry, and that he could do without. For hours he'd toyed with the notion of throwing himself on Honoria's mercy and asking for her aid. She'd give it, but it would come at a price; nothing was more certain. The present duchess of St Ives was not one to pass up a never-to-be-repeated advantage. It was a measure of his desperation that he even contemplated asking her.

In the end, he'd concluded that his promise – the promise the countess had so artfully phrased – bound him too tightly and left him no room to manuever. Thrown back on his own devices, he had come here tonight for the sole purpose of tracking her down.

Her – his houri – the woman who had captured his soul.

Raising his head, he scanned the room. The one feature she could not conceal was her height. There were a number of tall ladies present, but he knew them all – not one was an elusive countess. Alathea, he noted, was presently on the dance floor, partnered by Chillingworth. He looked away. At least the dance was only a cotillion, not a waltz.

'There you are. At last!'

Lucifer struggled free of the crowd. Gabriel raised a questioning brow.

His brother stared at him. 'Well, the twins, of course!'

Gabriel looked around, and spotted his fair cousins on the dance floor. 'They're dancing.'

'I know that,' Lucifer stated through his teeth. 'But it's more than time for you to take the watch.'

Gabriel studied the twins for one second more, then looked back at Lucifer. 'Not anymore. They don't need watching. Just as long as we're here if they need us.'

Lucifer's jaw nearly dropped. '*What*? You can't be serious.'

'Perfectly. They're halfway through their second Season. They know the ropes. They're not ninny-hammers.'

'I know that – God knows, they're sharp as tacks. But they're female.'

'I'd noticed. I've also noticed that they don't appreciate our endeavors.' Gabriel paused, then added, 'And they might have reasonable cause to accuse us of excessive interference in their lives.'

'Alathea's spoken to you, hasn't she?'

'She's spoken to you, too.'

'Well, yes . . .' Lucifer turned and surveyed the twins. After a minute, he asked, 'Do you really think it's safe?'

Gabriel considered the two bright heads spinning in the dance. 'Safe or not, I think we must.' After a moment, he glanced at Lucifer. 'I don't know about you, but I have other fish to fry.'

'Indeed?' One of Lucifer's black brows quirked. 'And here I thought your exceedingly unmellow mood was due to enforced abstinence and an overfamiliarity with your own hearth.'

'Don't start,' Gabriel all but snarled. His exceedingly thin facade threatened to crack.

Lucifer sobered. 'Who is she?'

With a definite snarl, Gabriel swung away, moving into the crowd, leaving Lucifer with his brows riding high and real concern in his eyes.

Whoever she was, she had to be here somewhere. Clinging to that conviction, Gabriel started to quarter the room.

Alathea was taking the long way back from the withdrawing room whence she'd retreated to escape her increasingly persistent cavaliers, when she came upon Gabriel in the crowd. As making any headway through the throng required constant tacking, despite being so tall, neither had any warning of the other's approach.

Suddenly, they were face to face – and very close.

They both jumped, tensed, Gabriel with his habitual reaction to her, instantly masked. Alathea saw it and prayed that he thought her reaction merely simple surprise, not the ground-shaking shock it had been. Her breathing had seized; her eyes had flown wide. She kept them locked on his. They were so close, she could sense his strength through every pore, could almost feel the shocking heat of that large body against hers. Wrapped intimately about hers, sunk deep into hers. She swayed slightly toward him, then caught herself. *Heaven help her*! Would it always be like this from now on?

His eyes narrowed. Dragging in a desperate breath, she stiffened her spine and lifted her head. His gaze rose to her beaded hairnet; she tilted her chin even higher and clung to her customary haughtiness.

'It might be gold, but . . .'

Temper came to her rescue. 'It is *not* tawdry. If you *dare* say it is . . .' She held his gaze for an instant longer – long enough to realize that she had to get away. 'I have nothing to say to you – I doubt you have anything civil to say to me. I have better things to do than stand here crossing swords with you.'

'Indeed?'

That was accompanied by an infuriating lift of one brow.

'Indeed – and I don't wish to hear your opinion of anyone else, either.'

'Because it might be true?'

'Regardless of their accuracy, to me, your opinions are neither here nor there.' With that, she tried to step around him but the crowd was so tight-packed she couldn't get past unless he gave way.

He didn't immediately. His gaze skimmed her face, searching – she prayed not seeing. Then he inclined his head and shifted. 'You will, as always, go to the devil in your own way.'

She bestowed a look of regal indifference upon him, then pushed past. Her breast brushed his arm, one thigh touched his. The tremor that rocked her nearly buckled her knees. Lungs locked, she held her spine rigid and forged on and away. She didn't dare look back.

Inwardly shaking his head, Gabriel waited for the muscles that had seized at her touch to relax. They'd touched little over the years but her effect on him hadn't waned. As his chest eased, he dragged in a huge breath—

She was close.

Instantly, he scanned the surrounding crowd. Not one woman in sight was tall enough, but he couldn't mistake that perfume. It was the essence of her, the scent that wreathed his dreams. He breathed in again. The perfume was still strong, but dispersing. She'd been very . . . close . . .

His muscles locked like stone. Slowly, he turned, and stared at the slender back of the exceptionally tall woman who had, just a moment before, stood very close to him.

It couldn't be.

For one finite moment, his mind flatly rejected what his senses were screaming.

Then reality fractured.

★   ★   ★

Alathea felt Gabriel's gaze on her back, like a knife between her shoulder blades. Her lungs seized; panic clutching her stomach she shot a glance behind.

He was tacking through the crowd in her wake. His eyes met hers, their expression primitive. For an instant, the sight paralyzed her. Then she whirled and tried to go faster, to slip through the crowd and escape.

The crowd only got denser. Lady Hendricks called and waved – Alathea had to stop, smile, touch fingers. Then she was on her way again, breathlessly dodging, weaving, desperately seeking an easier path through the crush—

Hard fingers locked around her elbow.

She froze. In the instant her panicked wits re-engaged, he bent his head and murmured, 'Don't bother.'

His lips brushed her ear. Suppressing a shiver, she stiffened. He stood at her right shoulder, her elbow in a viselike grip; even without his warning, she knew that grip would be unbreakable. And he was furious. Past furious. The anger pouring from him scorched her. What had given her away?

'This way.'

He'd been looking over the sea of heads; now he steered her toward one side of the room. She forced her feet to move. She could not cause a scene, not here. In his present mood he was capable of anything, even picking her up, tossing her over his shoulder, and stalking off with her.

His temper once aroused was a force to contend with; challenging it now would be foolhardy. As they moved toward one wall, she struggled to marshal her wits, her arguments, her denials, bracing herself for what was to come.

She didn't see the door until they stood before it; he opened it and marched her into an unlit and thankfully uninhabited gallery. He didn't stop until they were at the end where a long window, curtains wide, poured moonlight into the narrow room.

Placing her directly in the silver beam, he swung to face her.

His gaze raked her face, devoured her features as if he'd never seen them before. His face was chiseled, harder than stone, every edge sharp. Lips compressed, his jaw set, his heavy lids too low for her to see his eyes, he studied her. His gaze lingered on her jaw, then he lifted his lids and looked into her eyes. For a long moment, he held her gaze, hazel to hazel. Tense beyond bearing, her nerves stretched tight, she wondered what he could see.

'It was you.'

Although laced with wonder, his tone brooked no argument. She raised her brows. 'What on earth are you on about?'

His brows rose but his expression didn't waver. 'Denial? Surely you can do better than that?'

'I dare say if I knew what misbegotten notion you've taken into your fevered brain I could more specifically address it, but as I don't, denial seems the safest option.' She looked away, too afraid that if she continued to meet his eyes she would see his knowledge of her – his physical knowledge of her – blazoned in the hazel. Then she'd remember, too, and vulnerability would sweep her – and he'd pounce.

The touch of long fingers curving about her face nearly brought her to her knees. His grip firmed; deliberately, he turned her head until her eyes met his again.

'Oh, you *know* – there's no point denying it.' His words were clipped; fury raged beneath them. He hesitated, then added, 'Your perfume gave you away.'

Her perfume?

The tweeny. Tidying. Emptying her jewelry box onto the table. Then putting everything back in. Two identical flacons, one in, one out.

Her expression had blanked; her lips started to form an 'Oh.' Alathea caught herself and glared. 'What about my perfume?'

He smiled, not with amusement. 'Too late.'

'Nonsense!' She lifted her chin from his fingers. 'It's simply a particular blend – I dare say many ladies use it.'

'Perhaps, but none so tall. So . . . accomplished.'

When she merely raised a weary brow, he supplied, 'So capable of picking locks.'

Alathea frowned. 'Am I to understand that you're searching for some woman – a tall woman –

who wears the same perfume as I and can pick locks?'

'No – you're to understand that I've found her.'

His ringing certainty had her looking up – he trapped her gaze. His eyes narrowed, then his gaze dropped to her lips. Insidious, mesmeric attraction flared between them . . .

He stepped closer. Alathea's breath caught in her throat. Eyes widening, her gaze fixed on his hard face, she quivered—

The door from the ballroom opened; other guests ambled in.

Gabriel glanced around.

Alathea sucked in a breath. 'You're completely and absolutely mistaken.'

His head snapped back, but she'd already stepped around him. She swept past the other guests with a regal nod. Head high, in a glide just short of a run, she escaped back into the ballroom.

CHAPTER 13

A waltz was just starting. Alathea's mad dash nearly sent her into the dancers. She teetered on the edge of the dance floor— A hard arm collected her, sliding about her waist, swinging her forward, then expertly steadying her. She swallowed a shriek, then fought to catch her breath – and her balance, and her scattered wits, only to lose all three as Gabriel locked his arm around her, trapping her from breast to thigh against him. One hand held fast, he whirled her down the room.

Her body instantly came alive. Her breasts swelled. She fought to hold herself stiffly, but her body molded to his, thighs brushing evocatively at every turn. Their hips swayed together; memories churned.

Within seconds, she'd softened. She refused to meet his eyes, too busy struggling to master her whirling wits, to gather her resolution, to find some way forward. Her composure was all she had left; desperately, she clung to it.

He was holding her very close. As her head continued to whirl, as her body continued to heat

289

with every revolution, she fixed her gaze over his shoulder, and hissed, 'You're holding me too close.'

Gabriel looked at her face, so achingly familiar yet . . . had he ever truly seen it before? His temper was up and running, his emotions rioting; he had no idea what he thought or felt. He could barely believe the truth in his arms. His hold on his impulses was tenuous as he let his gaze roam the long slender lines of her throat, the creamy expanse of skin above her neckline, over the rounded swells, now firm, hot and tight, pressed against his chest. 'I've held you closer, if you recall.'

The gravelly rasp of his words affected them both; she shot him a shocked, breathless, scandalized glance, then looked away.

She said nothing more; her feet followed his, her body flowing with his, fitting so neatly, so totally attuned they could both have waltzed for hours without thought. Gabriel grabbed the moments to bring some order to the chaos in his brain. He frowned as he noticed the difference in her height, then recalled the high heels he'd dropped to the carriage floor three nights before.

Glancing down as they whirled through the next turn, he confirmed his guess. 'You never normally wear heels.'

Her breasts swelled as she drew in a tight breath. 'What *are* you talking about? You're making less sense than poor Skiffy Skeffington!'

His hold on his temper snapped. 'Indeed? In that case, I suppose there's no point in asking how long you'd thought to carry on your charade, or in inquiring as to its purpose. You can understand, however, that that last exercises me greatly.' He spoke through clenched teeth, his voice sharpened steel. He let his gaze rake her face; he saw only red. 'Did you think to trap me into marriage? Is that what this is about? Surely not—' He tightened his hold as she tried to free her hand until he knew he was crushing her fingers. 'You know I'd make your life a living hell, so why? Was it the challenge?' Already stiff, she went rigid. He glanced at her set face. 'That sounds nearer the mark.'

He looked up as they circled, then laughed mirthlessly. '*God*, when I think of it! – Lincoln's Inn Fields, Bond Street, Bruton Street.' He paused, then demanded, 'Tell me, in Bruton Street, did you flee into the modiste's because you couldn't contain your laughter?'

She reacted – her hand, crushed in his, jerked, the fine tendons in her neck tensed – but she kept her gaze fixed over his shoulder and her lips pressed stubbornly tight.

'Why did you do it?'

She gave him no answer.

'As the cat's caught your tongue, let me see if I can guess . . . you missed your chance with your own Season, but given you had to come to London to give Mary and Alice their turn, you thought to enliven your stay by taking a shot at me. Thanks to my fond mama, I'm sure you know my reputation.' His tone lashed. 'Is that what you thought? That bringing me to my knees as the mysterious countess would be just the thing to enliven your stay?'

Pale, her expression stony, she refused to look at him, to meet his eyes, refused to assure him that he'd got it all wrong, that she'd never betray him like that.

Betrayed was what he felt – not just by her but by her alter ego, too. No matter his devotion, no matter his patience and skill, no matter how deeply he'd come to worship her, the countess would never have revealed her identity to him. As for his dreams . . .

Bitterness welled, then swelled even higher. She'd struck much deeper than mere dreams. She'd struck straight to his core, just as she always had; she'd stripped away his armor, found his most vulnerable spot and laid it bare. He hadn't even known he possessed such a weakness until she'd uncovered it. He could only curse her for it – she was the very last woman on earth he would willingly reveal any vulnerability to.

But even that was not the worst. The most vital wound, the one that left him bleeding inside, was that, despite knowing him so well, she hadn't trusted him.

That, of it all, hurt the most.

'I always wondered when you'd get tired of your

life in the country. Tell me, now I've opened your eyes to the pleasures to be experienced in the capital, are you thinking of—' He didn't even hear what he said, as, element by element, he dismembered her character. Many considered his tongue too sharp for safety; he used it like a surgeon's knife to cut at her, to make her bleed, too. Just as she knew where to strike at him, he knew all her most sensitive spots. Like her height, like the fact she believed herself plain. And too old. He touched on each vulnerable point, savagely rejoicing when she stiffened, when her jaw locked.

He'd salvaged a tiny portion of his pride by the time the music slowed, and the red mist that had clouded his brain and his vision lifted enough for him to see the tears that stood in her eyes.

The music ended. They halted. She stood silent and still in his arms, her expression unyielding yet her whole being vibrating with suppressed emotion.

She met his gaze unflinchingly. Beyond the sheen of her tears, he saw his fury and hurt reflected back at him, over and over again.

'You do not have the first idea what you are talking about.'

Each word was distinct, carefully enunciated, underscored with emotion. Before he could react, she pulled roughly from his arms, caught her breath, turned, and swept away.

Leaving him alone in the middle of the dance floor.

Still furious. Still hurt.

Still aroused.

Alathea sat at the breakfast table the next morning in a state of deadened panic. She knew the axe would soon fall, but she couldn't summon the strength to run. She felt physically drained; she'd barely slept a wink. Maintaining an outward show of calm was imperative, yet it was all she could do to smile at her family and pretend to nibble her toast.

Her stomach felt hollow but she couldn't eat. She could only just manage to sip her weak tea. Her head felt steady enough, yet at the same time strangely vacant, as if blocking out all Gabriel's hurtful words had blocked off her own thoughts as well.

She knew she couldn't think – she'd tried for hours last night, but every attempt had ended in tears. She couldn't think of what had happened, much less of what might.

Picking at her toast, she let her family's cheery talk wash over her and drew a little comfort from its warmth.

Then Crisp paused beside her and cleared his throat. 'Mr Cynster is here, m'lady, and wishes to speak with you.'

Alathea looked up. *Here*? No – he wouldn't. 'Wh—' She stopped and cleared her throat. 'Which Mr Cynster, Crisp?'

'Mr Rupert, miss.'

He would.

Serena waved a plump hand. 'Do ask him if he's breakfasted yet, Crisp.'

'No! – I mean, I'm sure he would have.' Rising, Alathea placed her napkin by her plate. 'I'm sure he's not thinking of ham and sausages.'

'Well, if you're sure . . .' Serena frowned. 'But it seems an odd time to call.'

Alathea caught her eye. 'It's just a little business matter we need to discuss.'

'Oh.' Serena mouthed the word, and immediately turned back to her family.

Slipping out of the breakfast parlor, Alathea reflected that her last words were no deception. All that Rupert – Gabriel – wished to speak about had occurred because of their 'little business matter.'

That wasn't going to make the coming interview any easier.

Crisp had shown Gabriel into the back parlor, a quiet room overlooking the rear gardens. On sunny days, the girls liked to gather there, but today, with the clouds closing in and drizzle threatening, it would be a quiet, and private, haven.

It was unlikely they would be disturbed.

Alathea considered that and grimaced. She'd dismissed Crisp and come alone. Hand on the doorknob, she drew in a breath, gathered her wilting strength, and refused to think of what she would face on the other side of the door.

Outwardly calm, she turned the knob and walked in.

His head turned instantly; their gazes locked. He'd been standing by the windows looking out. He considered her unblinkingly, then, in a low voice said, 'Close the door. Lock it.'

She hesitated.

'We don't need any interruptions.'

She hesitated a moment more, then turned, shut the door, and snibbed the lock. Facing him again, she lifted her head, straightened her spine, and clasped her hands before her.

He continued to study her, his face unreadable.

'Come here.'

Alathea considered, but she felt the tug, the compulsion. The threat. She forced her feet to carry her forward.

It was the most difficult thing she'd done in her life – crossing the wide parlor under his eye. She kept her head up, her spine rigid, but by the time she reached his side and the light fell full on her face, she was inwardly shaking, her reserves of strength, of resolution, seriously depleted. As she stopped beside him and met his hard gaze, she realized that was precisely as he'd intended.

He searched her face, his gaze sharp, acute, his features warrior-hard. 'Now,' he said, *what the devil's going on?*'

Barely leashed anger vibrated behind the words. Drawing her gaze from his, she fixed it on the lawn and the enclosing trees. 'You know most of it.'

She drew in a breath, to gain time, to gain control. 'All that I told you as the countess is true, except—'

'That your supposed late husband is in fact your father, that the youthful Charles is Charlie, Maria is Mary, Alicia is Alice, and Seraphina is Serena. That much I'd guessed.'

'Well, then.' She shrugged. 'That's it.'

When he said nothing more, she risked a quick glance. He was waiting – he caught her gaze and held it.

A moment passed.

'Try again.'

His temper reached her clearly. There would be no escape. 'What do you want to know?' If she could cling to the straightforward, the matter-of-fact, she might just survive his inquisition.

'Is the earldom in as dire straits as you portrayed?'

'Yes.'

'Why did you create the countess?'

Straightforward. Matter-of-fact. She returned her gaze to the vista outside. 'If I'd written to you or visited you with the story of a suspect note *without* telling you of the family's financial plight, would you have undertaken the investigation yourself or handed it to Montague?'

'If you'd told me the whole story—'

'Put yourself in my shoes. Would you have told you the whole story? How close to ruin we stood? Still stand.'

After a moment, he inclined his head. 'Very

297

well – I accept that you would have avoided telling me that. But the countess . . . ?'

She lifted her chin. 'It worked.'

He waited, but she was too used to silence, to being silent with him, for the ploy to have any effect. His realization rang in his tone. 'I take it your father and Serena are not aware of your masquerade.'

'No.'

'Who does know?'

'No one – well, only the senior servants.'

'Your coachman . . . that was *Jacobs*?'

She nodded.

'Who of the others?'

'Nellie. Figgs. Miss Helm. Connor. Crisp, of course. And Folwell.' She paused, then nodded. 'That's all.'

He swore under his breath. '*All*?'

She shot him a frown. 'They're devoted to me. There's no need to imagine anything will come of it. They always do precisely as I say.'

He looked at her, then one brow quirked higher. 'Oh?' His tone had dropped to a whisper. Signaling her to silence, he crossed to the door, then flipped the lock and hauled it open in one movement, revealing Nellie, Crisp, Figgs, Miss Helm . . .

Alathea simply stared. Then she stiffened and glared. 'Go *away*!'

'Well, m'lady.' Nellie cast a wary glance at Gabriel. 'We were just wondering—'

'I'm perfectly all right. Now *go*!'

They shuffled off. Gabriel closed the door, relocked it, then returned to the window.

'All right. So much for your masquerade.' He stopped beside her; shoulder to shoulder, they looked out at the trees cloaked in dull shadow. 'You can now tell me why you took it upon yourself to rescue your family.'

'Well—' Alathea stopped, seeing the trap. 'It seemed most sensible.'

'Indeed? Let's see. A maid found the promissory note, which your father signed but somehow forgot about, and then you, your father, and Serena put your heads together, and they decided and agreed to let you pursue the matter – a matter that might destroy their lives – by yourself. Is that how it went?'

She regarded the trees stonily. 'No.'

'Well?'

The word hung in the air, insistent, persistent . . . 'I usually handle all the business affairs.'

'Why?'

She hesitated. 'Papa . . . isn't very good with money. You know how . . . well, *gentle* he is. He really has no idea – none at all.' She met his gaze. 'My mother managed the estate until her death. My grandmother managed it before her.'

He frowned. After a moment, he asked, 'And so you now handle all the estate business?'

'Yes.'

His eyes narrowed. 'Since when?'

When she looked back at the trees and didn't answer, he stepped between her and the window, leaving them all but nose to nose. His eyes bored into hers. 'When did your father cede his authority to you?'

Still she said nothing. He searched her eyes. 'Would you rather I asked him?'

If it had been any other man, she'd have called his bluff. 'Years ago.'

'Eleven years ago?'

She didn't reply.

'That's what it was, wasn't it? That was the reason you left town. Not chicken pox – I never did believe that – but money. Your father had brought the earldom to *point non plus*; somehow, you found out and took up the reins. You cut short your first Season before it had begun and went home.' He paused. 'Is that what happened?'

Her expression set, she shifted her gaze, staring out over his shoulder.

'Tell me the details. I want to know.'

He wouldn't rest until he knew. She drew in a tight breath. 'Wiggs came to the house one afternoon. He looked . . . desperate. Papa saw him in the library. I went to ask if Papa wanted tea brought in. The library door was ajar. I overheard Wiggs pleading with Papa, explaining how deeply in debt the estate was, and how the expense of giving me my Season would quite literally run us aground. Papa didn't understand. He kept insisting that all would be well, that far from ruining us, my Season would be the earldom's salvation.'

'He was counting on you making a good marriage?'

'Yes. Foolishly so.'

'It might have worked.'

She shook her head. 'You haven't considered. I would have had no dowry – quite the opposite. Any successful suitor would have had to rescue the earldom, and the debts were mountainous. I had nothing at all to recommend me except my lineage.'

'There are more than a few who would disagree.'

She glanced at him, then looked back at the trees. 'You forget – this was eleven years ago. Do you remember what I looked like at eighteen? I was painfully thin, even gawky. There was absolutely no chance I would make the sort of match required to save my family.'

When she said nothing more, he prompted, 'So?'

'When Wiggs left in despair, I went in and talked to Papa I spent the night going over the estate records Wiggs had brought.' She paused, then added, 'The next morning, we packed and left London.'

'You've been protecting your family – saving them – ever since?'

'Yes.'

'Even though it cost you your life – the life you should have had.'

'Don't be melodramatic.'

'*Me*?' He laughed harshly. 'That's the pot calling the kettle black. But if the shoe fits . . .' He caught

301

her eye. 'And it fits you.' He stood directly before her, his gaze locked on her face. 'You knew what it would mean from the very first – eleven years ago. If you'd shut your ears to your family's plight and seen out your Season, it's more than likely you would have married well – not, I grant you, well enough to save the earldom, but well enough to save yourself. You would have had a home, a title, a position – a chance to have your own family. All the things you'd been raised to expect. Your own future was there for the taking. You knew that, yet you chose to return to the country and struggle to resurrect the family fortunes, even if it meant you'd become an old maid. After your aborted Season, your family couldn't afford to have you come up again – couldn't afford to let anyone even guess. They certainly couldn't afford a respectable dowry, a point in itself too revealing, but you knew how it would be. So it all fell to you. You sacrificed your life – all of it – for them.'

He sounded angry. Alathea set her chin. 'You're making too much of it.'

He held her gaze mercilously. 'Am I?'

She couldn't avoid his eyes, the understanding lighting the hazel depths. The sacrifice of the years swept over her, the loneliness, the pain borne alone in the depths of the country. The mourning for a life she'd never had a chance to live. Dragging in a too-shallow breath, she fought to keep her gaze steady. When she was sure she had her voice under control, she said, 'Don't you *dare* pity me.'

302

His brow quirked in that way that was quintessentially his. 'It hadn't occurred to me. I'm sure you made the decision yourself – you set out to do precisely what you've done. I see nothing to pity in that.'

The dry comment gave her sensitivity, her vulnerability, the shield she needed. After a moment, she looked away. 'So now you know it all.'

Gabriel studied her face and wished that were true. In the hours since he'd learned the truth, he'd been buffeted, shaken, rocked to his soul by a tempest of emotions. Anger, raw fury, a desperate hurt, quenched pride; those were easily identified. Other passions, darker, more turbulent, much harder to define, had swelled the tumult to an ungovernable tide that had scored and ripped its way through him.

Now, in the aftermath, he felt, not empty, but cleared, as if the inner temple he'd built to house his soul had been smashed by the torrent, swept from its foundations and the bricks left scattered by the subsiding flood. Now he faced the task of building his inner house again. He could choose a simpler structure, one without the posturing, the false glamor, the boredom of which he'd grown so tired in recent months. Which bricks he chose to fashion his future was up to him, but the fact that he had a choice to make was due to her.

Only she could have caused such an upheaval.

His life from now on depended on what he did next, what he chose next. He'd come here, his anger still raging, fully intending to ring a peal over her. Now that he'd learned the whole story and finally understood what she'd been doing all along, his anger had resolved into something quite different, something intensely protective.

'What's the current state of the earldom's finances?'

She shot him a glance, then grudgingly offered a figure. 'That's the underlying security. The income from the farms adds to that.'

'What's that amount to per year?'

Bit by bit he drew the details from her, enough to confirm that not even his genius, not even Devil's touch with management, Vane and Richard's experience, not even Catriona's power could have done more to bail out the Morwellans.

I wish you had come to me earlier – all those years ago.

Thus spake his heart; he knew better than to utter the words.

'So there's nothing more that can be done there. Your family's as secure as it can be in the circumstances.' He ignored her offended stare. 'What about this man of yours – Wiggs? Is he reliable?'

'I've always found him so.' Stiffly, she added, 'If it hadn't been for his intercession with the banks, we would have sunk long ago.'

That had to be true. 'What's he think of your masquerade – or haven't you told him?'

She didn't meet his eye. 'He was very relieved when I told him I'd consulted you.'

'So he doesn't know you've been consulting in disguise.' He caught the look she threw him. 'I need to know – I'm bound to meet the man sometime over this.'

She blinked, arrested; at first, he didn't understand, then he did.

His jaw set. He felt like throttling her. 'I am not going to walk away and leave you to deal with this alone.'

Her relief was obvious, even though, sensing his reaction, she tried to hide it. The look in her eyes as they searched his made it clear she didn't understand his response.

Neither did he – not entirely. It was one of the long, vital list of things he didn't yet know, along with what he felt for her. Even now, standing no more than a foot from her, he had no idea what his feelings truly were. He had no intention of touching her – not yet. He couldn't yet contemplate dealing with the force that he knew would be unleashed when next he did, when next he took her in his arms. The time would come, but not yet, not until he'd realigned his mind and his senses to the new reality. The reality where he could stand so close to her and sense nothing beyond her warmth, a sensual, womanly, highly tempting warmth. No over-tense, flickering nerves, no prickling uncomfortableness disturbed him. Their decades-old affliction had died last night when he'd hauled her into his arms and waltzed her down Lady Arbuthnot's ballroom.

While he hadn't yet got a firm hold on what he felt, he had even less idea of what she felt about it all.

Some hint of what was in his mind must have shown in his eyes. Hers widened; sudden uncertainty flared.

He held her gaze ruthlessly; he made no attempt to hide his thoughts. She'd given herself to him, albeit in disguise. She was going to have to cope with the outcome.

'What are you thinking?'

Deliberately, he raised a brow.

She actually blushed. Her eyes widened even more, frantically searching his.

'I suggest,' he said, the words clipped and precise, 'that given the seriousness of the threat the Central East Africa Gold Company poses we set aside further discussion of the ramifications of your masquerade until we've successfully dealt with the company.'

He could almost see her feathers subside. A moment later, she nodded. 'Agreed.' She turned away. 'Not that there'll be any ramifications.'

He shot out a hand and shackled her wrist. She froze. The eyes that met his when he turned his head were wide. '*Don't* pretend.' After a moment, he continued, his tone less forceful, 'I said we'd defer discussion of the matter, not that we'd ignore it.'

'There's nothing to ignore.' Her tone was breathless; her other hand rose to her breast.

Turbulent emotion swelled, threatening to sweep

him away. Jaw set, he held it back, but allowed it to infuse his eyes. *'Don't tempt me.'*

The words, dark and low, vibrated with a power Alathea could sense; it gripped her, shook her, then held her, but lightly. If she tried to fight, the grip would tighten, would seize and pin her. For now, he was content to simply hold. Dragging in a shaky breath, she forced herself to look away.

She was immeasurably grateful when, an instant later, his fingers slid from her wrist.

'Have you learned anything since last we discussed the matter?'

The question gave her something to cling to, to respond to sensibly. 'Wiggs.' Dragging in another breath, she lifted her head. 'I asked him to find out the legal procedure involved in getting the note declared invalid. He sent a message yesterday saying he had an appointment with one of the Chancery Court judges tomorrow morning to discuss the possibilities.'

'Good. Anything else?'

She grew calmer. 'I've been looking for maps of the area to check the locations Crowley mentioned.'

'Detailed maps of that area are hard to find.'

'True, but I finally found one in a biography. It shows those three towns Crowley mentioned – Fangak, Lodwar, and Kafia. They're small, but there.'

'What did the biographer say about them?'

She hesitated. 'I don't know. I didn't read the text.'

He sighed through his teeth.

'I will! I only found it two days ago. Anyway,

what have you been doing? Have you located the captain?'

'No.' Gabriel frowned. 'It's not that simple. He's definitely not with any of the major shipping lines. There are scores of others to check, so we're checking. I've nosed about White's but no one remembers him. Incidentally, who saw him – Charlie?'

'No, Papa. But he doesn't remember anything beyond what I've told you. And I've made him promise to bring the captain home if he sees him again.'

'Hmm. I've got people searching, but it's possible he's no longer in London. Most of the senior seamen come ashore, then head off to visit family, often out of London, returning only a day or so before they're due to sail again.'

'So we might not see the captain again.'

'Not if we simply wait to see him. There are other possibilities I'm following up.' He glanced at the mantelpiece clock. 'Speaking of which, I have to be elsewhere.' He met Alathea's gaze. 'Are we agreed that we'll pool all information so we can settle this business as expeditiously as possible?'

Alathea nodded.

'Good.' He held her gaze for an instant, then he raised his hand.

Alathea's breath suspended; lost in the hazel depths of his eyes, she inwardly quivered as his fingers traced, then cradled her jaw. The pad of his thumb brushed slowly over her lips. She felt her eyes flare, her lips soften. Her wits whirled.

'And then,' he stated, 'we'll settle the rest.'

She was tempted to raise a brow; caution stepped in and prevented it. When she simply held his gaze, he nodded.

'I'll call on you tomorrow.'

She'd never been afraid of Gabriel; after careful consideration, Alathea concluded she still wasn't. It wasn't fear that tightened her nerves when she caught sight of him while strolling in the park; it was anticipation, but of what she wasn't sure.

Together with Mary, Alice, Heather and Eliza, she'd been strolling for twenty minutes. Lord Esher and his friend Carstairs, of the Finchley-Carstairs, young gentlemen of impeccable credentials, had joined the group, his lordship to chat with Mary, while Mr Carstairs manfully engaged the others, although his gaze strayed frequently to Alice's face.

Ambling in the rear, Alathea had watched the budding romances with an approving eye, until she saw Gabriel approaching. After that, she saw nothing beyond him, severely elegant in morning coat, buckskin breeches, and Hessians, the breeze ruffling his chestnut locks. His expression easy, he greeted her sisters and his with brotherly familiarity, appraised the suddenly tense young men, and nodded his approval. Then his gaze slid to her. Deserting the younger crew, he strolled to her side.

Alathea locked both hands on her parasol handle and prayed he wouldn't commandeer one.

His eyes met hers, then his brow quirked. 'I don't bite,' he murmured, as he halted beside her. 'At least,' he amended, voice deepening, 'not in public.'

Awareness swept her; she felt her blush rise. He viewed the sight, his brow quirked again, then he turned and surveyed the group moving far ahead of them. 'I suppose we'd better keep them in sight.'

'Indeed.' Alathea stepped out; he fell in beside her.

'Have you heard from Wiggs yet?'

'No – his appointment was scheduled for eleven.' It was only just past noon.

'Will you be at the Clares' ball tonight?'

'Yes.'

'Good – I'll meet you there.'

Alathea nodded. That was one benefit of the countess's unmasking; they could now easily meet to exchange information. 'I read that explorer's book, at least the relevant parts.'

As she jiggled her parasol and dug into her reticule, she felt Gabriel's gaze on her face.

'Burning the midnight oil?'

She flicked him a glance. She didn't need him to tell her she had rings under her eyes. 'When else would I get time to read?'

The tartness of the reply had no discernible effect. 'Running yourself ragged isn't going to help. What's this?' He took the sheet she thrust at him.

'That's the description the explorer gave of those three towns.'

He perused it as they strolled; his brows gradually rose. 'How very interesting. When was this explorer in these parts?'

'Only early last year. The book's just been published.' Alathea leaned closer, peering at the sheet. She tapped one paragraph. 'As I recall, Crowley said the company had purchased a large building in Fangak from some French government agency to house the workers involved in the construction of the company's mines. According to the explorer, Fangak is "a collection of flimsy wooden huts far from civilization".'

'Crowley also said Lodwar was on a major road. Instead, it appears to be a tiny settlement halfway up a rugged mountainside, "well away from the beaten track".'

Alathea glanced at his face. 'It's evidence, isn't it?'

He looked at her, then nodded. Folding the note, he slipped it into his pocket. 'But we'll need more.' He looked at the group ahead of them. 'How's that shaping?'

'Promisingly. Esher becomes more definite by the day, while Carstairs . . .' Tilting her head, Alathea considered the young gentleman. 'I think he's trying to screw his courage to the sticking point, but is having a hard time believing that it's actually happened to him.'

Gabriel snorted. 'Poor bugger.'

Alathea pretended not to hear.

They strolled on, following the others, then Gabriel halted. 'I'll leave you here.'

Alathea turned to him, only to feel his fingers close about hers. He raised her hand and considered it, slim fingers trapped by his. Then he lifted his gaze to her eyes.

She couldn't breathe, couldn't think. He was close; because of her height, her parasol shaded them both, creating an illusion of privacy in the middle of the park. They never exchanged the routine pleasantries, touching hands, bowing, but now he held her hand, and her, too; she wondered what he meant to do.

His lips twisted, wry and taunting both. 'I'll see you tonight.'

He pressed her hand briefly, then released it. With a nod, he left her.

Alathea stood still, breathing evenly, and watched him stride away. Part of her mind noted that he'd left just before their ambling stroll would have brought them into view of the carriage drive, presently lined with the carriages of the ton's matrons, including those of his mother and aunt. The rest of her mind was engrossed with the burning question of what he thought he was about, what tack he intended to take with her.

The situation between them had changed, yet he still wanted her, even though he now knew who she was. He still intended to have her, to continue their illicit liaison; amazing though that seemed, that much was clear.

Very little else was.

With the countess's unmasking, all control of their interaction had passed to him. She was completely in his power, a power she knew better than to imagine he wouldn't, if provoked, wield.

The little group she was watching were drawing ahead. Straightening her parasol, she set out in their wake.

What he had in mind she couldn't begin to guess, any more than she could be sure of his motives. Given their encounters in Bond Street and Bruton Street, let alone the rest, he might well wish to punish her. His present conduct might be a facade, adopted to ease their way while they pursued the company. He was more than honorable enough to put aside his own feelings until they'd dealt with the threat. *Then* he might consider retribution.

Luckily, he rarely held a grudge. By the time their investigations were complete, it was possible, even likely, that his interest in her would have waned, that he would have grown bored and shifted his sights to his next conquest.

A frown in her eyes, Alathea climbed the slope to the carriage drive, and wondered why the prospect of him growing bored with her and thus abandoning any notion of retribution did not bring her any sense of ease.

CHAPTER 14

Lady Clare's ball was yet another unrelenting crush. The Season was in full swing and everyone simply had to be seen at all the major events. Finally gaining Alathea's side, Gabriel cast a malevolent glance over the jostling throng. 'Manic,' he muttered.

Lord Montgomery, presently holding Alathea's attention, thought the jibe aimed at him. He bristled. Smiling serenely, Alathea pretended she hadn't heard. 'Have your mama and sister come up to town this year?'

Faced with such unequivocal interest, his lordship's hackles subsided. With a disdainful glance at Gabriel, he intoned, 'Indeed, indeed! They are, naturally, concerned as to the future of the estate. Why—'

Recently afflicted with a conviction that she would be just the wife for him, his lordship droned on. Alathea let her smile glide over the other eager faces, but did not linger long enough to encourage any to interrupt with his own tale. Completing her circuit brought her glance to Gabriel; he caught it, irritation behind his hazel eyes. He hesitated,

314

then, to her surprise, reached out and took the hand she hadn't thought to offer him. He held it, waiting with studied patience until Lord Montgomery's monologue rolled to a close, then he bowed. As he straightened, Alathea, off-balance and mystified, saw concern color his expression.

'My dear, you're rather pale.'

My dear? She nearly goggled.

Gabriel anchored her hand on his sleeve, drawing her within his protective orbit. 'Perhaps a stroll outside . . . before you faint from the stuffiness.'

She'd never fainted in her life. Her gaze trapped in his, Alathea waved a hand weakly before her face. 'It is rather hot in here.'

His brow quirked; one corner of his lips did, too. 'The doors to the terrace are open . . .'

The suggestion was greeted with numerous offers to accompany them; obedient to the fingers squeezing hers, Alathea smiled wanly. 'The noise . . .' She gestured limply. 'A few moments of absolute quiet would help, and then I'll be able to return to you.'

With that, they had to be content. Gabriel excised her from the circle and steered her down the room. Alathea hoped it appeared that he was dragging her off in brotherly fashion – for her own good – but the speculative frowns in too many eyes made her itch to box his ears. Next, he'd have the scandalmongers watching them avidly, and God only knew what they might see.

They gained the flagged terrace along which a number of couples were strolling. She tried to slide her hand from his sleeve to put greater distance between them. His fingers tightened; she knew better than to tug. 'You'll start people talking,' she hissed as, acquiescing, she continued to glide close beside him.

'No more than they're talking already of you and the aspirants to your charms. Why on earth do you surround yourself with them?'

'I assure you it's not by choice!' After a moment, she added, 'I suspect Serena's been busy on my behalf, *despite* the fact I made it plain that this was Mary's and Alice's Season and I have no interest in attracting a husband. Well' – she gestured to her braided cap – 'how much clearer can I make it? Can't they *see*?'

Eyeing the cap with savage dislike, Gabriel bit back the words 'Probably not.' Her caps offended him at some elemental level. There was, now he thought of it, one sure way of getting rid of them once and for all. Considering the prospect of never seeing another cap covering her hair, he guided her toward the shadowy end of the terrace, presently deserted. 'Did Wiggs report on his meeting with the judge?'

Reaching the balustrade at the end of the flags, they surveyed the thick bushes beyond the stone barrier, then turned and leaned against it, hip to hip, shoulder to shoulder, in oddly companionable comfort.

'Yes. It seems we can ask for a decision declaring the note invalid through a petition directly to the bench, without evidence or deliberations being heard in open court.'

'Good. That'll make things easier.'

'The judge said the speed at which a decision would be given will depend on the quality of our evidence. The more detailed and complete the evidence, the quicker the judgment. If the case was cut and dried, a decision could be formalized in a matter of days.'

Gabriel nodded. 'When we're ready, I'll alert Devil. He'll make sure it gets immediate attention.' Alathea's sudden grin caught his eye. 'What?'

She glanced at him. 'Just the way you operate.' She waved. 'Just like that – throw a duke into the equation.'

He shrugged. 'If one has a duke to throw . . .'

Her grin fading, Alathea asked, 'Have your people learned anything more?'

'No grand revelations, but Montague is making headway with all those figures and projections Crowley spouted. Needless to say, they don't add up. My contacts in Whitehall are still checking the claims he made about various foreign government departments and officials, and the permissions he said the company had already received. The more things that are false, the wider the front on which the company's claims are disproved, the easier it will be to convince the court.'

'But a witness – an eyewitness as it were – would

be the definitive proof. Have you heard anything more about the captain?'

'Yes and no. Mostly no. There are so many shipping lines, and at too many I have no contact from whom I can discreetly inquire. We can't risk any overt search, not even for the captain. Crowley's too powerful. He may well have contacts who'll report any unusual queries in all shipping lines dealing with his present area of interest.'

'Is he that omnipotent?'

'Yes. Don't underestimate him. He may not have attended any recognized school, but he knows how to play his connections well. Witness Archie Douglas.' After a moment, Gabriel stated, 'Whatever we do, we must never forget Crowley.'

The words disturbed Alathea. Frowning, she shook them aside. 'There must be some register of the ships and their captains, surely?'

'There is – it's kept by the Port Authority. There are two registers we need to look at – the log which lists all the ships as they enter the Pool of London along with their captain, and the main register of vessels, which shows which shipping line a particular ship sails for. Unfortunately, there was a scandal involving the last port registrar. Consequently, his successor is exceedingly resistant to the idea of allowing anyone access to either the log or the register.'

'Exceedingly resistant?'

'Short of an order from the Admirality or the Revenue, there's no way to view those books.'

'Hmm.'

Gabriel glanced at Alathea. 'Don't even *think* of breaking in.'

She focused on him. 'Why? Because you've already considered it?'

'Yes.' His lips twisted. He looked back along the terrace, then straightened. 'The office is manned around the clock. At present, searching the log and register is impossible.'

Following his gaze to Lucifer, strolling through the shadows toward them, Alathea murmured, 'Nothing's impossible when you're twelve years old.'

Gabriel shot her a look as Lucifer, brows high, joined them.

'What are you two doing out here?'

What do you think? burned Gabriel's tongue. He hadn't yet had time to steer their interaction into the arena he'd intended.

Alathea waved at him. 'He's looking into something for me. An investment.'

Turning his head, Gabriel looked at her; her gaze fixed on Lucifer's face, she ignored him.

Lucifer was looking at him. 'I think the twins have noticed. They're bubbling and fizzing and exchanging glances like fury. God knows what they'll do once they realize it's true.'

'Once they realize what's true?' Alathea asked.

Lucifer turned his dark gaze on her. 'When they realize *he's* not watching them anymore.'

'He's not?' Alathea looked at Gabriel. He'd

developed a consuming interest in his manicured fingernails.

The damned man had listened to her. Listened, and allowed her to influence his direction. She felt slightly giddy.

'He's not. And, at the moment, *I'm* not, either.' Belligerently disapproving, Lucifer looked from her to Gabriel and back again. 'I just hope you know what you're doing. That bounder Carsworth's sniffing about their skirts.'

Gabriel looked up. 'Has he approached either of them?'

The question was mild, the underlying tone anything but.

'Well, no,' Lucifer admitted.

'Have either of the twins encouraged him?' Alathea put in.

Lucifer's expression turned mulish. 'No. He intercepted Amelia – not overtly approaching her, just happening to come upon her in the crowd.'

'And?'

His reluctance was palpable, but eventually he conceded, 'She put on an act like Aunt Helena. Looked him down, then up, then stuck her nose in the air and swanned past without a word.'

'Well, there you are.' Straightening, Alathea slipped an arm through his. 'They've been very well trained. They're perfectly capable of managing, if you'll only let them.'

'Humph!' Lucifer let her turn him up the terrace. Arm in arm, they strolled back toward the open doors spilling light and noise across the flags. Although she spared him not a glance, Alathea was intensely aware that Gabriel prowled very close on her other side.

'Carsworth's a worm – no real threat.' Over her head, Lucifer exchanged a glance with Gabriel. 'But what happens when they try that trick with someone with a bit more' – he gestured – '*savoir faire*?'

Gabriel shrugged. 'So they'll learn.'

'Learn what?' Alathea asked as they stepped back into the ballroom.

'Learn what would happen if a lady tried such a ploy on, say, one of us,' Lucifer replied.

Alathea raised a brow at Gabriel.

He considered her, then flicked a glance at Lucifer. Confirming his brother's attention had wandered, he looked back, into her eyes. 'Try it – and you'll see.'

There was something in his eyes that reminded her forcefully of a tiger; the purr in his voice underscored the connection. Recalling what had happened the last time she'd tried, nose in the air, to brush past him, Alathea stiffened her spine and lifted her head. 'The twins will manage perfectly well.'

Lucifer, scanning the crowd, humphed again. 'Well, if you refuse to watch, then I may as well put my time to better use.' One black brow arching, he glanced at Gabriel, then, with an elegant nod to Alathea, he shouldered his way into the crowd.

If anything, the crush had worsened. Alathea felt Gabriel's fingers close about hers, then her hand was on his sleeve as he steered her out of the ebb and flow before the doors. The tack he took was in the opposite direction to where they'd left her cavaliers.

'Can you see Mary and Alice?' Why she felt so breathless she couldn't understand.

'No.' His lips were close to her ear, his breath a warm caress. 'But, like the twins, they'll manage.'

So would she, she vowed, as he found them a few square feet of space in which to stand comfortably. Although they were surrounded, they might as well have been alone for all the notice their neighbors took, too caught up in their own conversations.

'Now tell me, what did you mean about being twelve years old?' Gabriel trapped her gaze as she glanced up at him. 'In case it's escaped your notice, neither you nor I are.'

The meaning in his eyes was quite different from the subject of their discussion. Alathea reined in her skittering wits. 'I wasn't referring to us.'

'Good.'

The subtle easing of his lips did quite peculiar things to her nerves. She dragged in a breath. 'I meant—'

'My dear Lady Alathea.'

Alathea turned to see the earl of Chillingworth emerging from the crowd. He swept her a necessarily abbreviated bow. 'Such solace to discover a

322

divine delight in this unholy crush.' He sent a measuring glance Gabriel's way. 'So nice to know one's evening won't be a complete waste of time.'

Gabriel didn't respond.

Ignoring the burgeoning menace at her elbow, Alathea smiled and gave Chillingworth her hand. 'I believe the musicians her ladyship has hired are quite exceptional.'

'If only one could hear them,' Chillingworth replied. 'Are your sisters enjoying their Season?'

'Indeed. Our ball will be held next week – dare we hope you'll attend?'

'No other hostess,' Chillingworth avowed, 'will have any hope of enticing me elsewhere.' His gray gaze roved Alathea's face, then settled on her eyes. 'Tell me, have you seen the latest production at the Opera House?'

'Why, no. I had heard—' Alathea broke off as the sea of guests suddenly wavered, then parted. As the clamor of voices dimmed, the opening strains of a waltz filtered through.

'Ah.' Chillingworth turned to her. 'I wonder, my dear, if you would do me the honor—'

'I'm afraid, dear boy, that this waltz is mine.'

Gabriel's languid drawl did nothing to conceal the steel beneath his words. Chillingworth looked up; over Alathea's head, gray eyes clashed with hazel. Turning, Alathea stared at Gabriel's face, noting the hard edge fell determination lent his features. Relinquishing Chillingworth's gaze, he met hers. 'Shall we?'

He gestured to the rapidly clearing dance floor, then his arm shifted beneath her fingers and his hand closed about hers. His gaze flicked to Chillingworth. 'His lordship will excuse us.'

Giddy, slightly stunned by what she'd glimpsed in his hooded eyes, Alathea smiled apologetically at Chillingworth. The earl bowed easily. Without more ado, Gabriel led her forward. A second later she was in his arms, whirling down the floor.

It took a full circuit before she caught her breath. He was holding her too close again, but she wasn't going to waste what breath she had protesting that point. 'I don't suppose there's any sense in pointing out that this waltz wasn't, in fact, yours to claim.'

He met her gaze. 'Not the slightest.'

The look in his eyes stole her breath. She mustered her wilting temper for protection. 'Indeed? So whenever you feel like waltzing, I'm to expect—'

'You misunderstand. Henceforth, *all* your waltzes are mine.'

'*All?*'

'Every last one.' He expertly twirled her around the end of the room; as they joined the long line going back up the ballroom, he continued, 'You may dance any other dance with whomever you please, but you'll waltz only with me.'

All inclination to argue, to protest, evaporated. *Don't tempt me.* He'd warned her once – the words were again in his eyes. They rang in her head.

When she finally managed to draw in another breath, Alathea looked over his shoulder and tried to gather her wits and focus on his motives.

Only to fall victim to her senses, to the seductive shift and sway of their bodies, their long limbs twining, sliding, separating, then coming together again. He waltzed as he did all physical things – effortlessly, expertly, with an inherent grace that only emphasized the leashed power behind every move. He held her easily, his strength palpable, surrounding her, guiding her, protecting her.

She'd waltzed with others but none with his matchless authority, founded as it was in his knowledge, physical and sensual, of her. He knew she couldn't resist, that while in his arms she was helpless. That her heart beat unevenly, that her skin heated, that she would go wherever he led. He had her trapped in a web, one she had helped fashion, of passion, of yearning, of desire slaked by sensual reward. She was his and he knew it. What he meant to do with the knowledge, with her, remained an unsettling unknown.

The music ended and they slowed, then halted. She studied his face, the hard planes unyielding, uninformative, and inwardly sighed. 'I should find Serena.'

Releasing her, he placed her hand on his sleeve, and protectively steered her through the crowd.

The following evening, Alathea left her bed-chamber once again in a tearing rush. Heading for her office, she flung the door wide and dashed for her desk. Sitting, she pulled a sheet of paper free, settling it on the blotter as she flicked open the inkwell.

'You wanted me, m'lady?'

'Yes, Folwell.' Alathea didn't look up. Dipping a pen in the ink, she industriously scribbled. 'I want you to deliver this note to Brook Street.'

'To Mr Cynster, m'lady?'

'Yes.'

'Now, m'lady?'

'As soon as you get back from driving us to Almacks.'

A minute passed, the only sound in the room the scritch-scratch of the pen. Then Alathea blotted her missive, folded it, and scrawled Gabriel's name on the front. She dropped the pen and stood. Waving the note, she crossed the room to Folwell. 'There won't be an answer.'

Folwell slipped the note into his coat pocket. 'I'll drop it off on the way back from King Street.'

Alathea nodded. Lips compressed, she strode for the front hall where Serena, Mary, and Alice were waiting.

A minute later, she was in the carriage, rolling across the cobbles to the holy portals of the patronesses' dreary rooms. Almacks! She hadn't liked the place the first time she'd seen it, when she'd been a gawky eighteen. She sincerely doubted she'd enjoy her evening, but . . . her sweetly loving step-mother had turned stubborn.

She'd expected to remain home that evening and arrange some discreet rendezvous to discuss her urgent news with Gabriel. Instead, over dinner, Serena had announced that Emily Cowper had made special mention of hoping to see her that evening, having missed her in the park that afternoon. That afternoon, when she'd been off on an excursion to see just how much a twelve-year-old could pry from the otherwise impregnable Port Authority.

Jeremy's success had left her giddy. She desperately wanted to see Gabriel. She'd marshaled all her arguments against Almacks and spent the half hour after dinner laying them out, but Serena had stood firm. That happened so rarely, she'd been forced to acquiesce, which had left her little time to dress. Thankfully, Nellie was fully recovered; despite the rush, her hair was elegantly coiffed, her gloves, reticule, and shawl the correct accessories for her gown of pale-green silk.

Not that she cared. Given Gabriel wouldn't be there, her evening would be a complete waste of time. Still, tomorrow morning was, logistically speaking, no different from tonight.

That conclusion rang in her mind the next morning – mockingly. Scrambling to her feet, dusting earth from her cotton gardening gloves and quickly stripping them off, she told herself it didn't matter what he thought, how much he saw.

She looked up as he reached her. 'I didn't expect you this side of eleven.'

His brow quirked as he calmly took possession of one of her hands. 'You said as early as possible.'

One long finger stroked her palm. Alathea tried to stiffen. 'I thought, for you, as early as possible would be close to noon.'

'Did you? Why? I didn't go out last night, remember?'

'Didn't you?'

'No.' After a moment, he added, 'There was nowhere I wanted to go.'

Her gaze locked with his, Alathea felt unaccountably giddy. He couldn't possibly mean . . . Was he flirting with her? Abruptly, she cleared her throat and waved vaguely at her stepsiblings. 'We like to spend a little time in the garden every morning. Exercise.'

'Indeed?' His shrewd gaze swept the garden. He responded to Mary's and Alice's cheery greetings with an easy smile, to Charlie's familiar 'Hoi!' with a wave. Jeremy, helping Charlie lug a branch to the bottom of the garden, bobbed his head. Gabriel grinned, his gaze moving on to Miss Helm, who colored when he bowed. Beside the little governess, Augusta sat, Rose clutched in her arms, her wide-eyed gaze riveted on Gabriel.

'I can't recall seeing Jeremy since he was a babe in arms,' he murmured. 'And I don't believe I've met your youngest sister at all. What's her name?'

'Augusta. She's six.'

'Six?' He looked back at her. 'When you were six you gave me chicken pox.'

'I'd hoped you'd forgotten. You promptly gave it to Lucifer.'

'We three were always good at sharing.' A moment passed, then he said, 'Speaking of which . . .'

She waved at the house. 'If you'd like—'

'No need to interrupt your endeavors.' He looked down. 'The grass is dry.' So saying, he sat beside her mat, her hand still in his. Looking up at her, he tugged. 'You can tell me your news here.'

Alathea only just managed not to glare. She subsided with passable grace, settling once more on her knees, tugging her gloves back on. 'You know I hate gardening.'

His brows rose; from the corner of her eye, she could see him recalling. 'So you do. How very devoted of you, to keep your sisters company.' A moment passed, then he asked, 'Is that why you do it?'

'Yes. No.' Her gaze on the pansies, Alathea could feel her cheeks heating. Drawing in a breath, she reminded herself that he already knew more than enough to guess the truth. 'They think *I* love gardening, and Serena insists that they should understand the basics of borders and beds from the ground up, so to speak.'

She felt his gaze sweep her face, then he looked out over the lawns. 'I see. And Charlie and Jeremy are the pruning specialists?'

'More or less.'

He said nothing for a moment, one long leg stretched out, the other bent, one arm draped over his raised knee. Then he turned again to her. 'So what have you learned?'

Alathea yanked out a clump of grass. 'I've learned that being twelve years old can open the register at the Port Authority.'

His gaze switched to Jeremy. 'It can?'

'I took Jeremy on an excursion to learn about how ships are managed in and out of the Pool of London. The harbor master was extremely accommodating – he has a young boy of his own. Of course, being the son and daughter of a belted earl helped.'

'I dare say. But all we had was the captain's description. How on earth did you manage to learn more discreetly? I take it you have.'

'Indeed! I primed Jeremy – he has an excellent memory. I described the captain as Papa had seen him, and explained what we needed to find out. We decided it would be best to ask about the information in the log and register, and then ask what it might be useful for. That allowed us to suggest that it could be used to find out which shipping lines carried goods to different parts of the world. At that point, I suitably vaguely remembered a friend of ours, a Mr Higgenbotham, who—'

'Wait! Who's Higgenbotham? Does he exist?'

'No.' Alathea frowned. 'He's just part of our tale.' She yanked up another weed. 'Where was I? Oh, yes – this Mr Higgenbotham had dropped by with a friend of his, a captain whose ship recently docked from Central East Africa. That, of course, was Jeremy's cue to challenge the harbor master to see if his log and register would tell us who the captain sailed for.'

'And the harbor master obliged?'

'Of course! Men always like to demonstrate their abilities before an appreciative audience, especially one composed of a female and a youthful pup. It took him twenty minutes – there were quite a few ships to cross-check – but we think the captain must be one Aloysius Struthers who sails for Bentinck and Company. Their office is in East Smithfield Street. The harbor master recognized the description and is certain Struthers is our man.'

Gabriel resisted the urge to shake his head. 'Amazing.'

'Jeremy,' Alathea decreed, plonking another weed onto her pile, 'was simply magnificent. Even had you been the harbor master, you would have happily searched the log for him. He played his hand *just* right.'

Gabriel raised a brow. 'He's obviously like you – he must have inherited the same thespian tendencies.'

He waited, but Alathea pointedly ignored the comment, reaching instead for another weed. After a moment, she asked, 'So what's next?'

Gabriel looked across the lawns to where her stepbrothers were wrestling with a thick branch. 'I'll visit Bentinck and Company this afternoon.'

Alathea frowned at him. 'I thought you said any open inquiry was too dangerous?'

Completing his scan of the garden, Gabriel returned his gaze to her face. 'Surely you don't think you're the only one who can assume a disguise?'

Her lips twitched. 'What will you be? A merchant from Hull looking for a fast ship to carry his white-bait to Africa?'

'*Hull?* Good God, no. I'll be an importer of wooden artifacts looking for a reliable line to transport my wares, bought throughout Africa, to St Katherine's Docks.'

'And?'

'And I'll have received a recommendation for Struthers and the line for which he sails but, being an exceedingly fussy client, I'll insist on speaking directly to Struthers before making any decision. That should encourage the company to give me Struthers's direction with all possible dispatch.'

Alathea nodded approvingly. 'Very good. We'll make a thespian of you yet.'

She looked up, expecting some light retort – he was studying her, his hazel gaze steady and keen. He held her trapped, searching, considering . . . the sounds of the others, their chatter, their laughter, the bright calls of the birds and the distant rumble of carriage wheels, faded away, leaving just the two of them on the grass in the sunshine.

Then his gaze shifted, dropping to her lips, briefly sweeping lower before returning to her eyes.

'The trick,' he murmured, his voice very low, 'is not in assuming the role, but in knowing when the charade ends and reality starts.'

In his eyes, so like hers, lay living reminders of all they'd shared – the childhood triumphs, the youthful adventures, their recent intimacy. Deep in their gaze, Alathea simply existed. Reaching out, he caught a wayward lock of her hair lying loose along her cheek. Taming it, he tucked it back behind her ear. As he withdrew his hand, with the backs of his fingers he caressed the whorl of her ear, then lightly traced the line of her jaw.

His hand dropped.

Their gazes held, then Alathea drew a shaky breath and looked down. He looked away. 'I'll see what I can learn.'

Gathering his long limbs, he rose. Alathea kept her gaze on her pansies.

'I'll let you know if I'm successful.'

She inclined her head. 'Yes. Do.'

With no 'Good-bye,' he moved off, waving to the others, stopping to exchange a polite word with Miss Helm. Alathea hestitated, then gave in to the urge to turn her head and watch him as he strode away.

Twelve hours later, Alathea stood by the side of Lady Hendricks's overcrowded music room, enraptured by the composition faultlessly rendered by the capital's most sought-after string quartet. The first segment of the performance was drawing to a close when long fingers curled around her wrist, then slid down to tangle with hers.

Her head whipped around. Her eyes widened. 'What on earth are you doing here?'

Gabriel looked at her, an incipient frown in his eyes. 'I wanted to see you.'

He eased in beside her; she was forced to make room. The last thing she wanted was to draw more eyes their way. 'How did you know I was here?' They both spoke in whispers.

'Folwell told me where you were headed.'

'Fol—? Oh.' She caught his eye. 'You know about Folwell.'

'Hmm. Has he mentioned my new man?'

'Chance?'

Gabriel nodded. 'His tongue runs on wheels, out of my presence or in it. I knew Folwell was haunting my kitchen from the first. I didn't, however, connect his presence with you. I thought he was there to see Dodswell. I know better now, but Folwell does have his uses.'

With a sniff, Alathea returned her gaze to the musicians. 'I can't believe Lady Hendricks sent you a card for this – not even she could be that naively hopeful.'

'She didn't.' Gabriel settled close beside her. 'I simply walked in, secure in the knowledge she won't show me the door.' He studied Alathea's profile, watching it soften as the music drew her back. The line of her jaw fascinated him, a subtle melding of feminine strength and vulnerability.

She had always struck him that way – as much a partner as one to be protected. He'd recognized that quality in the countess; he'd known it in Alathea all his life.

Following her gaze to the players, he waited until they concluded their piece on an uplifting crescendo before murmuring, 'The captain is presently uncontactable.'

The outburst of applause distracted the crowd so none but he saw her disappointment. It filled her eyes as well as her expression. He moved across her, lifting her hand to his sleeve. 'Come to the window – we can speak more freely there.'

The narrow windows were open, a balcony, barely a ledge, beyond them. A cool breeze wafted the filmy curtains. Pressing them aside, they stood on the threshold, facing each other, hardly private but sufficiently apart from other guests to talk without being overheard.

Alathea leaned back against the window frame. 'What did you learn?'

'Aloysius Struthers is our man – the clerks at the shipping line confirmed the description, and also that he's something of an expert on East Africa, having sailed those coasts for the last decade and more. Unfortunately, the captain is presently away visiting friends – the company has no idea where. He has no family and no fixed abode in this country. However, he does call in now and then to check there's no change in his sailing schedule. He's not due to sail again for a month. I left a message guaranteed to bring him to Brook Street the instant he reads it, but he may not get it for a week or more.'

Alathea grimaced.

Gabriel hesitated, then continued, 'There's also the possibility that he might not be willing to help. The clerks painted a picture of an irascible old gent more concerned with his ships and Africa than anything else. I gather he doesn't have much time for non-sailors.'

'Do we have enough proof to mount a case without his testimony?'

Gabriel paused, then said, 'Montague's figures are strongly suggestive of deliberate fraud, but are not conclusive. A good barrister could argue his way around them. What else we have on the three towns – Fangak, Lodwar and Kingi – relies on the reports of explorers who are not themselves available to vouch for the details. As for information from the African authorities, my contacts in Whitehall are finding it exceedingly difficult to get any straight answers, which in itself is highly suspicious. For any serious investor, what we have would be more than enough to pass judgment on Crowley's scheme. For a court of law, we need more.'

'How much more?'

'I'll keep pressing Whitehall. Without more definitive proof, lodging a petition at this stage would be unwise.'

'Essentially, we need the captain.'

'Yes, but at the moment, there's nothing more we can do on that front.'

'And even if we do find him, he may not help.'

Gabriel made no reply. A moment later, the musicians laid bow to string. They both turned toward the dais as the crowd resettled for the next piece. A lilting air, it filled the room with a hauntingly sweet melody. Alathea watched the musicians, letting their art sweep her away, temporarily soothing her fears. Gabriel watched her. The short piece ended; applause rolled through the room. Alathea contributed her share, then sighed and turned to him.

'I'd forgotten you like music.'

Her expression turned wry. 'To my mind, it's one of the few charms of the capital – to be able to hear the most talented musicians.'

Gabriel merely nodded. His gaze went past her, and abruptly sharpened. 'Damn! That harpy's actually going to throw her daughter at me.'

Looking around, Alathea beheld their hostess bearing down on them, a beaming smile on her face, her pale, clearly reticent daughter in tow. 'Well, you are here, after all. She probably sees it as encouragement.'

The sound Gabriel made was derisive.

Alathea arched a brow at him. 'Shall I leave you to your fate?'

'Don't you dare. That poor girl always loses her tongue about me. God knows why. Conversing with her is worse than pulling teeth.'

Alathea smiled as she turned to greet Lady Hendricks. Gabriel appropriated her hand and placed it on his sleeve, thereby denying her ladyship any chance of whisking her off and leaving him alone with her daughter. Lady Hendricks accepted the situation with a puzzled look, settling for gushing over his presence before retreating, leaving her daughter with them. Alathea, who was acquainted with Miss Hendricks, took pity on all concerned and kept the conversation rolling, never straying from any but the most mundane subjects.

After one warning glance from her, Gabriel behaved himself, consenting to chat with debonair charm. When the musicians next took to the dais and, under Gabriel's direction, they parted from Miss Hendricks, the young lady was actually smiling. Gliding through the room on Gabriel's arm, Alathea felt sure Lady Hendricks would be pleased enough to forget her earlier puzzlement.

'Esher and Carstairs are sitting with your sisters.' Gabriel shot her a look as they passed out of the music room. 'How's that coming along?'

'Very well.' Halting in the foyer, Alathea drew her hand from his sleeve and turned to look back into the room. 'Inside two weeks, I should think.' Then she glanced at Gabriel, her expression growing serious. 'Have you . . . heard anything about either of them?'

'No.' He scanned her face. 'I've already checked – they're exactly as they appear. Both are wealthy enough to marry as they choose, and in both cases their respective families should be more than content with their securing an earl's daughters as their brides.'

'Thank heavens. I'd started to wonder if it was all too good to be true. I never imagined they'd both go off so easily.' She looked back at her sisters. 'This Season has proved far more felicitous than anyone could have expected.'

His gaze on her face, on the delicate line of her jaw, Gabriel slowly nodded. He hesitated, then touched her arm. 'Au revoir.' Stepping past her, he left the house.

He found her in the park the following afternoon, a willowy vision in pale green. The fine fabric of her gown clung to her hips, swaying evocatively as she trailed in the wake of her sisters and, unfortunately, his. Esher and Carstairs were once more in attendance; Gabriel resigned himself to speaking to both in the next few days regarding their intentions. A subtle prod wouldn't hurt.

His gaze fastened on Alathea. Lengthening his stride, he closed the distance between them. She whirled as he caught up with her. Surprise and awareness flared in her eyes, then she caught herself and inclined her head graciously. 'Have you heard anything?'

Taking her hand, an action that now seemed normal, even called for, Gabriel anchored it on his sleeve and drew her to stroll beside him. 'No. Nothing more.'

'Oh.'

He felt her questioning glance. She wanted to know what had brought him here. 'I thought you might be interested in the details Montague has put together.'

The distraction served; she not only followed his account, but posed a few shrewd questions on the Company's projected costs. He nodded. 'I'll get Montague to check—'

'Alathea! Such a pleasant surprise!'

The exclamation brought them up short; absorbed in their discussion, they had not been looking about them. Gabriel muttered a curse as his gaze fell on the countess of Lewes, approaching with her brother, Lord Montgomery.

Alathea smiled. 'Cecile! How lovely to see you.'

Suppressing a frown, Gabriel exchanged a terse nod with Montgomery. They both waited with feigned patience while the ladies exchanged far more detailed greetings. From references the countess made, Gabriel gathered she and Alathea were contemporaries; their acquaintance dated from Alathea's aborted Season eleven years before. From Montgomery's smug expression, Gabriel surmised his lordship imagined his sister's connection would put him on a closer, more personal footing with Alathea.

'And Mr Cynster!' The countess turned to him with an arch smile.

'Madam.' Gabriel accepted the hand she offered him, bowed easily, and released her. Alathea's fingers slid from his sleeve. Without looking, he caught her hand, enclosing it within his grasp. She stilled. He could all but hear her wondering what he was about.

'Perhaps,' the countess continued, ignoring the byplay, 'we could stroll together?'

Alathea smiled. 'Indeed – why not?'

Gabriel pinched her fingers, then made a great show of tucking her hand into the crook of his elbow. She shot him a sharp glance, then turned to Lord Montgomery. 'Is your mother well?'

Feeling distinctly unsocial, Gabriel turned to the countess. 'How's Helmsley these days?'

The countess colored and slid around his wicked question. She paid him back by describing her offspring and their illnesses, a subject guaranteed to send any sane gentleman fleeing. Gabriel mentally gritted his teeth and refused to yield. As they strolled on, he noticed that Alathea kept her gaze fixed on Lord Montgomery, paying no attention whatever to all the gory details about the countess's three children. Knowing her as he did, knowing how closely she'd been involved with the care of her stepsiblings, he at first found that odd. Then they reached the Serpentine and he glanced at her face.

She kept it averted; he couldn't see her eyes. He could see the underlying stiffness in her features. Smoothly, he turned to the countess. 'Do you plan to attend Lady Richmond's gala?'

The abruptness of the question made the

countess pause, but she took to the new topic with alacrity. With a query here and there, he kept her engrossed in the social whirl, well away from the subject of children. His awareness centered on Alathea, he sensed the gradual easing of her tension. She had, indeed, given up a lot to save her stepfamily, far more than she would willingly let anyone know.

'I say! Lady Alathea!'

'My dear lady!'

'Countess, do introduce me.'

A bevy of five gentlemen, including Lord Coleburn, Mr Simpkins and Lord Falworth, swept up to them from behind; if Gabriel had been able to see them, they wouldn't have managed it, but now he and Alathea were caught.

Alathea sensed his increasing irritation. She glanced at him; he was regarding Lord Falworth with an impassive expression and a dangerous glint in his eye.

'Don't you think so, Lady Alathea?'

'Oh – yes.' Recalling Falworth's question, she quickly amended, 'But only in the company of close friends.'

Dealing with her would-be suitors while knowing Gabriel was considering annihilating one or all of them played havoc with her normally unassailable nerves. Her relief was quite genuine when he closed his hand over hers, still tucked in his elbow, and halted.

'I'm afraid,' he purred, at his most urbane, 'that

we must shepherd Lady Alathea's sisters and mine back to our mothers' carriages. You'll have to excuse us.'

That last was said with enough underlying command to convince even Lord Montgomery that bowing and making extravagant adieus was the better part of valor.

Gabriel drew her ruthlessly away. He caught his sister Heather's eye and with one brotherly gesture redirected the group now well ahead of them back toward the avenue.

Side by side, strolling easily, their long legs a match for each other, they brought up the rear. Alathea sighed with relief.

Gabriel shot her a dark glance. 'You could try to discourage them.'

'I haven't encouraged them in the first place!'

They walked on in silence. As they neared the point where Serena's and Celia's carriages would come into view, Alathea slowed, expecting Gabriel to make his excuses and leave her. He tightened his hold on her hand and drew her on.

She looked at him in amazement. He cast her an irritated glance. 'I'm not escorting them.' His nod indicated the four girls and Esher and Carstairs ahead of them. 'I'm escorting you.'

'I don't *need* escorting.'

'Let me be the judge of that.'

His expression grimly resolute, that was all he deigned to say. Alathea was too surprised that he'd risk alerting his mother to any particularity between them to marshal any argument, and then they were within sight of the carriages.

With an inward sigh, she kept pace beside him. 'This is not going to make things any easier, you know.'

She thought he wasn't going to reply, but just before they reached his mother's carriage where Serena and Celia sat in matronly splendor, he murmured, 'We left "easy" behind long ago.'

Then they were at the carriage, joining with the girls and Esher and Carstairs. Over the heads, Gabriel fielded a glance from Celia; Alathea, watching closely, could interpret with ease – Celia wanted to know why he was there. Gabriel returned her gaze impassively with a slight lifting of his shoulders, giving Celia to understand he'd simply come upon them and walked them back. Nothing particular at all. His performance was so smooth, if she hadn't known better, Alathea would have believed that, too. Gabriel nodded and Celia smiled, waving him away.

He turned to her – their gazes met. In the folds of her gown their fingers brushed. With a brief nod, he turned and strode away.

Alathea watched him go, a frown in her eyes, an increasingly insistent question revolving in her mind.

CHAPTER 15

That question was answered two nights later. The Duchess of Richmond's gala was one of the highlights of the Season. The Richmonds' house on the river was thrown open; everyone who was anyone attended. Alathea arrived relatively early with Serena, Mary and Alice. Her father, out to dinner with friends, would look in later. Leaving Serena on a *chaise* with Lady Arbuthnot and Celia Cynster, Alathea hovered until the circle about Mary and Alice was established, Esher and Carstairs to the fore, then headed for a quiet nook by the wall.

Her attempt at self-effacement was frustrated by Lord Falworth, who spotted her in the crowd. Seconds later, her 'court' closed in.

To Alathea's relief, not five minutes passed before Chillingworth joined them. After exchanging the usual pleasantries, the earl settled by her side, displacing Falworth, who sulkily shifted back. As large as Gabriel, Chillingworth had a similar effect on her admirers; challenged, they exerted themselves to converse intelligently.

By the time the orchestra struck up for the first

345

dance, Alathea was feeling in considerable charity with the earl, very ready to grant him her hand. He did not, however, solicit it, calmly standing back while Lord Montgomery begged the honor. With no excuse ready, Alathea was forced to accede to his lordship's fervent plea but as the dance was a cotillion, she was spared most of his pompous declarations.

When at the end of the dance Lord Montgomery returned her to her circle, she was somewhat surprised to discover Chillingworth patiently waiting. Her gratitude bloomed anew as under his direction, the conversation remained lighthearted and general. Then the musicians struck up a waltz, and she realized why the earl was waiting.

The look in his eyes as he bowed before her was flatteringly intent. 'If you would do me the honor, my dear?'

Alathea hesitated, another large gentlemen very clear in her mind. She looked up – and found him watching her, waiting to see what she would do, ready to step in and claim her if she didn't fall in with his decree. His intent reached her clearly as the circle of her admirers, noticing him, parted like the Red Sea.

Tamping down a spurt of rebelliousness, accepting she dared not bait Gabriel in his present mood, she glanced at Chillingworth. 'I'm afraid, my lord, that I'm already promised. To Mr Cynster.'

That last was redundant; Chillingworth's gaze had

346

fastened on Gabriel's face. Primitive challenge flashed between them, then Chillingworth bowed. 'My loss, my dear, but only a temporary one. There'll be many more waltzes tonight.' Even more than his words, his tone signalled his intention.

With a grace to match Chillingworth's, Gabriel bowed and held out his hand. Alathea placed her fingers in his, conscious to her toes of the restrained strength in his grasp. He drew her to him, turning as she joined him, effectively cutting off her court. The dance floor was only a step away, and then she was whirling in his arms.

Alathea inwardly frowned. She was aware the outcome of that little scene had pleased him. It hadn't, however, pleased her. 'You're drawing too much attention to us.'

'In the circumstances, it's inevitable.'

'Then *change* the circumstances.'

'How?'

'Your insistence that I waltz only with you is ridiculous. It's going to cause comment. It's hardly something one can explain on the grounds of long-standing acquaintance.'

'You want me to let you waltz with other men.'

'Yes.'

'No.'

He whirled her through the turn. Alathea gritted her teeth. Why did he imagine he could dictate such things? Because of the hours she'd spent with him in the dark. She bundled the recollections aside. 'It isn't wise to attract the attention of the gabblemongers. People are starting to wonder.'

'So? They're not wondering anything that will reflect adversely on you.'

Yes, they were – if he kept on as he was, the whole ton would soon believe that he and she would marry, but that wasn't going to happen. By the time they'd dealt with Crowley and his company, Gabriel's attraction to her would have waned and he'd be off laying seige to his next conquest. Raising expectations destined never to be fulfilled was not a good idea. Worse, these were the sorts of expectations guaranteed to fuel the gossips' fires. She was too old – far too old – to be eligible.

Alathea seethed through the rest of the waltz, her temper not improved by the speculative glances thrown their way, or by his continuing – and she was quite sure deliberate – rasping of her senses.

By the end of the dance, she was ready to be returned to the safety of her court. He, it transpired, had other ideas. The reception rooms opened one into the other; on his arm, he paraded her through them. Only the increasing crush prevented them from being the focus of far too many eyes.

'Where are we going?'

'Somewhere less crowded.'

She could hardly argue with the wisdom of that; tall though she was, she was feeling hemmed in. The small salon to which he took her had palms and statues breaking up the space. Consequently, it boasted areas in which one could converse, not private but protected. Gabriel led her to a nook created by a trio of potted palms and an ornamental arch.

A footman passed with a tray. Gabriel collected two glasses of champagne. 'Here – it's only going to get hotter.'

Accepting the glass, Alathea sipped, relaxing as the bubbles fizzed down her throat. She scanned the room, then she sensed Gabriel stiffen. When she turned, her gaze collided with Chillingworth's as he joined them in their retreat.

'I count myself fortunate to have found you again, my dear.'

Gabriel snorted derisively. 'You followed us.'

'Actually, no.' Chillingworth snared a glass as the footman hove within reach. He sipped, his gaze on Alathea's face. 'I assumed, after that little display in the ballroom, that Cynster would retreat to some area more conductive to his purpose.'

'A tactic you would know all about.'

Chillingworth looked at Gabriel. 'That point has been puzzling me. You are, after all, a friend of the family. Your present tack is one I would never have expected.'

'That's because you have no idea what my present tack is.'

Chillingworth smiled tauntingly. 'Oh, no, dear boy. I assure you I'm far from being *that* unimaginative.'

'Perhaps,' Gabriel returned, sharpened steel beneath the words, 'it would be wiser if you were.'

'What? And leave the field to you?'

'Hardly the first time you've owned to defeat.'

Chillingworth snorted.

Glancing from one to the other, Alathea felt giddy. Despite her height, they were talking over her head, arguing over her as if she wasn't there.

'It would be more to the point,' Chillingworth opined, 'if, given the circumstances, you'd cease your present act and get out of my way.'

'Which act is that?'

'Dog in the manger.'

'*Excuse me*!' Eyes flashing, Alathea silenced first Gabriel, who'd opened his lips on a retort, doubtless equally graceless, then she rounded on Chillingworth. 'You will pardon me if I find this exchange somewhat less than gratifying.'

They both looked at her. She doubted either blushed readily, but slight color now graced their cheeks. The crude nature of their remarks was out of character for both, far from their usual unfailingly elegant poses.

'I am appalled.' Glancing from one to the other, she held them silent. 'It appears you believe I'm not only *unimaginative*, but deaf as well! For your information, I'm perfectly well aware of both your "acts" – permit me to tell you I approve of neither. Like any lady of my age and experience, *I* will be the arbiter of my actions; I have no intention of succumbing to the practiced blandishments of either of you. What, however, I find *unforgivable* is your propensity to single-mindedly pursue your own agendas, oblivious to the fact that your attentions are focusing unwanted and unwarranted attention on me!'

She ended glaring at Chillingworth. He had the grace to look contrite. 'My apologies, my dear.'

Alathea humphed, nodded, and turned to Gabriel. He looked at her for two heartbeats, then his fingers closed about her elbow. He handed his glass to Chillingworth, then took hers and handed that across, too. 'If you'll excuse us, there are a few pertinent details we need to clarify.'

'By all means,' Chillingworth returned. 'Once you've clarified the nonexistent nature of your claim, I'll be able to clarify my position.' He bowed to Alathea.

Gabriel frowned. 'Believe me, in this case, you don't have one.'

Before Chillingworth could reply, before Alathea could even see how he reacted, Gabriel drew her forward. Alathea fumed but didn't try to break free; a steel manacle would have been easier to break than Gabriel's hold on her arm. He marched her across the room to where a door stood ajar, giving access to a corridor.

'Where now?' she asked as they stepped through the door.

'Somewhere private. I want to talk to you.'

'Indeed? I have a few words to say to you, too.'

He led her up a flight of stairs, then back along a quiet wing. The door at the end stood open; beyond lay a small parlor, curtains drawn against the night. A fire burned in the grate. Three cande-labra shed golden light on satin and polished wood. The room was empty. Drawing her hand from his arm, Alathea swept across the threshold. He followed. Reaching the fireplace, she swung to face him, and heard the lock fall home.

'This ridiculous situation has got to end.' She fixed him with an irate glance. 'The countess is no more. She has faded into the mists, never to return.'

'*You*, however, are here.'

'Yes, *me*. Alathea-who-you've-known-all-your-life. I'm not some delectable courtesan that you have any real interest in seducing. You're annoyed because as the countess you thought I was – you now know better. And you know perfectly well that once you get over being annoyed, you'll be off after some other lady, one more suited to your tastes.'

He'd remained by the door; head tilted, he regarded her. 'So my interest in you is fueled by annoyance?'

'That, and perversity. A response to Chilling-worth and the others. It's almost as if, having relinquished your silly watch on the twins, you've transferred your attention to me!'

'And what's wrong with that?'

'You're obsessively protective! If you'll only stop and think, you'll realize there's no *need*. I need to be protected even less than the twins. Worse, hovering over me is exceedingly unwise. It calls attention to us – you know what people

352

will make of it. Before you know where you are, the ton will have imagined into existence something that simply isn't.'

A moment passed, then he asked, 'This something that isn't – this illusion you claim the ton will think it sees. What, precisely, is that?'

Alathea huffed out a breath. Across the room, she met his eyes. 'They'll imagine we have an understanding, that in the near future they'll read an engagement notice in *The Gazette*. As Chillingworth so sapiently stated, it's widely known that our families are close, that you and I have known each other for years. No one will imagine any illicit connection – they'll imagine we'll wed. Once that idea gains credence, there'll be hell to pay.'

'Hmm.' He started to walk toward her. 'And that's the bee that's buzzing in your bonnet?'

'I have absolutely no desire to spend the rest of the Season explaining to the interested why we aren't about to marry.'

'I can guarantee that won't occur.'

'Indeed?' She bridled at his patronizing tone. 'And how can you be so sure?'

'Because we *are* going to marry.'

Gabriel halted directly before her. A full minute passed while she stared at him, speechless. Then her eyes clouded.

'W-*what*?'

'I agreed to defer discussion of the matter until after we'd dealt with the company – that, however, is clearly not to be. So it may as well be now. As far as I'm concerned, we're getting married, and the sooner the better.'

'But you never had it in mind to marry me. Not when we spoke after Lady Arbuthnot's ball.'

'Thankfully, you never did learn to read my mind. I decided to marry you when I knew you as the countess. The morning after Lady Arbuthnot's ball, I was still adjusting to the startling discovery that it was you I'd decided to make my wife. As you might imagine, that was something of a shock.'

'But . . . you *must* have changed your mind. You don't want to marry me.'

'Not only do I *want* to marry you, I am *going* to marry you, a fact that makes my attitude toward you and other gentlemen perfectly understandable. I might be obsessively protective, but only about those of whom I'm obsessively possessive, such as the lady who will be my wife. The ultimate ramification of your masquerade as the countess will be marriage to me. There is, therefore, no false illusion for the ton to see – the only conclusion society will leap to will be the truth.'

'As you deem it.'

'As it will be.' He stepped closer; physical awarenes flashed in her eyes. She lifted her chin; he captured her gaze. 'This is *real*. I'm not going to grow out of it, or lose interest and become distracted. Marriage to me is your immediate and irrevocable future. If you hadn't realized, you'll need time to adjust, but don't imagine there'll be any other outcome.'

'But . . .' She shook her head dazedly. 'I'm *not* the countess. It was the countess who fascinated you – a lady of mystery and illusion. *I* don't fascinate you – you know everything there is to know about me—'

He kissed her, closed his lips over hers, then closed his arms about her. It was easy to do with her being so tall. Her resistance lasted a heartbeat, then vaporized like mist; she sank against him, her lips parting at his command, her mouth an offering he claimed.

Alathea clung to her wits. She yielded all else without a fight, knowing any fight would be futile, but she held on to reason. About her, the world whirled; her senses rioted. He'd shocked her with his declaration, but she surprised herself even more.

She wanted him. Her hunger was too strong, too sharp in its raw newness, for her to ignore or mistake it. The arms locked about her were a welcome cage, the hard body pressed to hers the essence of dreamed delight. He plundered her mouth, ruthless, relentless, not gentle. She took him in, lured him further, to give and take and give again.

He took and exulted in the taking. She knew it. She sensed the surge of passion, his and hers, and reveled in her power. The heady wave grew into a vortex of heat, swirling about them, flames licking, touching, but not yet consuming. Then, to her surprise, the world steadied.

He lifted his head.

She felt him draw breath, his chest swelling

against her breasts. It was an effort to lift her lids enough to see his face. Hard, each plane edged with desire, it gave her no clue to his direction. His eyes, glinting gold under lids as heavy as hers, were fixed on her hair.

His arms shifted. One hand splayed across her back, holding her against him. The other rose . . .

To her hair.

'What . . . ?' She felt a brusque tug; satisfaction gleamed in his eyes. Glancing to the side, she saw her beaded cap in his hand. 'Don't you *dare* throw that in the fire!'

His gaze returned to her face. 'No?' Then he shrugged and tossed the cap to the floor. 'As you will.' His hand returned to her hair, rifling the soft mass, searching and plucking. Pins tinkled across the hearth.

'What are you doing?' She tried to wriggle, but he held her too securely. Then her hair fell free.

'You appear to have formed a grossly inaccurate opinion of what fascinates me. Arguing with you always was so much wasted breath, so I'll demonstrate instead.'

'Demonstrate?'

'Hmm.' He speared his free hand through her hair, spreading his fingers, combing through the long tresses, holding them out, watching them drift down as his fingers pulled free. 'You never did understand why I hated your caps, did you?'

Mesmerized by the possessiveness investing his harsh features, Alathea didn't answer. He played

356

with the silken mass, then he gathered half of it in his fist, tipping her head back.

'What else?' His gaze fastened on her eyes. 'Ah, yes. Your eyes. Have you any idea what it's like to look into them? Not at them, but into. Whenever I do, I feel like I've fallen into some magical pool and lost myself. Certainly lost all sense.' His gaze lowered. 'And there's your lips.' He took them in a swift, achingly incomplete kiss. 'But we know why I like those.' The arm about her eased, his hand drifted from her back. He still held her by her hair. 'But I don't believe you have any idea about this.'

Long fingers feathered her jaw, tracing from her chin to her ear. Then he cupped her face, holding her steady as he bent his head and followed the same line with his lips.

Alathea shivered.

'That's right. *Vulnerable.*' The word caressed her ear. 'Not weak, but definitely vulnerable. Mine to seize.'

Her lids fell as his lips brushed the sensitive skin beneath her ear, then slid lower, laying heat down the length of her throat. Her mind told her to correct him; she wasn't his. Instead, when he fell to laving the tender spot at the base of her throat, she swayed into him. Her legs weakened. She clutched his lapels as her wits reeled.

He released her hair. His lips returned to hers and her hunger resurged. He matched it, fed it, incited her desire, then drank deeply, took, seized, claimed. Distracted, she had no inkling that his fingers had been busy until he closed his hands about hers and drew them down, then, breaking off their kiss, slipped her gown from her shoulders.

The ribbon straps of her chemise went, too. Her breasts, swollen and rosy-peaked, were in his hands before she lifted her lids, long before she drew in a breath.

He'd caressed her breasts before but only in the dark; she hadn't been able to see his hands cupping, caressing. She hadn't been able to see his face, to see desire engraved on his features, to see the fires of passion burning in his eyes.

His hands closed possessively.

'Beautiful,' he murmured. 'There is no other word. None to do you justice.'

He bent his head; Alathea closed her eyes and struggled to hang on to her sanity as he feasted. With lips, tongue, and teeth, he worshipped, heaping pleasure upon pleasure until she gasped. The guttural sound he made rang with masculine satisfaction, then he returned to repeat the torture.

His touch was exquisite; helpless, she arched in his arms, offering, entreating, yet still aware of every nuance of every touch, of the meaning invested in each caress. Although the vortex of their passions whirled around them, they yet stood at the still eye of their storm.

Gabriel knew it. Never before had he attained such a high degree of arousal while still retaining such absolute control. Not with any other woman. The woman in his arms was special, but he'd known that all along. All his life, even though he hadn't understood.

Lifting his head, drawing his lips from the sweet mounds of her breasts, he steadied her. Sliding his hands to her back, he eased her gown and chemise further down. They gathered about her hips. Eyes wide, one hand on his shoulder for balance, she met his gaze, stunned understanding in her eyes.

His lips curved. He raised his hands to the backs of her shoulders, then skimmed them slowly down, tracing the long planes of her back, the supple muscles on either side of her spine. 'I like the fact you're so tall. There's a lot of you, but you're so slender.' He spread his hands, spanning the back of her rib cage. 'I'm twice the size of you.'

He closed his hands about her narrow waist. Possessive lust flared; he knew it glowed in his eyes. 'Tall yet feminine. My ideal.'

His gravelly tone shook her. She sucked in a shaky breath—

He kissed whatever she'd thought to say from her lips. Thoroughly. Then he pushed her gown and chemise over her hips. They swooshed down her legs to puddle on the floor.

'Gabri—'

He cut her off with another kiss. Luscious curves filled his hands; he was no longer interested in verbal communication. Deepening the kiss, he drew her hard against him, fingers flexing, kneading, learning anew. He knew the feel of her, the contrast of feminine firmness and softness, yet his senses seemed starved, urgently needy for more and yet more of her.

Fascination was too weak a word to encompass his obsession.

As for her legs . . .

'Don't move.' Closing his hands about her hips, he sank to his knees. He heard her indrawn breath and pressed a kiss to her waist, then trailed lower to lave her navel. Her hands had fallen to his shoulders, her fingers restless. As he evocatively probed the slight indentation, her fingers slid into his hair.

He paid homage to her legs, sliding his hands down, then up the long, graceful limbs. She quivered, muscles tensing. When he bent his head and nuzzled her taut belly, she gasped.

'Gabriel?'

The word was an aching whisper, laden with entreaty. Alathea could barely believe it came from her. Her body was hot, her skin flushed, her wits in disarray, yet she felt every touch, every caress keenly. Desire throbbed in the air, passion heated it; this time, there was no darkness to shroud her senses, no veil to obscure the reality.

She stood naked before him, held by the thought that her nakedness captivated him. His head against her stomach was a warm weight; the touch of his hands both soothed and excited. His hair, silky locks sliding over her flickering skin as he turned his head, felt so right.

His only response to her plea was a hot, wet, open-mouthed kiss pressed to her quivering belly just above the curls at its base. She shuddered, and clung to his skull. He shifted one hand to her bottom, shoring up her precarious balance while the fingers of his other hand trailed up and down the sensitive inner faces of her thighs.

He shifted fractionally lower.

She expected him to touch the soft flesh between her thighs. She waited, nerves tensing. Then he did, and she nearly died. The hot, wet sweep of his tongue, the subtle probing, nearly brought her to her knees. Her exclamation was incoherent.

'Shh.' He caught her, steadied her. Grasping one of her knees, he lifted it over his shoulder. She had to shift her balance, curling that leg over his broad back, her fingers clenched on his skull. The position was more secure, but inevitably more intimate. Scalding hot, his tongue stroked her again. 'I'm going to taste you.'

Those mumbled words were all the warning she had before he did. Tasted, probed, stroked, lapped – whether she would have agreed to the intimacy was irrelevant. He simply took, and she gave.

Her nerves leaped, sensitized, excruciatingly aware; muscles tensed, clenched. Her wits reeled, yet some small part of her remained cogent, detached enough to catalogue his demonstration, sane enough to wonder if he had intended it that way.

Her very awareness was arousing; she could see and sense beyond the sensual plane. The air before her was cool, the fire behind her warm. And the man kneeling before her was the god of pure pleasure. He flayed her with it, lashed her with it, lavished it upon her until she sobbed, until her body became no more than a vessel of heated yearning.

She knew the instant his tongue and lips left her, felt the raw power as he surged to his feet. His hands closed hard about her thighs, and he lifted her.

Then he filled her.

The thick, solid length of him pressed in, breached the slight constriction, then slid up, in, thrust deep. With a gasp and a sob, she closed about him, sheathing him there, holding him there. His fingers flexed; she felt his chest strain. Locking her legs about his hips, winding her arms about his shoulders, she pressed herself to him, caught his head between her hands, and found his lips with hers.

The kiss was a true melding, drawn as much from her as from him; their bodies moved in similar harmony, in a slow, evocative rhythm as instinctive as their breathing. He lifted her; she slid sensuously down. She clung, then released; he withdrew, then returned.

It should, perhaps, have shamed her, this intimate yielding with her naked in his arms, her bare limbs wrapped around his fully clothed form. He'd only released his staff from the confines of his trousers. Every tiny movement rasped her sensitized skin with the fabric of his elegant evening clothes.

He'd planned it that way – at no stage did she entertain any other notion. He had said he would demonstrate his fascination; as he reveled in the slick heat of her body, drawing out every precious moment, holding the vortex at bay, she knew to her bones that he was playing no role.

She didn't need him to draw back from the kiss, chest laboring, eyes closed, concentration etched in every line of his face, to be convinced. Didn't need to feel her own body respond, undulating against him, upon him, to know she believed.

Didn't need him to lift his weighted lids, transfix her with a glittering glance, and say, 'You think I know you, but I don't – I don't know the woman you've become. I don't know how it will feel to run my hands through your hair when it's warm from sleep, or what it will feel like to slide into you as you wake in the morning. I don't know how it will feel to fall asleep with you in my arms, to wake with your breath on my cheek. To have you naked in my arms in daylight, to hold you when you're big with my child. There are lots of things I don't know about you. I'll spend my life with you, and still not learn all I want to know. I don't care by what name you go – you're still the same woman. The woman who fascinates me.'

She hushed him with her lips, but neither she nor he had the strength to prolong the kiss. They were clinging to sanity by their fingernails. She tucked her head down on his shoulder, nuzzled his neck, placed a breathless kiss on his heated skin.

His lips returned the pleasure, then he nipped lightly. 'You like this, don't you?' His voice was broken, strained; he gave a hoarse laugh. 'You're going to be the death of me in more ways than one.'

She deliberately tightened about him, something she'd noticed gave him pleasure.

His head fell back and he groaned. Then he caught the trailing ends of her hair and tugged her head back so he could look into her eyes. 'See? This is what you were made for – giving yourself to me.'

She kept her lips shut. She was afraid he was right. With a flick of her head, she pulled her hair from his grasp. The sudden movement shifted her. She sank even deeper onto him, and reflexively tightened even more.

He sucked in a breath, then his lips were on hers, urgent and demanding. His control was gone. The vortex closed upon them; the flames roared.

Passion took them, lifted them high on a swell of pure need, then shattered them. Release was so profound, neither was aware that they sank to the floor. The only reality their senses permitted them was the knowledge they were together, and one.

★　　★　　★

'You called me Gabriel.'

Slumped on his chest, still aglow in the aftermath, Alathea could barely think. 'I've been calling you Gabriel in my mind for weeks.'

'Good – that's who I am.' Sprawled on his back on the sofa he'd carried her to, his hand lingered on her hair. 'I'm not your childhood playmate. I'm your lover and I'll be your husband. I'm claiming the position.' His hand closed on her nape, then gentled, stroked. 'Just as my name doesn't really matter, what you call yourself changes nothing. You're the woman I want, and you want me. You're mine – you always were, and always will be.'

The bone-deep assurance in his words struck Alathea to the heart; she stirred—

'No – lie still. You're not cold.'

Her skin was still flushed. His body beneath her radiated heat. She wasn't cold – she was boneless, unable to summon the strength to reassert control and change direction. She was not even sure she wanted to.

They had, she recalled, once lain together on their backs looking up at the stars one summer night. They hadn't touched; instead, the tension between them had been so thick it had all but sparked. That tension had vanished completely. What surrounded them now was a well of peace, profound and enduring. Satiation deeper than she'd imagined could exist lapped them about; he seemed content to rest in its embrace, sharing the quiet.

She could hear his heart beating beneath her ear, slow and steady.

'Why are you here?'

He put the question evenly; mystified, she answered. 'You brought me here.'

'And you came. Now you're lying in my arms, totally naked – you took me willingly, willingly gave yourself to me, purely because I wanted you.'

She felt far more at his mercy now than she had before. How could he know the confusion and uncertainty hovering in her mind? But it seemed he did.

'You're good at that – giving. And what you have to give, I want.' His hand gently stroked her hair. 'You're a sensual woman, a Thoroughbred in bed, and I certainly don't care how old you are. You haven't even been in training for long and you still make my head spin.'

She shut her eyes. 'Don't.'

'Don't what? Speak the truth? Why, when we both know it?' His hand moved down, stroking her back, then he closed his arms about her. 'You love to give, and the only man you'll ever give yourself to is me.'

She didn't want to hear it because she couldn't deny it and it gave him far too much power over her. She struggled to sit up. 'We have to go.'

'Not yet.' He held her easily and nuzzled her ear. Then his lips touched her skin, and lingered. 'Just once more . . .'

CHAPTER 16

The next morning, Alathea sat in the gazebo tucked to one side of the back garden and watched Gabriel cross the lawn toward her. Bright sunlight struck red and gold glints from his hair; she remembered the feel of it beneath her palms.

Eyes narrowed against the glare, she watched him exchange greetings with Mary and Alice, who were weeding the bed about the fountain. She had excused herself from gardening on the grounds of feeling under the weather. It was the truth; she'd barely slept a wink.

If she'd needed unequivocal proof that Gabriel had read her emotions accurately, the second half of their encounter in Lady Richmond's parlor had provided it. Even now, hours after the fact, just the thought of the suggestions he'd whispered in her ear, of what she'd willingly done and let him do to her, brought color surging to her cheeks. He'd wanted, and she had wanted to give. Last night, he'd introduced her to the ultimate in giving.

She wasn't hypocrite enough to pretend she

hadn't enjoyed it, that the bliss she found in giving to him, whenever, however, brought the sweetest, deepest joy she'd ever known. In satisfying him, she found fulfillment. There was no other word, none that came close to describing the breadth and depth of what she felt. He'd labeled her a 'giver'; she had to accept he was right. What she didn't – couldn't – accept was his extrapolation.

He was fascinated with her. That had been no act. He of all men would appreciate the irony that he should find her – a woman he'd known from the cradle – so physically enthralling. And despite what he'd said, her age did matter, but not in the way it would matter to the ton. Because she was older and where he was concerned more assured than any other lady he'd seduced, she was more challenging, more demanding of his talents. That, too, he would appreciate.

His fascination was real. Fascination did not, however, lead to marriage.

As he left the girls and, loose-limbed and confident, strode toward her, Alathea drew calm certainty about her. He was an exceptional practitioner of the sensual arts; he knew how to use his talents to pressure her, to cloud her reason. But she knew him too well – far too well – to swallow the tale that fascination was behind his determination to wed her. She thought too much of him – *cared* too much for him – to meekly fall in with his plans.

He reached the gazebo and trod up the steps. Ducking his head beneath the trailing jasmine that covered the small structure, he stepped into the cool shadows. Straightening, he met her gaze. Stillness gripped him. 'What?'

Alathea waved him to the sofa beside her. She'd sent a note to Brook Street asking him to call. She waited while he sat; the wicker sofa was small – it left them shoulder to shoulder. He leaned back, stretching one arm along the sofa's back to ease the crowding. She drew breath and resolutely took the bit between her teeth. 'There is absolutely no reason for us to wed. *No*!' She cut off his immediate retort. 'Hear me out.'

He'd tensed; his expression hardened but he held silent.

Alathea looked out over the lawn to where her stepsisters and stepbrothers chattered gaily. 'Only you and I know about the countess. Only we know we've been intimate. I'm twenty-nine. As I keep trying to remind everyone, I've set aside all thoughts of marriage. I did so eleven years ago. I'm accepted as a spinster – your recent attentions notwithstanding, there's no expectation that I'll marry. Short of our liaison becoming common knowledge, which it won't for we're both too wise and too aware of what we owe our families and ourselves to bruit the fact abroad, then there's no need whatever for us to wed.'

'Is that it?'

'No.' She turned her head and met his gaze directly. 'Regardless of what you decide is the right

369

thing to do, I will not marry you. There's no reason for you to make such a sacrifice.'

He studied her. 'Why,' he eventually asked, 'do you think I want to marry you?'

Her lips twisted. She gestured to her stepsiblings, blissfully unaware of the clouds hovering on the family's horizon. 'You want to marry me because of that same quality I counted on when, as the countess, I asked for your aid. I knew if I explained the danger to them, then you'd help. I've told you before – you're obsessively protective.' He was her knight on a white charger; protectiveness was his strongest suit, and one of his most basic instincts.

He'd followed her gaze to the girls. 'You think I want to marry you to protect you. Out of some notion of chivalry.'

She'd tried to avoid that word; it sounded so melo-dramatic, even if it was the naked truth. Sighing, she faced him. 'I wanted to trap you into *helping* – I never intended to trap you into marriage.'

Gabriel searched her eyes, hazel pools of absolute sincerity. The vulnerability that had haunted him ever since he'd discovered the countess's identity evaporated.

She didn't know. She had no idea that he worshipped her, that his fascination was obsession, overwhelming and complete. He'd forgotten her naivete, that despite her age, despite knowing him all her life, in certain areas she was an innocent. She didn't know that she was so very different from all who had gone before.

370

He looked back at Mary and Alice while he mentally scrambled to reorient himself. 'At the risk of shattering your illusions, that's not why I want to marry you.'

'Why, then?'

He met her gaze. 'You can hardly be unaware that I desire you physically.'

Color touched her too-pale cheeks. She inclined her head. 'Desire in our circles doesn't necessitate marriage.'

She looked away, leaving him studying that all-too-revealing line of her jaw. Strength and vulnerability – she was a combination of both.

His reaction to the sight was immediate but no longer surprising – he now knew how primitive his feelings for her were. Last night, when she was fussing over her hair, trying to fashion it into some arrangement that would pass muster, he'd been visited by a violent urge to haul it all down again and march her through the house, past all Lady Richmond's guests, Chillingworth especially, so all would know that she was his.

His.

The powerful surge of possessiveness was achingly familiar. It was the same emotion she'd always evoked in him, the wellspring of that godforsaken tension that had gripped him whenever she was close. The emotion had clarified, crystallized. In unveiling the countess, other veils had been torn aside, too; he could now see his primitive impulse for what it truly was – the instinctive desire to seize his mate. *To Have and To Hold* was the Cynster family motto; hardly surprising he felt the impulse so keenly.

But how much was it safe to reveal to her? 'How long have we known each other?'

'Forever – all our lives.'

'Weeks ago, you told Chillingworth that our relationship had been decided for us. I agreed. Do you remember?'

'Yes.'

'The earliest memory I have of you, you must have been all of two years old. I would have been three. From our cradles, our parents told us we were friends. I was twelve when treating you as a sister started becoming difficult. I never understood why – all I knew was that something was wrong. You knew it, too.'

Her 'yes' was a whisper; they were both looking back down the years.

'Remember that time we had to slip out of old Collinridge's barn by the back window and your habit got caught on a nail? Lucifer was already mounted, holding the horses – I had to catch your hips and hold you up so you could unhook the material.'

He paused; a second later, she reactively shivered.

'Precisely. All that time, it was a peculiar blend of heaven and hell. I could never understand why I always gravitated to your side, always wanted to be near you, because whenever I was close,

I felt . . . violent. Crazed. As if I wanted to grab hold of you and shake you.'

Her laugh was shaky. 'I was never certain you wouldn't.'

'I never dared. I was too afraid laying hands on you – touching you in any way – would drive me mad, that I would behave like some bedlamite. That one dance we shared was bad enough.'

They both gazed blindly over the lawns, then he continued, 'What I'm trying to point out is that I've felt . . . possessive of you for a very long time. I didn't know what the feeling was until after that night at the Burlington, but it isn't something that only recently evolved. It's been there, between us, growing stronger for over twenty years. If our parents hadn't set us up as brother and sister, that feeling would long since have resolved itself in marriage. As it is, your masquerade has opened our eyes and given us a chance to rescript our relationship into what it ought to be.' He glanced at her; she was still stubbornly facing the lawn. 'I'm more than sexually attracted to you – you're the woman I want as my wife.'

She tilted her head. 'How many women have you known?'

He frowned. 'I don't know. I haven't counted.'

She looked at him, one brow high, disbelief in her eyes.

He gritted his teeth. 'All right. I did count at first, but I gave up long ago.'

'What number did you reach before you stopped counting?'

'*That* is neither here nor there. What point are you trying to make?'

'Merely that you seem to like women but, until now, that liking hasn't prompted you to beat a path to the parson's door. Why now? Why me?'

He saw the trap but was ready to turn the questions to his advantage. 'The now is simple – it's time.' The fateful words, '*Your time will come*,' resonated in his mind. 'I knew that at Demon's wedding. I just didn't know the who. You know how edgy Mama has been getting – much as it pains me to admit it, she's right. It is time for me to marry, to settle, to think of the next generation. As for the 'why you,' it isn't, as you seem determined to think, because you're a friend of the family and that because we've been intimate, I think I've ruined you and needs must make reparation.'

His increasingly clipped tone had her glancing his way; he trapped her gaze. 'What I'm saying is that you are the woman I want as my wife. Just that – I need no other reason.' He paused, then continued, 'You might have noticed I no longer suffer when I'm close to you. I can sit beside you, more or less at erase, no longer feeling caged to the point of madness, because I know I can take you in my arms and kiss you, that at some point in the not-overly-distant future, you'll lie beneath me again.' He let his voice drop. 'However, if you're witless enough to try to fight this – all

374

that's between us – if you try to refuse me and smile instead at Chillingworth or any other man, then I can guarantee that what has been between us through the years will be as nothing to what will be.'

She held his gaze steadily. 'Is that a threat?'

'No. It's a promise.'

She considered him, then opened her mouth—

He laid a finger across her lips. 'I'm deeply attached to you, you know that. Now I'm no longer blinded and forbidden by preconception, I can admit it. I desire you sexually, but that's only the half of it. I want you because I can think of no other I would rather share my life with. We suit. We could be successful life-partners. We've never been friends, not really, but with the difficulty between us removed, that's another relationship within our reach.'

Her eyes searched his – she was marshaling her arguments, still stubbornly resisting for all she was worth.

Releasing her lips, he traced her jaw, then let his hand fall to the sofa back. 'Thea, no matter how you struggle to refute it, you know what's between us. It might have been cloaked and veiled for years, but now we've stripped away the disguise, you can see what it is as well as I.' He held her gaze. 'It's an ardent and undying passion, not just on my part but yours as well.'

Alathea looked away. She didn't know what to do. It wasn't just her head that was spinning.

His words had evoked so many emotions, so many long-buried needs and barely recognized dreams. But . . . drawing herself up, she stated, 'You're telling me your emotions are engaged.'

'Yes.'

'That what's between us demands marriage as its proper state – its necessary outcome.'

'Yes.'

When she stared into the distance and said nothing more, he prompted, 'Well?'

'I'm not sure I believe you.' Facing him, she hurried to explain, '*Not* about what's between us so much as why you believe we should marry.' She searched his face, then, mentally girding her loins, she spoke bluntly. 'We *do* know each other well – very well. You claim that the feelings that have always plagued us were due to frustrated desire, that what's between us is that – physical desire – and I accept that that's probably so. You've said that your emotions are engaged and I accept that, too. But what I don't know is: *which is* the most prominent emotion?'

A scowl formed in his eyes. 'Whichever emotion it is that prompts a man to marriage.'

'*That's* what I'm afraid of. The emotion that's prompting, pressing, *spurring* you to marry me is the one dominant emotion you possess. You want to protect me. You've made up your mind that the right way forward is via the chapel and you're always successful once you fix your mind on a goal. Unfortunately, in this case, attaining your goal requires my cooperation, so I'm afraid your record of success is about to end.'

'You think I made all that up.'

'No – I think you were in the main sincere, but I don't believe your conclusions fit your facts. I think you're fudging. And if you want to know whether I think you would lie in pursuit of what you saw as a higher goal, then yes, I think you'd lie through your teeth.' With her eyes, she challenged him to deny it.

Lips compressed, he held her gaze intimidatingly, but didn't.

She nodded. 'Exactly. We know each other all too well. In creating the countess, I knew precisely what to say, how to pull the right strings to get you to do as I wished. I'm not so puffed up in my own conceit that I imagine you aren't clever enough to do precisely the same to me. You've decided we should marry, so you'll do whatever you need to to bring our marriage about.'

He looked at her steadily. She'd expected an immediate reaction, possibly an aggressive one. His silent appraisal unnerved her. She could read nothing of his thoughts in his eyes.

Then he sat up. The arm along the back of the sofa slid about her; his other hand rose to frame her face. A split second and she was held, lightly, in his embrace.

'You're right.'

She blinked. Was that a wry smile she saw in his eyes? 'About what?'

His gaze lowered to her lips. 'That I'll do whatever I must to bring our marriage about.'

Alathea mentally cursed. She hadn't meant to phrase it as a challenge. 'I—'

'Tell me,' he murmured. 'Do you accept that what's between us is an "ardent and undying passion"?'

It was a struggle to draw breath. 'Ardent, perhaps, but not undying. Given time, it will fade.'

'You're wrong.' He leaned closer and brushed her lips with his. The contact was too light to satisfy; all it did was make her hungry, too.

His breath was warm on her throbbing lips. 'The ardency that flooded you last night when I filled you . . .' His lips touched hers again, another achingly incomplete kiss. 'The passion that drove you to open yourself to me, to bestow whatever sensual gift I asked for. Do you think those will fade?'

Never. Alathea swayed. Her lids were so heavy, all she could see was his lips moving closer. Her hands, on his lapels, should have held him back; instead, her fingers curled, drawing him nearer. Her wits were drowning in a sea of sensual longing. In the instant before his lips completed her conquest, she managed to whisper, 'Yes.'

Lips touched, brushed, settled. An instant later, she surrendered on a sigh, giving him her mouth, thrilling to the slow, unhurried claiming. He touched every inch, then deliberately invoked the memory of their joining. Heady passion, ardent longing, had her firmly in their grip when he drew back and whispered against her lips, 'Liar.'

'Good morning.'

Alathea looked up, and only just managed not to gape. 'What are you doing here?'

Here was her office, her private, personal domain into which others ventured only by invitation. The room she had retreated to, ostensibly to tally the household accounts, in reality to search for some sure, safe, sensible path through her suddenly shifting world. Since their interlude in the gazebo, she was no longer sure what was real and what mere fanciful imaginings. As she watched Gabriel close the door, she resigned herself to making no progress on that front, not with him in the same small room.

'It occurred to me' – he scanned the room as he strolled toward her – 'that with the Season at its zenith, we can expect Crowley to call in his promissory notes in about two weeks.' Reaching the desk, he met her gaze. 'It's time we started framing our petition to the bench.'

'Only two weeks?'

'He won't wait until the very end. He's more likely to draw in his pigeons at the height of the whirl, when the ton provides maximum distraction. I suggest,' he said, lowering his long limbs into the armchair facing the desk, 'that you summon Wiggs. We'll need his input. I've brought Montague's figures.'

Alathea considered him, entirely at his ease in her chair. He smiled at her winningly, his expression studiously mild. With awful calm, she rose and tugged the bell pull. When Crisp answered, she requested him to send for Wiggs. Crisp bowed and departed; she turned back to discover Gabriel eyeing the ledgers on her desk.

'What are you doing?'

'The household accounts.'

'Ah.' A smile flirted about his lips. 'Don't let me disturb you.'

Alathea vowed she wouldn't, something much easier said than done. Pen in hand, she forced herself to tally column after column. Despite her intentions, the figures showed a distressing tendency to fade before her eyes. At full stretch, her senses flickered. She bit her lip, clenched her fingers tighter on the pen, and frowned at her neat entries.

'Need any help?'

'No.'

She completed three more columns, then carefully looked up. He was watching her, an expression in his eyes she couldn't place. 'What?'

He held her gaze, then slowly lifted one brow.

She blushed. '*Go away*! Go and sit in the drawing room.'

He grinned. 'I'm comfortable here, and the scenery's to my liking.'

Alathea glared at him.

The click of the latch had them both turning.

Augusta's shining head appeared around the door. 'Can I come in?'

Alathea beamed. 'Indeed, poppet. But where's Miss Helm?'

'She's helping Mama with the placecards for the dinner.' Shutting the door, Augusta came forward, studying Gabriel with the frank gaze of the young.

'You remember Mr Cynster. His mama and papa live at Quiverstone Manor.'

Gabriel lay there, a lazy lion relaxed in the chair, then he held out a hand. 'That's a big doll.'

Augusta considered, then turned Rose and held her out. 'I bet you can't guess her name.'

Gabriel took the doll; propping it on one knee, he studied it. 'She used to be called Rose.'

'She still is!' Augusta followed Rose, clambering onto Gabriel's lap.

As he settled her, he looked up – and met Alathea's astonished stare. He grinned and looked down at Augusta. 'Did your sister ever tell you about the time Rose got stuck in that big apple tree at the end of your orchard?'

Alathea watched and listened, amazed that he still remembered all the details, and that Augusta, so often shy, had taken so readily to him. Then again, he did have three much younger sisters; he could probably write the definitive thesis on bewitching young girls.

Seizing opportunity, she quickly finished the accounts, then opened another ledger and settled to check through receipts. The activity used only a small part of her brain; the rest grappled with the problem of Gabriel, and what she could and should do about him. The sound of his deep voice, rumbling low as he charmed Augusta, was familiar and oddly comforting.

Two days had passed since they'd met in the gazebo, two days since she'd last been in his arms with his lips on hers. They'd met that evening at a ball; although he'd claimed two waltzes, he'd claimed nothing more. He'd appeared the next morning to stroll through the park by her side. She'd been ready to counter any possessive move he made, any maneuver to demonstrate his claim over her. He hadn't made one. Unfortunately, the understanding in his eyes warned her that he knew how she felt, how she would react; he was simply biding his time until the battlefield better suited his purpose.

Of that purpose there remained not a smidgen of doubt. Marriage. The notion – not of marriage but of marriage to him – deeply unnerved her. Just thinking of him now unnerved her in a way she'd never had to deal with before. Intimacy, and all the emotions wrapped up with it, had thoroughly disrupted her inner landscape. Yet if he'd allowed her to disappear as she'd planned, to fade out of his life, while she might regret the brevity of their association, she would, she felt sure, have remained inwardly steady.

Instead, she was whirling, her stomach often hollow, uncertainty and excitement an unsettling blend. What she felt for him now she couldn't put a name to – was afraid to put a name to, to even study it at all, not while she had to refuse him.

He'd decided to marry her because he desired her and because he wanted her as his wife. The reason behind that want he'd refused to clarify; she felt sure he was motivated by a compulsion to protect her.

The prospect of him marrying her with protection his true aim chilled her. He would be kind, considerate, generous – even a friend – but as time passed, he would cease to be hers alone. He would cease to be her lover. They would grow apart . . .

With a little jerk, she returned to the present, to her office and the ledger open before her, to the rumble of Gabriel's voice and Augusta's piping prattle. Sucking in a breath, she held it, and tidied her pile of receipts.

She was *not* going to marry Gabriel – she couldn't let him sacrifice himself, or her. Turning him from his goal might not be easy, but marrying him would not be right, not for him or for her.

Marking off the last of the receipts, she opened a drawer and placed them in a box, then shut the drawer and shut her ledger. The slap of the pages brought Gabriel's and Augusta's heads up. Alathea smiled. 'I have to talk business with Mr Cynster now, poppet.'

Sliding from Gabriel's lap, Augusta gifted her with a confident smile. 'He said I could call him Gabriel. It's his name.'

'Indeed.' Rising and rounding the desk, Alathea hugged Augusta, then set her on her feet. 'Off you go now – Miss Helm should be nearly finished.'

Ducking around Alathea's skirts, Augusta waved to Gabriel and sang 'Good-bye,' then happily skipped to the door.

As it shut behind her, Alathea felt long fingers tangle with hers. She turned to discover Gabriel studying her hand, now entwined with his.

'What "business" do you wish to discuss?' He looked up, invitation in his eyes.

One part of her mind urged her to whisk her hand from his, to whisk herself out of his orbit. The rest of her reveled in the warmth that flooded her as his fingers caressed her palm. Alathea studied the sleepy, languid beckoning in his eyes, and was deceived not at all. She looked at the wall clock. 'Wiggs will be another twenty minutes, but we can make a start on a draft without him.'

Looking back at Gabriel, she raised a brow and gently detached her hand. He grimaced but let her go. 'All right. But you can write.' He rose as she resumed her seat behind the desk. 'We can start by noting the false claims we've identified.'

Unsurprised to find herself his amanuensis, Alathea set a sheet of paper on the blotter. They listed Montague's calculations derived from the figures Crowley had provided Gerrard, comparing them with those Crowley had claimed. Gabriel stated and she transcribed, adding and correcting as they went. He paced back and forth behind her, between the desk and the window, stopping now and then to read over her shoulder. When they reached the end of Montague's findings, Gabriel halted beside her, scanning the list. His hand closed on her shoulder, close by her neck, on skin left bare by her summer morning gown.

His hand nestled there, strong fingers gentle on her skin.

'What next, do you think?'

Her composure shattered, unable to breathe, Alathea heard the mild words and realized with a hot rush horribly akin to mortification that he hadn't meant to discompose her. He'd simply touched her as a close personal friend might, without any sexual intention.

She was the one thinking of sexual intentions.

Before she could gather her wits, he tipped up her face. He studied it; she scrambled wildly to find some expression to mask the truth. Then his gaze turned intent, and she knew it was too late. The fingers at her throat moved again, this time deliberately.

Sensual awareness flared in her eyes. Gabriel saw it. His lips curved. 'Perhaps' – he bent over her – 'we should try this.'

Her lips parted under his; her hand rose to cradle the back of his as he held her face steady. She gave her mouth freely as she always did; he took and drank and claimed. She was a delight in her sweet helplessness, her total inability to conceal her response, the womanly yearning that lay beneath the confidence of her years. Her tongue tangled with his; her fingers gripped his shoulder. Sliding his hand from her face, he lowered it to her breast, cupping the firm mound, then searching for its peak. Her hand followed his, cradling it still, feeling him knead and pleasure her. In one swift movement, he slipped his hand from under hers and reversed their positions, his hand covering and surrounding hers, pressing her palm to the heated flesh of her breast, guiding her fingers to her ruched nipple and squeezing them tight.

She gasped, swayed—

They both heard the creak of a board outside the door an instant before it opened.

Charlie looked in. 'Hello!' He nodded to Gabriel, lounging against the window frame, then transferred his gaze to Alathea. 'I'm going to Bond Street – Mama suggested I ask whether there's anything more we need for tomorrow night?'

Her pulse pounding, Alathea shook her head, fervently praying that, with her back to the window, Charlie couldn't see the flush heating her skin. 'No. Nothing.' Their ball would be held tomorrow night, formally introducing Mary and Alice to the ton. 'All seems in hand.'

'Good-oh! I'll be off then.' With a wave, Charlie departed, shutting the door behind him.

Drawing in a much-needed breath, Alathea turned her head and met Gabriel's gaze. She frowned balefully. 'Stop thinking about it!' Swinging back to the desk, she picked up her pen. 'Aside from anything else, there's no lock on that door.'

She heard his smothered laugh but refused to look his way. 'I think,' she said, stabbing the nib into the inkwell, 'that next we should note all we've learned about Fangak, Lodwar, and wherever else it was.'

He sighed dramatically. 'Kingi.'

Despite her hopes that all was in hand, the next morning saw a host of small commissions that simply *had* to be fulfilled. Leaving Serena in command, with Crisp and Figgs in their element. Alathea bundled Mary and Alice into the small carriage and escaped.

'It's a madhouse!' Face to the window, Alice peered back to where the red carpet was being shaken and swept. 'If they put that out now, it'll be a mess by evening.'

'Crisp will see to it.' Alathea sank back against the squabs and closed her eyes. She'd been up since daybreak, and had already met with the caterers and the florist. All the major components for the evening were thankfully falling into place. Opening her eyes, she scanned the list she clutched in one hand. 'Gloves first, stockings next, and then the ribbons.'

The carriage bore them home an hour and a half later. Mary and Alice were bubbling with excitement; Alathea watched them with joy in her heart. No matter how tiring the day might be, tonight would be its own reward.

As they turned into Mount Street, she glanced out of the window – and saw Jeremy's head almost in line with hers. 'What . . . ?'

Jerking forward, she stared, then leaned out of the window the better to view her youngest brother, laughing uproariously, arms flailing, seated atop a pedestrian curricle propelled full tilt down the pavement by Charlie and Gabriel.

She forebore to scream.

The carriage pulled up before their front steps. Mary and Alice tumbled out, paused but an instant to view Jeremy and company, then giggled and ran indoors.

Alathea descended from the carriage more slowly, then drew herself up and waited for the miscreants to arrive before her. They did so in an ungainly rush; for one instant she watched, horrified, expecting to see her worst nightmare unfold as, hauled to a halt, the unstable contraption slewed sideways, tipping Jeremy off the high seat—

Reaching forward, Gabriel caught him, swinging him clear, then setting him on his feet while Charlie neatly righted the curricle. Charlie and Gabriel grinned at her – Jeremy did his best to appear inconspicuous.

Alathea fixed her gaze on him. 'I believe I had your promise on no account to ride this machine in town?'

Eyes downcast, Jeremy squirmed.

Gabriel heaved a sigh. 'It was my fault.'

Alathea looked at him. 'Yours?'

'I arrived just as your footman was taking delivery and offered to show them how it was done.'

'*You* rode it?'

The look he bent on her was dismissively superior. 'Of course. It's easy. Would you like me to demonstrate?'

She nearly said yes. The notion of seeing him, hideously elegant as always, precariously perched on the awkward machine riding up and down the tonnish street was almost too good to pass up. But . . .' No.' She transferred her gaze to Jeremy. 'That's not the point.'

'Ah, but it is, because once I'd ridden to the corner, I simply put Jeremy on the seat and told him to hang on. It didn't occur to me that the machine had been bought for him but that he'd been forbidden to ride it.'

Alathea caught the swift upward glance Jeremy shot her. She pressed her lips together, then explained, 'The agreement I used to gain Serena's approval to buy the curricle was that Jeremy would only ride it on the lawns at the Park. He's prone to broken bones – to date, we've survived three broken arms and a broken leg. A collarbone in three pieces would never be welcome, but it would be even less welcome *today*.'

Jeremy glanced up again; Alathea caught his eye. 'You are extremely lucky that it was I who took

Mary and Alice to the shops, and not your mama – she would have swooned had she seen your performance.'

Jeremy shuffled his feet, but his eyes sparkled. A small smile played on his lips, just waiting to dawn. 'But she didn't see it – you did. Wasn't it *grand*?' His smile broke free.

Alathea twisted her lips in an effort to hold back her own. 'Potentially grand – you could do with a bit of practice, but don't you *dare* ride it here again.'

'What about the back lawn?' Charlie asked. 'That's thick – he wouldn't break anything if he fell on that.'

'It's got a nice slope to it, too,' Gabriel put in. 'And I promise I won't let him career into the rhododendrons.'

Faced with three male faces ranging in age from twelve to thirty but all with the same little-boy-pleading expression, Alathea threw up her hands. 'Very well – I'll go and prepare Serena.' She caught Gabriel's eye as she turned to the steps. 'At least it'll keep you all out from under our feet.'

His grin would have done his namesake proud.

Leaving them wheeling the curricle around to the back gate, Alathea crossed the threshold and entered a world of pandemonium. She first sought out Serena and reassured her of Jeremy's safety, embroidering on Gabriel's promise without a second thought as soon as she realized Serena was happy to place her trust in him.

For the next hour she was fully occupied dealing

with queries from the caterers, the florist, and most importantly the draper. Her novel idea to decorate the huge ballroom with swaths of cerulean blue muslin, which could later be given as presents to the female servants here and at the Park, had been given form and style by the earnest young draper – the white-and-gilt ballroom looked like a vision of heaven.

'Perfect.' With a brisk nod, she turned away from the sight. 'Please send in your account promptly, Mr Bobbins – we will only be in town for another few weeks.'

Mr Bobbins bowed low, incoherently assuring her that his account would be presented forthwith.

Alathea checked the supplies of salmon and shrimp with Figgs, then she and Crisp descended to the cellar. By the time they'd finished selecting the wines for the formal dinner preceding the ball, it was past noon. Retiring to her office, intending to do no more than catch her breath and check her lists for the next most pressing item, Alathea found herself drawn to the window.

On the lawn behind the house, Jeremy, Charlie and Gabriel were totally absorbed in the new toy. Gabriel had stripped off his coat; together with Charlie, he was coaching Jeremy in the difficult process of gaining his balance on the awkward machine. Alathea watched, quietly amazed at the patience Gabriel showed. None knew better than she that he was naturally impatient, yet in dealing with Jeremy he displayed both tact and steady encouragement, exactly what Jeremy needed. Under Gabriel's eye, he bloomed. Before she turned away, Alathea saw him free-wheel down the lawn, managing to steer the curricle away from the thick bushes.

As she left her office and plunged back into the melee, she reflected that, while he was not long on patience, Gabriel's second name could have been persistence, a fact she would do well to remember.

Half an hour later, he found her supervising the positioning of the trestles in the parlor they were converting into a supper room. Surveying the scene, he raised his brows. 'How many cards did you send out?'

'Five hundred,' Alathea absentmindedly replied. 'God knows how we'll manage if they all arrive at once.'

Gabriel studied her face, then calmly took her arm. Ignoring her resistance and her distracted scowl, he towed her to the side of the room. 'Where's the petition.'

'The petition?' She stared at him. 'You can't mean to work on that *now*?'

'*I* can work on it. I can write, you know.' Her frown suggested she wasn't convinced of it; he ignored that, too. 'I'll take it home and continue framing our arguments.' He glanced at the footmen and maids scurrying frantically about. 'It's too noisy here.'

She didn't look happy, but nodded. 'It's in the top drawer of my desk.'

'I'll take it.' Gabriel started to leave, then halted. Ignoring the many about them, he caught her chin. '*Don't* run yourself ragged. I'll see you at dinner.'

Before she could react, he ducked his head, kissed her quickly, and left.

'Lady Alathea – is this where you wanted this table?'

'What? Oh . . . yes, I suppose . . .'

Inwardly grinning, Gabriel headed downstairs.

CHAPTER 17

The formal dinner preceding a come-out ball was, in social terms, even more important than the ball itself. The earl, Serena and Alathea had agreed that this dinner should be the most glittering affair regardless of cost, one by which the assembled leaders of the ton would remember the Morwellans. Alathea had personally overseen every detail, from the guest list Serena had organized and the stiff white stationery on which the invitations had been inscribed, to the gleaming crystal, the silver service, the Meissen dinner service, and the crisp white damask. The dishes in all twelve courses had been carefully chosen to complement one another in a parade of culinary delight. The wine was superb. Not one of the fifty guests seated about the long table would entertain the slightest suspicion of the economies normally practiced at Morwellan House.

From her seat midway down the table, Alathea watched the sixth course being laid out. All was proceeding smoothly, the babel prevailing on all sides – conversations, laughter, the constant clink of porcelain and silverware – a reassuring testament. Her father, presiding over the event from the table's head, looked magnificent; Serena, resplendent in navy silk at the other end, was his match. Opposite Alathea, spread between their guests, Mary and Alice conversed with simple charm. Charlie was seated farther along the table to her right. All three were dressed to perfection, each a paragon of tonnish expectations. In her amber silk gown, a beaded cap perched atop her coiffed hair, Alathea contributed her part to their sartorial facade.

Her heart lifted as she gazed about her. They'd done it – they'd come to London and, despite the difficulties, claimed their rightful place in society. As if to illustrate their success, Sally Jersey caught her eye and smiled and nodded. Seated further along, Princess Esterhazy had already regally signaled her approval. Only as she followed Sally Jersey's gaze to Serena did it occur to Alathea to wonder what it was both patronnesses were complimenting *her* upon. Their appreciation of the dinner and company they conveyed to Serena, of course. So what was it she'd done to attract their approbation?

She turned to Gabriel, seated on her left. She'd been so absorbed with the dinner itself she hadn't registered his appearing at her side to escort her into the dining room as anything odd. She'd grown accustomed to having him near, to resting her hand on his arm and letting him steer her through crowds. It wasn't until she'd caught Lucifer's questioning look halfway through the fourth course that she'd realized. One glance at Celia's face, at her intrigued expression, confirmed that their sudden penchant for each other's company had not escaped notice.

The suspicion that their ease in each other's company was not escaping *anyone's* notice suddenly assailed her. Before she had a chance to frame the question: 'Did you plan this?' in any form likely to get an answer, Gabriel glanced at her and saw the frown in her eyes.

'Relax. Everything's going well.' He indicated a dish of game. 'This is excellent – what's in the sauce?'

Alathea looked at the dish. 'Muscat grapes and pomegranate syrup.' There was no point wrangling over how he'd come to be sitting beside her. He was there. She might as well take advantage. 'How's the petition?'

He shrugged non-committally. 'We've made a good start.'

'But not enough to be certain of a favorable judgment.'

His lips twisted; he didn't answer.

Alathea forged on, her tone barely a whisper as she considered a dish before her. 'Everything we have is open to argument – there's nothing cut and dried, no absolute and obvious falsehood. All our claims rely on the word of others, others we can't call on to verify the facts. Without a bona fide witness – without Captain Struthers – all Crowley need do is deny our claims. The burden of proof will rest on us.' She helped herself to beans in white sauce and passed the dish along. 'We have to find the captain, don't we?'

Gabriel glanced at her. 'The case would be certain with him. Without him, it's going to be difficult.'

'There must be something more we can do.'

Again she felt his gaze on her face. 'We'll find him.' Beneath the table his hand closed about hers. His thumb stroked her palm. 'But tonight, enjoy your success. Leave the captain and Crowley for tomorrow.'

Unable to meet his eyes, she nodded and prayed her blush didn't show. His hand wrapped around hers had evoked a sensual memory of his body wrapped around hers, stroking hers . . . When his hand slid away, she determinedly lifted her head and drew a steadying breath, looking along the table rather than at him.

'I take it Esher and Carstairs are both in earnest?'

Alathea refocused on Mary. Beside her, Lord Esher was quietly and persistently attentive, Mary sweetly appreciative. A similar scenario was playing out toward the other end of the table, where Mr Carstairs sat beside Alice. 'We believe so. Their parents were clearly pleased to be invited tonight.' With a nod, Alathea indicated Lady Esher and Mrs Carstairs; their husbands were farther down the table.

Gabriel followed her gaze, then transferred his

attention to the dish she passed him. 'Esher has a neat little property in Hampshire. He does well, and pays attention to his land. He's a likable chap with a sense of humor, but sensible and steady. From all I can gather, he's in a position to please himself – I doubt he'll cavil over Mary's lack of dowry.'

'She does have a dowry.'

'She does?' He hesitated, then asked, 'How much?'

Alathea calmly told him.

'Just enough to ensure not even the most censorious raise a brow. You have covered all the cracks.'

She inclined her head.

'Well, if Esher's unlikely to be concerned about money, Carstairs is even less likely to give it a second thought. While Esher's old money, well established, Carstairs is both old and new. They met at Eton and have been firm friends ever since, which should suit Mary and Alice admirably.'

'They are very close.'

'Carstairs's estate is just south of Bath – within easy visiting distance of Morwellan Park. His maternal grandfather had an interest in shipping, which Carstairs inherited. He's gaining a reputation as having a cautious interest in the right sort of ventures. He's ambitious in that area, and not about to become a silent partner.'

The approval in his tone was clear; Alathea shot him a glance. 'A useful contact for you, perhaps?'

Gabriel met her gaze. 'Perhaps.'

'How did you find out all this – about Carstairs and Esher?'

'I asked around. Quietly. I didn't think your father would have the right contacts to find out for you.'

'He hasn't.' Alathea hesitated, then inclined her. head. 'Thank you.'

She looked away, along the table, ostensibly scanning the guests, in reality letting her gratitude flare, then fade. The reprobate beside her – he who knew her far too well – needed no encouragement. She tried not to dwell on how much easier her life was with him beside her, supplying the reassurances she needed but could not gain for herself. Having his shoulder to lean on was a far too seductive proposition.

Her wandering gaze reached Lucifer, sipping his wine, his gaze on her and Gabriel. His expression was quietly considering.

Smiling serenely, Alathea let her gaze wander on, only to encounter more considering glances. It took her a few minutes to realize why Gabriel and she were so persistently raising questions in so many minds. It was the way they conversed with each other. They were so attuned to each other's tone, to every nuance in the other's repertoire, that they rarely needed to look at each other to be sure of the other's meaning. They talked as two who knew each other well, as two who, in the ton's parlance, shared an understanding of long duration.

They talked like long-standing lovers.

The last course was being removed before she again turned to Gabriel. All the guests were repairing directly to the ballroom. He was already standing; he offered her his arm. She placed her hand on his sleeve and allowed him to raise her – as soon as she was on her feet, he grasped her hand, tucked it in his arm, his hand possessively over hers, and led her to join the queue exiting the dining room.

The message he was sending the interested observers all about them was crystal clear. Although he could be devilish enough when he wished, she was certain that, at present, he wasn't deliberately putting on a show. His behavior was simply an instinctive extension of how he now felt about her.

He caught her glancing at him and lifted a brow. 'What?'

She looked into his hazel eyes, then, lips curving, shook her head and looked away. 'Never mind.'

There was no chance she could get him to change and, deep down, she knew she would miss their newfound closeness if he did.

The ballroom caused a sensation. Standing in the receiving line Alathea fielded numerous compliments on the unusual decor while helping Mary and Alice greet the more intimidating dowagers. Unfortunately, more than a few of the old battleships, when distracted from Mary and Alice, were only too ready to turn their cannons on her.

'Absolutely criminal,' Lady Osbaldestone declared, scrutinizing her silk-clad figure through her lorgnette. 'Waste, gel, *waste*!' One bony finger poked her in the ribs. 'God knows *why* you've hidden yourself away, but it's past time some rake rattled your stays.'

Others took a different tack.

'So, my dear, do you spend much time in charitable works?' Lady Harcourt, of similar age to Alathea, smiled insincerely. 'It must be so nice to live a quiet life.'

Alathea responded to all such queries with a serene smile and calm assurance. As soon as the incoming tide eased, Gabriel appeared and, with Serena's encouragement, drew her out of the line.

'But Mary and Alice—'

'Serena's with them. There's someone I want you to meet.'

'Who?'

His Great-aunt Clara was a sweet old lady, although a trifle vague. She patted Alathea's hand. 'Your sisters are lovely, dear, but we'll have to see you wed first.'

'Precisely what I've been telling her,' Gabriel put in.

Over Clara's head, Alathea narrowed her eyes at him.

'Indeed, yes,' Clara said, and patted her hand again. 'We'll have to find some nice gentleman for you – perhaps that nice Chillingworth boy.'

The look on Gabriel's face was priceless; Alathea

only just managed not to laugh. 'I don't think so,' she said, smiling at Clara.

'No? Well, then, let's see. Who else?'

Devil strolled up before Clara could consider other options. She released Alathea to clutch his sleeve. 'Is Honoria here?'

Devil grinned. 'She's on the other side of the room – I'll take you to her if you like.'

'Oh, yes – so kind.' Clutching her shawl with one hand and Devil with the other, Clara smiled in farewell and moved on.

'There are the Carmichaels.' Gabriel directed Alathea's gaze to a couple whose country estate lay not far from Morwellan Park and the Manor. They headed toward them.

For the next twenty minutes, they moved through the ever-increasing crowd, stopping here then there to chat, always at Gabriel's direction. Only when she spied Lord Montgomery, then Lord Falworth through the sea of heads did Alathea realize what he was doing. With them constantly moving from one conversation to the next, her court was given no chance to gather about her.

Alathea swallowed her protest – she'd rather move through the crowd on Gabriel's arm than stand surrounded by her all-too-often vacuous court. Feigning ignorance of his high-handed manuverings was definitely the sensible course.

Then the musicians started up and the crowd magically parted, clearing a wide space. As both

Mary and Alice had been given permission to indulge long since, the first dance was a waltz. Keen to see if her expectation that Esher would partner Mary and Carstairs would partner Alice would be fulfilled, Alathea eagerly accompanied Gabriel to the edge of the floor.

Sure enough, Mary and Esher took to the floor first, Mary blushing delightedly, her smile declaration enough, while Esher looked the picture of pride. Alathea smiled mistily as they waltzed past, then looked back up the room. Alice was already in Carstairs's encircling arms – both seemed lost in each other's eyes, oblivious to the crowd looking on.

Alathea sighed. With her sisters, her hand was played and she'd won – they would have the futures she'd wanted for them, and which they patently deserved. They'd be happy, and loved . . .

Alice and Carstairs waltzed past.

The next instant, Alathea, too, was on the floor, whirling in Gabriel's arms. Her eyes flew wide. There were as yet no other couples on the floor. 'What? . . .'

Gabriel raised a brow. 'My dance, I believe?'

She would have loved to tell him what she thought of his arrogance, but under the curious eyes of half the ton, all she could do was fix a smile on her lips and let him sweep her away. She did, however, glare at him.

He only smiled, gathering her closer as other couples took to the floor in their wake. He leaned closer as they went through the turn. 'Don't tempt me.'

The whispered words caressed her ear; Alathea shivered. 'I should take umbrage.'

'But you won't. You know I can't help myself.'

She limited her response to a sniff; prolonging such a conversation would do nothing for her serenity. The nagging observation that she enjoyed waltzing with him, enjoyed the feel of his hand burning through the silk at her back, enjoyed the sense of being captive to his strength, whirled so effortlessly around the room, was more than distracting enough.

That her pleasure in life was increasingly dependent on him was a thought she wished she'd never had.

After the dance, they once more meandered through the crowd, chatting with acquaintances. They were leaving one group when Gerrard Debbington hailed Gabriel. Gabriel stopped; sidestepping this way, then that, Gerrard eventually reached them.

He smiled vaguely at Alathea.

She smiled brightly back, completely forgetting that she hadn't met him in the receiving line. 'Hello.'

Gabriel pinched her fingers and introduced them. Alathea continued to smile as if she commonly spoke to gentlemen she'd never met. Gerrard, thankfully, was too well brought up to comment.

He looked at Gabriel. 'If I could have a word . . . there's something you should know.'

Gabriel gestured to Alathea. 'Thea knows of my interests – she knows of Crowley. You can speak freely.'

'Oh.' Gerrard's smile hid his surprise. 'In that case . . . I was leaving Tattersalls yesterday when I literally bumped into Crowley. He was with a gentleman Vane said was Lord Douglas. Unfortunately, Vane and Patience were right behind me, and Patience spoke. From what she said, it was obvious she was my sister.' He grimaced. 'Only a sister would say something like that. As she was on Vane's arm, it wouldn't need any great intelligence to guess the connection. Vane said I should tell you and ask what you think.'

'I think,' Gabriel said, 'that we should discuss the possibilities with Vane.' He looked over the sea of heads. 'Where is he?'

'Far left,' Gerrard said, craning his head. 'Close by the wall. Patience was with him.'

Alathea spotted the purple plume Patience Cynster wore in her hair. 'There – by the second mirror.'

They headed that way but in tacking through the crowd, Gerrard forged ahead. Gabriel drew Alathea closer. 'I need to talk to Vane about this – Gerrard could be in danger.'

Alathea glanced at him, concern in her eyes. 'From Crowley?'

'Yes. I need you to distract Patience while I talk to Vane.'

'Why can't you talk about the matter in front of Patience? Gerrard is *her* brother, after all.'

'That's why. And in case it's escaped your notice, Patience is increasing, so Vane will certainly not want her worrying over a threat to Gerrard that we're going to ensure never materializes.'

'So you want me to distract her? To connive at keeping her in the dark over something she has a perfect right to know' Alathea broke off, another idea overriding all thought of Patience's sisterly rights. 'Tell me – if there was any threat to Charlie or Jeremy, would you tell me, or make sure I never heard of it?'

The way Gabriel's lips sealed into a thin line was answer enough. She narrowed her eyes at him. 'Men! Why on earth you imagine—'

'Just tell me – who wants Crowley stopped?'

Alathea blinked. 'I do.'

'And who did you ask to stop him?'

'You.'

'I vaguely recall stipulating that you had to obey my orders.'

'Yes, but—'

'Thea, stop arguing. I need to talk to Vane and I don't want Patience unnecessarily upset.'

Put like that . . . 'Oh, very well.' She threw him a stern look. 'But I don't approve.'

They drew free of the crowd and advanced on Vane and Patience. With an assured smile, Alathea drew Patience aside; Gabriel hid a smile as he overheard her ask after Patience's condition. The perfect topic, the perfect excuse to exclude the menfolk from their councils.

The males in question quickly formed their own huddle.

'What do you think?' Vane asked.

'Altogether too dangerous. Crowley would have prised it out of Archie Douglas before they'd got to the first ring.' Gabriel looked at Vane. 'I take it Archie was sufficiently *compos mentis* to recognize you?'

'Definitely – he was remarkably sober, but then it was before noon.'

Gabriel looked at Gerrard. 'Nothing for it then – we've got to get you out of sight.'

Gerrard shrugged. 'I could go home to Derbyshire for a bit.'

'No – too far. You have to be within reach of London and the courts. We'll need you as a witness to corroborate the details of the company's proposal to investors.'

'How do you think Crowley will react?' Vane asked.

'I think,' Gabriel replied, 'that he'll pause and take stock. He's been in this game too long to act rashly. And he's very close to calling in his notes. I think he'll reason that Gerrard will have consulted me *after* the meeting – there's no reason he should suspect I knew anything about the meeting beforehand. Indeed, if Gerrard had mentioned one of Crowley's schemes to me *ahead* of any meeting, I would have advised against the meeting taking place.

So he'll imagine I was consulted afterward, and that I've advised Gerrard against the investment. He hasn't heard from Gerrard again, and now he'll know why. He's so close to getting his hands on a small fortune, he'll be very hesitant over unnecessarily rocking his boat. I don't think he'll come searching for Gerrard yet, but I do think he will, and with a vengeance, the instant he hears there's a petition lodged against the company.'

'How dangerous is he?'

Gabriel met Vane's gaze. 'He'll kill without a qualm.' Vane's brows rose. Gabriel continued, 'The information I've received suggests he's plowed every last penny into this venture – if the company's notes fail, he'll be ruined. And he'll likely have some rather unsavory and irate creditors after him, too. Basically, I'd rate Crowley as more dangerous than a rabid rat cornered.'

'Hmm.' Vane's gaze shifted to his wife, chatting animatedly with Alathea three feet away. 'I'm concerned about Patience. She seems rather pale, don't you think?'

Gabriel considered the bloom of health blushing Patience's fair cheeks. 'Definitely peaked.'

'A short sojourn in Kent would be just the thing to restore her. Fresh air, sunshine—'

'Scores of your workers in the fields surrounding the manor. Just what the doctor ordered.' Gabriel swung to Gerrard, who had listened in silence. 'Of course, as a dutiful brother, you'll accompany your sister into the country.'

Gerrard grinned. 'Whatever you say – I can sketch there as well as here.'

Vane gestured to Patience and Alathea. 'Shall we break the news?'

Ten minutes later, Gabriel and Alathea stepped once more into the crowd. Alathea smiled. 'That was very thoughtful of Vane to be so concerned over Patience, even if there is no need. She's perfectly well.'

'Yes, well, husbands have to do what husbands have to do, especially when they're Cynsters.' Gabriel glanced at her. 'Did you learn anything useful?'

'We were talking about pregnancy.'

'I know.'

Alathea took one more step, froze, then whirled on him. 'What do you—? You don't—?'

He opened his eyes wide. 'Don't what?' The musicians started up. Sliding one arm about her waist, he drew her to him, into his arms, onto the floor.

Staring straight over his shoulder, Alathea drew in a tight breath. Ignoring the color burning her cheeks, she categorically stated, 'I am *not* pregnant.'

His deep sigh feathered the curls about her ear. 'Ah, well, one lives in hope.'

His hand moved on her back in soothing little circles. Alathea bit her lip against a sudden compulsion to blurt out the truth – that she didn't know if she was or not. She was not, definitely not, going to talk about such things with him. Especially not with him.

'You will be pregnant with my child one day – you know that, don't you?'

She shut her eyes – tried to shut her ears to the words but they kept falling, straight into her mind, her heart, her empty, yearning soul.

'You love children – you want children of your own. I'll give you as many as you like.'

They circled, neither paying any attention to the dance, moving to a tune heard on a different plane.

'You want to have my child – I want that, too. It'll happen one day, Thea – trust me, it will.'

She shivered. To her immense relief he said nothing more but simply steered her around the floor. By the time the music ended and he released her, she'd regained her mental feet. She did not, however, meet his eyes; instead, she scanned the room. 'I should check with Serena—'

'Everything's fine – she told me to keep you from worrying.'

That had her searching his face. 'She didn't.'

'She did, and you know a gentleman should do everything in his power to satisfy his hostess.'

Her pithy retort was cut off by the descent of Lord and Lady Collinridge, the neighbors who owned the old barn with the narrow back window. The Collinridges had known them both from childhood but hadn't met Gabriel for years; with a sweet smile, Alathea encouraged Lady Collinridge to twit her tormentor for all she was worth.

In the end, Gabriel invented a summons from his mother to escape, taking her with him.

'Jezebel,' he whispered as they made their way through the crush, now as bad – as good – as any ball that Season. 'You enjoyed that.'

'You deserved that,' Alathea retorted. A sudden press of bodies brought them to a temporary standstill, him behind her.

'Hmm – and what else do I deserve?'

Alathea swallowed a gasp as one large hand slid over her hip to perform a leisurely, all-too-knowing circuit of her silk-clad bottom.

Closing his hand, Gabriel lowered his head and whispered in her ear, 'Perhaps you'd like to retreat to your office – I was, after all, ordered by your stepmother to do my very best to keep you amused.'

Alathea couldn't resist the urge to tip her head back and meet his eyes. Under their heavy lids, they glowed with golden fire. There was absolutely no doubt of what he was thinking.

Her gaze dropped to his lips. Did temptation come any more potent than this?

The crush about them eased, and she managed to draw breath. 'There's no lock on my office door, remember?'

She'd spoken before she'd thought – her cheeks flamed. The wicked chuckle he gave made her think of a buccaneer about to seize her, but his hand left her bottom – her fevered flesh – closing briefly, affectionately, on her hip before he released her. The flow of people resumed and they moved on.

Almost immediately they encountered Lady Albemarle, a distant Cynster connection, and stopped to chat. From her, they passed on to Lady Horatia Cynster.

'I have no idea,' she responded to Gabriel's query, 'if Demon and Felicity will return to town before the end of the Season. They're enjoying themselves hugely by all accounts. The last we heard, they were in Cheltenham.'

They chatted easily for some minutes, then once again moved on. When the next lady with whom they paused to exchange greetings proved to be another Cynster connection, Alathea had to wonder. It was true there were a lot of Cynsters and many more family connections. Nevertheless . . .

As they strolled on again, she caught Gabriel's eye.

'You're not, by any chance, introducing me to your family?'

'Of course not – they already know you. And those who don't were introduced to you in the receiving line.'

Alathea sighed exasperatedly. The look in his eyes, the set of his jaw, warned her any protest would be fruitless – his intention was fixed. The reins were presently in his hands and he was driving as hard as he could toward matrimony. She shook her head. 'You're impossible!'

His lips quirked. 'No. *You're* impossible. I'm merely immovable.'

She tried to smother her giggle but failed.

'Lady Alathea!' Lord Falworth pushed through the crowd to bow before her. 'Dear lady, I've been searching quite doggedly, I do assure you.' He shot a censorious glance at Gabriel. 'But now I've found you, I believe a cotillion is starting. If you would do me the honor?'

Alathea smiled. For all his foppish tendencies, Falworth was an amiable gentleman and an unexceptionable partner. 'Indeed, sir – it is I who would be honored.' It was, perhaps, time she put some distance between herself and her self-styled keeper. 'If you'll excuse me, Mr Cynster?' With a nod for Gabriel, she placed her hand on Falworth's sleeve and let him lead her to where the sets were forming.

As soon as the dance started, her thoughts reverted to Gabriel, Falworth forgotten. No other gentleman could vie with her nemesis. There was – and very likely always had been – only one man for her, the man she'd been closest to all her life. And now he wanted to marry her. He cared for her, but not in a way she could accept as a safe basis for marriage. What she should do – how she could take charge of the situation and steer a safe course for them both – she had no idea. With every day that passed, the pressure to give in, to surrender and be his wife, grew.

Her one bulwark against that was simple but solid. Fear. An unconquerable, unquenchable fear of a pain so vast, so deep, she'd never be able to survive it. A pain she sensed rather than knew, one she could imagine but had never felt. The sort of pain that no sane person invited or permitted to threaten them.

That much she knew: She was too afraid to ever consent to their marriage if all he felt for her, bar transient desire, was mild affection and a duty of care.

As she circled and swayed through the figures of the cotillion, she considered that truth, and the fact that it meant she would never bear his child.

She would never, ever, have children of her own.

But that had been decided eleven years ago. Fate had yet to revoke her decree.

From the side of the dance floor, Gabriel watched as Alathea gracefully twirled. She was thinking of something, some thing other than the cotillion – there was a distance in her gaze, a closed calmness in her expression that meant she was mentally elsewhere. He was certain she was thinking about him. He wanted her to think of him, but . . . he had a strong suspicion that her thinking at present was not following the lines he wished. His instincts prodded him to press her, to seize her however he might. Some other emotion – a stronger emotion – warned him the decision was hers. And he knew just how easy she was to influence.

At present, his campaign was mired in circumstance and his quarry was proving elusive. Every time he thought he had her in his grasp, she drew away, hazel eyes wide, slightly puzzled, not convinced.

Nowhere near convinced enough to marry him.

That fact left him feeling caged and not the least bit civilized every time she moved away from his side. There was no convenient wall against which he could lean and guard her, so he prowled the edge of the cleared area, unwilling to be waylaid by any of the ladies intent on catching his eye.

He was successful in avoiding all the encroaching madams, but he couldn't avoid Chillingworth. The earl loomed directly in his path.

Their gazes clashed. By mutual accord, they swung so they stood shoulder to shoulder, gazing over the dance floor.

'I'm surprised,' Chillingworth drawled, 'that you haven't tired of this game.'

'Which game is that?'

'The game of knight-protector, keeping the rest of us at bay.' Chillingworth's gaze raked his face. 'Being such a close friend of the family's, I can understand why you might feel compelled by the notion, but don't you think you're carrying the role a little far?'

'Now why, I wonder, should that so concern *you*?' Even as he asked the question, Gabriel felt an icy tingle at his nape.

'I would have thought that obvious, dear boy.' Chillingworth gestured toward the dancers, careful not to indicate Alathea specifically. 'She's an attractive proposition, particularly to one situated as I.'

Every word deepened the chill now steadily coursing Gabriel's veins. The uninformed might imagine Chillingworth meant he was considering seducing Alathea because he was presently amorously free. Gabriel knew better. The earl was of their class, from the same social stratum as the Bar Cynster; he was their contemporary in every way. He abided by the same unwritten code Gabriel himself had honored all his adult life. Ladies of good family and good character were not fair game.

Alathea was unmistakeably both. Seducing her was not what Chillingworth had in mind.

His expression impassive, Gabriel looked over the dancers, his gaze fixing on Alathea's face. 'She's not for you.'

'Indeed?' Challenge rang in Chillingworth's tone. 'I realize this may come as a surprise, especially to a Cynster, but the lady herself will ultimately be the judge of that.'

'No.' Gabriel uttered the word quietly, yet it held enough latent force to make Chillingworth tense. And wait.

Gabriel saw the danger clearly. Chillingworth was Devil's age but had yet to marry. He needed an heir, and for that he needed a wife. He could appreciate Chillingworth's taste in being attracted to Alathea; he was not, however, of a mind to approve.

Alathea loved him, but whether she knew that, or accepted it, he didn't know. She was headstrong and willful, used to charting her own course.

416

She also had that streak of considered recklessness he'd always found alarming. He could never
predict what it might lead her to do. She was
finding coming to terms with the notion of
marrying him difficult. If Chillingworth offered
for her hand, might she accept to escape the
impasse he'd created?

Despite loving him – or even because of it – might
she think to set him free of the chivalric bonds she
imagined compelled him by marrying Chillingworth
instead?

Over the heads of the other dancers, Gabriel
considered Alathea, and knew he couldn't risk
it. She felt friendly toward Chillingworth. The
earl could be charming when he wished and was,
after all, a gentleman in the same mold as he.
And Alathea was an earl's daughter. It would be
a felicitous match all around.

Except for one thing.

Turning to Chillingworth, Gabriel met his gaze.
'If you're imagining rectifying your lack of an heir
through an alliance with the Morwellans, I suggest
you think again.'

Chillingworth stiffened; the look in his eyes
suggested he could barely believe his ears. 'And
why is that?' he asked, his tone steely, his aggression poorly masked.

'Because,' Gabriel said, 'you would die before you
laid so much as a finger on the lady in question,
which might make getting your heir a trifle difficult.'

Chillingworth stared at him, then looked away,

resuming his previously noncombative stance. 'I can't,' he murmured, 'quite believe you said that.'

'I meant every word.'

'I know.' Chillingworth's lips quirked. 'How enlightening.'

'Just as long as you keep it in mind.'

Chillingworth looked to where, the dance having ended, Alathea was strolling on Falworth's arm. Both he and Gabriel stepped out to intercept her. 'I'll think about it,' Chillingworth replied.

Alathea could not believe how easily Gabriel tracked her through the crowd; she and Lord Falworth had barely begun to stroll before he loomed from the throng. She was, consequently, especially delighted to see Chillingworth by his side.

'My lord.' She gave Chillingworth her hand and smiled with real appreciation as he bowed. 'I hope you note I took your comments to heart. I could do nothing about the number of guests, but there are many waltzes scheduled tonight.'

Chillingworth sighed. 'What manner of torture is that, my dear? I assume that, as usual, you have no waltzes free.'

Alathea did not miss his sidelong glance at Gabriel. 'Unfortunately not.'

'However,' Chillingworth continued, 'unless my ears deceive me, that's a country dance starting up. Might I beg the pleasure of your company?'

Alathea smiled. 'I would be delighted.'

The dance was one that left them paired throughout. Chillingworth conversed easily on general topics. Alathea answered lightly, off the top of her head, her thoughts, as always, sliding back to Gabriel. She'd lost sight of him when the dance got under way; he was no longer where they'd left him. She wondered where he was, and what he was doing.

At the conclusion of the dance, she laid her hand on Chillingworth's sleeve. He led her from the floor, straight to Gabriel, who was waiting at the other end of the ballroom from where they'd parted.

Alathea resisted an urge to raise her eyes to the skies. Drawing her hand from Chillingworth's arm, she positioned herself between them, ready to jab an elbow into either of their ribs should they infringe her conversational standards.

Somewhat to her surprise, neither did. Chillingworth seemed careful, watchful. Gabriel was his usual arrogant self, the reality uncloaked given it was only Chillingworth, whom he patently regarded as an equal, with them. Then Amanda, escorted by Lord Rankin, joined them. A minute later, Amelia glided up on Lord Arkdale's arm.

'This is such a lovely ball, Lady Alathea.' Amanda beamed her delight. 'I'm enjoying myself hugely.' The minx batted her long lashes at Rankin, who, all unknowingly, glowed.

'It's a crush – a positive crush,' Amelia chimed in. 'There are so many here.' She smiled at Lord Arkdale. 'Why, I've never had the chance to chat with Freddie here, before.'

'I hope,' Alathea cut in, preempting Gabriel,

'that you're wise enough to take full advantage of the possibilities offered.'

'Oh, indeed,' Amanda assured her. 'Our dance cards are full. We've danced every dance with a different gentleman.'

'And spent every interval with still different gentlemen,' Amelia added. Both girls softened the news of their deliberate inconstancy with a ravishing smile at their escorts. Neither gentleman was sure whether to preen or not.

'Incidentally, Gabriel, we haven't sighted Lucifer.' Amanda fixed her angelic blue eyes on her cousin's face. 'Is he here?'

'He was.'

'He must have discovered something terribly interesting. Or someone,' Amelia ingenuously announced.

'I saw Lady Scarsdale, and Mrs Sweeney, too. She was wearing vermillion – a hideous shade. I don't think Lucifer would be with her, do you?'

'Perhaps he's with Lady Todd. I know she's here . . .'

The twins continued artlessly speculating on Lucifer's current obsession. Their escorts were totally bemused. Gabriel was not, but neither was he willing to deflect their attention. Alathea bit her lip, and let the twins have their revenge.

Under cover of the girls' bright chatter, Chillingworth touched Alathea's arm. Turning, she encountered a slightly rueful expression in the earl's eyes.

'I fear I'm going to desert you, my dear, and leave you captive to this bevy of Cynsters.'

Alathea smiled. 'They are a riotous lot, but the twins, you see, are celebrating a family victory.'

For an instant, Chillingworth's eyes held hers, then his gaze flicked to Gabriel, presently exchanging barbs with Amanda. Chillingworth looked questioningly at Alathea. 'Cynster, too, I think?'

Alathea didn't know what to think – and even less what to reply.

Chillingworth relieved her of the problem by bowing. 'Your servant, my dear. If you ever find yourself in need of help, know you have only to ask.'

He then nodded elegantly and stepped away, disappearing into the crowd.

Puzzled, Alathea watched him go, then turned back to Gabriel and the twins.

The next dance was a waltz.

Without so much as a by-your-leave, Gabriel, his temper sorely tried by the twins, closed his hand about Alathea's and drew her onto the floor. His arm came around her, holding her close. Their gazes met.

She grinned, but said not a word. She relaxed, following his lead without conscious effort. Scanning the room as they twirled, she saw no indication of any problem; their ball was in full swing and all was well.

She was about to refocus on Gabriel's face when Lady Osbaldestone's flashed past. The gleeful expression in her ladyship's old eyes reminded Alathea of the approval of Lady Jersey, Princess Esterhazy, and the others. How many more had had their eyes opened tonight, their censorious minds alerted?

'This is dangerous – you and me.' She looked at Gabriel. 'We're going to end as a high treat for the scandalmongers.'

'Nonsense. Who's been disapproving?'

No one. Alathea pressed her lips together. After a moment, she said, 'I'm too old. The entire ton is expecting you to marry – they won't approve of your marrying me.'

'Why not? It's not as if you're in your dotage, for heaven's sake.'

'I'm twenty-nine.'

'So? If that doesn't worry me, and you know damned well it doesn't, why should it concern anyone else?'

'Bachelors of thirty do not customarily marry spinsters of twenty-nine.'

'Probably because most spinsters of twenty-nine are that for good reason.' Gabriel caught her eye. 'You're that for a completely different reason – a reason that is no longer valid. You've done what you needed to do – you've set your family back on their feet. You've held the fort until Charlie can take over, and trained him to do it.' His voice

422

lowered. 'Now it's time to let go and live the life you should have lived. *With me.*'

Alathea remained silent, not sure she could trust her voice.

He continued, 'I haven't detected the slightest hint of disapproval – quite the opposite. The senior hostesses all knew your mother – they're thrilled at the thought of you marrying at last. Along with the rest of the ton, they've never understood why you didn't marry. To them, the notion of your marrying me is highly romantic.'

Alathea managed a sniff. After a minute, she risked a glance up.

Gabriel's gaze was gently ruthless. 'They'll cheer the announcement, when you consent to let me make it. *They're* not standing in my way.'

Only she was. Alathea looked away. There was, it seemed, to be no help from any quarter. She was swimming against a flood tide.

In the nearby card room, Devil Cynster, Duke of St Ives, strolled up to the earl of Chillingworth, who was standing by a wall watching a hand of piquet.

'Amazing. I never thought to see you pull in your horns.' Devil glanced pointedly toward the ballroom. 'I find it difficult to believe there are *no* possibilities in there. If you don't look quick, you'll be cold tonight. I, at least, have a warm bed to hie home to.'

Chillingworth looked amused. 'And what makes you think I haven't? The only difference between you and me, dear boy, is that your bed will be the same tomorrow night, while mine has at least a chance of being different.'

'On the other hand, there's something to be said for consistently high standards.'

'At present, I'll settle for variety. That aside, to what do I owe this questionable pleasure?'

'Just checking on your current interest.'

'To make certain we don't cross bows? Pull the other one.'

Devil settled his shoulders against the wall. 'Purely altruistic, on my part.'

Chillingworth hid a smile. 'Altruistic? Tell me, is it me you're interested in keeping whole, or another more nearly related?'

Devil studied the crowd in the ballroom through the arch directly before them. 'Let's just say that I've no wish to see any misunderstanding cloud the otherwise congenial relationship between your family and mine.'

Chillingworth said nothing for several minutes, also staring at the figures jostling in the ballroom. Then he shifted. 'If I was to say that I have no intention of disrupting the harmony currently reigning between our houses, would you do me one favor?'

'What?'

'Don't tell Gabriel.'

Devil turned his head. 'Why?'

His lips quirking wryly, Chillingworth pushed away from the wall. 'Because it's entertaining watching him rise to my bait, and,' he murmured, just loud enough for Devil to hear as he moved away, 'I consider that fitting consolation.'

CHAPTER 18

Their ball had been held on Monday night. Alathea did not set eyes on Gabriel again until Wednesday. Ambling in the park behind his sisters and hers, closely escorted by Lord Esher and Mr Carstairs, she was deep in disturbing thoughts of Crowley and the Central East Africa Gold Company when she heard her name called. Looking up, she saw the group ahead looking back at her. Heather Cynster pointed to the nearby carriageway – to where her brother held his team of restless bays, stamping impatiently. As she lengthened her stride, Alathea got the distinct impression that the horses were merely reflecting their master's state.

'Good morning.' Tipping her head up, she looked into his face, some way above her, courtesy of his high perch phaeton. The carriage held the interest of the girls and their beaux, leaving her to deal with its driver.

He beckoned. 'Come up. I'll take you for a tool around the avenue.'

She smiled. 'No, thank you.'

He stared at her.

The others had heard.

'Go on, Allie! You'll enjoy it.'

'We'll be safe enough.'

'It'll just be for a few minutes.'

'Carstairs and I will engage to watch over your charges in your stead, Lady Alathea.'

Alathea kept her gaze steady on Gabriel's face. 'When last did you drive a lady in the park?'

He studied her for an instant longer, then his lips thinned. 'Hold 'em, Biggs.' His groom leaped from the back and ran to the horses' heads. Gabriel tied off the reins and jumped down.

Without a word, he took her arm and waved the others on. Absorbed with their own concerns, the girls were happy to comply. By mutual accord, she and Gabriel waited until the group was far enough ahead so they could talk without being overheard, then set out in their wake.

'There's no reason you couldn't let me drive you about the park.'

'I have no intention of letting you declare your hand in such a public fashion.' She shot him a reproving glance. 'I'm not going to be swayed by such manuevers.'

'More fool you. How did you know, anyway?'

'Your mama is always full of your doings – yours, Lucifer's, and the rest of your cousins. The fact that none of you drive ladies in the park – ladies other than your wives – is well known to all, I gather.'

Gabriel had been counting on it. 'How does

Gretna Green strike you? We could be there in two days.'

'At present, I have matters to deal with here. As soon as those matters are settled, I intend retiring to the country once again.'

'Don't wager your mother's pearls on it.'

'Humph! Anyway, what have you learned? I take it you got my note last night?'

'Yes, but not until this morning. Last night I was busy trying to prise information from certain African dignitaries.'

'What did they say?'

'Enough to unofficially confirm that at least four of Crowley's claims of governmental approvals and permissions are false. I'm working on turning unofficial into official, but no government bureacracy works quickly. We won't have any official support for our petition by the time we have to lodge it.'

'And when's that?'

'I would advise against waiting longer than next Tuesday.'

'That soon?'

'We can't risk Crowley calling in his notes, and I'd wager my bays he'll do it late next week.' Gabriel glanced at Alathea, then continued, 'The petition's all but ready. Wiggs's clerk should have finished it – as far as we've gone – by tomorrow. Wiggs will bring it to me. If we have no more to add, with your permission, I'll ask my solicitor to make an appointment for Tuesday morning with one of the judges of the Chancery Court to submit our case. We don't dare wait longer – fighting a rearguard action once the promissory note is executed and the call on funds made will leave us in a considerably worse position legally.'

Alathea grimaced. 'If that's how it must be . . .'

'I'll alert Devil, and Vane, too. He'll bring Gerrard up to town when he's needed.' His gaze on her face, her profile, Gabriel opened his mouth on the words: 'Thea, it's a big risk,' but left them unsaid. If he had considered all the dangers and alternatives, she would have, too. There was no danger to her – he would marry her in an instant, and rescue both her and her family from penury – she knew that without his stating it. But what of Morwellan Park, and the title, the long unbroken line of Morwellans stretching back through time? What of her family's pride? That was what she'd set out from the first to protect, and it wasn't something that could be rescued other than by risking all.

Her motives needed no explaining to a Cynster. All he could do was stand by her shoulder and do whatever he could to bring about her victory.

And, perhaps, provide a distraction. 'Actually, the reason I came looking for you wasn't to tell you all that. I've tickets for Friday's performance of *The Barber of Seville*. I thought you and your family might like to attend.'

Alathea stared at him. 'Friday night's the last night – it's to be a gala performance.'

'So I understand.' The production had taken the ton by storm. The management had decreed the final performance would be a gala event, to thank both cast and patrons.

'But . . . the gala was sold out within hours of the announcement last week. How on earth did you manage to get tickets for us all?'

'Never mind how I got the damned tickets! Will you come?'

'Speaking for myself, of course I'll come! As for the others, you can ask them yourself.' Alathea waved ahead to where the group were gathered about the Morwellan barouche.

Gabriel was glad to see that his sisters had already said their good-byes and were heading for his mother's landau, drawn in to the verge a little way along. Celia saw him and waved but did not beckon him to attend her. Nor did she evince any surprise at seeing him again strolling with Alathea. Those facts declared that Celia, at least, understood his intention and approved; Gabriel knew he could rely on her for support should the need arise.

Joining the others before the Morwellan carriage, he smoothly issued his invitation, specifically including both Esher and Carstairs. Alathea looked at him curiously but said nothing. She didn't have to – everyone was eager to attend the gala performance of *The Barber of Seville*.

When she arrived with the others at the Opera House on Friday night, Alathea discovered Gabriel had not just secured tickets, but one of the two most sought-after private boxes overlooking the stage. He met them in the foyer, then with her on one arm and Serena on the other, led the way up the stairs and down the plushly carpeted first-floor corridor to the gilded door giving onto the box overhanging the left of the stage.

Eyes swivelled as they took their seats, the tonnish occupants of the less-favored boxes craning to see who had commanded prime place on this, the most celebrated evening of the season. Whispers abounded as, head high, her expression serene, Alathea regally sat in one of the chairs at the front of the box. Serena sat beside her, turning to murmur her thanks to Gabriel as he settled in the chair behind and to the side of Alathea's.

Alathea would gladly have boxed his ears, but not in public. As it was, all she could do was smile and return the gracious nods of the ton's matrons. Mary and Alice, wide-eyed, took the other front-row seats beyond Serena. Esher and Carstairs sat behind them. His lordship leaned forward and engaged Serena in some discussion. Alathea turned to Gabriel, intending to inform him she would box his ears later, only to find him leaning closer, a frown in his eyes.

'My apologies. I didn't realize we'd attract *this* much attention.'

Alathea grimaced, absolving him of intent. She refrained from acidly informing him that this was the degree of attention he, a Cynster, should expect in declaring his hand. 'I take it,' she whispered, glancing briefly at Serena to make sure she was occupied, 'that you haven't heard anything of the captain.'

'No.' His gaze lifted to her forehead. The frown in his eyes intensified. 'Stop worrying. One way or another, we'll see this through.'

Willing away all external evidence of her state, Alathea sighed. 'I've done all I can to be beforehand, just in case . . .' She gestured helplessly. 'I've paid all the accounts from the ball – the caterers, the milliners, the modistes – even the musicians. They all thought I'd run mad, demanding they submit their accounts immediately.'

'I dare say. If you've paid them all outright, the Morwellans will be the only family in the ton to finish the Season with a clear slate.'

'I thought it would be better – more ethical, in a way. I'd rather our honest creditors were paid before Crowley and his schemes lay claim to all we have.'

Gabriel's fingers closed on her hand. She only just had time to brace herself against the sensation of his lips caressing the backs of her fingers.

'Relax. Forget the Central East Africa Gold Company. Forget Crowley, at least for tonight.' With a nod, he indicated the stage; the curtain was rising to building applause. 'I've brought you here tonight, and the only thanks I want is for you to enjoy yourself. So stop worrying, and do.'

Turning her hand, he brushed her inner wrist with his lips, then released her. Alathea faced the stage as the house lamps were doused, and did as he asked.

It wasn't difficult – the production was a *tour de force*, the singers superb, the sets and orchestra unsurpassed. She had fallen in love with musical performances in those few short weeks when she'd first come to London. She'd felt starved ever since; the efforts of provincial theatres could not compare with the extravagantly superior London events.

Because of the additional scenes and special arias to be presented as part of the gala, there was to be only one interval, occurring after the second act. When the curtain swished down and the lamps flared to life, Alathea sighed contentedly and glanced back at Gabriel.

He raised a brow, then stirred his long frame. 'Time to stretch our legs.'

Alathea allowed him to draw her to her feet. She turned to Serena.

Her stepmother flicked open her fan and waved it before her face. 'I'm going to rest here – you may all stroll the corridors, but do be back in good time for the next act.' She smiled on them all, Esher with Mary on his arm and Carstairs beside Alice. Gabriel waved the others on ahead, then he and Alathea stepped from the box into a sea of parading humanity. There was nothing they could do but parade along with everyone else.

'Forget about watching the others,' Gabriel advised. 'But tell me, have they spoken yet?'

'*Both* have asked leave to call on Papa next Wednesday.' Alathea smiled. 'I understand they're very seriously preparing a joint presentation to win his consent. No one's had the heart to tell them there's no need. They're both dears, each in their own way.'

'Just leave them to it. Marriage is, after all, a serious business, not something a gentleman should embark on without due consideration.'

'Indeed? Then might I suggest—'

'No. You may not. Twenty-nine years of knowing you is consideration enough.'

A footman in full Beefeater costume appeared before them, flourishing a tray of glasses; they each took one and sipped. Countess Lieven hailed them through the crush; by the time they gained her side and suffered through her observations, the bell summoning the audience back to their seats was pealing.

Ten minutes later, they regained their box and sank into their seats as the curtain rose. An expectant hush fell over the audience. Gabriel angled his chair so he could see Alathea's face, illuminated by the light from the stage. Then he settled to watch – not the performance but the expressions animating her features, the signs of joy, of sorrow, of delight evoked by the unfolding story. The performers held the ton in thrall, but for him there was only Alathea.

The second half of the program exceeded the expectations raised by the first; at the end the audience was on their feet, applauding wildly, flowers raining down as the soloists took their bows. Finally, it was over, and the curtain fell for the last time. Gabriel watched as Alathea heaved a deep sigh and turned to him, a smile in her eyes, her lips curved, all worries temporarily banished.

Reward enough.

The others were exclaiming, discussing various highlights. Tilting her head, Alathea studied him. Her smile deepened. 'You needn't pretend you paid attention.'

'One of the numerous benefits of knowing each other so well – there's no need to prevaricate.'

She searched his face. 'Why did you do this – go to all this trouble, indulge in what I'm sure will prove a shockingly hideous expense?'

He returned her gaze steadily. 'You like music.'

It was that simple – he let her read the truth in his eyes. Then she shivered. He reached for the shawl she'd left over her chair and held it up. She hesitated, then turned so he could drape it over her shoulders. Releasing the fine silk, he closed his hands about her shoulders; leaning closer, he murmured, 'As with other pleasures, my reward is your delight.'

The glance she threw him was arrested, her expression not one he could place. But he had no chance to probe in the short time it took to escort her down the private stairway to where their carriages waited.

As he handed her up to the same black carriage he'd handed the countess into weeks before, she

435

squeezed his hand. Then she ducked and entered the carriage. He shut the door and stepped back as Folwell flicked the reins.

Alathea sank back in the carriage, frowning now the shadows gave her freedom to do so. Beside her, Alice chatted animatedly with Tony Carstairs, seated opposite. She left them to their dissection of the performance; there was another performance with which she was far more concerned.

A performance she was starting to think might not be an act at all.

If there was any possibility that that was so . . .

It was time to face her fear and the emotion that gave it birth. Both were new to her. She'd pandered to the former, while pretending the latter didn't exist. She couldn't do so any longer.

She remained absorbed through the drive back to Mount Street, absentmindedly responding as, together with Serena and her stepsisters, she bade farewell to Esher and Carstairs in the front hall. She climbed the stairs, murmured her good nights, then surrendered to Nellie's ministrations, all the while analyzing each of their encounters, trying to see past his warrior's shield. Finally alone, she hitched a shawl over her nightgown and curled up on the padded seat before her window.

Morwellan House was over fifty years old, built on the foundations of a much older residence. Morwellans had owned the site for centuries. How much longer they would continue here was in the lap of the gods. Her own life, however, was in her hands. She stared at the old trees at the bottom of the back lawn, then heaved a deep sigh, crossed her arms on the stone window ledge, and settled her chin on her wrists.

When had she fallen in love with him? Had it been when she was eleven? Had he sensed it – was that what had first made him edgy when near her? Or had it been later? Had love bloomed unknown to her sometime in her teens? Or had a girlish fancy slowly developed into something more?

Unanswerable questions now. All she knew was that sometime, it had happened. It didn't, in truth, feel like something new so much as something newly discovered, a vulnerability she hadn't known she possessed until fate and circumstance had revealed it. That was bad enough, but there was more she'd yet to face. She loved him, but her love had not yet fully blossomed. It was still a bud, newly burgeoning after an extended winter; it had yet to open. She'd yet to experience the full expression of her love, the total spectrum of her need. But she could feel the force, the power swelling within the bud; if freed, it would sweep her will before it – it would become the dominant force in her life.

That fact only added to her fear.

The two threads of her worry – her family and her love – were headed for simultaneous resolution. Regardless of what transpired in the Chancery

Court, he, she knew, would be there, ready to whisk her to safety be the outcome victory or defeat. If it be victory, he'd push for her surrender; if defeat, he'd wait for no permissions but simply claim her as his. From his point of view, all was straightforward; from hers, it was anything but.

Her fear she at least understood now that she'd acknowledged the strange notion of loving him. One benefit of being twenty-nine was that she knew herself well. Loving him as she knew she would if she allowed her love free rein would leave her wholly committed, totally enmeshed in their relationship. She wasn't capable of doing anything by halves – when she gave, she gave completely. If she gave her heart, it would be his, all his, forever. She hadn't done it yet, hadn't surrendered her love and her life into his keeping. If she agreed to be his wife, she would do precisely that.

But what would happen if he didn't love her?

The pain she feared flowed from that. She'd faced disappointment, misery and loneliness, the threat of servitude, of destitution, of seeing her loved ones in rags. She'd found strength when she'd needed it, yet she knew in her heart that the pain of his kindness would slay her.

For he would be kind, considerate, always gentle. Yet if he didn't love her in the same way she loved him, her love was of the sort that would destroy her from within. She couldn't contain it, simply hold it inside if there was no one to give it to, to lavish it upon. She'd waited too long for the bud to bloom – it would now bloom in glory, or wither and die. There was no other way. And if it died, so would she, in all ways that mattered.

Better the swelling bud froze again, and never bloomed.

She'd been certain he didn't love her. Not for a minute had she believed fate would be so amenable as to arrange for him to fall madly in love with her. Life had never been so kind. He cared for her, yes, just as he always had, in that guarded, rational way of his, where every emotion was nicely logical.

She was annoyed with him for that. How dare he be so logical when she felt so emotional? Yet that difference had seemed to confirm that love as she was coming to know it was not what he felt for her. He was presently in lust with her, he wanted to care for her, to protect her, to marry her, but he didn't love her. She'd held firm against his proposal, utterly certain she'd read him aright.

Until tonight.

It hadn't been the extravagance of the box, or even the fact that he didn't, as she well knew, appreciate music. The moment when her certainty had been rocked to its foundations was when he'd whispered, 'As with other pleasures, my reward is your delight.'

It was his tone that had struck her, so accustomed as she was to every nuance, every inflection he used. He'd uttered those words as if it was his soul speaking, not just his mind. The words had resonated within her, as if in that moment, heart spoke to heart.

Had she been wrong? Did he love her? *Could* he love her?

The question was: How to tell?

Raising her head, she looked up at the stars, at the moon slowly waning in the west. Asking outright was out of the question. If she wasn't prepared to confess her love for him out aloud, in words, then she could hardly expect him to do so. She felt far too vulnerable to make such a confession; she credited him with sensibility enough to feel much the same way. As for expecting him to go down on his knees and declare his heart . . .

Lips curving, she uncurled her legs and rose. Sobering, she walked to her bed. She slipped between the sheets, no clever plan of how to prompt his confidence revolving in her head, yet on that she was determined. If there was any chance that fate had at last smiled and sent love to touch them both, she could not live without knowing.

The next morning dawned leaden, the skies gray, the light gray, all of a piece with her mood. Toying with her toast, conscious of the subdued nature of the conversations around the breakfast table, Alathea struggled to shrug off a deadening sense of aftermath. The triumph of their ball had been eclipsed by persistent worry over the looming

440

prospect of their incomplete case failing to convince the Chancery Court to declare the Central East Africa Gold Company a fraud. The special magic of her night at the opera, with its seductive suggestion that perhaps, possibly, Gabriel, too, might be concealing the true nature of his feelings, had dispersed in the cold light of morning.

Despite numerous restless hours, she'd been unable to devise any plan guaranteed to make him lower his shield, the barrier with which, for as long as she'd known him, he'd protected his heart. She couldn't, despite their closeness, see into his soul.

She was no better – she'd always been careful to protect her innermost feelings. She wasn't about to drop her guard and let him see into her soul, either. Unfortunately, that seemed the one approach with any chance of success, but the risk . . .

Inwardly heaving a sigh, she reached for the teapot. There *had* to be something she could do, some positive action she could take to slough off her dour mood, if not in unraveling the complexities of her nemesis-turned-lover-and-now-would-be-husband, then in pursuing their investigations. There had to be something not yet done, somewhere not yet searched. Some stone as yet unturned . . .

She looked at Charlie. 'Have you and Jeremy visited the museum?'

'No.' Charlie shrugged. 'We did mean to while we were here, but . . .'

Jeremy brightened. 'Can we go today? The back lawn's too wet to run the curricle over it.'

Alathea glanced at Mary and Alice. 'Why don't we all go? We haven't gone out all together for weeks, and there's nothing else happening this morning.'

A tug on her sleeve had Alathea turning. Augusta looked up at her, brown eyes wide. 'Me, too?'

Alathea smiled; the grayness receded. 'Indeed, poppet. You, too.'

An hour later, Alathea stood in one of the cavernous halls of the museum, looking down at what purported to be a map of Central East Africa spread on a large table and protected by a glass case. Lodwar was marked, but neither Fangak nor Kingi, not even as Kafia Kingi, was shown. Worse, Lodwar appeared to be on the banks of a huge river – a river the explorer whose works she had studied had apparently missed seeing.

Alathea sighed.

She hadn't bothered with the museum before, reasoning that the clerk at the Royal Society would have mentioned any exhibits had there been any of use. In desperation, however, she'd been willing to draw a long bow. On inquiring of the custodian at the main door, and learning that the museum did indeed have an exhibit including a good map, her heart had leaped. Perhaps . . .

She'd left the others wandering, Charlie and Jeremy among the military exhibits. Mary, Alice and Augusta among the ancient pottery, and slipped into this hall – only to have her hopes dashed again. Other than the map, there was only a display of native artifacts, and a few watercolors of wildlife supposedly found in Central East Africa.

Her heart felt like lead. She'd lifted even this stone but, like all the rest, there was no help beneath it. With one last disgusted look at the unhelpful map, she stepped away—

She cannoned into a gentleman. 'Oh!' Falling back, she clutched her slipping shawl.

'Beg pardon, m'dear.' The gentleman bowed awkwardly. 'I was so incensed by this trumpery stuff, I wasn't looking out as I should.' His gesture took in the entire Central East African exhibit.

'On the contrary, it was I who didn't look.' Alathea took in the man's shaggy brows overhanging features weather-beaten to a walnut-brown. Grizzled whiskers framed them. His eyes were a washed-out blue, his old-style coat and corduroy knee breeches attire no longer common in town. The stance he adopted was unusual, too, his hands clasped behind his back, feet apart, legs braced.

Abruptly turning back to the exhibit, Alathea waved at the map. 'Is this incorrect, then?'

His derisive reply came immediately. 'Poppycock! All of it. It's nothing like that, upon my word.'

'You've been there?'

'In between my sailings, when I have to wait

443

months because of some flood or famine or skirmish between the tribes, an old prospector and I take to the hills. Why, we've crossed the whole continent a number of times.' The sweep of his hand encompassed the area in which the interests of the Central East Africa Gold Company lay. 'Not much improvement on the Great Desert, Central East Africa. Dusty wasteland, it is. This river shown here is nothing more than a trickle, and then only in the rainy season.'

'You sail?' Alathea held her breath. 'On a ship?'

'Aye.' The man dragged his hat from under his arm and doffed it in a bow from a bygone age. 'Captain Aloysius Struthers at your service, ma'am. Captain of the *Dunslaw*, sailing for Bentinck and Company.'

Alathea exhaled, dragged in another breath and held out her hand. 'Captain, you have no idea how glad I am to make your acquaintance.'

Struthers looked taken aback, but instinctively grasped her hand. Alathea shamelessly held on to his. She cast a swift glance around. 'If we retire to that bench, I'd like to explain. My interest is prompted by the Central East Africa Gold Company.'

The change in Struthers's expression was instantaneous. 'That blackguard, Crowley—' He broke off. 'My apologies, ma'am, but when I think of the damage that jackal has done, it fair boils my blood.'

'Indeed? Then you might be interested to learn

that a friend and I have plans to bring his latest scheme to naught.'

Slipping his hand from hers, Struthers offered his arm. 'I'd be devilish interested in hearing from anyone ready to thrust a spoke in that brigand's wheel. But what's a lady like you doing mixed up with the likes of him?'

That took some time to explain. Alathea hesitated, but, in the end, revealed her identity. If she wanted Struthers's help, it was only fair to be frank. She outlined Crowley's scheme, then detailed all the false claims they'd uncovered. To her relief, Struthers grasped the situation quickly.

'Aye – that's his game, right enough. A blood-sucker, he is. He's swindled the colonists right and left all through that area. And what he's done with the local tribes . . .' Struthers's expression hardened. 'I won't sully your ears with the tales of his infamies, my lady, but if ever there was a black-guard overdue in hell, it's Ranald Crowley.'

'Yes, well, I have to agree.' Alathea thrust aside the idea of an opponent steeped in infamy. 'Our problem, however, is that we have no absolute proof to disprove Crowley's claims. All our evidence is *surmised* from what we've learned from others. We desperately need someone who can appear before the judge and corroborate what we've learned – an eyewitness, as it were.'

Struthers straightened. 'Captain Aloysius Struthers is your man, my lady. And I'll do better than just give you my say-so. I know where I can get maps – signed maps, mark you. And if I ask around quiet-like, I'm sure I can get more on the holdings Crowley's claimed. They ring a bell, they definitely do. I'm not positive, but I think an old acquaintance holds the mining rights to those areas. I can ask, easily enough. You'll want as many nails in your hand as possible when the time comes to make sure Crowley's coffin's good and sealed.'

Alathea didn't argue. The captain's reaction to Crowley, the grim look in his eyes every time he mentioned him, frightened her far more than her previous glimpse of the villain.

Struthers nodded decisively. 'It'll be an honor to bring that blackguard down. Now.' Briskly, he turned to Alathea. 'How do I contact you when I've gathered my proofs?'

'The hearing will be on Tuesday morning . . .' Alathea dug in her reticule and came up with a pencil. 'In the judges' chambers at Chancery Court.' The only paper she carried was the entry ticket to the museum; the back was blank. She ripped it in half. 'If you need to contact me before that, this is my direction.' She wrote down her name and address. There was no point giving Gabriel's address; not only had the captain not met her knight, but her protector had a habit of galloping about town. At present, he was making a furious effort to prise some formal acknowledgment of the Central East Africa Gold Company's status from the African authorities' representatives in London. He didn't hold out much hope; neither did she.

The captain was their best hope – their savior, indeed. If he needed to contact anyone, it had better be her; they couldn't afford to lose touch with him now. She handed him the scrap of paper. 'Now, where are you situated?'

He gave her the address of a lodging house in Clerkenwell. 'I find a different place every time I stay in London. I rarely stay long.'

Alathea wrote down the address, then tucked the paper into her reticule. 'You won't be sailing again before Tuesday, will you?'

'Unlikely,' Struthers murmured, reading her address. Then he slipped the paper into his coat pocket. 'Right, then. I'd better set to.' They both rose. Struthers bowed to Alathea. 'Never fear, my lady. Aloysius Struthers won't let you down.'

With that, he clapped his hat on his head. With a grimly determined nod, he strode off.

Alathea watched him go. A rush of relief poured through her. Dizzy, she sank back onto the bench. Five minutes later, Mary, Alice and Augusta found her sitting there, smiling.

'Yes,' she replied in answer to their query. 'We can, indeed, go home.'

She sent a summons to Brook Street the instant they reached home; Gabriel arrived as they rose from the luncheon table. Barely giving him a chance to greet the rest of her family, Alathea dragged him out to the gazebo.

As if in tune with her mood, the clouds had

rolled away. The others followed them into the sunshine, spreading out on the lawn to relax and play, but no one attempted to follow them into the shadowed privacy of the gazebo.

'I presume,' Gabriel said, following her up the steps, 'that you're about to reveal the nature of your "fantastic discovery"?'

'Captain Aloysius Struthers!' Alathea whirled and sank onto the sofa. 'I've found him.'

'Where?'

'The museum.' Gleefully, she recounted their meeting. 'And he's not only agreed to testify as to the falsity of Crowley's claims, but he says he can lay hands on verified maps, and also on details of the relevant mining leases.' She gestured expansively. 'He'll be even more help than we hoped for.' Gabriel frowned. Surprised, she asked, 'What is it?'

He grimaced. 'I'd be content with the captain simply turning up before the judge – with his testimony to anchor our case, we won't need anything more.'

'It won't hurt to have a few more facts behind us.'

'Hmm. Did Struthers tell you where he's staying?'

Alathea drew a folded sheet from her pocket. 'I copied his address for you. Will you go and see him?'

Gabriel read the address; his expression turned grim. 'Yes. If he'd been staying in Surrey, I wouldn't have bothered, but, as it is, I think a visit might be wise.'

'Why?'

'To warn him. If he goes nosing about asking after maps and mining leases, he's liable to alert Crowley. We might be nearing the eleventh hour, but Ranald Crowley is not an opponent I'd ever turn my back on.'

'Indeed not, but the captain seemed to know him well.'

'Nevertheless, I'll speak to the captain. It won't hurt to underline the need for secrecy.' Sliding the note into his pocket, Gabriel looked at Alathea, then turned and sat beside her. 'Which brings me to another point.'

Shuffling to make space for him, she looked at him questioningly.

'Don't go anywhere alone. Not until we have the decision handed down – no, not even then. Not until we know Crowley has left England.'

'And I thought it was me who was melodramatic.'

'I'm serious.' Jaw setting, he took her hand. 'Crowley is not some predictable English villain – he recognizes no law but that of the jungle. From the minute he learns of our plans until he returns to the jungle, or some other uncivilized place, you will not be safe.' He trapped her gaze. 'Promise me you won't go anywhere alone, and that, even in company, you'll restrict your outings to the purely social. No visits to the museum, or the Tower – no more searching at all. We have enough to defeat Crowley now. There's no reason whatever for you to place yourself in danger.'

A gust of laughter had them both looking to where Charlie and Jeremy stood on the lawn, teasing Mary and Alice, seated on a rug.

'They're safe enough. While you remain within the ton, you'll all be safe – that's not an arena Crowley can move within without attracting immediate attention.' Looking at Alathea, Gabriel squeezed her hand. 'Promise me you'll take care.'

Alathea looked into his eyes. She saw urgency and an unaccustomed softness in the hazel depths. 'I'll be careful, but if—'

'No buts, *no* ifs.' In a blink, all softness vanished from his face. Her knight-protector all but glared at her. '*Promise.*'

A demand, no plea. Alathea glared back. 'I'll be careful. I won't do anything silly. With that, you'll have to be content. I've never been yours to rule.'

His expression, the granite hardness in his gaze, gave credence to his low growl, 'You're treading on thin ice.'

Yes, but what was underneath? Desperate to know, once and for all, Alathea returned his gaze haughtily. 'I am my own person – *not* yours.'

Hazel eyes fell into hazel. A long moment passed, then he looked away. His expression hardened as he gazed at Jeremy and Alice, Augusta and Mary. 'Let me tell you what's going to happen after we gain our judgment against the Central East Africa Gold Company.

'First, we're getting married. Not in any hole-and-corner fashion, but right here, in the heart of the ton. St George's Church one fine June morning. After that, we'll divide our lives between London and Somerset – the Season in London, and various trips as required for business, but we'll spend most of the year at Quiverstone Manor. Aside from anything else, from there you and I can keep an eye on Morwellan Park and lend a hand if Charlie needs it. And you'll be there to watch Jeremy and Augusta grow. We can sponsor Augusta for her come-out, and while in London you'll be able to catch up with Mary and Esher, and Alice and Carstairs.

'In between, you can learn about those of the Manor's tenants you don't already know, and help Mama with all the thousand and one things she does about the estate, so you'll be ready to step in when she eventually flags. And there are Heather, Eliza and Angelica, who, as you well know, will be thrilled to call you sister. You could try teaching them not to giggle – God knows, Mama hasn't managed it yet.

'The east wing will have to be redecorated, too. I never did more than order the old furniture cleaned. I don't even know the state of half of it, although my bed there is sound enough.'

Alathea swallowed the question, 'Sound enough for what?' The answer was not long in coming.

'And if all that doesn't keep you sufficiently amused, I have a number of other distractions planned – at least three sons and any number of daughters.' Turning his head, he met her gaze. 'Yours and mine. Ours. Our future.'

She held his gaze steadily, and prayed he couldn't see how much the thought tugged at her heart.

'Picture it – us sitting under the old oak on the south lawn, watching our children play. Hearing the shrill voices, the laughter, the cries. Picking them up to soothe them, to comfort them, or perhaps just to hold them.' He searched her eyes, his own hard as agates. 'You've always liked children, you always expected to have a tribe of your own. That was always your dream, your destiny. You gave it up for your family, but now fate's handing it back to you.' His gaze raked her face, then, as if satisfied with what he saw, he sat back and looked across the lawn. 'I know you too well to believe you'd turn your back on that dream a second time.'

His confidence tweaked Alathea's temper, but she shrugged the temptation to ire aside. His words – his *pronouncement* – should have chilled her; there'd been no lover-like softness in his words. He'd been all warrior – logical, practical – her knight-protector carrying her off to a new beginning, for which she should be duly grateful and acquiesce to all his decrees.

It was enough to make her laugh, but she didn't. If he'd been charming, presenting his arguments with the light, airy touch of which she knew he was capable, her heart would have sunk without trace. That was how he behaved in matters that did not touch him deeply. Instead, he'd presented her with his warrior side, all impenetrable granite and impregnable shield. She had to wonder what he was shielding. Lifting her chin, she fixed her gaze on his profile. 'And what about us? You and me. The two of us together. How do you see us?'

The question hit a nerve. His swift frown, an infinitesimal tensing of muscles otherwise under rigid control, told her so.

'I see us in bed,' he growled, 'and in a few other places, too. Do you want to know the details?'

'No. I'm quite imaginative enough to supply my own.'

'Well, then.' But his tone had softened, as if in thinking of her question, he'd seen more than he'd expected. 'I imagine we'll ride like we used to, every day. You always liked riding – do you still ride a lot?'

After an instant's hesitation, she said, 'I sold all the horses years ago.'

He nodded. 'So we'll ride every day. And, I just realized, you can help me with the estate accounts, which will leave more time for riding. And investing – studying the news, weeding out the rumors, checking with Montague and my other contacts. I manage all the Cynster funds. You've dabbled to good effect with the Morwellan treasury, such as it was, but I play a more aggressive hand.'

'I'm not particularly good at aggression.'

'You can take an interest in the defensive side, then – the bonds and capital.' He gestured expansively. 'That's how I see us.'

Alathea waited a moment, then softly said, 'You know perfectly well that's not what I meant. I wanted to know what you see *between* us.'

His head whipped around and he scowled at her. 'Thea – stop resisting. We'll be married soon. All I just said *is* going to happen – you know it is.'

'I know nothing of the sort. Why do you imagine I'll agree to your dictates?'

He hesitated, his narrowed gaze locked with hers. Then he said, 'You'll agree because you love me.'

Alathea felt her lips part, felt her jaw drop. Horrified, she searched his eyes. The comprehension she saw horrified her even more. How *could* he know? She snapped her lips shut and fixed him with a militant glare. '*I'll* be the judge of whether I love you or not.'

'Are you saying you don't?' His tone was a warning.

'I'm saying I haven't yet made up my mind.'

With a disgusted snort, he looked away. 'Pull the other one.'

Although he'd muttered, Alathea heard him. 'You *don't* know that I love you – you *can't* know!'

He looked her in the eye. 'I do.'

'How?'

After a moment, he looked away; this time, his gaze fastened on the jasmine, blooming in profusion over the gazebo, filling the arches, fragrant white blossoms nodding in the breeze. Catching a spray, he snapped it off. Looking down, he turned it in his hands, long fingers caressing the velvet-soft blooms. 'How many men have you allowed to make love to you?'

Alathea stiffened. 'You know perfectly well—'

'Precisely.' He nodded, his gaze on the jasmine. 'Only me. You don't know—'

Alathea waited; after a long moment, he drew breath and met her gaze. 'I know you love me because of the way you give yourself to me. The way you are when you're in my arms.'

'Well!' She fought down an urge to bluster. 'As you're the only lover I've yet known—'

'Tell me,' – his steely words cut her off – 'can you imagine being as you are with me, if it wasn't me with you but some other man?'

She stared at him. She couldn't begin to even form a mental picture; the idea was utterly foreign.

So foreign, she suddenly realized she'd lost sight of her agenda. 'You're avoiding my point.' It was a wrench to drag her mind from the avenues into which he'd lead it, to consider instead that if he knew she loved him, he'd be even more chivalrously inclined to wed her regardless of any other motive. The realization fueled a fresh rush of emotions, hope and frustration equally represented. Hope that the reason for his self-protective shield was a heart as vulnerable as hers; frustation over convincing him to lower his guard long enough for her to know.

She felt like clenching her fists, screwing her eyes shut, drumming her heels, and *demanding* he tell her the truth. Instead, she fixed her eyes on his and carefully enunciated, 'I will not marry you until you tell me why you want to marry me, and place your hand on your heart and swear you've told me all – *every last one* – of your reasons.'

Those who thought him the epitome of a civilized gentleman would never have recognized the harshly primitive warrior who now faced her. Luckily, she'd encountered him often enough not to quake.

'*Why?*'

The very air shivered beneath that one word, so invested with suppressed passions – anger, frustration, and barely leashed desire.

Alathea didn't blink. 'Because I need to know.'

He held her gaze for so long, she began to feel giddy, then he wrenched his gaze from hers and abruptly stood.

He looked out over the lawns, then glanced down at her. His expression was impassive. With a flick of his fingers, he tossed the sprig of jasmine into her lap.

'Don't you think we've wasted enough years?'

His gaze rose, touched hers, then he turned and strode down the steps.

Alathea sat in the gazebo mentally replaying their exchanges, wondering, if she had the chance, if she would say anything different, do anything different, or manage to achieve anything more.

At the end of an hour, she lifted the jasmine and inhaled the heady scent. She focused on the sprig, then, with a self-deprecating grimace, tucked it into her cleavage.

For luck.

She'd diced with fate for her sisters and won. She'd just played for her own future – had she told him she wasn't aggressive? She'd risked everything on a last throw.

She'd do it again in a blink.

With a sigh, she rose and headed for the house.

CHAPTER 19

Sunday evening. Gabriel let himself into his house with his latchkey. As he closed the door, Chance materialized from the back of the hall.

Gabriel handed him his hat and cane. 'Is there brandy in the parlor?'

'Indeed, sir.'

Gabriel waved a dismissal. 'I won't need anything more tonight.' He stopped with his hand on the parlor doorknob. 'One thing – did Folwell bring his report?'

'Aye, sir – it's on the mantelshelf.'

'Good.' Entering the parlor, Gabriel shut the door and headed straight for the sideboard. He poured himself two fingers of brandy, then, glass in hand, lifted Folwell's missive from the mantelpiece and slumped into his favorite armchair. He took a long sip, his gaze on the folded sheet, then, setting both glass and note down on a side table, he pressed his hands to his eyes.

God, he was tired. Over the last week, aside from the time he'd spent with Alathea and a few restless hours' sleep, he'd devoted every waking minute to

458

trying to shake formal statements – statements with legal weight – from a score of civil servants and foreign ambassadors' aides. To no avail. It wasn't that the gentlemen didn't want to be helpful; it was simply the way of governmental authority the world around. Everything had to be checked and triple-checked, and then authorized by someone else. Time, it seemed, was measured on a different scale in Whitehall and foreign parts both.

Sighing deeply, Gabriel stretched out his legs and leaned his head back, eyes closed. It wasn't his failure on the foreign front that was worrying him.

He'd called on Captain Aloysius Struthers that afternoon. Even from that short interview, it was clear that the captain was indeed the savior Alathea had thought him. His testimony, even in the absence of any further facts beyond those they'd already gleaned, would prompt the most reticent judge to a speedy and favorable decision. The problem was the captain had embarked on a crusade with all flags flying. He'd already contacted acquaintances in search of maps and mining leases.

Gabriel wasn't at all sure that was the way to sling a noose around Crowley's neck. Stealth might have been wiser.

He'd spent half an hour urging Struthers to caution, but the man hadn't wanted to listen. He was fixated on bringing Crowley down. In the end, Gabriel had accepted that and left, trying to ignore the presentiment of danger resonating, clarion-like, in his mind.

As long as Struthers appeared at Chancery Court on Tuesday morning, all would be well. Until then, however, the investigation and his nerves would teeter on a knife edge. One wrong move . . .

Opening his eyes, he straightened, reached for his glass, and grimly sipped. There was nothing more he could do tonight to bolster the Morwellan cause. It was, however, time and past that he attended to the other matter on his plate.

He was a coward.

A difficult fact for a Cynster to face, but face it he must. *She* had given him no choice.

He hadn't seen Alathea since their meeting in the gazebo the previous afternoon. Indeed, he didn't *want* to see her, not until he'd decided what to do, how to respond to her ultimatum. She made him feel so . . . *primitive*, so stripped of all his elegant attitudes, the patina of his social charm. With her, he felt like a caveman, one who had suddenly discovered heaven on earth was beyond the ability of his club to provide. He'd painted the details of their future life intending to lure her into admitting how desirable it would be, to show her how easily their lives would mesh. Instead, he'd opened his own eyes to how desperately he wanted all that he'd described.

He hadn't considered the details before – he'd known he wanted her as his wife and that had been enough. But now that he'd conjured up such visions in all their glory, they haunted him.

And pricked and prodded at his cowardice.

Was he going to risk that future – the glorious future that should be theirs – simply because he couldn't find the words to tell her what she wanted to know? Because the mere thought of what she truly meant to him closed his throat and rendered him incapable of speech?

But there *were* no words to encompass all she was to him, so how the devil *could* he tell her?

He swallowed a mouthful of brandy, and brooded on that fact. But he had to tell her, and soon. Patience had never been his strong suit – patience that entailed concomitant abstinence was utterly foreign to his nature. He'd endured more than a week without her; his stock of patience was stretched vanishingly thin. He certainly wasn't about to let the court case run its course and risk her slipping back to the country. If she did, he'd have to hie after her, and just think how revealing *that* would be to the now all-too-interested ton.

No – he had to speak before Tuesday morning. God knew how things would pan out after that, Struthers or no. And if, by some hellish twist of fate, things went awry and the decision went against them . . . if he waited until then to drum up his courage and speak, it might take forever to convince her he wasn't simply doing his all to whisk her into his protection. He'd probably go insane before he succeeded. Best to strike now, when their case looked strong, so she had less justification to attribute all his motive to his admittedly obsessive protective instinct. He wasn't sorry for that instinct – he wouldn't dream of apologizing for it – but he could see that in this case, it was going to get in his way.

So – how to tell her what she insisted on knowing before Tuesday morning?

He couldn't see himself doing the deed via a formal morning call, and trying to talk to her in the park would be insane. Reaching for Folwell's note, he scanned the list of Alathea's engagements. As he'd supposed, the next time he and she would unavoidably meet was at the Marlboroughs' ball tomorrow night.

They'd meet at Chancery Court the next morning.

Gabriel grimaced. How, between appearing in court and now, did fate expect him to declare his hand, let alone his heart?

'Send Nellie up to me, Crisp. I may as well get ready.'

'Indeed, Lady Alathea. I believe Nellie's with Figgs. I'll inform her immediately.' Crisp sailed on through the green baize door.

Alathea climbed the stairs, doggedly ignoring her constantly vacillating emotions. On the one hand, she felt almost hysterical with relief, buoyed to the point of frivolity over having the sword that had hung over the family's future for the past months all but effectively removed. The captain's

462

testimony would carry the day against Ranald Crowley. There were moments when she had to concentrate to keep a silly grin from her face.

She had mentioned to her father and Serena that matters were looking up. A superstitious quirk had stopped her from assuring them that the family was finally safe. That she would do later in the week, the instant the judge handed down his decision.

But they were safe. She knew it in her heart.

Her heart, unfortunately, was otherwise engaged, not at all inclined to share in her imminent joy. On a matter that had, to her considerable surprise, come to mean more to her than even her family, her heart was troubled. Uneasy. Unfulfilled.

Reaching the top of the stairs, she released her skirts and sighed.

What was he up to?

She hadn't seen him, or heard from him since he'd left her in the gazebo, his harsh words 'Don't you think we've wasted enough years?' ringing in her ears. So what now? Did he imagine she'd weaken and meekly acquiesce?

'Hah!' Lips compressing, she swept down the wing and flung open the door to her room. Nellie's footsteps came pattering after her.

'I want that ivory and gold gown – the one I was saving for a special occasion.'

'Oooh!' Nellie darted to the wardrobe. 'What's the occasion, then?'

Alathea sat before her dressing table; in the

mirror, she considered the militant light in her eyes. 'I haven't yet decided.'

She wasn't going to do it – weaken and give in. She was going to be tenacious, stubborn – she was utterly determined. As far as she could see, *she* was the one who had taken all the risks thus far – in demanding his sworn motives, in being so naively transparent. It was time he did his part and told her the full truth.

A tap on the door heralded her bathwater. While Nellie oversaw the preparations, Alathea unpinned and brushed her hair, then wound it in a simple knot. Nellie came to fetch her usual bath salts; she mumbled through lips clamped about hairpins, 'No – not those. The French sachets.'

Nellie's brows rose, but she hurried to the drawer where the expensive birthday present from Serena was secreted. A moment later, a lush scent reminiscent of the countess's perfume wreathed through the room.

Nellie's face was gleefully alight; without further direction, she assembled all required to turn Alathea out at her finest – at her most seductive.

It was nearly an hour later before they were done. As she settled a gold cap on her hair, Alathea studied her reflection, trying to see herself through his eyes. Her hair shone, her eyes were wide and bright. Her complexion – something she rarely considered – was flawless. The years had erased all traces of youth from both face and figure, leaving both honed, refined. She touched her fingers lightly to her lips, then smiled. Swiftly, she scanned the expanse of her shoulders and breasts revealed by the exquisite gown, one Serena had forced on her earlier in the Season.

Sending heartfelt thanks winging her step-mother's way, Alathea stood. The gown rustled as the stiff silk fell straight, the gold embroidery at neckline and hem glittering. Stepping back, she turned, studying her outline, the way the gown caressed her hips. Determination glowed in her eyes.

As far as she was concerned the next move was Gabriel's, especially given he'd been so helpful as to make her declaration for her. Being naively transparent was bad enough – having one's trans-parency explained to one was infinitely worse.

She wasn't going to budge. He was going to have to convince her, utterly, completely, beyond a shadow—

'Here!' Nellie turned from the door to which a tap had summoned her. 'Look what's come.'

Alerted by the wonder in Nellie's voice, Alathea looked around.

Reverently holding a white-and-gilt box, Nellie gazed delightedly on what it contained. Then she beamed at Alathea. 'It's for you – and there's a note!'

Alathea's heart leaped; her lungs seized. She sank back down on her dressing stool. As Nellie approached with the box, Alathea realized the reason for her awestruck expression. The box wasn't white – it was glass lined with white silk. It wasn't gilt, either – the decorations at corners, hinge and latch were all pure gold.

As Nellie gave it into her hands, Alathea could not imagine anything more exquisite. What on earth did it contain?

She didn't need to open it to find out. The lid was not lined. Through it, she saw a simple posy.

Simple, yes; in all other respects the posy was a match for the box. A group of five white flowers of a kind she'd never seen were secured with a ribbon of gold filigree. The posy nestled amid the white silk, all but hiding the note beneath. The petals of the flowers were lush, thick, velvety, the green of their stems a sharp contrast.

It was the most elaborate, expensive, extravagant come-out posy Alathea had ever seen.

Swivelling on the stool, she set the box on her dressing table and raised the lid. A drift of perfume reached her, sensual and heavy. Once inhaled, it didn't leave her. Carefully sliding her fingers beneath the flowers, she lifted the posy and set it aside. Then she drew out the note. Barely breathing, she opened it.

The message was simple – a single line in his bold, aggressive hand.

You have my heart – don't break it.

She read the words three times and still couldn't tear her eyes away. Then her vision misted; she blinked, swallowed. Her hand began to shake. Quickly folding the note, she laid it down.

And concentrated on dragging in her next breath.

'Oh, dear,' she finally managed, and even that wavered. Blinking frantically, she stared at the posy. 'Oh, heavens. What on earth am I to do?'

'Why you'll carry it, of course. Very nice, I must say.'

'No, Nellie, you don't understand.' Alathea put her hands to her cheeks. 'Oh, how *like* him to make it complicated!'

'Him, who? Master Rupert?'

'Yes. Gabriel. He's called that now.'

Nellie sniffed. 'Well, I can't see why you can't carry his flowers, even if he is using some other name.'

Alathea swallowed a hysterical laugh. 'It's not his *name*, Nellie, it's *me*. I can't carry a girl's come-out posy.'

He'd known, of course. She'd never had her come-out, never received a come-out posy, never had the opportunity to carry one.

'Damn the man!' She felt like weeping with happiness. 'What am I to do?' She'd never felt so flustered in her life. She wanted to carry the flowers, to pick them up, rush out of the door like an eager young girl, and hurry to the ball just so she could show him – her lover – that she understood. But . . . 'The scandalmongers are watching us as it is.' If she carried the posy, they'd be the *on-dit* of the night. Possibly the whole Season.

'Maybe I can wear them as a corsage?' She tried

it, angling the flowers this way, then that, at her right, her left, in the center of her neckline.

'No.' She sighed. 'It won't do.' One flower wasn't enough against the gold embroidery, but three, the number needed to balance the spray, was too much, too large. Far too visible. Aside from anything else, the spray would be in her constant vision – facing him over it, spending the evening with him by her side with his flowers so blatantly between them would be impossible. She'd never maintain her composure.

'I can't.' Dismayed, she gazed at the beautiful blooms – at the favor her warrior had sent her as a token of his heart. She desperately wanted to carry them, but didn't dare. 'Fetch a vase, Nellie.'

With a disapproving humph, Nellie left.

Alathea cradled the posy in her hands, and let all that it meant wash through her. Then she heard Mary's and Alice's voices; blinking, sniffing, she gently laid the posy back in the box and set it to one side of the table. In a daze, she finished her toilette, clasping her mother's pearls about her throat, placing the matching drops in her ears, lavishly dabbing on the countess's perfume.

'Allie? Are you ready?'

'Yes. I'm coming!' Her wits whirling, she rose. Her gaze on the posy, cradled in its delicate box, she breathed in, exhaled, then picked up her reticule and turned.

'Hurry! The coach is here!'

'I'm coming.' Reaching the threshold, Alathea

468

lingered. Her hand on the door, she looked back at the delicate box he'd used to send her his heart.

Her gaze lifted to the mirror beyond, to her own reflection.

A moment later, she blinked. Leaving the door, she recrossed the room.

Halting before the dressing table, she picked up his note. She reread his message, then looked again at her reflection. Her lips twisted, lifted. Tucking the note into her jewelry box, she raised her hands to her cap.

It took a moment to ease out the pins. Alathea ignored the chorus of calls wafting along the corridor. This time, her family could wait.

Laying aside the cap, she quickly unwound the posy. She wrapped the ribbon around the tight bun on the top of her head and tied it in a simple knot, the trailing ends interleaving with the surrounding curls. Fingers shaking, she separated three luscious blooms from the arrangement. By the time she'd threaded the stems into her thick hair and secured them with pins, she was smiling, her heart soaring, her face mirroring her joy.

Nellie rushed in, vase in hand, and abruptly halted. 'Oh, *my*! Well, now! That's better!'

'Put the others in water. I have to rush.' Whirling, Alathea squeezed Nellie's arm, then, breathless, ran to the door.

Brows high, Nellie watched her go, then, a broad smile wreathing her face, she bustled to the dressing table. She placed the two remaining blooms in the vase, then carefully carried it to the table beside the bed. Nellie wiped her hands and returned to the dressing table to tidy Alathea's combs and brush. She was about to turn away when the folded note poking out from Alathea's jewelry box caught her eye.

Nellie cast a glance at the door, then lifted the lid of the jewelry box and took out the note. She unfolded it, read it, then refolded it and replaced it. And chuckled delightedly. 'You'll do, my lad. You'll do.'

Gabriel saw his flowers in Alathea's hair the instant she appeared in the archway giving onto Lady Marlborough's ballroom. The sight transfixed him; joy, relief, and something far more primal locked his lungs. Pausing with her family at the top of the stairs, Alathea looked down, over the ballroom, but didn't immediately see him. His gaze didn't leave her as she slowly descended the broad sweep, one hand lightly skimming the balustrade as she searched the throng.

Then she saw him.

He drew breath and started toward her. His eyes didn't leave her face as he closed the distance between them; he had no recollection of those he passed as he cleaved through the crowd. He reached the newel post before her.

She descended the last steps, her gaze locked with his, pausing on the very last, higher than he,

470

then she stepped down to the floor and angled her head so he could study the blooms.

'I couldn't carry them – you do understand?'

Triumph washed through him, a rolling wave that nearly brought him to his knees. 'Your alternative is inspired.' He took her hand; uncaring of any who might be watching, he carried it to his lips. His eyes held hers. 'My lady.'

Some magical force held them trapped, hazel drowning in hazel, so close they could sense each breath the other took, each beat of the other's heart. Neither could manage a smile.

'And about time, too, but *do* get a move on! There's a seat on a *chaise* over there I want to snare.'

Alathea jumped and whirled. Gabriel looked up, into Lady Osbaldestone's black eyes. She grinned evilly and poked his arm. 'Don't let me stop you in your rush into parson's mousetrap, but *do* get out of my way!'

They did; Lady Osbaldestone pushed past them and stumped into the throng. Gabriel turned as Alathea took his arm.

'We'd better do as she says.'

Placing his hand over hers, he guided her into the already dense crowd.

'We were late,' Alathea murmured. 'Only by a few minutes, but it put us so far back in the queue of carriages . . .'

'I was beginning to wonder if something had happened . . .'

Something had. Alathea met his eyes; they were gently smiling, magnanimous in victory. She looked away. 'You know, I would never have expected flowers from you.'

She said nothing more; the muscles under her hand slowly tensed.

'There was a *note* with the flowers . . .'

Alathea turned smiling eyes his way. 'I know. I read it.'

He drew her to a halt, his eyes searching hers. 'Just as long as you *understood* it.'

His tone held aggression, uncertainty, and a strong undercurrent of vulnerability. Alathea let her expression soften, let her guard down enough for him to see her heart in her eyes. 'Of *course* I understood it.'

He looked deep into her eyes, then he released the breath he'd held. 'Just don't forget it. Even if you never hear or see the words again, they'll always be true. Don't forget.'

'I won't. Not ever.'

The noisy crowd around them had faded. For a moment, they remained in that world where only they existed, then Alathea smiled softly, squeezed his arm, and drew them both back to the present. She glanced about. 'You could have chosen an evening more conducive to your declaration.'

Gabriel sighed and they started to stroll. 'Our whole courtship – no, our joint *lives* thus far have been dictated by circumstance. I'm looking forward to shaking free of the shackles and taking charge of our reins.'

'Indeed?' Regally, Alathea exchanged nods with Lady Cowper. 'Might I suggest that you resign yourself to sharing the reins?'

Gabriel shot her a glance; his brow quirked. 'I'll think about it.'

They strolled on through the crush, encountering no member of either of their families. 'This is ridiculous,' Alathea stated as the press of bodies forced them to a halt. 'Thank heaven there are only a few weeks to go.'

'Speaking of time passing, has Struthers contacted you?' Surrendering to the inevitable, Gabriel drew her out of the parading crowd to a spot where they could stand and converse in reasonable comfort.

'No. Why? I thought you were going to see him.'

'I did. I told him my address and to get in touch with me if he needed any help, but he hasn't.'

'Well.' Alathea shrugged and looked about. 'Presumably that means all's well and we'll see him tomorrow in court.' She smiled and held out her hand. 'Good evening, Lord Falworth.'

Falworth took her hand and bowed. Gabriel inwardly cursed. Within minutes, her entire court had gathered. They must have located her by tracking him, tall enough to be followed through the jostling throng. Lord Montgomery prosed on; Falworth and others attempted to capture the conversation and steer it in their own directions. A social smile on her lips, Alathea pretended to follow, nodding and murmuring at appropriate moments.

The first waltz and she would be his again. Unfortunately, Lady Marlborough was of an older generation; she'd scheduled a great many cotillions and even a quadrille amid a host of country dances. He'd be waiting a while for his waltz.

Meanwhile . . .

'Dear Lady Alathea, I most earnestly implore your favor in this dance.' Montgomery bowed low.

Mr Simpkins regarded his lordship with unconcealed dislike. 'Lady Alathea, you need only say the word. I would be honored to partner you.' Simpkins's bow was abbreviated to the point of abruptness.

Alathea smiled serenely on them all, her gaze at the last touching Gabriel's. 'I fear, gentlemen,' she said, turning back to her court, 'that I will not be dancing, in general, this evening.'

They all heard the qualification. They'd all seen that swift, shared glance. Now they all wondered. Furiously.

'Ahem.' Lord Montgomery struggled not to glare at Gabriel. 'Might one enquire . . . ?'

Alathea waved at the crowd. 'It's far too exhausting to even imagine fighting one's way to the dance floor.' Again she favored them with a serene smile. 'I prefer to enjoy your conversation and' – her gaze slid to Gabriel's face – 'save my energies for the waltzes.'

His expression inscrutable, he met her gaze, then arrogantly raised a brow. If her court had not yet got the message, the moment, heavy with blatant sensuality, should have opened their eyes. The warrior within him roared in triumph; he hesitated, then inclined his head and tore his gaze from hers. While his primitive self gloated at her gesture, it was doing nothing for his composure, further eroding the thin veneer that, where she was concerned, was all that hid his true feelings from the world.

Now she'd all but publicly declared that she was his, surely his possessiveness could relax, triumphant? Unfortunately, he felt anything but relaxed. Alathea re-instituted a conversation with Falworth, regally ignoring the not-quite-convinced looks on Montgomery's and Simpkins's faces. Gabriel tried to stand easily beside her and not think of what he'd rather be doing.

Both proved impossible. She'd been right. Marlborough House filled to the rafters was not a useful venue for what he would prefer to be doing with her, to her. Finding an empty parlor tonight would be impossible. Was there any other way they could steal an hour or so alone? With the conversations about them droning in his ears, he considered all the options, regretfully rejecting every one. He slanted her a glance. The instant she and her family were free of Crowley's threat, he would have to kidnap her, for a few hours at least. Long enough to soothe the beast within.

Thinking of how he would soothe his clamorous needs did nothing to ease them. Gritting his teeth, he wrenched his thoughts onto a different track. Struthers. He'd sent Chance to call on the old sea dog at noon, offering his services in any helpful capacity. The captain had, not entirely unexpectedly, sent Chance off with a gruff but polite refusal. Chance had obeyed orders and kept watch on the run-down lodging house in the Clerkenwell Road. The captain had left late in the afternoon and headed for the City, then on toward the docks. Chance had faithfully tracked him, a talent learned in his previous existence, but the captain must have sensed he was being followed. He'd gone into a tavern and then disappeared. Chance had searched the three alleys the tavern gave access to, but hadn't been able to find the old man. Defeated, he'd returned to Brook Street to report.

If the captain was fly enough to lose Chance, then he could take care of himself. Presumably. The presentiment of danger that had struck Gabriel on first meeting the captain continued to nag at him.

Shifting, he glanced at Alathea. At least she was safe. From Crowley. She wasn't entirely safe – not in her terms – from him. They had nigh on a decade to make up for, and more than one event to celebrate. His gaze rose to her hair, to the gift he'd given her that had finally accomplished what he'd sought for so many years to achieve. He'd gotten rid of her damned caps. Never again would she wear one – he'd ensure she never even thought of it.

All of which added to his tension, to the impatience he could feel rising like a tide, a building pressure he could do nothing to release, not here, not now. He drew in an increasingly tight breath and refocused on her face, abruptly conscious that he was nearing the end of his severely strained tether. He glanced around at the gentlemen surrounding them; none posed as much of a threat to her as he.

Straightening, he shifted closer, all too aware of the countess's provocative perfume gently rising from her warm flesh. The thought of how much more strongly that scent would rise once her skin heated with passion had him clenching one fist.

Risking a scene at this point was senseless. He'd do better to take his clamoring instincts, possessive and otherwise, a short distance away.

A sudden gust of laughter from a nearby group had her court looking behind them. He seized the opportunity, touching the back of Alathea's arm, fingers light on the soft skin bare above her glove.

Vivid awareness streaked through him – and her. It was there in her wide eyes as she looked up. 'What?'

The word was breathless; she was as giddy as he.

'I'd better circulate. I'll be back for the first waltz.'

Her gaze dropped to his lips. They were so close, they could sense each other's breaths. She moistened her lips. 'Perhaps,' she whispered, 'that might be . . . wise.'

She lifted her gaze to his. Gabriel nodded.

He managed to turn away without touching his lips to hers.

Alathea watched him go, then, with an inward sigh, she returned her attention to her court as, the nearby ruckus abating, they turned back to her. She was relieved Gabriel had taken himself off; she'd sensed his suppressed tension. The fact that she now knew what caused it – what it truly was – did not make being its subject any less unsettling. Nevertheless, she would much rather have gotten rid of all her court, slipped away on his arm, and done all she could to ease him.

Keeping her social smile in place, she encouraged her court to entertain her. Her heart, however, wasn't in it. When a footman pushed through to her side, a folded note on a salver, that unruly organ leaped. Her first thought was that her warrior had found some bolt hole and was summoning her to his side.

The truth proved more disturbing.

Dear Lady Alathea,

I have secured all the information I sought and more. I have evidence enough to discredit Crowley's scheme but have been summoned back to my ship and must up anchor and depart on the morning tide. You must come at once – I must explain some of the details of the maps and documents in person, and it will be vital to your cause for me to make a signed deposition before witnesses, and leave the whole in your hands.

I implore you do not dally – I must weigh anchor the instant the tide turns. Take heart, dear lady – the end is nigh. All the necessary documents will shortly be in your hands and you will be able to send Crowley to the devil.

I have taken the liberty of sending a carriage and escort for you. You may trust the men implicitly – they know where to bring you. But you must come at once or all may be lost!

Your respectful servant,
Aloysius Struthers, Captn.

Alathea looked up. Her court were chatting among themselves, giving her a moment of privacy in which to read her note. She turned to the footman. 'Is there a carriage waiting?'

'Aye, my lady. A carriage and a number of . . . men.'

They'd probably be sailors. Alathea nodded. 'Please tell the men I'll be with them directly.'

The footman was too well trained to show any reaction. He bowed and withdrew to do her bidding. Alathea touched Falworth's arm and smiled at Lord Montgomery, Lord Coleburn and Mr Simpkins. 'I'm afraid, gentlemen, that I'll have to leave you. An urgent summons from a sick relative.'

They murmured sympathetically; she doubted

they believed her. Alathea inclined her head and left them. Stepping into the crowd, she lifted her head, scanning the throng. She couldn't see Gabriel.

'Damn!' Muttering under her breath, she started to quarter the room. He'd been tripping over her skirts for weeks. Now, when she needed him, he was nowhere to be found. The crowd was so dense, she couldn't be certain she wasn't crossing paths with him. She saw Celia, and Serena, and the twins, but their cousin was not to be found. Nor was Lucifer. Stepping onto the bottom of the ballroom stairs, Alathea cast an exasperated glance around, but could see no one – not even any of the other Cynsters – who might be of use.

'My lady?' The footman materialized at her elbow. 'The men are very insistent that you leave right away.'

'Yes, very well.' With one last disgusted glance about the packed room, Alathea picked up her skirts, turned – and spied Chillingworth talking with a group of other guests in the lee of the stairs. 'One moment.'

She left the footman and plunged into the crowd. With a laugh and a bow, Chillingworth turned away from his friends as she pushed nearer. He saw her instantly.

He started to smile, then he took in her expression. He searched her eyes. 'What's wrong?'

Alathea caught the hand he held out to her and pressed the note she held into it. 'Please – see this gets to Gabriel. It's important. I have to leave.'

'Where are you going?' Chillingworth closed his hand about both the note and her fingers. He glanced at the footman on the stairs as another liveried servant hurried down to whisper in the first's ear.

Alathea followed his gaze. 'I have to go with someone – that's a message. Gabriel will understand.' With a skill honed through years of wrestling with Cynsters, she twisted free of Chillingworth's grasp. 'Just make sure he gets it as soon as possible.'

The first footman had pushed through to her side. 'My lady, the sailors are growing restive.'

'*Sailors*!' Chillingworth grabbed for her arm.

Alathea eluded him. Pushing past the footman, she hurried to the stairs. 'I haven't time to explain.' She threw the words back at Chillingworth, following as fast as he could in her wake. 'Just get that note to Gabriel.'

Reaching the less-crowded stairs, she lifted her skirts and hurried up.

'Alathea! *Stop*!'

She didn't. She kept doggedly on to the top, then rushed through the archway and on out of the house.

Reaching the bottom of the stairs, Chillingworth stared after her. An influx of guests swept down, making it impossible for him to follow her. Other guests who'd heard him bellow cast him odd looks. His lips setting grimly, he ignored them. 'Damn!'

He looked at the note crumpled in his fist, then he turned and surveyed the throng. 'Serve Cynster *bloody* well right.'

He found Gabriel in the card room, shoulders propped against the wall, idly watching a game of whist.

'This' – Chillingworth thrust the note at him – 'is for you.'

'Oh?' Gabriel straightened. His tickle of presentiment changed to a full-blown punch. He took the note. 'From whom?'

'I don't know. Alathea Morwellan charged me to see it to you, but I doubt it's from her. She's left the house.'

Gabriel was busy scanning the note; reaching the end, he swore. He looked at Chillingworth. 'She's gone?'

Chillingworth nodded. 'And yes, I did try to stop her, but you haven't trained her very well. She doesn't respond to voice commands.'

'She doesn't respond to *any* commands.' Gabriel's attention was on the note. 'Damn! This doesn't look good.' His expression hardened. He hesitated, then handed the note to Chillingworth. 'What's your reading of it?'

Chillingworth read the letter, then grimaced. 'He's effectively told her to 'come immediately' three times. Not good.'

'My feelings exactly.' Retaking the note, Gabriel stuffed it into his pocket and pushed past

Chillingworth. 'Now all I have to do is figure out where the hell she's gone.'

'Sailors.' Chillingworth followed in Gabriel's wake. 'The footman said the men waiting for her were sailors.'

'The docks. Wonderful.'

They were nearing the stairs when Chillingworth, still behind Gabriel, said, 'I'll come with you – we can take my carriage.'

Gabriel threw him a look over his shoulder. 'I'm not going to feel *that* grateful, you know.'

'My only interest in this,' Chillingworth replied as they went quickly up the stairs, 'is in getting the damned woman back so she can plague you for the rest of your life.'

Reaching the top of the stairs, they made their way through the gallery, then descended the grand staircase and strode across the front foyer. They swept up to the main door, shoulder to shoulder—

Looking back over his shoulder, down the steps to the forecourt, Charlie Morwellan collided with them on the threshold. He fell back. 'Sorry.' He started to bow then recognized Gabriel. 'I say – do you know where Alathea's gone?' He looked toward the road leading to the City. 'I can't understand why she had to go with that rough lot—'

Gabriel grabbed him by the shoulders. 'Where did they go? Did you get any idea?'

Charlie blinked at him. 'Pool of London, Execution Dock, as a matter fact.'

Gabriel released him. 'You're sure?'

Charlie nodded. 'I was getting some air – terribly stuffy in there – and struck up a conversation with the sailor by the carriage.' He was talking to two departing backs; Charlie started down the steps in their wake. 'Here – where are you going?'

'After your sister,' Gabriel ground out. He shot a glance at Chillingworth. 'Which carriage?'

'The small one.' Chillingworth was striding along, scanning the ranks of carriages drawn up along the road.

'I might have known,' Gabriel muttered.

'Indeed you might,' Chillingworth retorted. '*I*, at least, had plans for the night.'

Gabriel had had plans, too, but—

'There it is!'

Together with a score of other coachmen, Chillingworth's coachman had left his master's unmarked carriage in the care of two of their number while the rest adjourned to a nearby tavern.

'I can run like the wind and 'ave your man here in a jiffy, guv'nor,' one of the watchers offered.

'No – we haven't time. Tell Billings to make his own way home.'

'Aye, sir.'

The carriage was wedged between two others; it took the combined efforts of Gabriel, Charlie, and the two coachmen to clear the way sufficiently for Chillingworth to ease his carriage free. He waited only until Gabriel swung up to the box seat

484

alongside him and Charlie leaped on the back before giving his blacks the office.

'Billings is going to have a heart attack.' Chillingworth glanced at Gabriel. 'But never mind that. What's going on?'

Gabriel told them, omitting only the extreme extent to which the Morwellans were at financial risk.

'So she thinks she's going to meet this captain?'

'Yes, but it's all too pat. Why tonight, the last night before the petition is lodged? I spoke with his shipping line only last Friday and they had no expectation of the captain sailing so soon. Struthers himself didn't expect to sail for weeks.'

'This Crowley character. What's his caliber?'

'Dangerous, unprincipled – a gutter rat grown fat. One with no known scruples.'

Chillingworth glanced at Gabriel, taking in the cast of his features, the granite-hard expression thrown into harsh relief by the street lamps. 'I see.' His own expression hardening, Chillingworth looked back at his horses.

'Alathea'll be all right,' Charlie assured them. 'No need to worry about her. She's more than a match for any rogue.'

Unslayable confidence rang in his tone; Gabriel and Chillingworth exchanged a glance, but neither made any move to explain that Crowley was no mere rogue.

He was a villain.

'Pool of London,' Chillingworth mused, reaching for his whip. 'Vessels can leave directly from there.'

With a flick of his wrist, he urged his horses on, clattering down along the Strand.

CHAPTER 20

The coach carrying Alathea rocked and swayed as it rumbled along the dock. Clutching the window frame, she peered out on a world of dark shadows, of looming hulks rocking on the wash of the tide. Ropes creaked, timbers groaned. The soft slap of black water against the dock's pylons was as inexorable as a heartbeat.

Alathea's own heart was beating a touch faster, anticipation high but in this setting, tempered by caution and a primitive fear. She shrugged the latter off as the product of a too-vivid imagination. For centuries, convicted pirates had been hung off Execution Dock, but if ghosts walked, surely they wouldn't haunt a site so steeped in justice? Surely it was a good omen that it was to this place in all the dingy sprawl of the London docks that the captain had summoned her. She, too, sought justice.

The coach jerked to a halt. She looked out, but all she could see was the black denseness of a ship's side.

The carriage door was hauled open. A head

swathed in a sailor's kerchief was outlined against the night. 'If you'll be giving me your hand, ma'am, I'll be a-helping you up the gangplank.'

While undeniably rough, the sailors had been as courteous as they knew how; Alathea surrendered her hand and allowed the sailor to help her from the carriage.

'Thank you.' She straightened, feeling like a beacon in the dark of the night, her ivory silk gown shimmering in the moonlight. She hadn't worn cloak or shawl to the ball; the night in Mayfair had been balmy. Here, a faint breeze lifted off the water, brushing cool fingers across her bare shoulders. Ignoring the sudden chill, she accepted the sailor's proffered arm.

The dock beneath her feet was reassuringly solid, the wide planking strewn with ropes, pulleys and crates. She was grateful for the sailor's brawny arm as she stepped over and around various obstacles. He led her to a gangway; she clutched the rope as they climbed, crossing the dark chasm above the choppy water between the dock and the hull.

She stepped onto the deck, grateful when it did not heave and tilt as much as she'd feared. The movement was so slight she could easily keep her balance. Reassured, she looked around. The sailor led the way to a hatch. As he bent to lift the cover, Alathea inwardly frowned. When the captain had said he plied cargo from Africa, she'd imagined a ship rather bigger. This vessel was larger than a yacht, yet . . .

The thud of the hatch cover had her turning. The sailor gestured to the opening, lit by a lamp from somewhere below.

'If'n you'll just climb down the ladder, ma'am . . .' He ducked his head apologetically.

Alathea smiled. 'I'll manage.' Gathering her skirts in one hand, she grasped the side of the hatch and felt for the top rung with her foot. Carefully placing her slippered feet, she stepped down the worn wooden rungs. A rope formed a handrail; once she'd gripped it, the rest was easy. As she descended, a corridor opened up before her. It ran the length of the vessel, with doors on both sides staggered along its length. The door at the very end was half open; lamplight shone from beyond.

As she stepped onto the lower deck and let her skirts fall, Alathea wondered why the captain had not come out to greet her.

The hatch clanged shut.

Alathea looked up. A thick iron bolt slid heavily across the hatch, locking it in place. She whirled, clutching the ladder's rope—

Her gaze locked on Crowley's face.

Through the open rungs of the ladder, he watched her, black, bottomless eyes searching her face, watching, waiting . . .

Alathea's lungs seized. He was watching to see her fear. Waiting to gloat. Mentally scrambling, her wits all but falling over themselves in panic, she drew herself up, clasped her hands before her, and lifted her chin. 'Who are you?'

She was pleased with her tone – regal, ready to turn contemptuous. Crowley didn't immediately react. A faint trace of surprise gleamed in his eyes; he hesitated, then deliberately stepped out from behind the ladder.

'Good evening, my lady.'

Alathea was seized by an overwhelming urge to stuff him back behind the ladder. She was used to tall men, large men. Both Gabriel and Lucifer were as tall as Crowley, possibly even taller. But neither they nor any of the men she knew had Crowley's weight. His bulk. He was massive – a bull of a man – and none of it looked like fat. Hard and mean, his presence at close quarters threatened to smother her. It was an effort to bristle rather than flee. She raised one brow. 'Are we acquainted?' Her tone made it clear there was no possibility of that.

To her increasing disquiet, Crowley's thick lips curved. 'Let's not play games, my dear – at least, not *those* games.'

'Games?' Alathea looked down her nose at him. 'I have no idea what you mean.'

He reached out, not quickly but without warning; there was nothing she could do – no space – to avoid the thick fingers that closed about her wrist. Her gaze locked on his, Alathea refused to let her rising panic show. Her chin set. 'I have not the faintest idea of what you are talking about.'

She tested his grip. It was unbreakable – and he wasn't even trying.

'I'm talking,' he continued, ignoring her futile attempt to break free, 'of the interest you've shown in the Central East Africa Gold Company.' He brought his black gaze fully to bear on her eyes. 'One of my enterprising schemes.'

'I'm a lady of quality. I have absolutely no interest whatever in any "enterprising schemes." Least of all yours.'

'So one would have thought,' Crowley agreed equably. 'It was quite a surprise to learn differently. Struthers, of course, tried to deny it, but . . .' Locking his grip on Alathea's wrist, he drew her arm up, forcing her to face him.

'St-Struthers?' Alathea stared at him.

'Hmm.' Crowley's gaze locked on her breasts. 'The captain and I had a most satisfactory conversation.' His gaze swept down, raking her insolently. 'It was impossible for Struthers to explain why a paper bearing your name and direction in what was obviously a lady's hand was so carefully placed with his maps and the copies of those damned leases.'

Returning his gaze to her face, Crowley smiled unpleasantly. 'Swales remembered the name. After that, it wasn't hard to put two and two together. You Morwellans have decided to try to weasel out of honoring the promissory note your father signed.' Crowley's gaze hardened. Fingers tightening on her wrist, he shook her. 'Shame on you!'

Alathea's temper flared. 'Shame on *us*? I hardly

think the notion applies to chousing a cheat out of his ill-gotten gains.'

'It does when I'm the cheat.' Crowley's jaw set pugnaciously. 'I know how to hold my own, and as far as I'm concerned, your father's wealth became mine the instant he signed that note.'

He shook her again, just enough to let her feel his strength and how puny hers was pitted against it. 'Family honor – *bah*! You can forget all concerns about that. You'll have more than enough to concern yourself with, with what I've got planned for you.'

The pure malice in his snarl seized her; Alathea fought down her fear. Some fleeting flare must have shown in her eyes – his demeanor changed in an instant, the change itself so quick it was frightening. 'Oh-ho! Like *that*, is it?' Eyes gleaming, he shoved her against the wall. 'Well, then, let me tell you what I've planned.'

He leaned closer; Alathea fought not to turn her head away, forced herself to meet his black gaze without a single flinch. He was breathing heavily, rather too fast even given his bulk. She had a nasty suspicion he was one of those men who found fear in others arousing.

'First,' he said, enunciating each word, his eyes locked on hers, 'I'm going to use you. Not once, but as many times as I wish, in whatever way I wish.'

He looked down at her breasts, at the ivory mounds so enticingly displayed by her rich gown. Alathea felt her skin crawl.

'Oh, *yes*. I've always had a hunger to taste a real,

bred-to-the-bone lady. An earl's eldest daughter will do nicely. Afterward, of course, even if you live, I'll have to strangle you.'

You're mad. Alathea swallowed the words. His voice had deepened and slowed, slurring slightly. He continued to gaze at her breasts. She tried hard not to breathe deeply, but her pulse was racing, her mouth dry, her lungs laboring.

'Mind you' – his tone was that of one pondering aloud – 'I suppose I could sell you to slavers if you survived. You'd fetch a good price along the Barbary Coast. They don't see many white bints as tall as you, but . . .' He drew the word out, head tilting as he considered. 'If I wanted to get a good price, I'd need to be careful not to mar the goods too obviously. That's hardly fun. And I would never be one hundred percent certain the threat was gone. No.' Shaking his head, he raised his eyes to hers.

They were flat, bottomless, utterly without feeling. Alathea couldn't breathe.

His face a malignant mask, Crowley stepped back, hauling her away from the wall. 'I'll get rid of you after I've had my fill. That way I won't need to exercise the least care in taking you.' Abruptly changing direction, he thrust his face into hers. 'A fitting punishment for your meddling.'

With a leer and a laugh that echoed manically, he started along the corridor, dragging her behind him. 'A fitting punishment, indeed. You can join your friend Struthers on the morning tide.'

Alathea dug in her heels. 'Struthers?' Throwing her weight against Crowley's pull, she managed to jerk him to a halt. 'You killed Captain Struthers?'

Crowley scowled. 'You think I'd let him go with all the information he had?' He snorted and pulled her on. 'The captain has caught his last tide.'

'He had information that threatened you, so you simply *killed* him?'

'He got in my way. People do disappear. Like him. Like *you.*'

Alathea scratched at the hand locked about her wrist. 'You're crazed! I can't just disappear. People will notice. Questions will be asked.'

He threw back his head and laughed. The concentrated evil in the sound shook Alathea as nothing else had. The laugh ceased abruptly; Crowley's head snapped around. His black gaze pinned her. Unable to help herself, she shrank against the corridor wall.

'*Yes.*' The word was vicious. Crowley rolled it on his tongue and smiled. 'People will indeed notice. Questions will indeed be asked. But not, my beauty, the questions you think.' He stepped closer, crowding her against the panelling, the gloating she'd noted before more pronounced. 'I did a little checking of my own.' His voice had lowered. Raising a hand, he went to caress her cheek. Alathea jerked her head away.

A second later, his hand closed like a vise about her jaw. Fingers biting cruelly, he forced her face to his. 'Perhaps,' he rasped, his gaze falling to her lips,

'I'll keep you alive long enough to see it – what's going to happen to your precious family and who everyone will think is to blame.'

He paused. His very nearness made Alathea feel faint. She tried not to breathe deeply, to smell his smell. The sheer bulk of him closed in on her. Her head started to spin.

His lips curved. 'Your disappearance is going to coincide with the calling in of the promissory notes. I can guarantee your family is going to be beating off the bailiffs almost immediately. They'll be in turmoil. No one will know where you are, or what to make of your disappearance. All the precious ton will see is your family thrown out of their home in *rags* and you nowhere in sight.' His gloating deepened. 'I've heard there are offers in the wind for your sisters. Those offers will evaporate. Who knows?' He pressed closer, his gaze locking with hers; she felt the panelling hard against her spine. 'If I enjoy breaking you, I might just send some "gentlemen" I know to make an offer for your sisters. All *three* of them.'

Alathea's temper erupted. 'You *blackguard*!' With the full force of her arm, she slapped him.

Crowley swore and jerked back, hauling her arm up, pulling her off balance. Alathea screamed. He clapped a hand to her mouth and she kicked him.

That hurt her; the pain only infuriated her more and lent her strength. Swearing viciously, Crowley let go of her arm and caught her around the waist. She jabbed him in the ribs. He juggled her, then locked his beefy arms around her, trapping her with her back to his chest. Half lifting her, he bundled her down the corridor.

Toward the open door at the end.

Alathea wriggled and squirmed. No use. The man was as strong as an ox. She kicked back with her legs, but that was worse than useless. Dragging in a panicked breath, she thought back to her days of fighting with two young sprigs who had always been taller than she.

Gulping in another breath, she stretched and reached back. She grabbed Crowley's ears and tugged as hard as she could.

He howled and jerked his head back. Her nails scored his cheeks.

'*Bitch*!' His voice grated in her ear. 'You'll pay for that. For every last scratch.'

She could only be glad that, broad as he was, the corridor was too narrow for him to easily strike her. To do so, he'd have to risk letting her go.

Cursing freely, he half carried, half pushed her on before him. Alathea fought and twisted furiously, but did no more than slow him. His strength was overwhelming, suffocating; the notion of being trapped beneath him sent panic sheering through her.

Two yards from the open door, Crowley halted. Before she realized what he intended, he flung open another door concealed within the paneling and started to push her through.

Alathea saw the bed fixed against the wall.

She grabbed the door frame and redoubled her resistance, but inch by inch, Crowley forced her forward. Then he slammed his fist down on her fingers locked about the door frame.

With a yelp, she let go, and he thrust her across the threshold.

Footsteps pounded overhead. They froze, and looked up.

Alathea sucked in a breath and screamed for all she was worth.

Crowley swore. He shoved her into the room.

She tripped on her skirts and fell, but immediately scrambled up. '*Gabriel*!'

Crowley slammed the door in her face.

Flinging herself against the panel, Alathea heard a key scrape, heard the lock fall home. She crouched and put her eye to the keyhole.

And saw the paneling on the corridor's opposite wall. '*Thank God*!' Crowley had taken the key. She reached for a hairpin.

Outside the door, Crowley stared at the ladder. Footsteps moved over the deck above, checking one hatch after another.

'*Gabriel?*'

A smiling sneer curved his lips, then he laughed, turned, and strode for the open cabin.

Gabriel found the main hatch. He hauled on the heavy cross bolt and heard it grate. Swearing under his breath, he shot it fully back. Chillingworth

497

appeared and helped him lift the hatch cover, easing it over. They looked down on a circle of lamplit corridor and the rungs of the ladder leading down.

Looking at Chillingworth, Gabriel shook out his hands, then signaled that he was going down. His face felt expressionless. He had no difficulty acting nerveless. His blood was ice-cold, his veins chilled. He'd never known fear like this – a cold cramping fist closed about his heart. He'd known Alathea forever but he'd only just found her. He couldn't lose her now, not when he'd finally bitten the bullet and opened his heart – and she'd been poised to give him hers. No – he thrust the idea aside. It was unthinkable.

They were not going to lose each other.

He grasped the hatch's rim and swung himself into the hole. Locating the rungs, he quickly descended. He was so tall, he reached the floor before the corridor came fully into view. Stepping onto the lower deck, he looked straight along its emptiness – directly into the maw of the pistol Crowley had pointed at his heart.

Gabriel heard the trigger click. He dove for the floor.

The corridor wall exploded outward. A door swung across, blocking Crowley's shot. Alathea burst into the corridor. The door panel splintered beside her shoulder. She instinctively ducked.

The percussion of the shot boomed and echoed, the sound bouncing deafeningly around the corridor.

'*Get down!*' Gabriel roared.

Alathea looked at him, then at the door. They both heard Crowley curse, heard his pounding footsteps nearing. Alathea shrank back along the corridor wall.

Crowley slammed the door shut. He didn't look at Alathea but at Gabriel, coming to his feet, the promise of death in his eyes.

Crowley turned and raced back to the main cabin.

'Wait!'

Alathea heard Gabriel's bellow but she didn't even look back as she raced straight after Crowley. He would need to reload. Gabriel was unarmed. She could at least slow Crowley down.

She rushed into the cabin, expecting to see Crowley at the desk or bed, frantically reloading. Instead, she saw him fling the pistol across the room as he strode past the desk. Reaching the wall, he grasped the hilt of one of the twin sabers hanging in crossed scabbards between two portholes.

The saber left its sheath with a deadly hiss.

Alathea didn't pause – she flung herself at Crowley, trusting in her sex to keep her safe. It never occurred to her that Crowley might use the saber on her.

It did occur to Gabriel; he crossed the threshold just in time to see her grapple with Crowley, now brandishing a cavalry saber. One swing and he could cleave her in two – Gabriel died another death. He should have felt relieved when Crowley flung Alathea aside, much as an ox would swat a gnat.

She fetched up hard against the wall, shocked, shaken, but essentially unharmed.

Gabriel saw it all in an instant – the instant before blind rage took possession of his senses. After that, all he saw was Crowley.

Crowley settled his weight evenly, taking a two-handed grip on the saber, his very stance declaring he'd never used one in battle.

Gabriel smiled a feral smile. Crowley shifted. Reaching out, Gabriel pushed a small table out of his way – it slammed against the wall. His eyes didn't leave Crowley's face. Slowly, he circled.

It was Crowley's move; he was the one armed. Despite his pugnacious expression, his overweening belligerence, uncertainty flickered in his eyes. Gabriel saw it. He feinted to his left. Crowley raised the saber and slashed—

Gabriel was nowhere near the space the saber whistled through. From Crowley's other side, he stepped inside his guard, left hand closing about Crowley's fists on the saber hilt, right fist slamming into the man's jaw. Crowley grunted. He tried to turn on Gabriel; Gabriel's hold on his fists prevented that, but Crowley's double-fisted grip also prevented Gabriel from gaining any hold on the hilt.

Crowley bunched his muscles to throw Gabriel off. Gabriel released him and spun away. Crowley slashed again and again, following Gabriel as he circled. Each slashing stroke threw Crowley off-balance. Gabriel feinted again; again

Crowley fell for it. Gripping the saber hilt, Crowley's fists and all, Gabriel landed a swinging left on Crowley's jaw. Crowley roared and fought back. Wrenching the hilt free of Gabriel's restraining hand, he slashed and found his mark.

Ignoring the stinging bite of the sabre along his left arm, Gabriel flung himself at Crowley, locking both hands on the saber's pommel. Crowley was off-balance; Gabriel forced him back across the desk, pressing the saber closer and closer to his face.

Eyes locked on the blade inching nearer, Crowley gritted his teeth, gathered his strength, and shoved Gabriel and the blade to the side. Reading the move, Gabriel sprang back. The saber flew free, clattering on the floor.

Crowley reared upright – to be met by a solid punch to the gut. He bellowed and swung, starting after Gabriel, his clear intent to grapple with him.

Gabriel wasn't about to give Crowley the satisfaction of breaking his ribs. The man was a bruiser, the sort who'd learned his science in tavern brawls. Given his size and lack of agility, he relied on his brawn to win. In any wrestling match, Crowley would triumph easily. Fisticuffs, however, was another game entirely, one at which Gabriel excelled.

He landed blow after blow, focusing on Crowley's face and gut. Crowley laid not a finger on him. Crowley bellowed and raged, staggering into punch after punch. Gabriel concentrated on softening him up, on enraging him further. On finally beating him to the ground.

But the man's skull felt like rock; knocking him unconscious was not going to be accomplished by one lucky blow.

Backed against the wall, Alathea watched, her heart in her mouth, her breath suspended. Even to her untutored eyes, the fight was a battle between steely reflexes governing strength honed and refined, pitted against sheer brawn and a blind belief in the power of weight. Gabriel was clearly winning, even though he was now risking more to step closer, well within Crowley's reach, to where he could deliver his blows with more force. One of Crowley's swinging fists caught him as he retreated, snapping his head back. To her relief, Gabriel didn't seem to feel it, returning the blow with one that connected with a sickening crunch.

Crowley couldn't possibly last much longer.

Crowley must have come to the same conclusion. The vicious kick came out of nowhere. Gabriel saw it, but only had time to swivel. It caught him high behind his left thigh. Crowley clumsily pivoted. Gabriel lost his footing and fell.

Alathea smothered a scream.

Gabriel's head hit the desk's edge with a dull thud. He slumped to the floor and lay still.

Massive chest heaving, Crowley stood over him, fists clenched, blinking his piggy black eyes, both bruised and half-closed. Then his teeth flashed in a vicious smile. He looked around, then swooped on the saber, scooping it up, hefting the blade as he took up a stance beside Gabriel's twisted legs. Crowley shuffled his feet apart as he settled his hands about the saber's hilt.

Gabriel groaned. His eyes were closed, his shoulders flat to the floor, his spine twisted. He lifted his head slightly, struggling up onto his elbows, frowning, blinking dazedly, shaking his head as if to clear it.

Crowley's gloating expression filled his face. His eyes glittered. He smiled as he slowly raised the saber.

Alathea inched along the wall, unable to breathe, barely able to think through the flood of emotions swamping her. But fear and fury were the strongest; she knew what she had to do. Setting her teeth, she passed behind Crowley, creeping silently further along the wall.

Crowley stretched upward, raising the saber high above his head, tensing for the downward stroke—

Alathea leaped the last feet, grabbed the second saber, and yanked it from its sheath. The angry hiss filled the room.

Crowley's head snapped around. Teetering, he took an instant to regain his balance. He started to shift his bulk, to realign his saber, turning to swing at her—

The weight of the saber flying out of its sheath swung Alathea away from Crowley. With a gasp, she hauled on the heavy sword and sent it arcing back toward him—

Shoulders and torso still turning, Crowley raised his saber—

Gabriel finally refocused – what he saw stopped his heart. Hauling up his legs, he kicked at Crowley, catching him high on the thigh.

Crowley stumbled. His weight shifted. He staggered helplessly sideways toward Alathea, into the arc of her wildly swinging saber.

Powered by its own weight the saber flashed in, burying itself in Crowley's side. Alathea gasped and released the hilt. The saber remained, its glistening tip barely disturbing the front of Crowley's coat, the hilt quivering behind his back.

Crowley's face leached of all color; shock overlaid all expression. He regained his balance, both feet settling square, the other saber held tight between his fists. Slowly, he looked down, then, equally slowly, turned his head and looked over his shoulder at the saber sticking out from his back. His expression said he didn't comprehend . . .

He shuffled his feet, turning to Alathea, still holding the other saber—

In a rush of footsteps, Chillingworth appeared in the doorway. He took one glance, raised his arm, and shot Crowley.

Eyes wide, Alathea made no sound as Crowley jerked. The ball had found its mark in the left of his huge chest. Slowly, he turned his head to stare uncomprehendingly at Chillingworth. Then his features blanked, his eyes closed, and he pitched forward.

Gabriel pulled his legs clear and struggled to sit up. Still dizzy, his head ringing, he leaned his shoulders against the side of the desk.

Chillingworth stepped into the room, frowning as he took in the saber sticking up from Crowley's back. 'Oh. You'd already taken care of it.' Then he looked at Gabriel, back at Crowley, then back to Gabriel, frowning even more. 'How the devil did you manage that?'

Gabriel looked at Alathea's white face. 'It was a joint effort.'

Chillingworth followed his gaze to Alathea, still pressed back against the wall, her stunned gaze locked on Crowley's body.

Footsteps approached; Charlie looked in. 'I heard a shot.' Eyes growing round, he peered around Chillingworth. 'I say – is he dead?'

Gabriel smothered a crazed laugh. 'Very.' His grim expression only tangentially due to the pain in his head, he studied Alathea, then softly asked, 'Are you all right?'

She blinked, then she lifted her head and looked at him. 'Of course I'm all right.' Her gaze traveled over him. Wild concern flared in her eyes. Picking up her skirts, she leaped over Crowley's body. '*Good God* – the bastard cut you! Here – let me see.'

Gabriel had forgotten about the cut on his arm. Now he looked and discovered his coat ruined, blood pouring afresh thanks to Alathea's probing. Crouched beside him, she was tweaking the slashed material, trying to see . . .

'Can you stand?' She looked into his eyes, then grimaced. 'No, of course, you can't. Here.' She waved Chillingworth closer as she wriggled a shoulder under his. 'Help me get him up.'

Frowning, Chillingworth lent his aid.

'Just watch out for that damned dress.' Hauled to his feet, Gabriel settled against the desk.

Alathea pressed close, pushing his hair out of his eyes to peer into them. 'Are you all right?'

Exasperated, Gabriel opened his mouth to tersely inform her it would take rather more than a severe blow on the head and a shallow cut on his arm to incapacitate him. Then he caught a glimpse of the arrested expression on Charlie's face, and substituted, 'Of course not.' He gestured to the blood darkening his sleeve. 'See if you can stop the bleeding. Just be sure you don't damage that gown.'

The gown was a fantasy he had every intention of peeling from her, inch by sweet inch.

'Crowley must have some linen stored here somewhere.' Alathea glanced at her brother. 'Charlie – look around.'

By the time Charlie returned, Alathea had eased Gabriel's coat off and laid bare the wound. It was a shallow but wide cut, lifting inches of skin but nowhere deep enough to be dangerous. It had, however, bled copiously and continued to do so.

'Here.' Charlie handed Alathea a pile of clean shirts. He glanced at Crowley. 'He won't need them anymore.'

Alathea didn't spare a single glance for Crowley as she picked up a shirt and started ripping.

Straightening from examining the body, Chillingworth stepped around it. He glanced at Gabriel's wound, and stilled. Alathea bustled to the sideboard in search of water or wine. Chillingworth watched her go, then sent a disgusted glance at Gabriel.

Who met it with a bland if not challenging stare.

Chillingworth raised his eyes to the skies. Alathea returned, a bowl of water in her hands. Chillingworth surveyed the room. 'While you're having your strength restored, perhaps Charlie and I should search.'

'Good idea,' Gabriel concurred.

'So what are we looking for?' Chillingworth rounded the desk.

'The promissory notes?' Alathea paused in her dabbing. 'Would they be here?' She looked at Gabriel.

He nodded. 'I think so. Presumably, the reason Crowley is here tonight and not in Egerton Gardens is because he got the wind up when he learned of our investigations.' His expression grew grim and he glanced at Alathea. 'I assume Struthers's activities kicked up too much dust. Did Crowley say?'

Alathea's eyes dimmed. 'He killed the captain. He said so.'

Chillingworth cast a dark glance at Crowley's body. 'Obviously destined for Hades.'

Gabriel caught Alathea's wrist. 'Are you sure the

507

captain's dead? Crowley didn't just say it to frighten you?'

Alathea shook her head sadly. 'I think he's already thrown the body in the river.'

Gabriel caressed her inner wrist, then released her.

Chillingworth grimaced. 'Nothing we can do for the captain now. The villain's already savored his just deserts. The best way to avenge the captain's death is to make sure Crowley's scheme dies with him.' He pulled out a desk drawer. 'You sure these notes will be here?'

'I expect so.' Gabriel looked around. 'This is not a ship of any line – it's a privateer, and a small one at that, built for speed – for fleeing. My guess is that Crowley moved his operations here, ready to depart at an instant's notice. With Alathea and Struthers removed, he would plan on calling in the notes immediately, and leaving England as soon as he had his hands on the cash.'

Alathea started to bind his arm. 'Crowley did say he'd call the notes in immediately.'

Chillingworth continued searching the desk. Charlie drifted off, saying he'd search the other rooms.

Just as Alathea was tying off her bandage, Charlie reappeared, dragging a small seaman's chest. He brandished a document. 'I think this is what we're looking for.'

It was – a thick stack of promissory notes filled the chest. Alathea held the one Charlie had brought in, and started to shake. Gabriel slid an arm around her waist, drawing her closer until she rested against him. 'Take it home, show your father, then burn it.'

Alathea glanced at him, then nodded. Folding the note, she handed it to Charlie with a strict injunction not to lose it.

Charlie shoved it in his pocket, then went back to reading the names on the handful of notes he'd extracted from the chest.

Chillingworth was doing the same. 'He preyed on small fry, for the most part. From the addresses, some of these must be shopkeepers.' He pointed to another pile he'd laid aside. 'Those are the peers, but most are not the sort who usually invest in such schemes. And the amounts pledged! He'd have turned half of England insolvent.'

Gabriel nodded. 'Greedy and unscrupulous. That should be his epitath.'

'So.' Chillingworth re-stacked the notes. 'What are we going to do? Burn these?'

'No.' Alathea was frowning. 'If we do that, then the people involved will never know they're free of the obligation. They might make decisions assuming they're in debt to Crowley, when that debt will never be realized.'

'Are the addresses on all the notes?' Gabriel asked.

'Far as I can see,' Charlie replied. Chillingworth nodded.

'Perhaps . . .' Gabriel stared into the distance.

509

'Find something to wrap them in. I'll take them to Montague. He'll know how best to return them to their owners, apparently properly and legally canceled.'

'Our petition, if successful, will cancel the notes.' Alathea looked at Gabriel.

He shook his head. 'We won't be lodging it. We won't be doing anything to link ourselves with Crowley.'

'No, indeed.' Chillingworth glanced at the body on the floor. 'So what should we do with him? Simply leave him here?'

'Why not? He's got enemies aplenty. He doubt-less gave orders to his crew to stay away from the ship tonight.'

'All except the guard,' Charlie put in. 'But he never even saw you.'

Gabriel nodded. 'Two of the sailors – the ones who delivered the note – will know Alathea was lured here, but no one will know anything more. No woman could have overpowered Crowley. When his men return to the ship, they'll find him here, alone and very dead. They'll assume Alathea left, and *then* someone killed Crowley.'

'I sincerely doubt anyone will mourn him.'

'Other than perhaps Archie Douglas, although even that's uncertain.'

'Crowley probably had his hooks into him, too.'

'Very likely.' Gabriel considered, then continued, 'It's my guess that without Crowley, and without those notes, the Central East Africa Gold Company

510

will simply cease to exist. It has no capital, and Swales, from all I've been able to glean, is not the sort to drive this type of enterprise on his own.'

Chillingworth considered, too, then nodded. 'It'll do. We'll simply leave and take the notes, and get your Montague to return them to their owners.'

They wrapped the notes securely in a blanket and Charlie carried them off the ship. Alathea helped Gabriel. Chillingworth was their lookout. When he joined the others in the shadows by his carriage, he nodded. 'All clear.'

Alathea sighed with relief. 'Help me get Gabriel inside.'

Chillingworth stared at her, then, hauling open the carriage door, cast a narrow-eyed look at Gabriel. 'I assume,' he asked in a sweetly inno-cent tone, 'I should drive directly to his house?'

'Of course!' Alathea scrambled into the carriage, then turned and reached out to help Gabriel in. 'I need to tend that cut properly as soon as possible.'

Gabriel shot Chillingworth a wicked grin, then bent his head and stepped into the carriage. Chillingworth slammed the door shut. 'Who knows,' he said, loudly enough for Alathea to hear, 'it might even need stitches.'

With that, he climbed to the box seat, took up the reins Charlie was holding, and set his carriage rolling back to London.

CHAPTER 21

Chillingworth let Gabriel and Alathea down in Brook Street.

'I'll go straight home,' Alathea called to Charlie as she went up the steps beside Gabriel, her grip on his arm firm and supporting. 'I don't know how long this might take. Tell your mama there's no need to wait up for me.'

Gabriel grinned as he reached for his latchkey. He could just imagine Chillingworth's face. Chillingworth had somewhat curtly offered to drive Charlie back to Marlborough House. That probably entitled him to yet another quota of Cynster gratitude. Given they could never be sure just how incapacitated Crowley had been before Chillingworth shot him, tonight had seen the earl's stocks rise high indeed.

Charlie called an acknowledgment. Chillingworth's horses stamped, then the carriage rattled away. Sliding his key into the lock, Gabriel turned it. Glancing at Alathea, he twisted the knob and opened the door.

This would, after all, shortly be her home. He was simply jumping the gun a trifle. He wasn't,

512

however, foolish enough to sweep her off her feet and carry her over the threshold.

He let her shoo him in, instead, fussing like a mother hen.

Chance appeared at the end of the hall. He was in his shirtsleeves, clearly taken aback to see his master returning so early. When he saw who his master was with, he goggled, and started to silently back away . . .

Alathea saw him and beckoned. 'You're Chance, I take it?'

'Hmm.' Chance ducked his head, warily edging closer. 'That's me, mum.'

Alathea shot him a sharp glance, then nodded. 'Yes, well, your master has been injured. I want a bowl of warm water – not too hot – brought up to his room directly, with some clean cloths and bandages. And some salve, too – I assume you have some?' All the while she'd been progressing down the hall, towing Gabriel with her.

'Umm.' Falling back before her advance, Chance looked helplessly at Gabriel.

'This is Lady Alathea, Chance.'

Chance bowed. 'Pleased to make your acquaintance, mum.'

'Indeed.' Alathea waved him away. 'I want those items, and I'll need your help upstairs momentarily.' When Chance stared at her blankly, she leaned forward and looked him in the eye. '*Now*. Immediately. Sooner than soon.'

Chance jumped back, all but tripping over his feet.

'Oh! Right. Straight away, mum.' He scurried through the baize door.

Alathea watched him go, then shook her head and tugged Gabriel on toward the stairs. 'Your eccentricities never cease to amaze me.' She proceeded to propel him up the stairs.

She couldn't have done it if he hadn't been willing – very willing – despite the fact that he hated being the object of any woman's fussing. Her fussing he was willing to endure given that she'd yet to make any formal statement – a clear and unequivocal acceptance of his heart.

He wanted to hear it, but she was perennially stubborn; encouraging her to let her feelings run riot, as they presently were, would make it all the harder for her to draw back, to balk at the final hurdle. So he meekly climbed the stairs, biding his time, letting her imagine he was weak. He did feel a little lightheaded, relieved that it was over, that Crowley was dead, never to darken their horizon again, and eager, buoyed with anticipation like some callow youth at the realization that she was his.

All he needed now was to hear her admit it.

'Here.' He stopped by his door and leaned against the door frame, letting her turn the knob and set the door wide. Without the slightest hesitation, she urged him inside, steering him to the wide bed.

She pushed him to sit on its side. Her fingers going to the improvised bandage, she glanced frowningly at the door. 'Where is that man?'

'He'll be here in a moment.' Gabriel stood to ease out of his coat. She stripped it from him and promptly pushed him back down again, then busily set about unlacing his cuffs.

Gabriel twisted his lips to hide a grin. How far would she go if he let her?

'Are you in pain?'

Hurriedly straightening his lips, he shook his head. 'No.' He searched her face, drowned in her eyes, in the concern that filled them, the love that gave it birth. 'No.' He reached out and closed one hand over hers. 'Thea, I'm all right.'

Frowning, she shook off his hand and slapped a palm to his forehead. 'I hope you don't develop a fever.'

Gabriel dragged in a breath. 'Thea—'

Chance rushed in, balancing a bowl of water on his wrists, a towel over one arm, cloths balanced upon it, with a pot of salve clutched in his other hand. 'Is this all you wanted, mum?'

'Indeed.' Alathea nodded approvingly. 'Just bring that table nearer. And the lamp, too.'

'Oooh! Lot of blood there.' Chance moved the table closer. He glanced at Alathea. 'Perhaps you'll want some brandy, mum? To clean the wound?'

'An excellent idea!' She lifted her head. 'Is there any here?' Her glance fell on the decanter on the dresser.

Gabriel stiffened. 'No! That's—'

'Perfect!' Alathea enthused. 'Bring it here.'

'Thea . . .' Horrified, Gabriel watched Chance

515

dart to the dresser and bring back the decanter filled with superbly aged French brandy. 'I really don't need—'

'*Do* be quiet.' Alathea stared into his eyes, peering into one, then the other. 'I keep worrying you'll start raving any minute. Please – just let Chance and me fix this. Then you can rest. All right?'

He looked into her eyes – she was perfectly serious. Gabriel bit his tongue, glanced at Chance, then nodded.

For the next fifteen minutes, he suffered their combined ministrations. He'd forgotten that Chance had reason to want to repay him with kindness. Sitting silent on his bed, he was smothered by kindness, by concern, by love. It was pleasant, even if he felt a fraud.

With Chance's help, Alathea stripped off his shirt, then gently tended his wound, apparently unaffected by the sight of his bare chest. Gabriel itched to change that, but . . . Chance was still in the room. Alathea lovingly cleansed the long cut, then bathed it.

He kept his gaze glued to her hair. Despite all she'd gone through, the three blooms were still firmly in place, his declaration acknowledged. He wasn't about to remove them, not intentionally. Not until he'd had their promise converted into words. Multiple times. While she fussed over his arm, he fell to rehearsing all that was to come, and how best to wring from her the words he wanted to hear without disturbing those blooms.

Leaving his arm to dry, she straightened and stepped closer, the warmth of her breasts bare inches from his face. He tried not to breathe while she investigated the bump on his head.

'It's the size of a duck egg,' she pronounced, suitably horrified.

Gabriel shut his eyes as she probed, and tried not to groan. The cool cloth she laid upon the bump helped, easing the dull ache in his head. There was only one remedy for the ache in his groin. When she finally turned her attention to binding up his arm, Gabriel caught Chance's eye. It took a moment for Chance to understand his message. When he did, he looked shocked, but when Gabriel scowled, he hurriedly collected the cloths, towels, and bowl and eased himself out of the door.

The click of the latch coincided with Alathea's benedictory pat to the knot she'd tied in the bandage around his arm. 'There.' She lifted her gaze to his face. 'Now you can rest.'

'Not yet.' Gabriel clamped his hands about her waist and took her with him as he fell back on the bed. Her surprised yelp was smothered as he rolled, shifting them further onto the cushioned expanse, simultaneously trapping her beneath him.

'Be careful of your arm!'

'My arm is perfectly fine.'

She stilled beneath him. 'What do you mean, it's "fine"?'

'Just that. I did try to tell you. It's only a surface cut – I'm not likely to die from it.'

She scowled at him. 'I thought it was serious.'

'I know.' Bending his head, he nibbled at her lips. 'That did become apparent.'

He surged over her; the sensation of her long, supple form tensing beneath him sent a wave of primitive possessiveness through him. A possessiveness colored by desire, by need, and by another emotion almost too vital to contain.

Still frowning, she braced her hands against his bare chest. 'It must hurt. Your head *must* be throbbing.'

'It aches, but it's not my skull that's throbbing.' He shifted suggestively, thrusting his hips to hers.

Her eyes widened slightly as she shifted beneath him to cradle his erection at the apex of her thighs. Confirming his state. The look she sent him was the epitome of feminine – wifely – resignation. '*Men*!' With renewed vigor, she pushed him back and struggled to sit up. 'Are you all the same?'

'All Cynsters, certainly.' Gabriel rolled to the side, watching bemusedly as she reached for her laces. She was doing it again – taking a tack he hadn't foreseen. It took him a moment to fathom the why and wherefore, then he decided to follow her lead. He reached for her laces. 'Here, let me.'

He'd fantasized about peeling the white-and-gilt gown from her; in it, he could easily see her as some priestess, some pagan female designed to be worshipped. As he eased the gown from her shoulders, he worshipped, his lips anointing each silken inch of skin revealed. She shivered. Surging up beside her, he filled one hand with her breast, the soft flesh firming at his touch, heating as he kneaded. His other hand rose to cradle her head, long fingers searching for the pins that anchored the tight knot of her hair, careful not to dislodge the three white flowers adorning her crown – the evidence of his adoration. Her hair fell loose; his fingers tightened about her nipple. On a moan, she let her head fall back, offering her lips. He took them, took her mouth greedily, hungrily, aware there was no longer any need to hold back. She was with him. The same need drove them both, a fervent desire to hold, to possess, to reassure their souls they had survived the threat whole, still hale. To take a first tantalizing taste of the future, of the freedom to love that they'd won.

His plans degenerated into a sweet, reckless flurry of searching hands, of incoherent, breathless moans, of sweet caresses and heated kisses, of urgent fingers and quivering flesh. They stripped each other of every last stitch, content only when they lay skin to skin, long limbs entwined, cocooned within the chaos of his covers. He gathered her to him, moving over her, surrounding her. With one stroke, he sheathed himself in her heat.

She gasped and welcomed him in, her body arching, tensing, easing, then melting about him.

Her surrender was implicit. Gabriel held tight to their reins. Tonight, he wanted explicit. So he rode her slowly, joining with her in long, slow, rolling thrusts, melding their bodies as they would meld their lives – deeply, completely. When he would have risen over her, she clung to him, holding him to her. He acquiesced and stayed, their bodies in contact from chest to knees. She undulated beneath him, all shifting silk and velvet lushness, a glory of womanly need.

He filled her again and again, until she gasped and clung.

He stilled, savoring her glorious climax, luxuriating in her satiated sigh. He waited until she'd softened fully beneath him. Then he moved again.

Still slow, still unhurried. He had all night and knew it. Not even this – the glory of her giving – was going to distract him tonight.

It was a minute or two before she stirred, before her body instinctively searched for, then found his steady rhythm. Her lids lifted, just enough for her to stare at him. Her tongue touched her lips; he delved deeper and she arched.

A glint of surprise glowed in her eyes.

An instant later, he felt her hands trailing, gently questing down the planes of his flexing back, down to caress his pulsing flanks.

She caught his gaze. 'What?'

His grin was partly grimace, over gritted teeth. She was warm and soft and so inviting beneath him. 'I want to hear you say it.'

The words were low, gravelly, but sufficiently distinct. She didn't ask what it was he wanted to hear.

Beneath him, beneath the steady, relentless onslaught, she stirred. 'I have to go home.'

He shook his head. 'Not until you say the words. I'm going to keep you here, naked and hot and needy, until you admit you love me.'

'Needy? It's not me—'

He cut the words off with his lips. When he'd wiped them from her tongue and her brain, he drew back, rising up on his braced arms to drive deeper into her slick heat.

She gasped, panted, bit back a moan. Writhed just a little. 'You . . . you know I do.'

'Yes. I know. Even if I hadn't known before, I'd certainly know now, after your performance tonight. Now even Charlie and Chillingworth know.'

Her state made her slow to respond. She stared at him, blinked, then weakly asked, 'What? Why should they think . . . ?'

He couldn't grin, although he wanted to. It was hard enough to find the strength to answer. 'You half killed a man to save me tonight, and for the last two hours, you've been fretting and fuming over what anyone could see was little more than a scratch. You nearly made poor Chillingworth bilious.'

Alathea wished she could summon a glare, but her body was prey to the sweetest heat, her senses far too interested in the glory building between them. Her mind was clinging to sanity by a thread.

'I didn't know it was just a scratch. I was being led by the nose—'

'You were being led by love.' He lowered his head and found her lips in a kiss laden with sensual promise. 'Why don't you just admit it?'

Because she'd only tonight come to a full understanding of what this joint love of theirs entailed. The shared joy countered by the fear of loss – the sudden desperation when he, her life, had nearly been slain before her. There was a lot more to loving than she'd imagined. Loving this deeply was a frightening thing.

Lifting her head, she brushed her lips along his jaw. 'If it's so obvious . . .'

He lifted his head out of her reach. 'Obvious it might be. I still want to hear you say it.'

He was filling her with long, slow, languid thrusts, enough to keep her fully aroused but not enough to satisfy. Her temper, unfortunately, was thoroughly subsumed by desire. 'Why?' She arched, desperate to lure him deeper yet.

'Because until you do, I can't be sure you know it.'

She opened her eyes fully and looked into his. Beneath his heavy lids, she could detect not the slightest glimmer of humor. He was serious. Despite all, despite the way her heart ached simply when she looked at him. *Of course I* love you.'

The set of his face – features etched with passion but with his expression somehow driven – didn't change. 'Good. So you'll marry me.'

There was no question in the words. Alathea sighed, struggling not to smile. He wouldn't appreciate it. The reins were in his hands and he was driving hell for leather for the church.

He didn't even appreciate her sigh. He stilled within her, looking down at her almost grimly. 'You're not leaving this room until you agree. I don't care if I have to keep you here for weeks.'

Despite her best efforts, her smile dawned, even though she knew the threat was not an empty one. He would do it if she pushed him.

He was a Cynster in love.

Letting her smile deepen, she reached up and brushed aside the lock of hair hanging over his forehead. 'All right. I love you, and I'll marry you. There – is there anything more I need say to get you to go faster?'

She only just glimpsed his victorious smile as he bent to kiss her, but see it she did. She made him pay for his smugness by demanding more and even more of his expertise.

She nearly drove them both insane with wanting.

But it was worth it.

Later, when they lay wrapped in his sheets, not asleep but too deeply sated to move, Alathea lay with her head on his shoulder and hazily considered a lifetime filled with such peace.

For it was peace that filled her, an unutterable sense of having found her true home, her true place – her true love. That his love surrounded her, and hers him, she had not the smallest doubt. Only that, a deeply shared love, could fill her heart to this extent, so that she could not imagine any joy more fulfilling than lying naked in his naked arms, his breath a soft huff in her ear, his arm heavy about her waist, his hand splayed possessively over her bottom.

They were so alike. They would need to go slowly into their future, eyes open, careful not to step on each other's toes. There would be adjustments to be made by both of them – that was implicit in their natures. Yet while that future beckoned, rising like a new sun on their horizon, she was too comfortable, too sensually sated, to attend to it just yet.

She was comfortable, yes, and that was a discovery. That even now, fully aware of the latent strength in the body beneath hers, in the muscled arms that yet held her so gently, in the steel-sinewed limbs that pressed all along her length, even now, she was soothed, relaxed. Aware of the crisp hair beneath her cheek, exquisitely aware of his hair-dusted limbs tangled with hers. Aware to her soul of the warmth within her, of the firm member angled against her thing. The entire reality left her deeply content.

Profoundly happy.

In bliss.

She closed her eyes and indulged.

He eventually stirred, his arms tightening about her, tension returning to his limbs. He held her close, then pressed his lips to her temple. 'I'm never going to let you forget what you said.'

Alathea smiled. Was she surprised?

'So.' He shook her fractionally. 'When are we getting married?'

They had, apparently, arrived at the church.

Opening her eyes, she dutifully turned her mind to weddings. 'Well, there's Mary and Esher, and Alice and Carstairs, too. A joint wedding might be best.'

His snort said no. 'They may be your stepsisters, but they're sweet, innocent, and full to bursting with the usual romantic notions. They'll take months to decide on the details. I have absolutely no intention of waiting on their decisions. You and I are getting married first.' He tightened his grip on her. 'As soon as possible.'

Alathea grinned. 'Yes, my lord.'

Her teasing tone earned her a finger in her ribs. She gasped and squirmed; he sucked in a breath. He settled her again, his touch converted to caress, idly fanning her hip.

'I've already spoken to your father.'

Alathea blinked. 'You have? When?'

'Yesterday. I saw him at White's. I'd already arranged to send you the flowers.'

His hand continued its slow stroking, soothing, subtly calming.

Alathea looked into the future, the future he was so swiftly carrying her into. 'They'll miss me. Not just the family but the household – Crisp, Figgs and the rest.'

The slow stroking continued. 'We'll be close – only a few miles away. You'll be able to watch over them until Charlie takes a bride.'

'I suppose . . .' After a moment, she added, 'Nellie will come with me, of course, and Folwell. And Figgs is your housekeeper's sister, after all.

'Tweety's sister?'

'Hmm. So I'll certainly hear of any problems.'

'*We'll* hear of any problems. I'll want to know, too.'

She lifted her head to look into his face. 'Will you?'

He trapped her gaze. '*Anything* that happens in your life from now on, *I* want to share.'

She studied his eyes, read his feelings on the years gone by, on the question that would always be with him – could he have saved them those eleven years if he'd known, if he'd opened his eyes and truly looked at her?

She lifted her hand to his cheek. 'I don't think anything serious will happen, not with both of us watching.'

Stretching up, wantonly undulating in his embrace, she pressed her lips to his. He lifted her and settled her, stomach to ridged abdomen, then filled her mouth with caresses that stirred her to her toes.

She was simmering when he drew back. Brushing his lips across her forehead, he murmured, 'I fantasized for weeks about having the countess reveal herself to me.' His palms skimmed down her naked back to cup her bottom, making it abundantly clear just how forthcoming he'd wanted the countess to be.

'Are you disappointed?'

His hands closed possessively. He shifted her, then rocked his hips, his erection parting her curls, impressing her belly. Alathea caught her breath.

He chuckled. 'The revelations I've suffered were better by far than any fantasy.' She looked up; he trapped her gaze. 'I love you.' The words were simple and clear. He searched her eyes, then his lips relaxed. 'And you love me. As revelations go, those are hard to beat.'

Alathea tucked her head into the hollow of his shoulder so he couldn't see her eyes as the words slid through her, into her heart. After a moment, she sighed. 'I still can't quite believe that our troubles are all over, that Crowley is dead. We don't need to worry about him anymore – I don't have to worry about the family's finances any more.'

Abruptly, she stiffened and went to sit up; Gabriel restrained her. She lifted her head. 'The notes! Charlie has ours, but all the rest . . . we left them in Chillingworth's carriage.'

Gabriel started to stroke her again. 'He'll send them around. Don't worry. Stop worrying. You've been worrying for the past eleven years. You don't need to worry about *anything* anymore.'

Alathea subsided back into his arms. 'That's not going to come easily, you know.'

'I'm sure I can find any number of engrossing subjects with which to distract you.'

'But you manage your own estate – there won't really be anything for me to do estate office-wise.'

'You can help. We'll be partners.'

'Partners?' The idea was strange enough to have her lifting her head to look into his face.

He continued to stroke her bare back. 'Hmm.'

She frowned. 'I suppose . . .' Turning over, she settled comfortably, wrapping her arms over the hand he splayed over her waist. 'I'll do the household accounts, of course. Or does your mother do those?'

'No – by all means, you can do them.'

'And if you like, I can do the estate tallies. Or does your father do those?'

'Papa handed over the Manor estate to me two years ago. Neither he nor Mama is any longer involved.'

'Oh.' Alathea wriggled. 'So it's just the two of us, then?'

'Mmm. We can divide the duties any way we like.'

She drew in a breath. Held it. 'I'd like to continue actively managing my own investments. As I did with my family's funds.'

Gabriel shrugged. 'I can't see why not.'

'You can't?' She tried to look up at him but he held her fast. 'I thought you'd disapprove?'

'Why? From all I saw, you're good at it. I'd disapprove if you weren't. But if we're going to be partners generally, there's no reason we can't be real partners in that sphere, too.'

Alathea relaxed. After a moment, she murmured, 'Who knows? We might even be friends.'

Gabriel closed his arms about her. 'Who knows? Even that.' It was a peculiarly attractive thought. 'I'd enjoy that, I think.'

Another moment passed, then she murmured, 'So would I.'

Lips curving, Gabriel tightened one arm about her, splaying his other hand over the smooth curve of her belly. 'Given our present circumstances, I suggest we concentrate on the most pertinent – the most immediate – aspect of our partnership.'

She sucked in a breath as he slid his fingers further, twining through the springy curls to reach the softness they shielded. With one broad finger, he stroked. She shuddered.

'I really think you need to pay more attention to this.' With a grin, he rolled and lifted to come over her. She reached for him and found him. It was his turn to groan.

'Convince me.'

The words were a challenge – precisely the sort she knew his Cynster soul delighted in. He threw himself into meeting it, heart and soul.

When she was writhing beneath him, hot and ready and yearning, he filled her with one long thrust. Braced above her, he watched her face as, eyes closed, head thrown back, she arched and took him in. His flowers still glowed against the rich brown of her hair. He withdrew and thrust slowly again, just to watch her accept him, to see the flowers quiver, then he settled to a steady, easy rhythm, rocking her relentlessly, taking the longest route he knew to heaven.

She gasped, clung, but there was a subtle smile flirting about her lips. He bent his head and laved one furled nipple, then nipped it. 'By the time Jeremy and Augusta have grown, I can guarantee that if you pay attention to this aspect of our partnership, you'll have a tribe of your own to watch over in their stead.'

Her lids lifted fractionally; she seemed to be weighing his words. 'A tribe?'

She sounded intrigued.

'Our own tribe,' he gasped as she tightened about him.

Alathea grinned. Reaching up, she curved her hand about his neck and lifted her lips to his. 'Just as long as that's an iron-clad guarantee.'

The laughter started in his chest, erupted in his throat, then spilled over to her. They shook and clung, giddy as children. Then abruptly the laughter was gone; something much stronger swirled wildly about them, through them, then closed upon them and lifted them from the world.

Finally they settled to sleep, the city silent about them, the future settled, their hearts at peace.

Alathea slid into Gabriel's waiting arms and felt them close about her. Whatever the future, they'd create it together, manage it together, *live* it together. That was so much more future than she'd ever thought she'd have.

She slid her arms about him, hugged him once, then relaxed, content in his embrace.

The next morning, Lucifer stood on the front steps of the Brook Street house and watched the departure of the lady who, somewhat to her surprise, had spent the night warming his bed. And him. Raising a hand in salute as her carriage rumbled off, he turned inside, letting his victorious smile show. She'd proved a challenge but he'd persevered and, as usual, triumphed.

Success had proved very sweet.

Replaying honeyed memories, he headed for the dining room. Breakfast was just what he needed.

Courtesy of Chance, the door was ajar. Lucifer pushed it wide; it swung open noiselessly.

On a scene guaranteed to freeze the blood in his veins.

Gabriel sat at his usual place at the head of the table, sipping coffee. On his right sat Alathea Morwellan, dreamily staring straight ahead, a tea cup in one hand, a piece of nibbled toast growing cold in the other.

She looked radiant. And a trifle flushed. As if . . .

Stunned, Lucifer looked again at Gabriel. His brother appeared a great deal too well fed for someone just about to tuck in.

531

The dread conclusion hovering in his mind grew weightier, steadily taking on substance.

Gabriel sensed the draft from the door and looked up. He met Lucifer's astonished gaze with one of transparent unconcern, raising a querying brow as he gestured to Alathea. 'Come welcome your sister-in-law-to-be.'

Lucifer plastered a smile on his face and stepped across the threshold. 'Congratulations.' Alathea, he noted, still looked a trifle lightheaded, but then, he knew his brother. 'Welcome to the family.' Leaning down, he gave her a brotherly buss. He couldn't help muttering as he straightened, 'Are you sure you haven't both run mad?'

It was Alathea who frowned him down. '*We* were never the ones to run mad, as I recall.'

Lucifer abandoned that tack, along with any hope of ever understanding. He made all the right noises, said all the right words, while he floundered to make sense of any of it. Alathea and Gabriel? He knew he wasn't the only one who had never thought it. Which just went to show.

'The wedding,' Gabriel informed him, 'will be as soon as we can arrange it, certainly before we or the Morwellans, or indeed, the rest of the ton, desert the capital.'

'Hmm,' Lucifer returned.

'You will be there, won't you?'

At Alathea's pointed look, Lucifer summoned a smile. 'Of course.'

He'd be there to see his brother, the last of his

confreres still free, take up the shackles of matrimony. After that, he'd leave.

He was going to disappear.

London – indeed, the ton in its broadest sense – was far too dangerous for the last unmarried member of the Bar Cynster.

The Season ended as it always did, with a rash of tonnish weddings, but this year, amid the many, one stood out, very definitely 'the wedding of the Season.' The tale of how Lady Alathea Morwellan had turned her back on her own prospects to help her family in the country, only to return eleven years later to tame the most distantly aloof member of the Bar Cynster, fired the romantic imagination of the ton.

St George's Church off Hanover Square was filled to bursting on the day Lady Alathea took her vows. The crowd outside the church was just as dense, those not invited to the festivities finding reason to be passing at the time. Everyone craned to catch a glimpse of the bride, regally radiant in ivory and gold, three unusual flowers anchoring her long veil. As she appeared at the top of the church steps on the arm of her proud husband, flanked by a troop of imposing Cynster males and a bevy of beautiful Cynster wives, the crowd let out a communal sigh.

It was just the sort of fairytale romance the ton and all of London delighted in.

At three o'clock, long after the crowds had

retreated to savor all they'd seen, to recount the details and embellish their memories, Gabriel was still giving thanks that they'd managed to fight clear of the crowd of well-wishers before the church and repair to Mount Street for the wedding breakfast.

Standing by a window in the drawing room of Morwellan House, he peered through the fine curtains, reconnoitering the street. There was a small crowd waiting to watch them leave, but it was manageable.

'Almost free?'

Gabriel turned as Demon strolled up. His cousin looked disgustingly pleased with himself; Gabriel reasoned that Demon was yet too newly wed for his expression to ease into the deeply content expressions Devil and Vane now habitually wore. Richard was harder to read, but the glow in his eyes when they rested on Catriona was equally revealing. Gabriel knew a vain hope that *he* would not be quite so easy to read. 'Almost.' He turned back to the window. 'Add the guests inside and it'll still be a goodly crowd, but hopefully we'll make it away in reasonable time.'

'Where are you headed? Or is it a secret?'

'Only from Alathea.' Briefly, Gabriel outlined his plans to whisk Alathea off on a quick tour of the shires, visiting cities like Liverpool and Sheffield that she'd never visited before but that featured prominently in his business dealings. 'We'll end by going directly to Somersham for this summer celebration our mamas have planned.'

'Miss that at the risk of your life – or worse.'

Gabriel grinned. 'Richard's obviously taking no chances.' He nodded to where his cousin's black head was bent over his wife's fiery locks.

'Not on any count,' Demon agreed. 'He says they'll be on the road north the day after the celebrations. He's not at all sanguine about having Catriona traveling in the condition she'll be in then.'

'I'm sure Catriona will have everything precisely planned. Even if she hasn't, she'll just pass a decree and matters will fall out as she wishes – comes of being Lady of the Vale.'

'Hmm. Still, I can understand Richard's feelings.'

Gabriel glanced at Demon, wondering if that meant . . .

Before he could form a suitable question, Alathea appeared.

She swept into the room, and his heart stopped. She'd changed into a traveling gown of watered mulberry silk, the high upstanding collar a frame for her hair, rich and lustrous in the afternoon light. Her mother's pearls were coiled about her throat, the matching drops in her ears. She wore no other decoration, acquiescing to his anathema toward anything covering the glory of her hair. No other decoration except for the three white blooms fixed in a spray trailing over one breast, a filigree gold ribbon looped between.

They were the flowers from her veil, the flowers he'd sent her that morning, with another note even simpler than his last.

I love you.

That was all he'd wanted to say, but he knew as only a Cynster could that he'd be looking for ways to tell her that for the rest of his life.

She scanned the room, saw him, and immediately smiled. Her fine eyes bright, she glided to his side.

Gabriel raised a brow as she slid her hand onto his arm. 'Ready?'

She wrinkled her nose at him. 'We have to give Augusta and Jeremy a few more minutes.'

Not even that news could dim his anticipation; he knew his wife well enough to know the younger Morwellans would not have stepped over the line. All he wanted to do was to leave, and have her to himself again.

Flick, Demon's young wife, joined them in a froth of blue skirts, face animated, her eyes lit with an inner glow – an inner glow, Gabriel suddenly realized, now he'd grown accustomed to the sight in Alathea's eyes, that all the Cynster brides shared.

Interesting.

'Come on!' Flick claimed Demon's arm. 'It's almost time for them to leave.'

'Why are you so afire?' Demon asked. 'It's not as if you need to catch any bouquets.'

'I want to see who *does*.' Flick tugged. 'The steps are filling up.'

Demon gave a little ground, looking back at Gabriel. 'Where's Lucifer?' His demonic grin surfaced. 'Thought I'd give him a little advice.'

Gabriel scanned the crowd, then lifted a brow at Demon. 'I suspect he's already fled.'

Demon snorted. 'Fool!' He cocked a brow at Gabriel. 'Care to wager it'll do him no good?'

Gabriel shook his head. 'Some things are meant to be.'

Demon acknowledged the comment with a swift smile and a nod, then surrendered to Flick's impatience.

Gabriel turned his gaze on Alathea, and simply smiled. After a moment, she looked up at him. 'Ready?' he asked.

She held his gaze. 'Yes.'

'At last.' He covered her hand where it lay on his sleeve.

They walked out of the room, out of the house, and set out on a journey to last the rest of their lives.